PRAISE for...

Hit & Mrs.

If you're in the mood for a cute chick-lit mystery with some nice gals in Montreal, Hit & Mrs. is just the ticket.—Globe and Mail

Crewe's writing has the breathless tenor of a kitchen-table yarn...a cinematic pace and crackling dialogue keep readers hooked.—Quill & Quire

Shoot Me

Possesses an intelligence and emotional depth that reverberates long after you've stopped laughing.—Halifax Chronicle Herald

Relative Happiness

Her graceful prose...and her ability to turn a familiar story into something with such raw dramatic power, are skills that many veteran novelists have yet to develop.—Halifax Chronicle Herald

Amazing Grace

LESLEY CREWE

Amazing Grace

Vagrant Press is an imprint of
Nimbus Publishing Limited
3731 Mackintosh St, Halifax, NS B3K 5A5
(902) 455-4286 nimbus.ca

Printed and bound in Canada

Design: Heather Bryan
NB1196

This novel is a work of fiction. Names, characters, places, and incidents are either the product of the author's imagination or are used fictitiously.

Library and Archives Canada Cataloguing in Publication

Crewe, Lesley, 1955-, author
Amazing Grace / Lesley Crewe.

Issued in print and electronic formats.
ISBN 978-1-77108-316-4 (paperback).—ISBN 978-1-77108-317-1 (pdf)

I. Title.

PS8605.R48A66 2015   C813'.6   C2015-904314-X
                                 C2015-904315-8

Nimbus Publishing acknowledges the financial support for its publishing activities from the Government of Canada through the Canada Book Fund (CBF) and the Canada Council for the Arts, and from the Province of Nova Scotia through Film & Creative Industries Nova Scotia. We are pleased to work in partnership with Film & Creative Industries Nova Scotia to develop and promote our creative industries for the benefit of all Nova Scotians.

For my little sister, Nancy

CHAPTER ONE

NOW

The whole point of going to this wearisome church meeting is to ask the woman in charge of lunch how she makes her coconut balls. Fletcher loves them. I know damn well she's leaving something out of the recipe; I cannot replicate the delicate texture no matter how hard I try. And that ticks me off.

All of these church women give me indigestion, but dang, if you want something done around this rural community, go ask the seventy- and eighty-year-olds who frequent the parish halls in their aprons. At sixty, I'm pretty much the youngster in this crowd, and they know I'm not the religious type, but they're so hard up for fresh blood and volunteers, they tolerate me.

Up to a point.

Last year at the Christmas tea and sale, I was so frustrated at a woman dithering in front of the fruitcakes I blurted, "Jesus Christ, take me now." The ladies gathered round in case I trembled with ecstasy and crashed to the floor. They were mightily displeased when they realized that wasn't my problem. The city slicker and her wallet left in a huff, and I got a lecture from the eighty-two-year-old selling her woollen mittens.

I bought the fruitcake and a pair of mittens and gave them a twenty-dollar donation.

Tonight, all I'd like to do is sit in front of the fire with my feet up and listen to Fletcher snore in his recliner. I'm into a good book and have half a bottle of red wine on my kitchen counter. The cats are ready to settle in for the night and the dogs are lying like lumps in front of the wood stove. I can hear the wind howl outside on this cold November night.

I can't believe I'm going to get up and leave this paradise. The church hall is only five miles down the road, but it might as well be on another planet. Then I look at Fletcher's gigantic, callused hands resting on his round tummy and think I'm going to make those coconut balls if it kills me.

The wind nearly takes the back door out of my hand as I leave. Yellowing dry leaves fly through the air like bats as I hurry to the truck. When I turn the headlights on, I can see one of the small pumpkins we carved a few weeks ago rolling down the dirt driveway.

It's one of those absolutely pitch black late fall nights. I don't take the truck out of third gear in case Harvey Trimm next door is on the side of the road with his two fat Labradors, giving them their nightly pee. There's also a little fox that lives behind the blackberry bushes and I've nearly killed him several times. He thinks it's a game to dart out in front of the truck. I swear he waits for me, but tonight he's nowhere to be seen. Probably curled up in his foxhole, lucky sod.

The village of Baddeck in Cape Breton is like a picture postcard during the day, nestled in and around the Bras d'Or Lakes and rolling hills, but driving at night on the outskirts of town with no streetlights is a challenge when you have middle-aged eyes. I've become one of those old lady drivers, the kind men and teenagers love to scream past, like I don't deserve to live. I usually roll my window down and holler, "Asshole!" at the disappearing tail lights.

When I park the truck next to the Knox Presbyterian Hall, I see elderly Janet Pickup hanging on to her car door handle, afraid to let go. I honk the horn to get her attention, to tell her to wait for me. She jumps with fright instead. Now I've probably killed her. She has a bad heart. I exit my vehicle and have a tough time shutting the door.

"Wait for me, Janet! I'll be right there!"

"What?"

A great gust blows me over to her. I ask her if she's okay, which is ridiculous. She's frozen in terror.

"Just hang on to me!" I shout in her ear.

"What?"

Fortunately for us, Gladys Nicolson pulls up. She's a stocky woman, just what we need for ballast. The three of us are carried along and mercifully saved when we pile against the hall door. Inside, we're greeted by six other ladies, all clucking about how it's not fit for man nor beast out there.

Then why the hell are we here?

Before they start reading minutes and saying their unnecessary prayers, I hurry over to Delima Garland. "I think I'm missing an ingredient in your coconut ball recipe. What am I doing wrong?"

"The recipe I gave you is correct."

"Are you sure it's only one stick of butter? Because it seems to me—"

She holds up her hand to stop me. "I cannot help you. Some people are just born bakers." She hurries off, her orthopaedic shoes squeaking on the tile floor.

Old bitch.

I always sit by Gladys in the fall and winter because heat radiates from her bulk.

"Can you believe that woman? Won't give me her recipe."

Gladys leans towards me in conspiratorial fashion. "If it's her coconut balls, add another stick of butter."

"Thank you, Gladys."

Looks like the trip to town was worth it.

Fletcher and I live in a large trailer partway up a steep hill, overlooking the water. We have a gorgeous view of lakes, the rolling fir-covered mountains, and the sky, with its ever-changing cloud formations offsetting the beauty of eagles, hawks, and seagulls as they dip and soar, carried along by the wind that whistles down from the headland.

Fletcher has had many Americans and Germans offer him big money to buy his land, but he tells them to go to hell. His enormous rounded metal garage is to the left of the trailer, with a large yard in between, where people leave their cars to be fixed by the best mechanic on the island. While I don't see a whole lot of him during the day, I sure like being with him as he dozes in his recliner in the evenings.

Living with Fletcher is easy. I feed him, and since he hates dealing with money, I do his banking along with my own. If I were the criminal type, he'd be in trouble. We buy what we need, take care of our pets, and enjoy each other's company in front of the fire at the end of the day. There's no hanky-panky going on. We're roommates, even if no one in town believes it. Let them think what they want. It really doesn't matter to Fletcher and me.

The next day I make the coconut balls. It's amazing what another stick of butter will do. I put some on a plate and carry out a mug of tea for Fletch. He's bent over an open car hood, covered in grease.

"Thought you might be hungry."

He stands upright and towers over me, wiping his hands on a cloth, his brown eyes lost in his streaked dirty face. "Thanks." Taking the mug, he swallows half of the tea in one gulp before looking at the plate skeptically.

I extend my offering. "Just try them."

He takes one and puts it in his mouth. As he chews, he nods approval. "Delicious."

"I'll leave these here for you." As I put the cookies on his bench, I point at the two fellas at the back of the garage who like to gossip with Fletcher while he works. "You can't have any, so don't ask!"

"Who'd want them? They were as dry as dust last time."

The dogs join me at the clothesline. Daffy and Donald were strays, mangy-looking things, but with hearts as big as all outdoors. After I gather the sheets to finish drying them on a rack by the wood stove, I take the dogs on a hike up the hill out back. This is their favourite thing to do. They love to run ahead of me, but always scramble back to make sure I'm coming.

I know that feeling, so I always stay in the open where they can see me.

We get home when it's coming on dusk, almost time for supper. I take off the orange jacket that Fletcher makes me wear so the goddamn hunters can see me in the woods. That goes for the dogs too. I made their jackets myself. Wouldn't I love to see one of those hunting bastards in front of me. I've hollered at plenty of them from afar. "Go get your meat at Sobeys!" Some of them sit in their warm and cozy huts with bushels of apples scattered around outside to entice the deer to come. And they call that fair game. Fletcher knows how I feel, so he passes on the deer or moose steaks that some fellas try to trade for car repairs. But he says he won't stop eating meat, so I have a beef stew simmering on the stove. I didn't know this cow personally and it didn't live on my hill, and I tell myself that makes a difference. But it doesn't.

Fletch scrubs his dirty arms up to his elbows at the kitchen sink and then sits at the table. I dole out his beef stew with every intention of not eating any, but the smell is glorious. Damn it. I sneak a spoonful on my plate, to eat with my rice and beans. Fletch pretends not to notice. We get caught up with our news, enjoying the company of the cats, Tom and Jerry, who stare at us from the counter. The boys wait patiently for the scraps. When Fletch cleans his plate, I get up and offer him a piece of apple pie, which is a quarter of the whole thing. It will be gone by tomorrow.

Fletch and the animals make a move to settle in the living room to watch television. He enjoys ATV's *Live at 5*, because he's in love with the female host, Starr Dobson. "A damn fine woman, that one," he mutters every blasted time she comes on the screen.

Once I wash the dishes, I sit at the kitchen table to finish my tea, the *Cape Breton Post*'s crossword puzzle in front of me. That's when the phone rings. I'm tempted not to pick it up because I don't want to be roped into making sandwiches for Lenny Baxter's funeral.

"Get that," Fletcher yells. "I'm expecting a call from the auto parts store."

"Hello?"

"Mom?"

I'm so startled, I spill my tea all over the newspaper.

"Jonathan?" I pick up my cigarettes and light one to give myself a second to think. "It's nice to hear your voice after such a long time. How are you, dear?"

"Not great."

Jonathan is never great. "What's wrong?"

"It's Melissa."

Now this does make the hairs on my arms stand at attention. "Is she all right?"

"I'm going to kill her."

"There's not many parents out there who don't want to kill their sixteen-year-olds from time to time."

"I wasn't with you when I was sixteen, so how would you know?"

I take a drag of my cigarette. "Since I don't know anything, I'm surprised you're calling me for advice."

Fletch shows up at the kitchen door. He points at the phone and mouths, "Jonathan?" When I nod my head, he rolls his eyes and disappears.

"If I had anyone else I could call, I would."

"So talk."

"Melissa refuses to listen to me. I think she's on drugs. She stays out all night and knows more curse words than you do. She might be drinking, too. I caught her with a boy in her bedroom and she had the nerve to be furious with me!"

"So call her mother."

"Why do you think Melissa lives with me? Her mother doesn't want her."

"That's not true."

"Of course you'd side with her. Deanne's not picking up her phone. She and her new husband are on their honeymoon in some exotic island in the Pacific, while I'm left to worry about my kid being raped while she's shooting up in a crack house."

Jonathan always was a drama queen.

"It might help if you didn't accuse your daughter of doing those sorts of things."

"How do you know she's not? When was the last time you came to visit? Two years ago?"

"Sorry, kiddo, I was a bit busy with my chemo."

"So why are you still smoking? If you cared about us, you wouldn't, but it's always been about you."

That's enough. "I have to go, Jon; there's someone at the door. Good luck with Melissa." I put the phone down before he can give me any more lip.

When I curl up on the loveseat by the fire and stare into the flames, Fletch knows that's my signal for *Don't talk to me*, so he doesn't. He switches the channel and turns on NASCAR racing instead, which has got to be the most idiotic pastime on the planet. Racing around the same track over and over again. After a while I grab the remote and shut it off. He leans back in his recliner and folds his big-knuckled hands over his chest, waiting for me to start talking. The man is very sneaky.

I tell him what Jonathan said.

"You better go help him out."

"He insults me, he insults you, and my beloved granddaughter is a brat. Why should I put myself through that?"

"You're family."

Of course he's right, but I'm tired. "I'm going to bed."

"Can I just point out it's not even six o'clock?"

"Don't forget to give Donald his pill before bed."

"Righto."

Before I crawl under the covers, I have a bath. The kind that lasts so long that you have to keep adding hot water to be comfortable. Just me and my thoughts. It's that word. *Family*. It gets me every time. Sometimes I forget I have a family, since no one is ever around. How can you be a family when everyone is missing?

THE ADDED COST OF FLYING OUT OF SYDNEY TO GET TO NEW YORK IS BANANAS, so that weekend Fletcher drives me to Halifax in the truck. It's about three hours, which isn't bad, but the dogs are in the back seat and have a nasty habit of licking our ears. When we pull up to the airport drop-off spot, Fletcher takes my suitcase out of the back and puts it on the pavement. I pat the boys goodbye and join him.

"You're not going to drive all the way home now, are you?"

"We're fine. I'll get me a few Tim Hortons road rockets and a big box of Timbits for the jokers in the back seat and we'll be there before you even land in New York."

"I'll call you when I get there."

"Don't piss him off first thing. Let him talk."

It's hard to be mad at this man, because with his red sweater on, he looks like Santa Claus, white beard and all.

"Go on now." He pats my back goodbye.

I give him a quick hug and carry my suitcase into the airport. The flight to New York City doesn't leave for two hours, so I buy a coffee, sit on a seat, and wait. The egg sandwich I made this morning gives off a sulphurous smell when I unwrap it from the wax paper. A couple of young girls texting on their phones make a face at each other and move three seats down. It doesn't stop me from enjoying my sandwich.

As we get closer to departure, the seats around me fill up, and I head for the nearest washroom to spend some alone time in a stall. It's a trick I learned a long time ago. There's not much I can do about sitting pressed against someone on the plane, but popping a few pills helps.

Flying is unnatural. I usually close my eyes when the plane takes off and don't open them again until we land. Flight attendants don't like me—not that I can see them politely glaring at me when I ignore them, but I can feel their pissed-off energy poking into my eyeballs.

We get to New York in one piece and I follow the herd of human cattle streaming out of the arrivals gate. A sea of people look past me and around me, looking for their loved ones. I don't have to search for Jonathan. He'll be further back, looking at his watch every ten seconds with a pained look on his face.

It's too bad he doesn't scowl less; he's a good-looking lad when his mug isn't screwed up with anxiety. Jonathan finally spies me and heaves a great sigh. "I thought you missed the plane. Is this your only bag?"

"Hello to you too."

"Don't start." He leans over and gives me an obligatory kiss on the cheek. "We have to go or traffic will be hell. Why did you have to come at rush hour?"

"Isn't it always rush hour?"

He hurries me along, with one hand on my back and the other holding my bag.

"You look good," I say.

"You look terrible. Why don't you get some new clothes and shoes while you're here? You look like a washerwoman. I live in Manhattan, mother. You could at least make an effort."

Let him talk, Fletcher said.

The air is cold and damp as we hurry outside, and the wind whips our hair every which way. "Your weather is worse than ours."

"But at least I live in the city. If a storm descends, I'm not stuck in the back of beyond like you. You're getting older, Mom. You're living with a giant teddy bear who's not even your husband. It's ridiculous."

He rushes me into a very shiny BMW. The dash looks like a cockpit, with lights of every colour flashing urgently. Then it starts to talk and my son answers. He and the car are having a conversation. I wish Fletcher was here.

We emerge out of the parking lot and drive towards the streets of New York. I never did belong here. This was my husband's world. Old money and rules. Lots of rules.

"Mother! Are you listening to me?"

"Sorry. I thought you were still talking to the car."

Jonathan gives me a sideways glance. "Please don't make fun of me and the way I live."

"I didn't mean to." Sneaking peeks at his profile, I can see his hair is thinning and he has a small paunch, though he hides it well under his thousand-dollar suit. "May I smoke?"

"Of course not! You have cancer! And this is a brand new car!"

"I don't have cancer. I got my tits cut off months ago."

We're at a red light, so Jonathan has a chance to throw his hands in the air while he lectures me. "Do you hear the way you talk? Who says tits in front of their son?"

Fletcher's voice rattles in my brain. "You're right, I'm sorry. Now how can I help you?"

My surrender surprises him. It takes him a minute to gather himself. "How long can you stay?"

"A week."

"A week? What good is that?"

I turn in my heated seat and face him. "Believe it or not, big shot, I have a life in my hillbilly haven."

"Doing what? Are you still in that disgusting trailer?"

"Pull the car over."

Now he panics. "What? You can't get out here."

"Watch me." I gather up my purse and unlock the door. When I open it, he hollers and pulls over. I get out and light a smoke. He sulks in the car and I sulk out of it. Then I crush the butt under my shoe and get back in the car, grateful to be in the heated seat once more and out of the biting wind.

"Can we start over? I'll help you as much as I can."

He nods and starts the car. Off we go into the city.

Jonathan doesn't live in the brownstone my husband Aaron owned. He sold it, which is too bad, since it had character and gorgeous architectural detail. Riding up to the thirtieth floor in this sleek tower he lives in is about as nauseating as blasting to the moon. The elevator doesn't make any noise. Shouldn't it make some noise? I want to ask him, but he's rubbing his temples at the moment. I guess he's still getting migraines. We get off in a hallway that is completely empty and painted a dull mushroom colour. How depressing.

"This way." He turns left and we walk and walk. The dogs would love this. It's the last door, which is a good thing—there's nowhere to go but out the window.

He unlocks his sleek front door and we go inside. "Melissa!"

It's silent. I look around. This place has all the charm of a waiting room.

"I told her to at least have the decency to be here when you arrived."

As he takes my coat, a fluffy ball of brown and cream fur comes out of nowhere and wiggles at my feet. "Hello there."

"Don't touch it. It'll give you mange."

"Don't be so foolish." I pick up the puppy and wrap it under my sweater. "It's trembling."

"She does that. The damn thing cost me eight thousand dollars. Melissa begged me to get it and now she hardly looks at it."

Fletcher wouldn't want me to say "You're an idiot!" so I say "What kind of dog is she?" instead.

"A Pomeranian. Some mini variety."

"What's her name?"

"Beulah. Not my idea."

A sudden weariness comes over me. "May I go to my room for a minute? I need to lie down. It's been a long day."

He takes my suitcase and leads me to what looks like a luxury hotel room. "Would you like a drink of some kind? Club soda? Cola?"

"Whiskey."

"Mother, you know I only drink wine. Why would I have whiskey in the house?"

"There's always hope."

He makes a face and leaves me to look around. I sink into a bed that is so high off the floor I'll have vertigo. Once I kick off my shoes, I pull up a blanket to keep around Beulah. Poor little thing stops trembling, closes her eyes, and sleeps. I'm not far behind.

When I wake to raised voices echoing down the hallway, I don't know where I am. It takes me a few minutes to get my bearings. Beulah licks my ear.

Before I do anything, I need to pee, and then remember I was supposed to call Fletcher. I put Beulah in my sweater pocket, and once I've finished with the loo and washed my hands, I follow the shouts. My son and granddaughter are scowling at each other from opposite sides of the kitchen island.

"Hi, Melissa."

She turns around and smiles. "Hi Gee." That's been her name for me since she was two. She comes over and gives me a big hug. I kiss the top of her head.

"How long will you be here?"

I glance over at Jonathan. "I'm not sure. Could be a while. Let me look at you."

Melissa is a beautiful girl, with long blonde hair like her mother and a nice figure, but she has black circles under her eyes, and dull, acne-prone skin that she hides under makeup. If I saw her on the street wearing that short skirt, those leggings and high boots, I'd say she was twenty-five. That's not good.

"And look at you!" she giggles. "Remember that book, *The Paper Bag Princess*? That's you, Gee."

"I never did understand the fascination with clothes."

Melissa looks at me more closely. "There you are!" She picks up Beulah right out of my pocket. "I thought Dad had pushed her down the garbage chute."

"Don't be such a drama queen," he says.

She kisses the dog with big smacks, Beulah wiggling with happiness. Then she drops her on the floor and picks up her cell phone instead.

"Dad's trying to make me feel guilty about going out on your first night here, but I have a party I can't miss. You don't mind, do you Gee?"

Beulah comes over to me, so I pick her up and put her back in my pocket. "I do mind."

My granddaughter looks at me.

"But—"

"I've come a long way to see you and I'm hungry. Why don't you scramble up some eggs, put on some toast, and we'll get caught up on our news."

"I don't know how to scramble eggs."

"I'll teach you."

"Are you kidding me?"

Jonathan clears his throat. "You heard your grandmother. Call your friends and say you can't make it."

She's obviously horrified and gives us a death glare before she grabs Beulah from me once more and stalks off. We hear her bedroom door bang shut.

"Welcome to my world," Jonathan says.

"You hungry?"

I make the eggs and butter the toast. Instead of talking, Jonathan monkeys around with some sort of machine.

"What's that?"

"It's an espresso machine. It makes coffee."

"Got any tea?"

"Green or herbal?"

"I'll have the coffee."

At least he's taken off his jacket and tie. He looks much younger now, even with his furrowed brow. Jonathan takes our plates and moves to go into the dining room.

"I'd like to eat in here," I say.

"In the kitchen?"

"Yeah. That's what the stools are for."

He reluctantly returns and puts down the plates on the island. He pours our coffee and we sit, me on the end and he in the middle.

The eggs are good. Must be free-range hens. "How long have you had this place?"

"We moved shortly after your visit the last time."

"Pass me the salt, please. And do you like being this far off the ground?"

He hands me the shaker. "I very rarely get to look out a window. The dramatic views are lost on me."

"So why buy it?"

"It's a good investment."

"Jonathan, is that really a good way to decide where you're going to live? How much money you can get out of it?"

"Beats any other reason."

His face looks weary. I'd like to take his hand in mine, but I better not. "So how's your job? Is your grandfather still bossing you around?"

My son stabs the eggs with his fork. "Does he ever do anything else?"

"How many millions is he worth now?"

Jonathan laughs. "Millions? It's billions."

"No shit!"

"Mother! Why do you insist on cursing?"

"Oh, fiddle-dee-dee. Is that better? Why this hang-up about swearing, anyway?"

"Dad told me not to."

I put the last of my toast in my mouth. "He told you that when you were five. He didn't mean for the rest of your life."

"I don't remember you cursing before you disappeared and left me alone with Grandfather."

I didn't realize Melissa was standing by the kitchen door until she said, "You left Dad when he was a kid? Who does that?"

"I'm not discussing this right now. It's been a long day."

"Dad might be a total jerk sometimes, but he always takes me with him."

I've had enough of these two. "I'll say good night. Sweet dreams."

"Don't get all huffy, Mom. You're supposed to help me, remember?"

After putting my dishes in the sink, I grab Melissa's cell phone right out of her hand and take it to my room. After I light a cigarette, I pick up a fancy doodad to put the ashes in.

Fletch picks up on the first ring. "How's it going?"

"I'm going to fucking kill both of them."

"Don't use rough language around him. You know he hates it."

"Is he frigging royalty? I don't think so. Did you eat the shepherd's pie I left you?"

"The boys and I had it along with the chocolate cake Dora made."

Dora is Harvey Trimm's wife, our neighbour with the two labs. She's been in love with Fletcher since third grade. "Didn't take her long."

"Dora's a kind soul."

"She's a bitch."

"Get some sleep."

"Yeah. Don't work too hard."

There's an ensuite attached to this bedroom, so I have a bubble bath and smoke a few more ciggies. It's only when I get out of the tub and look at my mangled chest that I feel guilty about smoking. I'm in pretty good shape for my age. Must be all the walking. I get a pang every now and again about my breasts, but I don't miss them that much. Men liked them. It's just as well they're gone.

Before I go to bed, I sneak out of my room and knock on Melissa's door. "May I come in?"

I hear a muffled, "Whatever."

She's on the bed with her laptop, looking down-in-the-mouth. Beulah spies me and wiggles over to the end of the bed.

"I came to give you back your phone." I toss it to her.

"I'm getting the new iPhone tomorrow anyway." She looks up from her laptop. "Do you even like my dad?"

I sit on the edge of the bed and put Beulah in my lap. She scratches at my fluffy robe to make a nest, circles a few times, and curls up in a ball.

"I love your father, but our relationship is difficult."

"Well, if you went away without him, no wonder. And you won't move here. I guess his unhappiness is your fault."

"Does he really want me to live here? I had no idea."

"He sometimes says that our family is too small. Everyone is 'gone with the wind,' he says. Do men get menopausal? He's acting weird lately."

"Being a grown-up can be complicated. Let me ask you this. Do *you* even like your father?"

There's a small smile. "Sometimes."

"He's doing his best. Cut him some slack."

As I look around her room, it reminds me of a boutique, with racks of up-to-date fashions and a jewellery counter. There's even a huge flat-screen television mounted on the wall. Where are the books I've sent her over the years?

She reaches over and touches my thick, straight, shoulder-length hair. "I wish I had silver hair. Dad won't let me."

"What does a sixteen-year-old need with grey hair?"

"Platinum silver is super hip now. Do you think I'll get it when I'm your age?"

I shrug.

"Will I get breast cancer?"

Now I see my three-year-old Melissa, afraid of thunder and lightning. "No. Your mother doesn't have it, so you'll be fine."

"That's a total lie." She stares at me. "It's pretty messed up that you still smoke."

"That's me. One messed-up broad. Do you smoke?"

"God, no. It stinks."

"What about weed?"

She laughs. "I can't believe you're so nosy."

"So that's a yes."

She cocks her head to one side. "Are you here to do some sort of intervention? You know nothing about my life and I don't appreciate you thinking you can fix me. I thought you were visiting, like a normal person. If you want to be a shrink, go work on Dad. He's fucked up."

She waits for my reaction.

I give her back her dog and walk to the door. "You shouldn't swear. Good night."

CHAPTER TWO

I'm an early riser, a five-in-the-morning person. Sleep has never been easy for me. It's often the enemy, in fact, and so over the years I've developed a system whereby I take cat naps during the day. That way I only have to sleep about four hours a night. More often than not, in the hours before dawn, I reach over to my bedside table and grab my iPad so I can log in to my missing persons websites. They're from all over the world. It's comforting to know that there are other people out there like me.

Searching. Always searching.

I'm truly sorry our dinner ended on a sour note last night. I want to make amends by whipping up buttermilk pancakes, if I can find the ingredients in the endless wall of handle-less grey cupboards that wrap around three walls of Jon's kitchen.

First things first. Standing on the heated floor of the bathroom, which is kind of great, I'm trying to figure out how to turn on the shower. There are chrome openings on every surface. After messing around for a couple of minutes, I give up and have a shallow bath.

With my old jeans and pullover on, I feel better. It takes me a while to make my bed. You can put your back out trying to lift a mattress that's two feet deep. When I open the bedroom door, there's Beulah curled up on the floor. She's shivering.

That's enough.

I pick her up and put her inside my sweatshirt to warm up, but it's hard to hold a dog like that when you don't have a bra you can stuff it into. Once she's toasty, I put on my old sweater and put her back in the pocket. It seems to be her favourite place.

There's something I have to do before I make pancakes. I take my bathrobe and tiptoe down the main hall. The kitchen light is on, so I figure Jonathan must be up. When I walk in, a middle-aged Asian woman is sweeping the floor with a broom.

"Oh!"

She looks up and nods. "Hello, miss."

"You work here?"

"Yes."

She takes the dust pan and empties it in the sleek garbage can.

"Jonathan makes you come in this early?"

"I live here. Yesterday was night off."

"I'm Jonathan's mother, Grace." She hesitates before shaking my hand, as if unsure she should.

"Yes, I know. Mr. Willingdon said you were coming. Can I get you something to eat?"

"No, heavens. I was going to make buttermilk pancakes for everyone. Would you like some…I'm sorry, I don't know your name."

"Linn. But no, Miss Grace. I will cook for you. You are guest."

She seems adamant, so I give in. "That would be nice. But before you start, do you have a sewing kit and scissors?"

Off she goes and comes back with the requested items. "I can put on button."

"No, thanks."

When I get down on the kitchen floor and spread out my bathrobe, she looks a bit horrified. "I'm making Beulah a nice warm outfit."

I cut a piece off the bottom of my bathrobe and proceed to make a sweater. I'm good with a needle and thread and making patterns. By the time I hear the other two stir, Beulah is in her soft jumper with collar and cuffs. She dances around me when I put it on her. Linn and I smile at her antics. Then Beulah wants up, into my pocket. What am I going to do when I leave?

Linn steers me into the dining room, where the table has already been set. There are three different newspapers to read from. She pours me a glass of orange juice and a cup of coffee. "Would you like to eat now, miss?"

"I'll wait for Jonathan, thank you."

Linn picks up a remote and points it at the window. Ivory shades begin to rise up as if by magic. I get up from my chair and walk over to the floor-to-ceiling windows, but step back—I'm sure I'll fall to my death if I get any closer. New York City is at my feet. It is a spectacular view if you like concrete buildings, but since they don't turn me on, Beulah and I go back to the table.

Linn is pouring me a second cup of coffee when Jonathan shows up. He looks miserable as always, but he's dressed impeccably. There's something attractive about a man in a suit. A vision of Fletcher wearing one crosses my mind. No dice.

Linn pours him a cup of coffee as he sits at the table and brandishes a linen napkin.

"Thank you, Linn. Good morning, Mother. I trust you slept well?"

"Yes, thank you."

Linn serves us pancakes, which she didn't have to make but I appreciate. Jonathan always loved them. My son eats a plateful while looking at his Blackberry and glancing at the newspapers. How does he take in all that information at the same time? If he's purposefully trying to ignore me, he's doing a good job. It's like I'm not here.

My coffee cup clatters back on the saucer, a little harder than I intended. "How can I help with Melissa?"

He puts the paper down. "I don't know. Talk sense into her? Talk to her mother when she gets back. Tell her that life isn't all about her. What do grandmothers generally say? The ones who don't talk like sailors, I mean."

"It's a bad habit. I'll stop."

He looks at me with a sceptical face.

"All I can do is try! Jesus."

He leans back in his chair. "A whole half-second. A new world record."

"Holy God. No wonder Deanne left you. Do you always walk around with a poker up your ass?"

Jonathan bangs his mug on the table. "Believe it or not, I'm a great guy when I'm not with you."

"Then why the heck do you want me to come live in New York?"

"Who said that?"

"Melissa. Is it true?"

He looks like a little boy. "The fact that you've never even entertained the idea says everything."

This is not going well. "Just take a deep breath, Jon. I know we don't always see eye to eye, but I did come to support you. If you'll let me."

He closes his eyes for a moment and then opens them. "I don't know what to do."

We both turn when we hear Melissa approach. She's dressed to leave and has her school bag over her shoulder. She's already texting with her mitts on, the ones with no fingertips. "Later."

"Just a minute!" I say. "Come and have some breakfast. You can't go out with an empty stomach."

"I'll get a Starbucks on the way to school."

Linn comes in with more pancakes. "Melissa, your favourite."

Melissa sighs and rolls her eyes. "What part of 'I don't like pancakes' do you not understand? They're Dad's favourite, not mine, and if you paid more attention you'd know that. And by the way, you weren't supposed to put my new sweater in the wash. What is it with adults? You're all hopeless."

She walks out the door.

And her father and Linn remain where they are.

I hand Beulah over to Jonathan and then I'm out the door, running down the corridor. Missy has her earphones on and doesn't hear me. I grab her from behind, scaring the life out of her.

"What are you doing? Are you crazy?" She tries to escape. Fortunately she has about six layers on for me to grab. I haul her, squirming and yelling, back down the hall. We go back into the apartment and I push her into the dining room, where Linn is still holding the platter of pancakes and Jonathan is still holding Beulah.

"You apologize to Linn for your rude and dismissive comments. Who do you think you are? Show her the respect she deserves."

"You can't treat me like this!"

"Why is it okay to bully Linn, but not you?"

"I didn't touch her."

"Your words touched her! Do you know how awful words can be? They're the most powerful force of all. Now say you're sorry to Linn."

Melissa huffs and puffs and looks at her dad to intervene, but he keeps his mouth shut. "All right! I'm going to miss school thanks to you." She turns in the general area of Linn but doesn't look her in the face. "I'm sorry."

"You're sorry for what?" I prompt.

Melissa clearly wants to hit me. "I'm sorry I was rude. It won't happen again. Can I go now?"

"Have fun at school."

She marches over to the front door and slams it shut as hard as she can. I scoop Beulah out of Jon's hands and sit back at the table.

"Was that helpful?"

Linn can't keep the grin off her face, and she disappears into the kitchen.

"You shouldn't have put your hands on her. Technically, that's assault."

Okay. Now I know what I'm dealing with.

WHILE JONATHAN IS AT WORK AND MELISSA IS AT SCHOOL AND LINN IS CLEANing an already spotless apartment, Beulah and I go snooping.

In Melissa's room.

I have no qualms about her privacy. She doesn't pay the rent here. It's a huge job, because the kid has so much stuff, she just piles it out of the way. One girl does not need forty pairs of jeans. I grab a garbage bag and toss in half of them. I'll ask Linn to take them to Goodwill. I'm her favourite person at the moment.

It doesn't take me long to find the dope or the pills or the alcohol. She's not very inventive when it comes to hiding places. The top of a closet and a Kotex box are where you look first. At least I have evidence to back me up.

Then I spy her laptop. Melissa is so sure that her father wouldn't dare look at it, she's still logged on. What I see when the screen comes up is Melissa biting her lip in an attempt to look sexy, holding her t-shirt up around her neck and exposing her breasts. I scroll through her pictures, hoping this is a one-off, but she has several inappropriate images, and worse, she's posted them online.

A deep anger comes to the surface, along with the need to get rid of it. I get dressed in my down jacket because the six televisions in this apartment are blaring that it's cold outside. Beulah is now happily tucked into my jacket, her little head poking out enjoying the sights. She's the only thing that keeps me from weeping.

I walk for a long time. How I wish I was on my hill with the dogs. I want to run away from this place. It's too noisy, too busy, too vast. There's no air to breath, no silence to enjoy, no stopping on the sidewalk to look up at a patch of blue sky. Big cities frighten me. I'm alone here. Even when Fletch isn't home, I'm never alone in that trailer.

By the time I get back I have a plan, but then Melissa texts her father to tell him she's going to a sleepover at her best friend's house.

I'm wolfing down Linn's amazing pad Thai for dinner. "And you believe her?"

Jon hasn't even changed out of his suit. He looks done in. "I'd like to believe her. I'm almost too exhausted to care."

"Jonathan, did it ever occur to you that you could quit your job and do something else?"

He gives me a smirk. "Tell Grandfather that I'm going to paint pictures in Paris, or sail around the world? How do you think that would go over?"

"Who cares what he thinks?"

"I do, Mother. He's got me completely involved in every aspect of the business." He takes his fork and pokes at his forehead. "I've got it all up here. He doesn't trust anyone else, which is paranoia, but that's what I'm dealing with. If I go, he'll cut me out of his will. He told me so. And the company I've been slaving away for will belong to someone else."

I refill my empty wineglass. "And would that be so bad?"

Now he drops his utensils on the plate, and takes that starched linen napkin and wipes his mouth. "Bad? I have a daughter I'm trying to raise here. How am I going to do that with no job? You know darn well Grandfather will make sure no one hires me in this city."

"So move."

He leans back in his chair. "I've worked all my life for this company, and I think Dad would be proud of me. This was his legacy. I'm not going to throw that away just because Grandfather can be difficult. It's a terrible thing to say, but he's not going to last forever. I'd like to pass it on to my daughter."

I finish this glass of wine and set it on the table. "Speaking of daughters, you need to see something. Come with me."

He reluctantly gets up from his chair and follows me down the hall. I open Melissa's bedroom door.

"You can't go in her room. That's private."

"Parents your age believe a lot of bullshit."

It's all on her bed. The bright assortment of pills, the bags of weed, the bong, the bottles of vodka, all on display in front of him.

"Dear God." He moves slowly forward and puts out his hand to touch it, but covers his mouth instead.

"This is a shock, I know. She's lying to you. That's what they do."

"But…"

"And there's this."

I open her computer to show him the first picture. "You're trying to be her friend, but you're her father. She needs guidance."

His face is white. "How could she do this to me?"

"Why is she doing it at all?"

"I don't know what to do."

"I do."

MELISSA EVENTUALLY SHOWS UP AROUND NINE THE NEXT NIGHT. SHE SEES HER father and I sitting in the living room and gives us a brief nod and keeps going.

"Melissa."

"What?"

"Could I speak to you for a moment?"

She drags her feet on the shiny hardwood floor. "I'm exhausted and I have to write a paper for Monday." She keeps looking down at her phone.

"This won't take long. Sit down."

"Dad! I told you. I've got stuff to do."

"Sit."

She groans and flops on the couch. "What am I apologizing for this time?"

"For this."

Jonathan reaches for the paper bag that is by his chair. He takes each item out of the bag one at a time and puts them all in the middle of the area rug. I watch her eyes get big. He brings out her computer and opens it. Melissa's blood drains from her face and she slowly turns to look at me. "What have you done?"

"She's done what I should have done months ago. Now I'm going to tell you what's going to happen." He falters a little and glances at me.

"You've got this," I tell him.

"I called your principal today—"

"On a Saturday?"

"—at her home number, and told her you're taking some time off."

"She won't let you."

"She did."

Melissa's mouth opens and she stares at her dad. "Do *not* send me to rehab! I'm not into drugs full-time. I'm not an alcoholic. I'm not doing anything different than my friends. It's no big deal. Everybody does it."

"I'm sending you away."

"You're not serious."

"I have to do something. I cannot let this continue."

Melissa looks furious. "So your solution is to take me away from my father and my mother? You must be reading some great parenting manuals. As soon as your kid makes a mistake, kick them out of the house."

"Stop with the 'woe is me' routine," I say. "When you start behaving like a responsible young woman, you'll be dealt with accordingly."

She turns around and curls her lip at me. "It's all your fault! Everything was fine until you walked in here. Just go away!"

"I am going away. But guess what? You're coming with me."

CHAPTER THREE

When I call Fletcher to tell him I'm bringing home a pissed-off devil child, he doesn't seem too bothered. But then, nothing bothers Fletch. Of course, he's never lived with a teenager. A teenager who's just been told she can't have her laptop or phone. She's allowed one suitcase of clothes and Beulah. That's it. (As if I'd leave Beulah behind.)

After three hours of screaming into her pillow, she eventually falls asleep on top of her bed. I don't feel sorry for her. I tell Jonathan to get some sleep; he looks dreadful. I, on the other hand, make sure to sit by front door all night. It's not like I have to worry about her going out the window. She shows up on the dot of three with a bulging knapsack.

"I can't believe you're sitting here."

"I can't believe you thought I wouldn't be."

She stomps back to her room.

In the morning, I knock on Jonathan's bedroom door. He opens it, wearing pyjamas that Cary Grant would have on in a forties movie. They're even pressed.

"Did you get any sleep?"

He nods. "A little."

"I think Melissa and I should leave today. She tried to escape last night, and I don't want her to slip through our fingers."

"I can change your reservation, but it'll cost more."

"It's going to cost you a lot more than that. Hire a private plane. I'm not holding this girl down on a commercial flight while she screams she's being kidnapped."

He looks uncertain. "Are we kidnapping her?"

"Who cares? Do you want your daughter back?"

Jonathan nods. "How are you going to fix her?"

"You leave that to me."

"You're not going to strap her down and starve her, are you? Or hang her by the toenails?"

24

"Are you going to give me a hard time, Jon? Just make the arrangements, please."

DRIVING TO THE AIRPORT WITH THE WEEPING MELISSA IS A REAL TREAT. She's getting a lawyer. She's calling the media and child services. She's suing. She'll escape and live with her mother. She'll become a nun. She'll kill herself. She'll jump off a bridge. Her father will never get another Christmas gift from her and as for me, well, I can whistle Dixie. Finally, she says she hates us and is never speaking to us again.

Perfect.

When we get to the airstrip and Melissa spies the private plane, she realizes her plans for making my life hell in coach are thwarted. She looks defeated, but she has one more blow to deliver. She refuses to say goodbye to her father and hurries aboard before he can hug her.

"Do you think this will work?" He looks desperate.

"All I can do is try. If it doesn't, you can bring her back and make appointments with the best therapists in New York, but I don't think there's a pill for spoiled rotten. Say goodbye to Beulah."

He grimaces at my furry friend. I pat his arm and kiss his cheek. "See ya, Jon. Please don't call her. I'll let you know how things are going. Take care of yourself."

"You too. Thanks Mom."

Poor little bugger. I walk up the stairs and duck my head to get in the cabin.

I don't know what Melissa does while we are in the air. I keep my eyes closed. As long as she's quiet I don't care.

Since my son is paying for this flight, we're flying into Sydney instead of Halifax. Fletcher meets us at the airport. My blood pressure returns to normal just looking at his face. He puts his arm around my shoulder and squeezes it.

"Hey Fletch, you remember Melissa."

"Hello, Melissa."

She ignores him. We ignore her and wait for the bags. Then we head out to the truck, with Melissa walking a good thirty feet behind us.

"You know what you're doing?" he asks.

"Not really."

He grins at me. "I brought the dogs."

Melissa spends the hour ride to Baddeck in the back seat with two wiggly fiends trying to lick her ears. Since she's not talking to us, she just pushes them aside. But Daffy and Donald are very enthusiastic. They only listen to Fletch and he's keeping quiet. They pester her non-stop. I've got Beulah in my doggie carry-all. She's not going to be introduced until we get home.

As soon as Fletch pulls into the yard and turns off the truck, Melissa is out the door, the dogs jumping up and down on either side of her. She stands in the middle of the gravel driveway and shrieks.

"These are the stupidest dogs ever! Tie them up!"

Fletch and I depart the truck as well. He reaches into the back and takes the suitcases. "This is their home. I can tie you up if you like."

Another shriek and she stomps off behind the trailer and up the hill. The boys think this is great. It's Sunday, no hunters about. Off the three of them go.

"Is this a good idea?"

"She'll be back. She's not dressed properly."

While I was gone we had a snowfall. Just a coating, but enough that I can see Melissa's grassy footprints through the white film of newly fallen snow. The dogs zigzag back and forth.

When I enter the trailer, a sense of peace comes over me. It won't last long, and so I savour it. I introduce Fletcher to Beulah.

"This dust bunny cost eight thousand dollars."

His big belly laugh fills the air. He laughs so long and hard he's got tears in his eyes. "I didn't pay that much for this trailer."

He holds out his massive hand and I place Beulah in the palm of it. He brings her up to his face. "Well, if you don't beat all. Nice to meet you, Beulah."

The dog starts to wiggle and her two paws disappear into his beard as she tries to kiss him. I can see he's delighted with her. They look ridiculous, of course. Beulah weighs five pounds and Fletch around three hundred, but I do believe they're kindred spirits.

We are eating our dinner of pan-fried haddock, boiled potatoes, beets, and green chow-chow when a frozen child and two exhausted dogs return. Beulah is asleep in her sweater in the centre of the table, curled up in a wicker bread basket.

Melissa's face is vivid red with cold and outrage. "You're *eating*? You just left me out there and it's dark out!"

"We saved you some dinner. It's in the microwave."

The boys run to their dishes for their supper and my granddaughter stands glaring at us. She wants to stalk off, but she's hungry. She keeps looking at our food. "I don't like fish."

"Today's menu is take it or leave it."

She slumps into a kitchen chair, too tired to bother with this performance. I get up, re-heat her food, and bring it to the table. She grudgingly puts the fish to her nose, sniffs it, and makes a face, but it doesn't take long for the plate to be empty.

"There's a mess of chocolate brownies under that tinfoil over there." Fletch points at it while I bring his tea. "Courtesy of Dora."

I grunt.

Now that the food is bringing Melissa back to life, she summons enough interest to say, "Dora the Explorer?"

"Dora the snake-charmer."

Fletcher shakes his head when I put the plate of brownies in front of him. "I don't know why she bothers you so much."

"That woman can't wait for me to drop dead. Then she'll wheedle her way in here."

"What's she gonna do with poor old Harvey?" Fletch asks.

Melissa's mouth is full of chocolatey goodness. "Who's Harvey?"

"Her long-suffering husband. After I'm gone a week, Harvey will have an unfortunate accident—a fall down the cellar stairs, maybe, or his brakes will fail coming down Kellys Mountain. You mark my words."

"You have a vivid imagination," Fletch laughs.

The dogs finish their food. They pick up Beulah's scent and sniff the plastic tablecloth. Fletch takes the basket with Beulah in it and tells them to sit.

"Now, this little lady is Beulah. You boys have to treat her nice."

He holds out the basket but has his enormous hand covering her, letting the dogs smell but not touch her. They are in a frenzy of sniffing. Tom and Jerry are on the counter, watching every move. Fletch takes his hand away and Beulah sleepily opens her eyes. Her nose goes twitchy and she jumps up. She sees her four new roommates and has a conniption fit. Her shrill yapping sends both the cats and dogs running for cover.

Fletch starts his belly laugh, and no one can resist that—even Melissa smiles. Then she looks at me and it disappears.

Fletch leaves with his new best friend and heads for his recliner. "Come on, Beulah, time to meet Starr Dobson."

Melissa looks around. "Where's my room?"

"I'll show you after we finish these dishes."

"How long are you going to keep up this prison-warden charade? You let me nearly freeze to death outside and now I'm your housemaid."

"I'll wash. You dry."

"No."

"No food for you, then."

Melissa jumps up and clenches her fists. "You think you're going to bend me to your will by being all mean and tough?"

I turn to look at this exhausted, overwhelmed, and totally messed-up kid. "Have you ever done dishes?"

"No."

I throw the dish towel to her. "It's easy."

We do the dishes. When she grabs an entire handful of cutlery at once, I let it slide.

"I'll take you to your room."

We walk by Fletch, who's snoring on his recliner. Beulah has made herself comfortable on the outer edge of his beard.

Melissa points listlessly. "She's my dog."

"She's not going anywhere."

We go past Fletch's room first and then she automatically enters the next room down. "This is pretty small. It's like a walk-in closet."

"Sorry, this is my bedroom, and it's luxurious compared to yours."

She spins around and faces me. "I thought you and Fletcher were a couple."

"We're roommates."

"Friends with benefits?"

"That's none of your business."

"So you have no excuse not to leave this place. You really could come to New York. You just don't want to."

I take her by the shoulder and steer her out into the hallway. "There are things I have to do before I die, and being in the States will not help me."

"You are a very confusing woman, Gee."

I open the door to the spare room, which is not what you'd call attractive. There's a bed and a bunch of stuff I throw in there when I'm in a hurry. Fletch was nice enough to make the bed and put towels on the end of it. Her suitcase is on the floor.

"This is where you'll sleep. The cats may visit you through the night. You might as well keep your door cracked open, because they will scratch until you let them in. The bathroom is down the hall to your right. I'll leave a night light on. Feel free to use any toiletries. There's a new toothbrush in the medicine cabinet."

I imagine the look on her face is identical to that of people who have encountered aliens. She blinks several times. "Are you for real? I have no phone, no laptop, no music, no television. What am I supposed to do?"

"There's a pile of books over there you might enjoy before bedtime. If you need anything, just holler. I'll let you get sorted."

When I leave the room, I close the door to give her some privacy. I hear her weeping. That's a good thing. She needs to let a lot of stuff out.

I'm too tired to do anything but get ready for bed. Fletch usually sleeps out on his recliner until about eleven. Then he'll let the dogs out for their last pee, make sure the doors are locked once they come in, and bank the fire in the wood stove. When I hear his bedsprings groan, that's the signal that our day has come to an end. We're snug in our nest, dogs, cats, and people snoring until morning.

And Melissa will be snoring, despite her misery. She was outside in that crisp air for three hours. She's not used to pure, clean oxygen.

MELISSA IS STILL ASLEEP AT NOON, WHICH MAKES FOR A PLEASANT MORNING. Gladys Nicholson calls to ask something trivial. She has gossip on her mind. Doesn't everyone in a small town?

"Len was talking to Harvey, who was talking to Fletch, who said your granddaughter is visiting from New York."

"That's right."

"How nice for you. Did I hear someone say her father is quite wealthy?"

"He has a bit of money."

"Too bad he doesn't give some to you and Fletch."

"Fletch and I are just fine. Did you want something, Gladys?"

"Janet Pickup wants you to organize the food drive this year."

"I can do that."

"How about the craft table for the Christmas tea and sale?"

"Fine."

"Delima was wondering if you could make up the advent calendars to sell for the hospital auxiliary?"

"Guess what Delima can do with her advent calendars *and* her coconut balls."

Gladys giggles. "You are a breath of fresh air, Grace Willingdon."

Melissa eventually stirs. The bathroom door closes and soon after that I hear the shower go on, and then a yelp. "OMG!"

Let's see. She could be furious at the one showerhead, the low water pressure, the unheated floors, or maybe the clunking of the water pump. I'll have to ask her.

She eventually vacates the bathroom and her bedroom door closes. She stays in there, rejecting my breakfast and lunch. But I did promise her father I wouldn't starve her, so I put a chicken sandwich, a glass of milk, and more brownies on a tray. I knock on her door.

"Go away."

"I'll leave your lunch outside the door. It's up to you whether you want the dogs to get it."

I'm not down the hallway before I hear the door open and close. She stays in her room all afternoon while I go about my business.

It's only when the spaghetti sauce for supper is simmering on the stove, and Beulah and I are watching a nature documentary on beavers that Melissa comes out of her room and sits on the loveseat by the wood stove. I turn off the television.

Her hair is flat, her face unadorned. I can see her freckles. She looks sixteen.

"Did you have a good sleep?"

"Your pillows and mattress suck."

"Didn't seem to stop you from sawing wood for twelve hours."

She stares at Beulah. "She's my dog."

"She's not going anywhere."

Melissa slumps over and puts her head on the armrest. "Why do you want me here? How is this going to help anything?"

"It might not. It's purely up to you which way your life will turn out. We can't stop you from smoking up or drinking, but we can make it difficult."

"Now I wish I'd gone to rehab. At least they have hot tubs and a spa."

"Did you hear that, Beulah? Melissa wants us to fill the tub and stir the water."

Melissa laughs for the first time in two days. "I always tell my friends that you're nuts and they think it's great."

"You can always bring your friends here for the summer. We'd love to have you."

"Here? I mean...not that it's not great, but it's...so small...you know..."

She's trying to save herself. I look around the living room. The ancient panelling is dented and the colour of tobacco. The wood chips around the stove, the tattered recliners, the television that's only twenty inches wide, with crocheted afghans thrown everywhere and the dogs' beds taking up major floor space...she has every right to be dismayed. Fletch and I don't see it anymore. It's just home.

"I wasn't thinking of this place. You might like to spend time at my farmhouse."

"I didn't know you had a farmhouse."

"I have lots of secrets. Your dad never wanted to stay there on his quick visits, as he and your mother preferred hotels, but I have a feeling you might like this old place."

"Okay, when can we go?"

"Later on; there's no rush. Let's go for a quick walk before supper."

Melissa races up the hill out back with the dogs. They bark their excitement as Beulah and I saunter behind. The cats think we're nuts. They're still in front of the fire.

When we get to the top of the hill, Melissa is thrilled to see there are two weathered Adirondack chairs under a huge poplar tree. "Are these yours?"

"This is my reward for all that hiking."

"Good thinking."

We both sit and turn our faces to the lowering of the sun. All around us are dark shadows and a chill that reminds us that winter is just out of sight. Everywhere you look there are shades of dark blue and grey splashed across the landscape.

"I wish I could paint," I say. "Maybe I'll take it up."

"Fletcher should build you a studio up here. When you're not using it, you could rent it out to writers or other artists who want to get away from everything. People need to be alone to think."

I smile at her. "That's a very good idea. You are a clever girl."

When we eventually wander back down the hill, I tell myself that the only thing I need to do for now is to make sure Melissa has good homemade food, plenty of exercise, and lots of sleep.

Imagine getting a Starbucks coffee for her breakfast. And having that damn laptop and phone in her bedroom at night. She's probably up till all hours staring at those screens. It makes me shudder.

Three days into my Melissa mission, I call Jon. "She's doing well. She's still cranky sometimes, but then, so am I."

"What are you doing with her?"

"We baked a pie the other day, and I showed her how to make boiled icing. And I'm teaching her to sew. We're making more outfits for Beulah."

"That sounds very *Little House on the Prairie*, Mother, but how is it going to help her when she gets back to the real world?"

"Believe it or not, Jonathan, this is the real world too. You should remember that."

And then comes the day I take her to my farmhouse. I tell Fletch where I'm going.

"The old homestead, eh?"

"I'll just show her around. We'll be back by suppertime."

"You and I both know that there are ghosts in that house. Are you sure you want to wake them up?"

"Where is this place?"

"In Marble Mountain."

"Sounds like a Disney ride." She leans her head against the side window of the truck.

"It's a very beautiful spot about forty minutes from here. They used to mine for marble in a quarry on the mountain. Hence the name. The beaches have white sand because of it."

We drive down winding roads and pass two old churches. There are driveways that disappear into the woods, the houses too far back to see from the road. You'd think no one lived here, and not many do now; mostly summer residents.

At the bend of a blind hill, I turn and drive slowly down an overgrown dirt laneway. The tree branches close in and create a tunnel effect. Melissa looks nervous as we continue on.

"What is this? It's like the set of a scary movie."

I remember feeling that way the first time I set eyes on this place.

An old farmhouse, crooked and settled into the earth, comes into view. The white shingles have faded and the paned windows are empty. The front porch runs the length of the house, with ivy and brambles covering a good portion of it. The front door was red at one time, but it's mostly peeling now. Trees are taking over what was once a garden and meadow.

I pull the truck right up to the front porch and turn off the engine.

Melissa gives me a horrified look. "I thought the trailer was bad, but this? It's the house time forgot."

"This is a special house."

"It looks cold, damp, and mouldy. Why would you want me and my friends to stay here?"

"It wasn't always like this. Come inside."

It takes a few seconds for the key to cooperate and open the front door. A loud creak accompanies the motion.

"I'm not sure I like this place," says a small voice behind me.

"It's just old, like me."

When I open the parlour door, my heart skips a beat. It always does. The old-fashioned furniture bring back so many memories. The voices come rushing into my ears. "We're still here...."

Melissa pokes my arm. "Gee?"

"What? Sorry." I try and gather myself. Melissa looks unsure and that's the last thing I want her to be.

"Come. I'll show you around. This is the parlour, or at least that's what my aunts called it."

Melissa looks about. "You had aunts? I didn't know that."

"I had parents, too. I didn't just drop out of the sky."

The stuffed sofas in their big-blossomed patterns look shabby against the worn rose wallpaper. Nothing matches and everything clashes, but I personally love this look. A chintz cottage, Aunt Mae once called it. Two armchairs flank the small fireplace in the centre of the room, the white scrolled mantel chipped and covered with old candle sticks and porcelain figurines. There are a pair of tiger salt and pepper shakers, a Humpty Dumpty egg cup, two cow creamers, and a donkey hauling a wagon of wooden matchsticks. I've thought about taking them home with me, but they firmly told me they like it right where they are.

Beside one of the armchairs is a floor lamp and a frilly lamp on a walnut side-table. The dusty braided rug covers most of the linoleum, which is a blessing. Faded lace curtains hang like cobwebs at the dirty windows.

Seeing the house through Melissa's eyes makes me aware that I have neglected this property for far too long. Everything is neat and tucked away, but its heart is in a deep sleep. I should never have let that happen.

We explore the kitchen, with its imposing wood and coal stove on one side of the room, and the large farmhouse sink on the other. There is even wallpaper in here, a village scene with peasants, wooden shoes, and Swiss cuckoo clocks. A large strip of wallpaper over the stove is hanging on for dear life.

Melissa points to the right. "What's that small room for?"

"That's the pantry. It's where my aunts would bake. Cans and jars of all kinds lined the shelves, and flour, brown sugar, and molasses were stored in big barrels under the counter. It always smelled like cookies in here."

My granddaughter loves the old claw tub in the bathroom and gets a kick out of the elaborate metal headboards on the beds upstairs. I show her the quilts that are stored in the trunks, and she falls in love with Aunt Pearl's old vanity dressing table with a round mirror and a plush stool sitting underneath. The handles are made of ivory and Aunt Pearl's brush and comb set are still on the mirrored tray, along with her perfume atomizer.

"This looks like one I saw in *Vogue*! They were doing a piece on the thirties! That was such a glamorous era. Were you born then?"

"Thanks a bunch. Don't they teach you math at school? If I'm sixty, then when would I have been born?"

"In the fifties?"

"Bingo. Now come downstairs and I'll show you how to light a fire."

WE SIT IN THE ARMCHAIRS, WITH WOOL THROWS OVER OUR SHOULDERS. I DON'T want to turn on the oil stove to drive away the damp—the fireplace will do for now. There is no sound other than the flames crackling. This is so far removed from the place Melissa calls home, but if you want to know who you are, you need to stay very still and very quiet.

"Is this a solution?" she finally says. "Keep me away from civilization in the hopes that I'll forget about my life and be a farmer and milk cows?"

"No."

"So what are you trying to prove? Eventually my mother will be back from her perfect honeymoon with the boy wonder and she might notice I'm gone."

I sip tea out of a thermos. "So you don't like her new husband?"

"He's only ten years older than I am."

"Yikes."

"Exactly."

"Is she happy?"

"I'm assuming so. I don't see her all that much, and when I do she's usually on her phone with him."

"It must get lonely."

She takes a gulp of hot chocolate. "I know what you're doing. It's not going to work."

"Melissa, I know kids your age mess around with alcohol and weed. It's usually a phase they grow out of. But I want to know, why the Melissa show on the computer?"

"It's none of your business."

"Perhaps not."

After I add another log to the fire, I gaze into the flames. The smoke rising from the chimney makes it feel as if the house has started to breathe again.

"This is almost the last of the apple wood. One of the apple trees was blown down by a wild storm years ago and I cut it up and stacked it in the back shed. Do you smell it?"

She nods.

"Imagine. Even though it's been here for years drying out and forgotten, it's still here for us to enjoy. No matter how deeply we bury ourselves, our true essence stays with us, even when we think it's gone."

Melissa makes a face. "You're talking like a shrink again."

I don't respond.

"But you're better at it than most."

"Have you been to a psychiatrist?'

"Once, when Mom and Dad got the divorce. They thought it might help, but it made me furious."

"Why?"

"They could have just asked me how I was. Instead I had to sit with this old guy who had bad breath."

This makes me smile. She sees it.

"What?"

"You're an awful lot like me."

"I'm more fashionable."

"So true."

I poke at the fire once more. Melissa watches me. "Why did you bring me here?"

"To the farmhouse?"

Melissa nods.

A deep sigh escapes my lips before I can stop it. "This house, and the women in it, saved me. It is one of the only places where I feel truly safe, and what I'm about to tell you is terrifying."

Her eyes get big.

"I brought you here to tell you the story of a little girl named Amazing Grace."

CHAPTER FOUR

THEN

The first time my sister and I go to the bog, our mom takes us there. She makes us run faster and faster, telling us to hurry up. I laugh with delight as we tear through the woods, stumbling on the wet ground as we wave branches out of the way.

"Over here!"

We hide behind an outcropping of rock and then sit, leaning against the warm, hard surface.

My heart races. "Did I do good, Mama?"

She nods. "You're the fastest."

"I can run faster than the devil himself."

My sister turns on me. "Shut up, Grace. You can not."

"I'm Amazing, thank you very much! Amazing girls can do anything!"

Mom puts her hands on our shoulders. "Hush now. We don't want anyone to find out about this spot. We can have picnics here and play cards. Would you like that, Gracie?"

"No. I hate playing cards. It's too boring. Remember?"

"Okay then, what about cops and robbers?"

"I hardly think so," Ave Maria tsks. "I am *twelve*."

I forget what we played that first time, but it's a place we return to often, just to get away from the others. I'm not sure who all the others are. Mom's always vague with her answers and Maria, who thinks she knows everything, doesn't tell me a thing because I'm only nine. Who does she think she is?

One thing I know is that my mother loves hymns, and that's why my sister is Ave Maria and I'm Amazing Grace. My name is so much better than Maria's, but I don't tell her that, because she's usually grumpy, but I'm always happy. Mom calls me a chatterbox.

"Your mouth will get you in trouble one day."

We live on a farm with a lot of buildings. Some of the adults call it a compound, others a camp. I'm not sure who my father is, but I must have at least forty brothers and sisters. Everything is the same day after day. We play outside, we come indoors for school, and every night we sit together in the barn and the man talks about God and Satan. Then we sing hymns, sway our arms, and praise Jesus before we go to bed.

It's a pretty good life. Mom, Maria, and I share a bed, and that makes me feel safe. But some nights the man comes in and makes my mother get up and leave us. She comes back after a while, but she must get tired of that.

Sometimes I wake up first and I watch my mother and sister sleep. They look very much alike, with pale skin and silky hair. I'm afraid that I'll turn over in my sleep and smother them, since I'm pretty clumsy.

One night my mom goes with the man and comes back with a red line around her neck. That happens a lot. I reach out to touch the dark skin and she flinches.

"Sorry, Mama."

She takes my hand and holds it against her chest. "Promise me something."

"Okay."

"Don't believe everything you're told, no matter who says it. If something doesn't feel right, don't do it. Trust yourself."

"All right."

"You are amazing, Grace. Don't forget that. I forgot it and look where we are."

"Where are we?"

She pulls the blanket over our heads. "We're in our own cocoon. Someday you'll be a butterfly."

I giggle.

"A butterfly with a big mouth."

Then she giggles too.

My friend Helen is either my sister or cousin. It depends on who you talk to. We have a tree fort at the edge of the property and we like to pretend we're spies. The man who comes at night, the one who talks a lot about the devil, walks over to our tree and asks us if we'll do something for him. I'm sort of afraid of the man, but I don't let him know that. Helen is a softie. She trembles beside me.

"I want you two to tell me if you see your mothers talking to the new man, the one with red hair. Can you do that?"

Helen nods.

"Why do you want to know?" I ask.

In an instant he has a tight grip on my arm and shakes me really hard. My neck is going to snap.

"Don't you dare talk back!"

Helen wets her pants. I can see the pee run down her legs.

His black eyes stare at me. "You have a demon in you."

"I do?"

Next thing I know, I'm on the ground, not quite sure how I got there. My nose is bleeding, and as the man walks away, I gather up the bottom of my shirt and stuff it against my nostrils.

Helen is shaking. "You shouldn't talk to him." She runs away.

My afternoon is spent in the tree house, looking up through the cracks in the wood planks, to catch glimpses of the fir trees waving in the wind. There is a lot I don't understand and I find if I stay still, a bubble of air grows around me and I'm protected.

Coming on dark, Maria finds me.

"What happened to your face?"

"The man hit me."

Maria licks her fingers and rubs the skin under my nose. "What did you say to him?"

"He wants me to spy on Mom and I asked him why."

Maria closes her eyes. "Please don't talk back to him."

"Is he God?"

"No. He's the boogeyman. Stay away from him."

"Don't tell Mom he did this. She'll be sad."

Maria nods. "I saved you some supper."

Mom keeps me close to her in the circle that night, even though I didn't tell her a thing. She pretends to sing with the others. The man keeps looking at her. That's when I notice the red-haired man. He's very enthusiastic, but the new ones always are.

The man stands up and we have to look at him. I only watch him with one eye. The other eye doesn't want to.

"There is evil here," he says softly. "Do you feel it? Do you see it? Be on your guard. Only your father knows how to keep you safe. You must listen to the father."

I can't help it. "Which father? You or the one in heaven?"

Mama catches her breath and Maria pokes me in the ribs. So I say, "Sorry. I didn't mean that."

The man with the slicked black hair grins. "It's all right, child. A good question. What father am I talking about?"

Lots of kids put up their hands. "The one in heaven!"

"The one in heaven is correct, but who represents the one in heaven?"

"Jesus," I say. "And maybe cows. They were with Jesus the night he was born."

There's a smattering of laughter from my brothers and sisters.

The man shouts, "Who else? Who does Jesus rely on in this compound?"

Everyone shouts back, "The Master."

"And I am the Master. Those who follow my rules will have a place in heaven. Those who do not, will burn in hell."

Not for the first time do I wonder where hell is. Once I thought it was the furnace that comes on at night and then I wondered if it was the big bonfire that the men build to get rid of brush around the property.

That night the man comes into our room. At first I think I'm dreaming, because instead of taking my mother, he takes Maria. He has his hand over her mouth as he leads her away. Maria tries to kick him and my mother throws herself at him and grabs his leg. "No. No. No. No. No. Not her! Take me!" He drags my mother across the floor and kicks her in the face before he slams the door shut. She weeps by the door and can't get up. I run over to her. She grabs me and holds me in her lap.

"I'm so sorry. I'm so sorry. It's all my fault."

"It's not your fault, Mama. He's a bad man."

"We need to get away."

My stomach turns over. "Leave here? Where do we go?"

"I don't know, child. I have to think. Let me think."

That's the last I remember.

When I wake in the morning, my mother is sitting on the side of the bed trying to rub my sister's forehead, but Maria is turned to the wall and slaps Mama's hand away. "Don't touch me."

"I'm making a plan, Maria. I'm going to get us out of here."

"I don't believe you. You've said that before."

"I mean it this time. The three of us will go away and he'll never find us."

"What did he do?" I ask my sister.

"He married me."

"Why did he do that?"

"Because that's what we're here for. Isn't that right, Mommy? You knew he'd come here one night and you just let it happen."

Mama looks desperate. "Where's my duffel bag? My mother's address and phone number are written on the inside of it. That's where we'll go."

"What's her name?" I want to know.

"Rose Fairchild."

"Our last name is Church, isn't it?"

Maria sits up. "It's a fake, like everything else. What's your real name, Mama? Is it Church, or Fairchild, or Smith, or Webster? You don't even know who you are. You're a nobody!"

Mama grabs Maria by the arms. "My name is Trixie Fairchild. My mother's name is Rose Fairchild. She lives in Nova Scotia."

"When was the last time you talked to her?"

"When I was pregnant. I didn't tell her about you—I was afraid she'd make me come home."

"So she might be dead by now."

"I am going to get you out of here, Maria. I promise you. I'm taking you and your sister out of here and we're not looking back. Start packing. I can borrow a bit of money from the crazy lady. And I'll gather some food. We leave tonight. Hurry!"

When she goes out the door and shuts us in, we look at each other. "Do you think she means it?" I ask.

"If she doesn't, I'm going anyway."

Now for the first time I'm really frightened. I hug my sister. "Don't leave me here. I don't know what to do."

She wipes my tears. "I'm not going to leave you behind."

We get our belongings together and sit on the bed and wait. It's been too long. I'm hungry but I don't want to worry Maria. She spends her time peeking out the bedroom door and moving the curtains aside to see if she can see Mama coming.

Finally she says, "I can't stand this. What is she doing?"

"She wouldn't leave us here alone, would she?" I ask.

Maria turns to me. "I wouldn't put it past her. She only thinks of herself, Grace. It's always about her. And I'm sick of it."

"Yeah! Me too!"

"I'm going to see where she is. Maybe she had trouble getting money together." Maria points at the bed. "I want you to get under the covers and make it messy so you can hide under the blankets and no one will know you're here. I'll be back as soon as I can."

"Promise?"

"I promise."

Both Mama and Maria leave me and now I'm alone. I get under the covers and stay alert, ready to spring into action. Now I just have to wait.

I wait for three days before someone notices that I'm not at school or prayer meetings or in the lunch room. I do my business in the wastepaper basket; if I leave the room, I might miss Mama and Maria coming to get me. There's a bottle of water on the windowsill and I drink that.

Nights are the worst. I think the man will come in and drag me away too, so I stay under the bed in the dark, with Mama's nightgown wrapped around my neck. When I close my eyes, I can pretend she's with me in a cocoon.

Eventually the woman who cooks comes into our room. She doesn't see me at first under all the covers.

"My god! What's that smell?" She goes over to the window, puts the blinds up and opens the window. "What happened in here?"

Then she sees my eyes peering at her from under the blanket. She grabs her chest. "Merciful God!" She pulls the blanket off me and I grab it back. "Grace, what are you doing?"

"I'm waiting for my mama."

"Child, your mama's gone. I thought you were with her!"

When I try to stand up on the bed, I get violently dizzy and fall back against the wall. "You're a liar! My mama and Maria are coming for me! You're a liar!" I can't catch my breath.

"Here. Come here." She tries to grab my hand but I won't let her touch me. I know I'm crying because I can taste the salt on my tongue, but there's no sound.

"Wait here." She runs towards the door.

"NOOO!"

She turns back, grabs my foot and hauls me off the bed in one fluid motion. The last thing I remember is being carried in her arms while she hurries down the corridor.

When I open my eyes I'm on a bed in Helen's room with her mother, Iris, sitting beside me. Helen's brothers and sisters stare at me until Iris shoos them away. Helen hovers close by. Iris holds a bowl of something hot.

"I want you to drink this. Be a good girl now."

I'm too hungry not to drink it and finish the bowl quickly. Then she tears up bread and feeds it to me a piece at a time. The food makes me sleepy but I try to keep my eyes open.

"You'll never guess!" Helen blurts. "Maria and your mom ran away!"

Iris slaps Helen on the wrist. "Be quiet, child."

"They did not! You take that back!"

Iris looks sad. "I'm sorry, Grace. It's true."

I push away the bread. "But what about me? Why would they leave me?"

Iris takes me by the hands. "I believe your mother knew we'd look after you."

"But she wanted me to go too. We were all going to run away."

"Then she was very foolish. Look child, I'm only saying this for your own good. Your mother was a very selfish woman…"

"Leave me alone." I roll over and face the wall. I don't believe them. That couldn't have happened. They're lying.

No one knows what to do with me. I sleep on a cot in Iris's room, but I hear snatches of conversation between the women and children when they think I'm asleep. Even the man looks in the doorway from time to time. One day he tries to talk to me.

"Grace."

"Amazing Grace."

"Grace."

"Amazing Grace, how sweet the sound, that saved a wretch like me..."

"Stop it this instant."

"...I once was lost but now I'm found, was blind but now I see."

He walks over, slaps my face, and leaves the room. Iris kneels down by my cot.

"You don't want to bring attention to yourself. Try to be invisible."

That man lost my mother and sister. I'm going to make him pay.

I do what everyone wants me to do without complaint. I don't talk back, I do my chores, I wave my arms and sing to Jesus. I even smile at the man when it's required, like the time some people come to take a tour of our camp. They carry clipboards and I notice the man is nervous. These clipboard people must be important if the master is in a sweat, so I spy on them. They're very nice. One lady even sees me out of the corner of her eye and motions me forward. The man is beside her.

"Hello dear. What's your name?"

The man puts his arm around my shoulder. "This is Grace. Say hello, Grace."

"Hello."

"Do you like living here, Grace?"

"Oh, yes. I have a tree house."

She smiles. "Isn't that nice?"

"I built it for her," the man says as he squeezes me. "Our Grace loves to hang out in trees!"

They move on and I can see the man is relieved that I kept my trap shut. I was right. These people are important. Before they leave I copy down their licence plate numbers. Helen's brother told me cops collect stuff like that.

While I pretend to be happy and eat my food and do my homework, the whole time I make plans. They aren't plans that make sense, but one day I'll be ready to use them. My mama said if something didn't feel right, I need to trust myself.

And everything about the man tells me he's dangerous. I don't know why the adults here don't see it. A lot of the kids see it, like the boys who are punished in the barn, or the girls who shrink from the master when he comes too close.

But now I notice that even the other men who live here don't dare talk back to him. What does he do to make grown men keep their heads down?

Slowly over the months, I take important things to the bog. I bury my mother's duffel bag at the edge of the rocks we sat behind so long ago. The licence plate numbers go there. A few cans of food and water bottles I've managed to sneak out of the kitchen are stashed there. Then I collect dark clothes, a blanket, some grocery bags. Once the man asked me where I was going with a pot and I told him I was playing house in the tree fort. He believed me. I feel bad about stealing another girl's running shoes, but they are much better than mine.

And so these things wait. And I watch.

I see the man caressing the hair of girls who wear it long and loose, so I sneak into the kitchen, grab a pair of scissors, and hack my hair off. Iris is furious with me and the girls say I look stupid, but I don't care. Now I've even stopped wearing dresses, which is a constant fight with the other mothers, but no matter how many slap me in frustration, looking like a boy makes me feel better.

But nothing happens. I can't make anything happen. The adults keep their schedule and we're not allowed outside the gates. Sometimes I see a yellow school bus go by if I'm up in my tree house and I wonder what it would be like to be those kids who get to drive on a bus. It looks fun and free.

I'm so lonely that I forget to smile. But then I find a cat, a very skinny black and white cat, and I ask Iris if I can keep it.

"Cats belong in a barn."

So now I sleep in the barn. No one knows I'm here. Well, Iris knows, but she doesn't stop me. The cat and I are best friends. I call him Buddy and I won't let anyone near him. One day the man watches me play with the cat and that makes my stomach knot so tightly I run into the woods and go to the bog. Buddy and I try to catch butterflies while we sit on the rock.

Three years later, I'm twelve, and I almost forget what my mother and sister look like. They didn't want me so I don't want them anymore. I'm not running away now; I'm in charge of the chickens and I'm happy about that. Helen and I are still friends and I like when the teacher talks about books and geography. The cook is even teaching me how to make bread. I'm also knitting. I made a sweater for Buddy but he doesn't like wearing it, so I gave it to Helen's little sister to put on her doll.

Helen and I still go to the tree house but mostly we just talk there and laugh. Sometimes the women bring back comic books from the store and we read them and drink Tang. We hang from the branches with our legs and look at the world upside down. Iris comes running over and tells me to get inside. I think I'm in trouble, but no. She just looks in Helen's closet and takes out one of her bras.

"You're becoming a woman now," Iris says. "Your breasts are growing and we have to cover them up."

"Why?"

"To avoid temptation."

"What will I be tempted to do if I leave them hanging out?"

Iris looks at the ceiling. "Grace, you'd try the patience of a saint. Now tell me, have you started bleeding yet?"

I know what she means. The older girls told me about it, and Helen got hers months ago—I wasn't frightened when it first happened to me. But I'm private and everyone doesn't need to know my business.

"Not really."

"When it happens, come to me and I'll give you some rags."

I know how to collect rags. Iris is becoming entirely too bossy.

And then the man shows up in the barn one hot summer night. I see his shadow in the doorway. I know right away he's come for me. I grab Buddy and burrow under the hay, because I can't get out without him seeing me. He's going to hear my heart thumping. It will lead him right to me. He comes closer and says very softly, "Grace. Grace, come to me. I can see you."

I don't think he can see me but I don't know for sure. Buddy is wiggling and I'm so afraid to lose him that I jump up out of the hay and run. But the man doesn't stop me. All he does is grab the cat right out of my arms.

"NO. Give me my cat."

The man holds Buddy by the back of his neck.

"You're hurting him! Let him go."

"I'll let him go as soon as you stop shouting."

I close my mouth and watch Buddy dangling off the floor, helpless and frightened. I feel my body get hot, so hot that I'm burning up.

So this is hell. This is where hell lives. Within.

But I'm not losing the only family I have left.

"Do what you want. Just let Buddy go."

And that's the night he married me.

I THINK ALL THE WOMEN WHO LIVE HERE KNOW EXACTLY WHAT'S GOING ON. I may not be the best disciple Jesus ever had, but I know that this isn't right. There is no love between the man and I, no matter how much he moans that he loves me. If he loved me, he wouldn't hurt Buddy. And I tell him if he ever picks Buddy up like that again, I'll stab him with a pitchfork. He laughs and shakes a finger at me. "Don't make me mad."

Now I have to pretend to like everyone again. The cook who bakes with me, the teacher who teaches me, Iris who makes sure I have hand-me-downs and the occasional bag of treats. The adults are in on this. All these women run around and tell me to be modest and obedient and stay invisible, like that's going to protect me, but they know the man is going to come and get all the girls at some point. They pretend they care but they don't. And now the red-haired man wants to marry me.

I have to think of a way to make them all pay.

FIRST I STOP EATING AND HOPE SOMEONE NOTICES, BUT THEY DON'T REALLY. There are so many of us that we're easy to overlook. The mothers pay attention to their own kids. Iris does the best she can but she has seven to look after. All it does is make me feel weak, and I need to be strong. So then I eat a lot, so much that even the man notices. He pinches the skin on my stomach.

"You're getting porky. I don't like fat girls."

Perfect. I'll get so fat he'll have to roll me everywhere, but as hard as I try, I can't eat enough to get any bigger. I think it's because I'm taller and the fat seems to be smoothing out over my bones. So that idea doesn't work.

But setting the barn on fire does.

I make sure the chickens and cats and our two goats are all outside when I light the match and hold it against the straw. It's the spot where the man first touched me. I'm burning him in those flames. I want him dead. I almost forget to leave but sneak out before anyone smells or sees smoke. I run to the treehouse to watch.

Deep down I know it's a sin to destroy something, but I only need to get the attention of strangers, hopefully the fire department. At some point I'll grab one of them and make them take me out of here. Me and Buddy.

But I didn't count on the wind, or remember that the summer was a dry one. The crispy October leaves fly though the air like tiny lanterns spreading out in the late afternoon sky. They fuel the flames that get bigger by the minute. Soon everything is on fire. People scream and run around, carrying things out of the houses. The sirens I hear way off come closer and closer. All the men have to open the gates to let in the fire trucks and policemen. I want to watch it all but I've forgotten something. Mom's duffel bag has my grandmother's address and phone number on it. That's all I have left that ties me to anyone. I know Buddy isn't going to like it, but I stuff him in a burlap bag I keep in the tree house and put him over my shoulder. A fireman sees me come down the ladder and hollers for me to get away from the trees, but I run as fast as I can into the woods to get the duffel bag, Buddy occasionally scratching me through the burlap. I know he doesn't mean it.

There are voices behind me and one of them is the man's voice. The devil is coming after me. I run so hard my chest might explode. I'm tearing through the woods, stumbling on the wet ground and brushing branches out of the way.

I hear my mama's voice. "Over here!"

I hide behind the outcropping of rock, and frantically dig in the mud to get the duffel bag.

49

"Is he still out there, Mama?"

"Stay very quiet."

That's hard to do because I'm breathing too hard. People call my name. "Grace! Grace!"

The man screams, "Get out here now, Grace!"

I grab the duffel bag, stand up and scream back. "I'm Amazing!"

There are two firemen with the man and when they see me cut up and bloodied by the branches and filthy with mud, they look concerned. Like they're actually seeing me.

I know what to do. I point at the man. "He married me. You have to get me out of here! Please help me!"

The firemen both turn at the same time to look at the man.

"Why, you little bitch!" The man lunges at me but one fireman holds him back and the other steps towards me and picks me up in his big arms.

"I have to take my cat. He's in the bag."

"You can take your cat. I've got you now."

CHAPTER FIVE

NOW

I cannot go any further. By the time I come out of my story trance, the fire is out and it's dark outside.

"My god, it's so late. I'm sorry, we should go."

"Are you kidding me? You're going to leave me hanging! What the heck happened?"

"That will have to be for another day. Fletcher will be worried."

I rise from my chair and Melissa follows me. We fold up our blankets.

"Well, all I know is I hate that man! He's horrible. I hope you never saw him again."

"There were others."

Her mouth drops open. "Others?"

"I was young and alone, with no parent or family to protect me. That's when the devils crawl out of the sewer and wait for their chance to eat you alive."

Her eyes moisten. "That's not fair. I don't think I want to hear this."

"You don't. But you will. Just not right now."

Melissa sidles up and puts her arms around me. "Poor Gee. I don't want to sound mean, but I think it's horrible that your mom and sister left you behind."

I pat her back. "People are capable of anything."

We close up the house and head back to the trailer. Melissa is quiet most of the way home, staring out at the dark through her side window. Maybe this was too much for her. But I can't stop now.

"I have an idea," I eventually say. "Why don't you and I fix up the farmhouse while you're here? We can paint or move the furniture around. Just spruce it up so it will be ready if you do decide to come here for the summer."

"Will you tell me what happened after the firemen arrived?"

"Yes, but I need about two good sleeps before I start again. I didn't realize how exhausting this was going to be."

When we pull into the yard, I see Fletcher look out the kitchen window. That reminds me of something.

"Melissa, don't say anything to Fletcher about this. He knows some of the story, but he doesn't know the gory details. He's a big softie and it was a long time ago."

"Maybe I'm a big softie, too."

"No. You're not."

We both laugh.

As soon as we enter the trailer, a menagerie of furry creatures come to greet us. Beulah does a good job yapping at the others to go to the back of the queue.

Fletcher's at the stove. "I made a meat loaf. Are you hungry?"

"Yes!" says Melissa. "She starved me all day."

We talk about nothing in particular at supper. Melissa asks if she can call her father after she does the dishes, which is a nice surprise. Fletcher takes me aside. "You got a letter today in the mail." He hands me the envelope. "I didn't recognize the return address."

"Maybe this is it."

"Fingers crossed."

I go to my bedroom and shut the door. As I open the letter, my mouth is suddenly dry, and my heart thumps in my ears. I scan the letter quickly, looking for answers.

Dear Mrs. Willingdon,

I'm sorry to inform you that I am not the Maria Fairchild you are looking for. Firstly, my name is Maria, not Ave Maria, and I am from England originally, although we did move to Guelph, Ontario, many years ago. I do not have a sister, only two brothers.

I'm sure you will be very disappointed, but I encourage you to keep looking, and I pray you find your sister someday.

Yours Truly,

Maria Fairchild

My hand drops the letter into my lap. It's always the same answer. *Sorry, I am not your sister.* Why do I get my hopes up after forty-eight years? It's ridiculous. Obviously my mother is long gone, unless she's still alive in her late eighties, but I doubt that. At the same time, something compels me to keep searching for Maria. I don't think she's dead, but I'm pretty sure she's forgotten all about me.

I get in the tub and scoop the bath water from the tap into my hands and throw it at my flushed and mottled face. That way I can pretend I'm not crying. I don't need anyone to hear that nonsense.

There's a soft knock at the door. It's Fletch. "You okay, Gracie?"

"Yeah. It wasn't her, but I'm all right. Just tell Melissa I'm going to bed."

"Sure thing. Good night."

I toss and turn until dawn, finally falling into a heavy sleep around five in the morning. When I open my eyes, the clock says 2:00 p.m.

"Holy macaroni!" I jump out of bed and open the door. "Anyone here?"

There's no answer. There's no animals here either. What the hell?

Once my bathrobe and slippers are on, I rush to the back door and open it, yelling, "Hello?"

There's no answer; now I'm really concerned. I put on my old billy boots and tramp outside, calling. Finally Daffy sticks his head out of the garage door.

"What are you doing?" I ask him, as if he's going to answer me. He sheepishly disappears back into the garage. Obviously something more important is going on.

When I finally cross the yard and look into the garage, there's Fletcher with his radio blaring, showing Melissa how to change a tire. The dogs and cats are watching this procedure as if it's fascinating. I suppose it is, in a way. I don't think Melissa would ever change a tire in New York.

She looks up at me, and her cheeks are flaming red from the cold, since Fletcher never shuts the garage door unless there's a blizzard outside. I have to smile. She looks like I remember her, eight years old, with a saucy grin.

"Look, Gee! If I ever get a car, I can change my own tires! This is so awesome!"

I shout over the music. "You guys want some lunch?"

"Okay!" they shout back, so off I go to whip something up. Beulah decides she's had enough of the cold weather and chases me back to the trailer.

The next few days I start making plans for the food drive and craft sale. Christmas is only three weeks away. Something Jon reminded me of when he called the night before.

"If this keeps up, she may not pass her semester. When are you bringing her home?"

"First you can't wait to get rid of her and now you're annoyed she's staying with me. Make up your mind."

"You don't have to shout. I'm concerned."

I take a deep breath. "I'm sorry, but at this point, I think I'm making progress, although she hasn't opened up about everything, and that's what I'm waiting for. She can always make up her courses. She's as bright as a button, just like you were."

"Her mother comes home later this week. I think Melissa should be here, or Deanne will be furious with both of us."

When I get off the phone I tell Melissa I have to go to the church hall and ask her to come with me, but she puts the kibosh on that. "I don't want to meet a bunch of old women. I think I want to go back to New York. I miss Dad."

"Would you like to return to the farmhouse one more time before you leave? I can tell you the rest of the story." Talk about bribery.

"Instead of cleaning the place up, would you make a fire with more of the apple wood? And can we bring hot chocolate?"

She thinks this is fun. I hope I have the strength to see this through.

CHAPTER SIX

THEN

In my head I imagine the lady with the clipboard will magically appear and take me away to her house. She called me dear—I'm sure she's kind. But I never see her. I sit in the back of a police car and don't understand what the policeman's saying to the voice on the radio. He puts a blanket around me and gives me a chocolate bar.

"Do you have some cat food? My cat is hungry."

"Wait." He opens up a piece of tin foil. "I have a tuna sandwich my wife made this morning." He passes it back to me. I feed it to Buddy. He licks the tuna off the bread. When the policeman isn't looking I eat the bread myself.

"Can I come home with you? Your wife sounds nice."

He glances back at me in the rear-view mirror and clears his throat. Another police officer gets in and they drive me away from the chaos of the farm. I see Helen standing by her mom as she holds her little sister. They're all crying. I wish Helen was with me, but maybe she'll hate me now.

We drive out of the gates and into the world. All my life I've dreamt of this and thought it would be like flying in the sky. But it's nothing like that. I get up on my knees and look out the back window.

"I need to go back! My mama and sister might come looking for me! Stop!"

They keep driving.

THE NEXT FEW DAYS ARE JUMBLED UP IN MY MIND. A LADY TAKES BUDDY AWAY, despite my wailing. She tells me he'll be looked after. I throw up when she walks out the door with him, because he cries and meows for me. I never see him again. I hope the policeman with the nice wife took him in.

In the hospital they give me lots to eat and I gobble everything. But then a doctor comes in and wants to look at me. I scream blue murder because he's a man. Finally a woman comes in wearing a stethoscope around her neck. She sits beside me on the bed.

"Hello," she smiles. "I'm Doctor Stevens. What's your name?"

"Amazing Grace Fairchild."

She looks delighted. "Imagine! You must be very special, to have a name like that."

"I think so. My sister is Ave Maria and she's special too."

"I'm sure she is. Now Amazing, I want to tell you what's going to happen. I need to look at you, to check your body, to see if you've been molested. Do you know what that means?"

"I think it means he married me."

Dr. Stevens gathers herself. "I'm going to put a sheet over you, so no one else will see but me. Do you trust me to do that? I promise I won't hurt you."

She does have a nice smile. "Okay."

It's over pretty quickly and she doesn't hurt me. She takes off her rubber gloves and throws them in the wastepaper basket. Then she comes close to me and puts her hand on my shoulder. "All done."

"Do you believe me?"

"Yes, I believe you."

"What will they do to him?"

"Hopefully he'll go to jail."

"Can I come home with you?"

She quickly turns her head. "Let's just get you better. You rest now and I'll be back to check on you."

"Okay."

But I don't see her again either. A nurse comes in instead and she's very brisk. I don't ask to go home with her. She probably hates cats.

Then another man comes to see me—I pull up the blankets around my neck.

"Grace, I'm Detective Grant. I want to ask you a question."

"Am I in trouble?"

"No, not at all. But before we can proceed further, I need to know if you'd be willing to testify against Mr. Wheeler."

"Who's Mr. Wheeler?"

"The man who did this to you."

"What does testify mean?"

"Tell your story in a courtroom to a judge and jury. All you have to do is tell the truth."

"Will the man be there?"

"Yes, I'm afraid so. But you'll be protected from him, I promise."

Promises don't mean anything. "No."

"Don't you want him to go to jail?"

What a dumb question. He tries hard to change my mind but gives up after a while.

A few days later I'm eating rice pudding when a heavy woman comes into my room. Her skirt looks like it's going to split up the seam. I wait for her to sit down to see if she pops out of it, but she only stands at the end of my hospital bed.

"Grace Fairchild, I believe."

"Amazing Grace."

"Grace, I want you to get dressed. You're coming with me."

My bowl of rice pudding drops in my lap. "NO! I don't want to come with you."

"Whether you want to or not makes absolutely no difference. You are a ward of the state until your family is found. In the meantime you'll be placed in a foster home. It's for the best."

I grab the sheets and pull them over my head. "Go away!"

"Nurse!"

When two or three adults want you to do something, it usually gets done, even when you're limp and don't co-operate. By the end of the struggle, the looks on their faces are the same as the adults in the camp. Grown-ups get mad really fast. As they escort me out of the hospital I ask them, "Where's my duffel bag? I need it."

"There's no duffel bag."

"I have to have it! It's my grandmother's."

"If I find it I'll give it to you." The fat woman only says that so I'll be quiet. They put me in a car and I slump over so my head is on the seat.

"Get up."

I don't, and what's she going to do about it? She has to drive the car. So I don't see where I'm going, only hear the motor and feel the wheels go over the bumps and dips in the road. It almost puts me to sleep, but the car stops before that happens. The fat lady gets out and she's gone for a while. Then the back door opens and a man's face appears.

"Get out of the car, please."

No way am I getting out of this car.

"Do you hear me?"

Pretend he's not there.

He grabs my arms and pulls me out all at once. He places me on the sidewalk and points his finger at me.

"You will not get away with this sort of behaviour in my house. Do you understand?"

"Yes."

There's a woman behind him. She's got an apron on. "I'll take you to your room."

"Goodbye, Grace," the fat woman says.

I ignore her. She says to the man, "Do you see what I mean? You'll have your hands full."

The woman walks ahead of me, but does turn around to look at me when she talks. "I know this is frightening and unfamiliar, but we'll do the best we can until your family situation gets sorted. My name is Sandra. My husband is Lloyd. We have three foster kids with us at the moment. I'm sure you'll make friends quickly."

It's a big, rambling sort of place, set back on a street with a lot of other big homes. There's a part of me that's interested in being inside, since I've never been in a house on an actual street before. The minute I walk over the threshold, the smell is different. Do all houses have their own smell?

Sandra walks me up a big flight of stairs. "Do you have any luggage?"

I shake my head.

"That's all right. I'll gather some things for you before dinner."

There are a few closed doors on the landing, with radio music coming from behind them. And some shouting from upstairs on another level. She points out the bathroom and then opens a door to a small room that is at least neat and clean. "Why don't you rest here and I'll call you down to supper when it's ready. You can meet everyone then."

She smiles at me. Maybe this place isn't so bad. I have a bed with a quilt on it and a bureau and some towels on a chair. There's even a stuffed dog on the pillow. But that reminds me of Buddy, and I throw it on the floor. But then I pick it up again because it looks sad down there.

My eyes take in everything. There's no lock on the door. Another man could come in here. I put the chair under the doorknob. I saw Helen do that once when the red-haired man kept trying to see her.

When I look out the window I see the man, Lloyd, mowing his lawn. I'm glad he's forgotten about me already. But after a while he sees me staring at him, so I drop the curtains and move away from the window.

I lie back on the bed and listen to doors bang and voices come and go. I don't know these people. How could I be so stupid? Why did I set the barn on fire? I miss Buddy and my chickens and my tree house. I miss the bog and Helen laughing. I've ruined everything.

When Sandra comes up at suppertime and knocks on my door, I don't answer it. This doesn't seem to bother her. "There's some chicken pie on a tray outside your door. And a glass of milk and some cookies. We'll see you at breakfast. There's also a nightgown and some clean underwear for you."

I wait until I don't hear a sound outside the door before I open it and grab the food and the clothes. The chair goes back in position. The meal is good and the nightgown fits. I get into bed but leave the light on.

I'm so tired.

In the morning when I open my eyes and turn over, I realize the worst has happened. I've wet the bed. Everything is soaked. I don't have any other sheets to use. Sandra will be mad at me. Maybe I should throw them out the window, but instead I stuff them under the bed along with the nightgown, and pull the blanket over to hide the damp mattress. Now I have nowhere to sit except on the hard chair. I lean against the wall until there's a knock on the door.

"Grace. Are you awake? Please open the door. Being difficult won't help you in the long run."

When I open the door, I wring my hands. "I wet the bed."

"It happens all the time." Sandra comes in and gives me more clothes. "Why don't you have a bath and then come downstairs for breakfast. I'll take care of this."

Now that I wasn't expecting.

MY TIME WITH THIS FAMILY IN WATERLOO LASTS EIGHT MONTHS. I LIKE EVERY-one, even Lloyd. School is hard and I'm way behind in my studies, but I catch up quickly and on the last day I get my certificate saying I can advance into eighth grade. This makes me happy. I don't have any friends, but the kids at the foster home make things not quite so lonely.

But then Sandra gets cancer and we all have to be farmed out to someone else. I assume we'll go together but that doesn't happen. I'm taken to Brampton, to another foster home, and I never see those kids again.

It happens twice more after that, first to a foster home on the other side of Brampton, which means going to a new school, where I might as well be a thousand miles away. Then I'm back in Waterloo. I make it a point to look for the province of Ontario, on the big Canadian map at school, just to see where I am. I also look for Nova Scotia, but it seems very far away. Doesn't matter. No one there even knows I exist.

On my fifteenth birthday I make a vow that I won't feel anything anymore. The price to pay for not crying or being homesick or missing mom and Maria, is to not laugh or smile or enjoy even the smallest pleasure. I don't even hold animals in my arms in case someone takes them from me.

Soon the man who runs this foster home introduces me to liquor and dope. This is a much better way to zone out.

He lets me and another girl, Tracy, go down in his basement, and he hides bottles of beer, wine, and joints for us. His wife is always hollering at us to come upstairs. I think she suspects what we're do-ing, but doesn't want to know. The two of them argue about it in their bedroom at night.

In the back of my mind I know what he's doing is wrong, but it's the first time in a long time that someone's just wanted me to be happy.

And if we have to let him touch us for it, why not? Like Tracy says, who's it hurting? He's not asking us to take our clothes off.

I have friends now. I'm cool and hanging with the fast crowd, as my homeroom teacher calls us. Mr. Ferguson is always trying to get me to stay after school, and one day I finally do.

"Grace, your English assignments are amazing. You really need to be a member of our writing club."

"Thanks, but no." I walk towards the door.

"Then how about the drama club, or the glee club? You're a bright student and would be an asset to whatever after-school activity piques your interest."

"Terry says he's going to help me be a model."

"Terry James is a thug. Listen to what I'm saying. Stay away from him, Grace."

I feel sorry for Mr. Ferguson. He hates everybody.

Terry is blonde with blue eyes and he's very good-looking. All the girls want him, and I'm pleased as punch that he wants to be with me. Every day after school he meets me in the park and gives me presents—cigarettes, a leather jacket, earrings, a necklace.

He even takes me to a restaurant, like a grown-up. After that we go back to his place and he says that he loves me, and that if I love him, I'll do it. When I hesitate, he gets pissed off. "What? Are you a virgin or something?"

"No, of course not."

"Then get over here and stop making me wait."

I think I'm in love with Terry; he's so nice to me. When he asks me to go on a date with one of his friends as a favour, I figure I owe him. It'll probably just another boy in our gang.

When I get in my date's car, he's as old as the man. I'm so high I can't get out of the car fast enough. I try and fight him off, but I lose that battle. It's a good thing I only remember bits and pieces of that night.

The next week, Terry picks me up with another guy and the three of us go out on a date. I'm not sure how I get home, but when my foster mother opens the door, she grabs my neck and curses before kicking me in the backside when I fumble up the stairs.

"I don't have time to waste on you useless bitches! You think this is how I want to spend my life? Cleaning puke off the floor?"

And then one day at school I'm at the back of the room and blood starts seeping between my legs. I try and stop it, but there's more and more. One of the other girls sees it and starts screaming. Mr. Ferguson hurries out of the room to get help. Everyone looks at me with disgust. I need to get out of there, but when I try to stand up, I crash to the floor.

At the hospital they tell me I had a miscarriage.

"I was pregnant?" I ask the nurse.

"Yes, but you lost the baby."

All sound goes away except the ringing in my ears. I had my own little baby and I lost it? It's gone? I had Mama, and Maria, and Buddy, and my baby, and I lost them all?

I left my baby on the floor at school. I'm evil. God doesn't want me to have anything.

I don't remember crawling out on the ledge of the hospital's fifth-storey window, but I almost get to fly away before someone grabs my ankle and drags me back inside.

The psychiatric facility where I live for six months is no different from anywhere else. It's a constant struggle to get me to eat something and most of the time the adults are impatient with me, even though they try to be nice.

One morning as I stare at the ceiling a woman comes in my room. She looks like a social worker of some kind. They all have the same look; like they know everything. No doubt she's here to tell me something that means nothing.

"How are you, Grace?"

I gave up telling people I'm really Amazing a long time ago.

"I have some news."

Close your eyes and she'll go away.

"We found your grandmother's family."

"No, you didn't."

She doesn't correct me or get huffy. She sits in the chair by the bed and opens her folder. There are a lot of papers in it, official-looking documents.

"Why don't I show you what I have here and you can decide for yourself if what I'm saying sounds like the truth?"

When I don't say anything, she proceeds.

"Your name is Amazing Grace Fairchild. Your mother's name is Trixie Fairchild. Your grandmother's name is Rose Fairchild and your grandmother's sisters are named Pearl and Mae Fairchild. Pearl and Mae still live in a place called Marble Mountain in Cape Breton."

"My grandmother came from Nova Scotia."

"Cape Breton is a part of Nova Scotia."

"I don't believe you."

"That's okay."

"Not that it's true, but how did you find them?"

"A lot of hard work."

"If you know who these people are, why can't you find my mother or sister?"

"We're trying, but so far not much luck. We hope this is a start."

My heart beats a little faster, which annoys me. Don't feel anything. It's probably all lies. "So, who cares about them? What am I supposed to do with this? You find two old women who don't know me and I'm supposed to be grateful?"

She takes out a letter. "They sent this to me. It's for you."

When I keep my hands where they are, she places the letter on my bedside table. "I'll be back."

The letter is staring at me. It won't leave me alone. Everywhere I turn, it shows up in my line of vision. It's sticking its tongue out at me. I dare you, Amazing. I dare you to open me.

So I shout at it, "No! Go away!"

It doesn't. It's breathing on my side table, but I'm not fooled. I won't be sucked into another hole that leads to nowhere. It stays there all night, glowing in the dark, calling to me.

When morning comes, nothing's changed. It's there and so am I. The trouble is, my head is about to explode and my brains will be dripping down the walls. Who needs to see that?

I open the envelope and take out the letter. The handwriting is thin and spidery. How am I supposed to read this?

Dear Amazing Grace,

Trust your mother to come up with a name like that. She always was a handful. But regardless, kin is kin. Your grandmother Rose died years ago. I think she died of a broken heart, what with the worry over your mother, Trixie, but Mae says I need to be more charitable. So officially she died of complications from diabetes, but I have my doubts.

Rose was a change of life baby, much younger than Mae and I. Since both of us are spinsters, we felt it was our duty to take Rose in when her good-for-nothing husband left her with a baby to look after. That baby was your mother and I'm surprised I'm not deaf from all the hollering that went on here. Rose was too soft and Trixie was a hippy-dippy from the time she could talk, so I'm not surprised to hear that she abandoned you. They tell me your sister, Ave Maria (absolute nonsense) is gone too. You people have a terrible habit of losing track of one another.

Despite all that, Mae and I are Christian women, and as such, we cannot abandon you to the mercy of strangers, now that we know you exist. They tell us you've been bounced around from foster home to foster home. No doubt you have some terrible habits and no table manners, but kin is kin.

We would like to offer you a home with us. We don't have much and the house is old, but we have good neighbours who help us from time to time. As long as you promise not to be a hippy-dippy, I suppose we'll muddle through.

Yours truly,

Pearl Fairchild

I put the letter back in the envelope and tuck it under my pillow. She sounds like an old goat. Imagine saying stuff like that about my mother and grandmother? Who does she think she is?

The social worker knocks on my door the next day.

"So what do you think? Would you like to go home when you're released?"

"Yes."

I'VE NEVER BEEN ON A PLANE BEFORE. THE THOUGHT OF TAKING OFF INTO the air and flying seems very romantic, but only if you've never been on a plane. The first thing I do is throw up into the little bag. Then I lock myself in the toilet and my insides run out. Eventually someone knocks on the door and asks me to hurry up. I want to die.

It's bumpy from the time we take off to the time we land in Sydney. No one speaks to me, no one looks at me. That's the way I like it. My hair is hanging in my face, I have on a brown wool poncho and old bell-bottom jeans. My wooden Dr. Scholl's sandals click against the floor. Everything I own is in my crocheted shoulder bag.

As soon as I walk through the airport door, I get out of the way of the people coming behind me and stand to the side. I'll close my eyes so that if no one is here to pick me up, I can say I must have missed them. The time ticks by. I knew it.

"Amazing Grace?"

A tall, thin old woman in a coat down to her ankles purses her lips at me.

A short, fat old woman with a similar coat smiles at me and sings, *"How sweet the sound..."*

"Mae, for crying out loud. You're in an airport. Can we presume you are Amazing Grace?"

"Of course she is, Pearl," Mae beams. "She looks just like Trixie."

"Hardly. I see her good-for-nothing grandfather around her eyes. Don't you?"

"Gracious, no. How are you, dear? It's so wonderful to meet you. I'm your great-aunt Mae and this bag of hot air is my sister Pearl. You can call us aunts. It's easier."

I stand stiffly as Aunt Mae tries to put her arms around me, but they're too short; she pats my shoulder instead.

"It's polite to say hello," Aunt Pearl points out. "Has no one taught you manners? I can see we have our work cut out for us, Mae."

"Don't be so foolish. I'm sure Amazing Grace is a simply wonderful child. Aren't you, dear?"

There she goes again with that "dear." I should reward her with something.

"Yes."

Aunt Mae claps her hands together. "What did I tell you, Pearl? She's wonderful."

Aunt Pearl grunts. "Do you have a suitcase?"

"No."

"Land sakes! They send you down here with not a stitch of anything? People in Ontario think they're God's gift to humanity, but it's obvious they're lacking in brains. Who throws a child on a plane with nothing? Remind me never to go there."

They scurry me out to the car, obviously their pride and joy. Mae tells me it's a 1955 two-toned blue and cream Pontiac, with chrome detail. I settle into the biggest back seat I've ever been in. My aunts talk over one another from the front seat—not that I can see Aunt Mae's head, but she bobs to the side every now and again.

"We have to leave right away," Aunt Pearl says. "I don't like driving in the dark."

Aunt Mae's gloved hand appears with something wrapped in tinfoil. "We thought you might be hungry."

I take it and then she passes me a thermos.

"Say thank you!" Aunt Pearl glares at me in the rear-view mirror.

"Thanks."

Aunt Mae pats her sister on the shoulder. "Let's not start with the rules just yet. Amazing has had a long day."

Aunt Pearl shakes her head. "I have no idea what's going to happen when she goes to school. That Turner kid from up the road will eat her for breakfast."

The fat egg sandwich with moist homemade bread hits the spot. I drink all the milk, too.

They talk back and forth to each other, but I slide over to the window and look at the scenery. It's very pretty here, with the green grass and blue water. Where are all the people?

It's been a long day and it's an even longer ride to get to their house. They live in the woods, with only a winding hilly road breaking up the trees and water. The sun is starting to set by the time Aunt Pearl puts her blinker on and pulls into a dirt driveway.

At first it seems creepy; the trees make me feel like I'm going to be swallowed whole. But there's an outside light shining above the red front door and the swing on the front porch looks inviting.

Even though it's August, the air is cool as the sun goes down. Once I'm out of the car, my arms are full of goosebumps and my toes are cold.

Aunt Pearl notices my feet as she searches for the key to unlock the door. "Are those the only shoes you own? You won't get far in those once December hits."

Aunt Mae puts her hand on my arm. "Then it's a good thing we have lots of time to get you new shoes before the snow flies."

They mutter and putter while putting away their coats and purses and insist on taking my poncho to hang on the hooks in the inside hall. When the door opens into the living room, with its rose wallpaper and rose-covered chairs, it's hard to know where to look first. There is absolutely no room for another knick-knack whatsoever. I've never been in a house so full of stuff. They insist I sit in front of the fire while they attend to supper. The flames in the fireplace make me think of the burning barn. I wonder where Helen is now. I wonder if my mother and Maria ever came back to look for me.

My eyes keep closing in this heat, but Aunt Pearl's strident, "Supper's ready!" jolts me to attention. I join them in the kitchen. There's a pine table already set with dishes in the middle of the room and my aunts in their full-length aprons standing by it.

"Sit down, my dear." Aunt Mae pulls out my chair, so I sit in it.

Aunt Pearl zooms over with a plate of fried chicken, mashed potatoes, green beans, carrots, peas, and gravy. "Eat up. You're too pale."

They join me at the table, the two of them in their pearls. I get why Aunt Pearl wears pearls, but Aunt Mae seems to love them too. She has three strands that cuddle into the folds of her neck.

"Let's say grace." Aunt Mae bows her head and folds her hands together. "Thank you, oh Lord, for these thy gifts we are about to receive, and thank you for bringing Amazing Grace back home to us. Amen."

I pick up the chicken with my fingers and their eyes get huge. I put it down.

"Fork and knife. Always fork and knife," Aunt Pearl instructs. She stabs the air a few times. So I pick up my utensils and cut into the chicken. I have to say, it tastes better than when I rip it off the bone with my teeth.

Aunt Pearl clears her throat. "Your napkin goes on your lap, not tucked into your collar."

Here's me trying to impress them. I pull the napkin out and drop it on my lap. This woman is going to be a pain fairly soon.

"Let the child eat," Aunt Mae smiles. "What sorts of things do you like to do, Amazing?"

Aunt Pearl's hands go up. "I'm sorry, but I'm not calling this child Amazing. I don't care if that is your given name, it grates on my nerves every time someone says it. Your name is also Grace. A very lovely name, as it happens. It belonged to our grandmother, and I wish you would do us the courtesy of using it while you are in this house. It's not much to ask, is it?"

"I have a great-grandmother?"

"Of course you do, child! Grace would be your great-great grand-mother. Where do you think you came from? The cabbage patch? Your great-grandmother's name was Mehitable, which we all agree was regrettable."

Aunt Mae grins at me. "Pearl pretends she doesn't have a sense of humour, but she does."

At that moment a fat black and white cat waddles into the kitchen and sits beside me. He looks up with a sweet face and meows at me.

Tears pour out of my eyes and onto my plate. They are springing out, gushing out, and I have no idea how to stop them. My arms are limp by my sides as I howl. My two great-aunts sit with their mouths open, completely speechless, which I have to say is probably a rare state for them. My nose starts to run, I have saliva running out of my mouth. I am a crying machine that is stuck on the freak-out setting. It's all too much.

Eventually, the crying slows and I'm just a hot red mess with a snotty face. I'm still whimpering but the shock is over for my dinner companions. Aunt Pearl gets up and grabs a whole lot of tissues and rubs the residue off my face. Aunt Mae comes behind her with a damp, cool tea towel and holds it against my burning cheeks.

"There, there, sweetheart. You're here with us. You're safe now."

CHAPTER SEVEN

NOW

Melissa is grinning at me. "So it all worked out in the end."

"No."

Her face falls. "What do you mean? You can't possibly still be in trouble. I think you're making this up."

"Is your life that simple? Is anyone's?"

"You're safe. You have two old ladies cooking for you. There's no man lurking in the bushes anymore."

"I was a train wreck who smashed into the world of two elderly ladies who wore gloves to drive the car. It wasn't easy for any of us."

I have to move, and so I get up to stretch my legs. "Let's go for a walk."

"Do I have to?"

"No."

"I'll stay here then."

"Okay, but you'll miss the best part of the story." I bundle up in my outer gear and leave the house. Before I'm down to the apple trees, she's running after me. She's out of breath when she catches up.

"You can't just leave me here."

"How often do you go for a walk at home?"

She puts her hands on her hips. "Why? Are you going to tell me I'm too fat?"

"Why on earth would I tell you you're fat?" I keep walking and she follows along.

"I don't wear a size zero."

I tip my head back and look up at the grey skies. We're going to get rain before the day is out. "I don't think I'd survive if I went to high school now."

We walk through the soggy leaves down by the water. I point to the big rock further along the beach. "I used to sit there when I was your age. It was my refuge. Where do you go when things get tough?"

Melissa wipes her nose with the back of her coat sleeve. "Nowhere. My room, I guess."

"But how can you shut everyone out when they're attached to you day and night by an electronic umbilical cord? When do you just sit in silence?"

She picks up a rock and throws it in the water.

"You don't strike me as the sort of girl who would want to have naked pictures of herself posted online."

"You don't know me very well then, do you?" She grabs a whole handful of rocks and throws them into the lake. "If you're going to bug me about it, I'll go back to the house. I don't need a lecture."

"Okay. Let's keep walking and I'll tell you the next chapter of the story."

CHAPTER EIGHT

THEN

There are a lot of cool things happening in the early seventies, but they're not happening to me. I'm in a backwater with two old fuddy-duddies who take their job as guardians to heart. Their charm wears off after a week. Not that I'm not grateful, but I went from a life of complete abandonment to a jail cell. It's bound to end badly.

They don't want me to go anywhere.

"You'll get lost," Aunt Mae frets. "There's acres and acres of trees out here and if you wander off you won't find your way back."

"Can I go down to the water?"

Aunt Pearl is peeling onions. "Don't go in the water. You might drown."

"That might be sweet relief." I slam the back screen door, but not before hearing, "Talk back and you'll get a hiding!"

"Now Pearl," Aunt Mae tsks.

The only place they'd like me to go is to church. I'm at breakfast when they bring this up. I dip a bread soldier in my egg yolk. "That is the last thing I need. Trust me."

Strangely, they don't challenge me on this. I thought for sure they'd start pecking away at me. I'm just grateful they leave it alone.

Mostly what I do is sit on my rock and smoke cigarettes. I'm running out and I don't have any money. School starts in a week and I need some clothes, although who knows what they wear in this backwater. The thought of going into another school gives me hives. In the whole nightmare of the last few years, the agony of meeting new kids is the worst, because kids can smell desperation and I reek of it.

The aunts take me shopping. I'm mortified walking around with these two clucking behind me. Everything I like they hate, so I turn on my heel and walk out the door. I'm sulking when they find me, puffing on my last cigarette.

Aunt Pearl walks over and grabs it out of my hand. "Have you no shame? Standing here smoking like a common prostitute!" She grinds it under her shoe.

I point my finger at her. "That's exactly what I was before I met you, and it's what I do best."

She slaps me in the face.

Aunt Mae hops about, wringing her hands. "Now Pearl! Was that necessary?"

"Who do you think you are?" I shout.

Aunt Pearl grabs my earlobe and hauls me over to the car. "I'll tell you who I am, missy. I have the misfortune to be one of your relatives. A relative who will not put up with another spoiled brat living under my roof. Now get in that car!"

I yank the door open and slam it shut behind me. Then open it and slam it again. "You old bag!"

Aunt Mae clutches her chest. "Oh, dear. Oh, my. That really isn't necessary. Pearl! Pearl! Where are you going?"

Aunt Pearl is ramrod straight as she walks back into the store with Aunt Mae running behind her. They come out with a shopping bag fifteen minutes later.

"I can't believe this," I say to no one. "What the hell is she doing?"

They get in the car and she throws the bag at me. "Clothes for school. If you don't like them, you can go naked."

So that's how I end up wearing black slacks and a white blouse on the first day of school. My jeans were in the wash. A convenient coincidence?

The kids on the bus stare at me and I ignore them as we bounce towards higher learning. I'm in grade eleven now. This year and one more and I'm out of here. But then what? I've never made plans this far ahead. It's always been pointless.

At lunch, one of the boys approaches my table with a bit of an attitude. He wouldn't last a day in my former school.

"You seem to be the type who likes a good time. I'm Devon."

"Fuck off, Devon."

He grins. "Ouch! She bites!"

No sense in wasting this opportunity. "Do you have a smoke?"

"Sure thing. Come with me."

He leads me through the hallway and out to the side door. There are a group of kids smoking cigarettes at the edge of the school property, all of them intent on sucking them down to the filter. We join them.

They want to know where I'm from. I tell them Chicago and they look impressed. So gullible.

"Do you drink?" asks Devon. "I've got some beer in the trunk of my car."

I end up skipping my afternoon classes, getting drunk with Devon and rolling around in the back seat of his car.

He eventually takes me home but drops me off at the top of the driveway. "I'm not tangling with that skinny bitch. The fat one's not so bad."

He backs out onto the road and squeals his tires as he leaves. What a dork.

My aunts are in their rocking chairs looking mighty displeased.

"The school called," Aunt Pearl says. "You disappeared after lunch. Where did you go?"

I plunk down on their flowered sofa. "I went driving around with a guy."

"Who, dear?" Aunt Mae says.

"Devon."

Aunt Pearl looks disgusted. "Devon Hibbs is an idiot! His father's an idiot and so is his grandfather. The elevator doesn't go to the top floor in that family."

"Now Pearl," Aunt Mae tsks.

"I forbid you to see that boy again."

"Just how are you going to stop me?"

"Try me."

I've had enough for one day. "Good night, ladies." Staggering up the stairs, I'm aware that the sisters are whispering to each other. "I love you too!" I shout behind my shoulder.

As my aching hangover head goes around and around, I'm aware I'm being a big shithead. I just can't summon the energy to care. But before I drift into semi-consciousness on my flowery quilted bed, it occurs to me that it's nice that someone wondered where I was.

In the morning I apologize. Aunt Mae beams and Aunt Pearl grunts.

We have this hostile truce for a couple of months. I mess up plenty, drinking, smoking, toking on weekends with other kids, but I stop skipping school. That's the thing that bugs the aunts the most, and I think that as long as I rinse with mouthwash, air out my clothes, and stop drinking a couple of hours before I go home, they're none the wiser.

That's how stupid you are when you're young.

While I congratulate myself on how well I'm hoodwinking these fine ladies, they hatch a genius evil plan.

I start seeing a pattern.

"Grace, could you bring in more firewood from the shed? Thank you, dear!"

"And make sure you clean out the grate this time. The chimney doesn't draw properly if you leave a pile of ashes."

"Grace, dear, do you think you could help me put up a few wreaths?"

"While you're out there, shovel the snow off the porch."

"Dearest, is there any chance you could cut down a small tree and bring it inside? You can help decorate it. Isn't that exciting?"

"Do you see these arthritic hands? Mix up that fruitcake for me. I'm surprised I have to ask."

Then they inform me that in their day, the house had to be clean from top to bottom, walls and everything, so that the neighbours would be impressed when they came to socialize over the holidays.

"Do you have many visitors? No one's come since I arrived."

Aunt Pearl takes her rolls out of the oven. "That's because we told them to stay away."

I grab a banana from the fruit bowl and peel it. "Well, thanks a lot."

"Now that you're housebroken, we can send invitations."

Naturally they start to do the chores themselves, hanging off a ladder or standing on a chair to dust their endless knick-knacks.

"Give me that before you kill yourself," I shout.

"Why, thank you, dear."

"About time!"

I'm exhausted by Christmas Eve. But I have to say the place looks like a little dollhouse. I take a weird pride in it. I even fluff a pillow.

All I want to do is sit, but no. The two of them come downstairs in their finery.

"Where are you going?"

"To church, obviously. It's Christmas Eve. The whole reason we're celebrating? We've let your lack of interest in religion slide, but we must insist, on tonight of all nights. Go get dressed."

"Wear your red sweater, dear! It's so Christmassy!"

"No fucking way."

It's like I shot them with bows and arrows. They both flail backwards and Aunt Mae starts to weep while she looks for a handkerchief in her purse.

Are you proud of yourself, Amazing? "That didn't come out right. I meant to say, I'll be down in five minutes." I bolt up the stairs.

Can I be any meaner? Why am I such a bitch? All these questions go through my mind as I put on the red sweater and tie a red bow in my hair. I even steal Aunt Mae's red lipstick and slap that on too.

They are composed when I come back down.

"You look very nice, dear," Aunt Mae sniffs.

"Your great-great-grandmother Grace was a lady. How proud do you think she'd be, knowing her namesake spews filth like that?"

"You are absolutely right. I will never say that word again. I'm very sorry."

Aunt Pearl straightens her shoulders. "I should think so. Now let's go."

The little white church in the snow is crammed with people and twinkling lights. All these old ladies gather round and shake my hand as my aunts introduce me. My cheeks are scarlet, thinking of what transpired back at the house.

I'm squished between the aunts and I try desperately not to listen to the man in the pulpit asking us to follow God's son Jesus, to praise the name of Jesus, to love one another and obey the master.

I panic, leaning over to whisper in Aunt Pearl's ear. "Did he say obey the Master?"

She gives me a look. "No. Clean out your ears."

Now we have to stand up and sing the hymn "Silent Night." My knees buckle and I put my face in my hands and cry and cry and cry. The kind of crying you can't ignore.

The minister, organist, and choir keep going. There's an uncomfortable atmosphere around us and a murmuring of the crowd. Aunt Pearl puts her arm around my shoulder and leads me and Aunt Mae out of our pew, down the church aisle, and back to the car.

When we get to the house, Aunt Pearl sits me at the kitchen table, while Aunt Mae puts the kettle on.

"I'm sorry I ruined your night," I sniff. "I'm not sure what happened."

Aunt Pearl takes off her gloves and sits beside me. "No, I'm sorry we made you go. I should have known better."

"What do you mean?"

Aunt Mae also sits at the table. "Before you came to us, the social worker sent us your case file so we would know what we were up against. She told us we had every right to refuse to take you in. That because of your upbringing, you had a lot of baggage, and she needed to know if we could handle it."

The kettle starts to sing. Aunt Mae gets up while Aunt Pearl continues.

"We know what happened to you at that farm."

"You do?"

Aunt Pearl looks down at her lap. "I know about the leader of that miserable cult you were in. God knows what you suffered. I didn't want the details, which I realize now was selfish on my part. If you were courageous enough to survive him, then I should be courageous enough to hear it."

So over toast and tea, I tell them about the man. Aunt Mae sheds copious tears and Aunt Pearl keeps patting my hand. They're outraged on my behalf, which is comforting.

"And he calls himself a Christian!" Aunt Mae keeps yelling. "He deserves to be doused in honey and buried in an anthill!"

We both look at her.

"Well, why not? Or cut his pecker off!"

When I open my eyes the next morning, I have a dull headache, no doubt from reliving some of the worst days of my life. If only memories could be shut off like a tap.

I lay in bed awhile, listening to the sounds of the house. The aunts are up, because the house is toasty, the smell of bacon is in the air, and someone has opened my door a crack—Lulu, the fat black and white cat, is curled up at the end of my bed. There's Christmas music playing on the radio, which is kind of nice.

Christmas wasn't celebrated when I was a kid. Well, it was as far as learning that Jesus was born on Christmas Day and the three Wise Men showed up, but the man never let any of us have presents and we never saw Santa Claus. We all knew about him of course, the few times we saw television, but the man said that greed was a sin and we wouldn't partake in such blasphemy.

I think he was just cheap.

The calm, peaceful mood this morning almost puts me back to sleep again but then I hear a sound.

"Psst! Psst!"

I lift my head. Aunt Mae's head is poking through the doorway.

"Good morning," I say.

"Good morning," she grins. "Have you forgotten it's Christmas morning? We've been waiting downstairs for hours."

"Oh. Sorry."

"Don't tell Pearl I was up here. She'll get mad. Just come down soon or your bacon will be charcoal." She disappears.

It's while I'm putting on my housecoat and slippers that I realize that maybe my aunts have bought me Christmas gifts. I have nothing for them. It never crossed my mind. Frantically, I look about the room, but there's nothing that's not theirs already.

"Lulu! I'm such a jerk."

Lulu rolls over and exposes her belly for immediate attention but I don't have time. There's only one thing I can do.

When I go downstairs, the aunts are in their bathrobes and slippers. There's a fire burning in the fireplace and candles lit even though it's morning. Our small Christmas tree's lights are on and there are a few presents underneath.

I'll make sure I remember this. What families are supposed to look like.

"Merry Christmas!" the aunts shout. They then come over and hug me. "Breakfast first, and then we'll open our gifts."

"I don't have any gifts," I mumble as we go in the kitchen.

"Matters not a whit." Aunt Pearl puts a bowl of porridge with brown sugar in front of me. Aunt Mae pours the cream. Afterwards we move on to orange juice, bacon, eggs, and toast.

If this is all they do, it's still the best Christmas I ever had.

After breakfast we go back in front of the fire. The aunts hand me my presents to open. They look more excited than I am. I receive a pair of handmade mitts, a new nightgown, two books, scented bubble bath, and a pair of earrings—pearls, of course.

I'm overcome. "Thank you. I don't deserve this."

Aunt Pearl gets annoyed. "Don't be so foolish. I'll have no more of that kind of talk. You deserve as much happiness as anyone else. Remember that. You're not a victim."

Aunt Mae then gives Aunt Pearl a new Mixmaster and a cookbook. Pearl gives her sister perfume, stockings, and a pretty sweater. Both are equally happy with their gifts.

They make a move to get the turkey in the oven, but I call them back. "I wrote a poem."

"Did you, dear? That's nice." The aunts continue into the kitchen.

"For you guys."

They both turn at the same time and come back to the couch.

"I hope you like it."

The Kid

When you have no home, and no one loves you, life is dark and bleak.
Then Aunties come and hold your hand and make you want to speak.
They listen to your stories, they give you food to eat.
They get upset and cross with you, which means you're not so weak.
They want a better life for you and this is what they seek.
I wouldn't be the girl I am, without Aunt Mae and Pearl,
So thank you for your loving arms, a place to rest and curl.

They both rise from the sofa and disappear upstairs. I think that means they liked it.

WHILE I SIT AND EAT BREAKFAST ONE MORNING IN THE NEW YEAR, THE AUNTS COME in together and try to be nonchalant as they join me. It's not working.

"So," says Aunt Pearl. "Any plans this weekend?"

"No."

Aunt Mae can't contain herself. She shakes the car keys at me. "Wanna learn how to drive?"

This is how I end up slipping and sliding over snowy roads in rural Cape Breton, with a cheerleader in the back seat and a sergeant-major in the front.

"You're coming to a turn! Slow down!"

"I *am* slowing down!"

"Not enough!"

I brake a little too quickly and fishtail a bit, but we manage to navigate the turn.

"Well done!" squeaks Aunt Mae. "You'll be driving to Sydney in no time."

"We have to get to Baddeck first!" Aunt Pearl hollers. "Watch out! There's a gravel truck coming! Don't be nervous! Don't look at him! Keep your eyes on the road! Slowly release the gas! No! You're too far over! Watch the ditch!"

The gravel truck roars past us.

"Well done!"

"My nerves."

You should always learn to drive in the worst conditions possible, because then you're not afraid of anything. The three of us drive everywhere that winter. Whenever I'm not in school I'm ferrying them around to their friends' houses, the grocery store, the gas station, to church, and finally to take my driving test in Sydney.

They wave as I go into the room to write the test and then wave when I go out with the driving instructor. They stand when I get back, clutching their purses in front of them. I give them a thumbs-up. We go to K-Mart to celebrate.

Later that night, Aunt Pearl asks me to come into her bedroom. This is an unexpected privilege. I sit on her bed as she sits on the stool of her makeup table. Not that she has any makeup; just powder, scent, and her mother-of-pearl brush and comb set. She does have one lipstick for special occasions, unlike Aunt Mae, who has dozens.

She looks at me in the mirror. "I bought you something." She reaches into one of the dresser drawers by her side and hands me a rectangular box. Inside are a pair of leather gloves.

"Everyone needs gloves to drive a car. It's safer."

I don't tell her that I'll never, in a million years, drive the car with those gloves on. And the next time I'm behind the wheel, I wear them. Why is anyone's guess. I just pray none of my friends see me.

I'M FIRST IN MY CLASS THAT YEAR. AND THE NEXT. AT MY HIGH SCHOOL graduation, I see the two of them in the audience, Aunt Mae beaming as she gives me little waves, Aunt Pearl with her hands in her lap. We go out for dinner that night and Aunt Pearl says I can order lobster if I want to, but I choose a cheeseburger. We all have chocolate cake for dessert.

One of our neighbours lets me borrow his lawnmower and I spend about a week cleaning up the grass that threatens to drown us around the house, but I leave the field alone because the buttercups, daisies, and Indian paintbrush look so lovely swaying in the wind.

Aunt Mae likes to sit outside and sketch from time to time. She shows me a drawing she did while I was working. It really does look like me, with my auburn hair pulled into a messy knot at the back of my head. I didn't realize I was so pretty. And I'm smiling, which is almost more shocking. I tuck the picture into the mirror over my dresser so I can look at it sometimes. That's when I realize I have no pictures of myself. If I die tomorrow, there's no evidence that I lived.

At dinner that night, we're lazy and have tomato soup and grilled cheese sandwiches. Aunt Mae pours us tea so we can dunk our gingersnaps.

"Remember you asked me what I'd like for a graduation present?"

They nod.

"I'd like a camera."

"That's a great idea," Aunt Pearl says. "Clever girl."

By midsummer I have about a thousand snapshots of this house, Lulu the cat, the field, the lake, the islands, my rock, and the kids I hang out with sometimes, but my favourite ones are of Aunt Mae and Aunt Pearl. At first I have to chase them around, and Aunt Pearl gets mad if I catch her with her slip on, or her hair in curlers. Aunt Mae only ever has one pose: she throws her arms over her head and pretends she's a movie star. "I'm Marilyn Monroe!"

That camera is my favourite thing in the world. All of my allowance that the aunts insist I take goes into buying and developing film.

Late one night, Aunt Mae's already gone to bed and I'm at the kitchen table putting my pictures in albums. Aunt Pearl comes in for her nightly cup of hot water, but instead of taking it upstairs she sits at the table with me.

"What was your mother like?"

I don't know what to say.

"You don't have to be polite. It's between you and me."

"She was what you said, hippy-dippy. I wanted to protect her."

Aunt Pearl shakes her head. "That's a terrible burden for a child."

"Ave Maria helped me."

"Was Maria good to you?"

"Oh yes, but she worried a lot."

"How did Trixie get taken in by this psychopath?"

"Maybe she was lonely."

"More like Trixie didn't like rules. She completely cut her mother off, and it broke Rose's heart."

"What was my grandmother like?"

"Your Aunt Mae, times two."

"Oh."

"Thank the Lord I'm exactly like my father, otherwise my sisters would've starved. You can't live on rainbows and marshmallows."

I smile at her and she smiles back.

"Aunt Pearl, how did you become a bank manager?"

"I started as a teller. Just goes to show what happens when you work hard." She sips her hot water. "Now that you're finished high school, what would you like to do? Any ideas?"

"Find my mother and my sister."

It's the first weekend in September, when I'm in a rush to go to an afternoon movie with some girlfriends. The aunties want me to take them for groceries first. I'm already late and a little pissed off, if the truth be told. The two of them are nattering about coupons and whether the new cashier added them up correctly. They pass the receipt to each other between the front and back seat.

I'm about to yell, "Does it really matter?" when Devon Hibbs comes screaming up behind our car and passes me on a double line. There's a car coming towards us, so he veers back in front of me, clipping my front end. The jolt takes the wheel out of my hand momentarily, and before I can recover, we're in the ditch.

It happens so fast I'm not sure I even believe where we are, but I do see that ass-hole's taillights disappear over the hill. The other car stops and a couple of men run over to us.

"Are you guys all right?" I taste blood on my tongue.

Aunt Mae groans a bit from the back seat. "What happened? Ouch, my neck."

I reach over to Aunt Pearl. She's dazed but coming around. "I think I hurt my arm."

One of the men opens my door. "Are you all right, Miss Pearl? Miss Mae?"

"Hello, Joe," they say in unison.

"This must be your great-niece. Pleased to meet you. Let me help you out."

So now I'm on best terms with Joe MacPherson and his brother Burt. Their friend Hank from Christmas Island happens by, so we put the ladies in his car and Joe and Burt pull my car out of the ditch. They insist on driving it to a garage to get checked out. In the meantime Hank takes us to outpatients at the hospital to make sure we're all right.

I only need a few stitches in my lip, and Aunt Mae has some whiplash, but poor Aunt Pearl has broken her arm. Wait till I get my hands around Devon's neck. That bastard is going down.

But before we go home, Aunt Pearl has a fainting spell and the doctor wants to keep her overnight. This throws Aunt Mae in a tizzy and now she won't leave. Joe and Burt deliver our car back to the hospital, bless their hearts. They tell me I need a new bumper but otherwise it's good to go.

Aunt Mae eventually nods off in the chair by Aunt Pearl's bed. I can't sleep. I'm sure I'm overreacting, but when I look at Aunt Pearl's face, I don't think she looks well.

The doctor comes in the next morning and he seems concerned. He motions me out to the hall.

"I'm going to keep your aunt in for another day or so. Just to be careful."

"Something's wrong. I know it."

"Any injury or shock to the system with the elderly has to be monitored and we're doing that. Why don't you take Mae home and you can visit with her later today. She needs to rest."

So that's what I do, with Aunt Mae resisting the entire time. I call their friend Erna and ask if she can come and sit with Aunt Mae while I go back to the hospital. Erna's over about fifteen minutes later with a pan of squares and a hot water bottle.

I hold Aunt Pearl's hand while she sleeps, and tuck the blankets around her. I must have drifted off for a minute because she has to squeeze my hand to get me to open my eyes. I jump off the chair.

"Hi, how are you feeling?" I reach for a soft cloth and gently rub her forehead.

She stares at me, her thin, wrinkled face ageing before my eyes.

"What's wrong, Aunt Pearl? Your arm is going to get better. I'll take care of everything."

"Stop talking. Now listen to me. Mae and I had our wills done up recently—"

"Don't talk like that!"

She gives me a look, and I stop.

"We're leaving you the house. I expect you to look after Mae when I'm gone. I have a goodly sum of money that will help you to do that. Anything left over, I want you to take and use for your education. I always wanted to go to university, but my sisters needed me and I've had a good life. Although I do regret never seeing a Broadway show. Regardless, it's a miracle that you came back to us, and I'm forever grateful to God for that."

My hands are shaking. "Please don't die on me."

"Knowing you'll be here for Mae gives me peace of mind."

"But you're not sick! You just broke your arm!"

"I have breast cancer. I've had it for a while, but I didn't want to upset Mae. Our mother died of it and it terrifies her. The doctor knows, I asked him not to say anything."

"Oh no. Oh no."

She squeezes my hand again. "You'll be fine. You have survived more in your young life than a body should have to. You are Amazing Grace, don't forget."

She dies three days later.

The first thing I do is drive to the abandoned quarry, where I know Devon and his deadbeat friends are hanging out, and race the car right up to him. He has to jump out of the way.

"Whoa! What the fuck is your problem?" he says as I get out of the car.

I march up to him and punch him in the face. He's so shocked, I punch him again and knock his front tooth out. Then I jump on him and kick the crap out of him, his idiot friends laughing to kill themselves. He's still on the ground when I point at him. "You are a piece of shit. And if you ever come near me or my family again, I'll kill you. Do you hear me? I'll kill you, because I have nothing to lose. Do you understand?"

He gives me a nod. When I get back in the car I spin my wheels and spray dirt and gravel all over the bastard.

Aunt Mae is never the same after that. I look after her as best I can. She's like a little girl at first, always wanting to be near me. I bathe her and wash her hair. She loves it when I rub cream on her hands and asks me to read to her at night by the fire.

While the winds howls outside and the fire crackles, we slip into the world of L. M. Montgomery.

"I swear if Matthew Cuthbert was alive and well, I'd marry him," she says.

About two years pass before her senility creeps up behind us and robs her of her cheery self. She starts a fire in the kitchen one morning, and it's only luck that I manage to control it before it gets out of hand. But the worst is the night she gets lost on me.

My routine is to check on her before I go to bed, but she isn't in her room. Panic rises up in my throat as I holler her name over and over. She's not in the house, and now I see the back door open. It's early spring and the air is damp and cold. She's outside in her nightie and slippers.

The first thing I do is call the neighbours, even though it's late. Many cars speed down our driveway and over twenty people start looking in the dark with me, all of us carrying flashlights and calling her name. What if she goes down to the lake? I'm responsible for her safety. I'm such an idiot.

When someone shouts, "Over here!" my relief is instant. We run in the direction of the voice. It's Bruce Samuels who finds her slumped under a fir tree down by the water. She's trembling with cold and Bruce takes off his jacket and wraps it around her. Someone else has a blanket, and when Bruce lifts her to carry her back up the field, they drape that over her as well.

Erna's husband has his car running as Bruce and I manage to get her in the back. We race to the hospital and the doctors take over. I can only slump in a chair and rock back and forth. Erna sits down beside me.

"It's not your fault, dear. You've done your very best, but you can't do it anymore. She needs to be in a home with twenty-four-hour care."

"She doesn't want to go! She thinks Aunt Pearl is still alive. She refuses to leave her alone in the house. How am I supposed to deal with that? I can't let her lose her sister."

Erna pats my back. "There, there now."

Aunt Mae never does go in a home. She develops pneumonia. I stay with her every day in the hospital, making sure she drinks her juice through a straw, and brushing her hair to soothe her. She doesn't know who I am, but I know she likes having me there. She dies a couple of weeks later.

After the funeral, everyone wants me to come back to their place for some food, but I want to go home. I spend the night at the kitchen table and go through my photo albums. There's one picture of the two of them that I love. Aunt Pearl is standing by our Thanksgiving turkey with the fork and carving knife at the ready, trying to teach me how to carve a bird. Aunt Mae is behind her with a butter knife pretending to cut her own throat, with her tongue hanging out.

Goddamn it. I'm going to miss them.

CHAPTER NINE

NOW

We've been walking the entire time, and now Melissa is weeping. I put my arm around her and she leans on me as we tramp back to our sanctuary. The minute the house comes into view, her lip goes down.

"I wish I'd met them. I'm so proud of you for beating up that guy. I wish I was that brave. That's exactly what I need to do with Kurt."

"Who's Kurt?"

"He's the creep who made me take the pictures. I thought he was my boyfriend. He said if I didn't do more, he'd show them to the whole school, so I did, but he put them online anyway and now everyone at school calls me a skank and I'm not! I've never even been with anyone. I'm such an idiot."

I let her cry as we cross the field. The minute we get back she curls up in her chair by the fire. Her cheeks are apple red. Now she looks like a real girl. A very sweet girl. We share a package of cashews.

"You're like the best cook."

"Hardly."

We munch together and I wish I could keep her here, but that's not the way life works.

"Do you mind if I make a suggestion about the Kurt issue?"

"Like how to knock his teeth out?"

"Unfortunately, in this day and age you'd be up for assault and that will solve nothing. I think you should tell your father about Kurt."

"No! That will make it worse! If Kurt finds out I ratted on him, I'm dead."

"That pimply-faced pervert is not the mafia. He's a joke and he needs to be put in his place."

"By you?"

"Your father is quite capable of dealing with it."

"I'm not sure about that. I don't think he's thrown a punch in his life."

"A man is not a man by virtue of his fists. He loves you and he's concerned enough that he called me, a woman he's not that fond of, because he thought it might help you."

"Why doesn't he like you very much?"

"That's another story, but it's for his ears, not yours."

"I think you're pretty cool, even though you act like Aunt Pearl."

This makes me laugh. "I'm not like Aunt Pearl!"

"Trust me. You are."

I smile at her. "Really? I'll take that as a compliment."

She watches the fire. "What's going to happen now?"

"We're going to go back to Fletcher's place and leave for New York in a couple of days. Before your mom gets home. She'll be missing you."

"I love this place."

"As I've said, you and your family and friends are more than welcome to come all summer. I'll have the place spruced up by then, seeing as how we didn't get much done this trip."

"I wish I had my phone with me. I want to take some pictures of the farmhouse."

"Take my cell. I'll send them to you."

Melissa takes ten pictures of every room, paying special attention to Aunt Pearl's bedroom. That gives me a great idea.

"How about I give you Aunt Pearl's makeup table? I can have it shipped to your Dad's."

Her delight is obvious. "Do you mean it?"

"Yes, but you have to promise me to treasure this. Don't hide it under mounds of clothes or let laptops scratch it. It's very precious to me, but I know you love it and I think Aunt Pearl would be tickled for you to have it, instead of it gathering dust here. Make it a showpiece in your room."

"You are so awesome, Gee! I love you!" She throws her arms around me.

That night I call her father and tell him the plans.

"So after a couple of days with you, she's suddenly cured?"

"For the love of Pete, of course she's not cured. She's relieved, that's all. We'll tell you about it when we get there."

"Does she miss me?"

"Of course she does. You're her father."

"What's to stop her from reverting right back to old behaviours after you leave? Maybe I should have gone the psychiatrist route first."

"Sweet Jesus."

"I thought you were going to stop swearing."

"You would try the patience of a saint! Goodbye!"

After I hang up I try to remember who said that to me once. It sounds familiar.

The night before we leave for New York, I go in to say good night to Melissa and she's reading a book from the pile I showed her the first night she got here.

"Can I take this home?"

"Feel free."

Perhaps I should wait to tell Jonathan first, but I'm so upset about this Kurt kid, I need to blow off a little steam. I tell Fletcher when we're outside with the dogs for the final time that night. He closes his eyes and shakes his head. "What is this world coming to? You know, it kind of makes me glad I never had kids. Now I wish I'd left the dogs at home when we picked her up. Poor little mite."

Flights back to New York are booked. No private plane needed for this jaunt. We pack up our suitcases and Fletch takes them out to the truck. Melissa is saying goodbye to the critters when he comes back in. "All set?"

Melissa picks up Beulah. "I guess you better say goodbye to Beulah. Thank you for being so nice to her."

Fletch nods. "Bye, Beulah. Thanks for keeping me company."

I can't watch. I'm about to go out the door when Melissa laughs.

"She's not going anywhere."

"What?"

"She belongs with you." Melissa kisses Beulah's head and passes her over to Fletcher. "She'll be a lot happier here. But can she come for the ride?"

I could kiss her.

Fletch does kiss her when he says goodbye, and she has a giant hug for him.

"I don't know how long I'll be," I tell him as I give him a squeeze at the airport.

"You plan on staying awhile?"

"There are some things I need to say to Jonathan; we may need a little time. He's in worse shape than she is."

"Good luck. We'll be here waiting for you when you get home."

Then he and his five-pound sidekick drive into the sunset.

THE MINUTE MELISSA SEES HER FATHER, HER DEMEANOUR CHANGES. IT'S LIKE she wants him to know she's still suffering and that he was the one who put her through the wringer.

Kids are a pain.

On the way out to the car, Jonathan says, "I thought you said she missed me."

"Hormones."

We're back in the tower and I can feel my blood pressure rising. What is it about this building that makes it hard for me to breath?

Linn offers to take our suitcases and I'm back in the hotel room. It feels like I never left. Melissa immediately runs to her room to pick up her electronic gadgets. Jonathan says he has to make a few phone calls. In the space of a minute, this tiny family has disappeared into their own private worlds. Whatever happened to "How was your trip?"

No time like the present. I open the door to Melissa's room. "Stop texting and get out here."

She doesn't look up. "Give me a minute! I just got home."

"Now!"

She throws the cell on the bed but she follows me. The two of us walk into Jonathan's study and he's on his cell talking shop.

"Get off the phone. If I made her do it, you can too."

Jonathan gives me a dirty look. "Sorry Frank, can I call you in the morning? Something's just come up. Thanks." He clicks off the phone. "Can't this wait for five minutes?"

"I don't have five minutes and she certainly doesn't have five minutes. I don't want her sucked back into the despair that is her life at this particular moment. You asked me to help and this is me helping you, believe it or not."

"All right."

"These days, with the wonderful inventions called cell phones, tablets, and laptops, if a boy happens to take a picture of a girl in a compromising position, and let's face it, that's almost every day, they can use that image to threaten them with ridicule over the Internet if the girl doesn't keep sending naked pictures of herself, which is blackmail in my books. It's a real phenomenon and it's happening under your watch, because you don't know what's going on in your daughter's life. You know the symptoms of the problem, the drinking, the doping, but you don't know the actual problem because you didn't bother to find out. Stop being so wrapped up in your own concerns. You're disregarding this child—something you've accused me of for years, and you are a hundred percent right. I've done that to you, and I want to ask your forgiveness. But first I want you and Melissa to come up with a plan that will stop this torture instantly, and I don't care if that means taking her out of that disgusting preppy school you've got her in, or letting her stay with her mother—and believe me, you're going to tell her mother. This ends tonight. Melissa is a delightful child who's being ignored to death."

I fall into the nearest chair, out of breath and dizzy. Both my son and my granddaughter stare at me.

"I started this conversation. You two better finish it right now."

Jonathan looks sick. "Is this true, Melissa? Why didn't you tell me?"

She gets upset. "You think I want my dad to know that I was stupid enough to send pictures of my boobs to a guy? Yeah, I'm going to scream that from the rooftops. I didn't want you to be mad at me."

Now she's crying and he gets up and puts his arms around her. Finally, someone is doing something constructive. After they part, I hand them a box of tissues and the two of them sit back down, Melissa near me and Jonathan back behind his desk.

"So what are you going to do about this?" I ask him.

"I'm going to call the school, and I want to know who this boy is. I will be contacting his parents."

Melissa jumps up. "You can't! They'll know and then everyone in school will make it ten times worse! I'll figure it out myself."

"You will do no such thing," he says.

"So you're going to let me go to school and be hated more than I already am?"

"No, I'm taking you out of that school. There are plenty of others. I don't want you in that building."

"But...my friends..."

"These people are not your friends, Melissa. What friend would cause you this kind of pain?" He stands up and walks to his wall of windows. "So much for wanting your child to hobnob with the best families in the best schools. That little sonofabitch. He and his family will pay for this."

Now, that's probably not going to happen, but it's sure impressing Melissa.

"When your mother finds this out, she'll want to help, and I think she can do that by keeping you with her until we can devise a plan for another school. That way you aren't even in the neighbourhood. I don't want you bumping into these little creeps even accidentally. No, you're going to your mother's. I'm calling her right now."

I wonder if he noticed these were all my suggestions. Who cares? I'm proud of him.

FORTUNATELY, MELISSA'S MOM, DEANNE, IS BACK FROM HER EXOTIC HONEY-moon and is appropriately horrified by the situation. The next day she leaves lover boy at home and comes charging into the apartment with steam coming out of her designer ears. Despite her boob job and puffed-up lips, I like Deanne. She always wore the pants in the family, and I'm grateful she's on board.

"Oh my God! How did this happen? Hi, Grace. You look well. Where's my darling girl? Melissa!"

Melissa comes out of her room and Deanne runs down the hall to her. I notice Melissa's face crumble before her mom gives her a bear hug, and then they disappear behind Melissa's bedroom door. You're never too old to need your mother.

I go to the kitchen and Linn pours me a cup of tea and serves me a slice of lemon loaf.

"Thanks, Linn. I need this. Pour yourself a cup and sit with me."

She sits and has the tea but no loaf, which is probably how she's as slender as a reed.

"It's good you come here," she says.

"I should've been here more often. I'm not a good mother, Linn."

"You are excellent grandmother."

"You're very kind. I'm hope I can mend fences with Jonathan, but he has every right to be angry with me."

"He needs you."

"My thoughts exactly."

We hear Jonathan come in the front door, so we talk about the weather. He shows up in the kitchen with a look of satisfaction.

"There. That's done. I tore a strip off that principal and demanded her tuition back. Thirty thousand dollars a year to send my child to their lousy school."

"Thirty thousand dollars a *year*? Are you crazy?"

He instantly deflates.

Rats.

"I'm glad you made them pay it back. That took guts. Did you get in touch with the boy's parents?"

"I spoke to the father, and naturally he said it was my brat of a daughter who sent pictures of herself to his son, and what kind of girl does that? How dare I try to damage his child's reputation."

Linn and I look at each other.

"Is no one responsible for their actions?" I yell. "You've got idiot parents out there defending their idiot offspring, who refuse to admit their mistakes and pin the blame on their victims!"

"It's pathetic," he says.

"So what did you say to this asshole? Sorry, I forgot."

"No, you're right. He is an asshole. And he doesn't know it yet, but I run the company his company is trying to get into bed with. Too bad he didn't recognize my name. His little merger is going down in flames, which will make life very difficult for him."

"Good. But what about his wormy kid?"

"What can I do? The kid has 'rights' and he knows it."

"You have to be crafty."

"Mother."

"Trust me. I'll think of something."

Deanne and Melissa join us. Melissa's face has been ravished by tears, a sight I'm sick of, but she nevertheless looks better.

"Hi, Deanne. Did you have a nice honeymoon?"

"Yes, thank you, Jonathan. It was grand."

Linn takes our cups and makes herself scarce. I should do the same, but I'm too damn nosy.

Melissa sighs. "Don't be all stiff with each other. I thought you were here for me."

"What's the plan, people?" I ask.

"Melissa will have to live with me. There's no other solution. I don't want her anywhere near this neighbourhood."

"But not forever," Jonathan reminds her.

"This is the scene of the crime, darling. Do you want her here after what she's just told you? It's either let her live with me full-time or you relocate and get out of this part of Manhattan altogether."

"It's not quite as easy as you make it seem."

Deanne sighs. "Jonathan, dear, you always panic. It *is* that easy. You get a realtor to find you another apartment and you sell this one. You get a moving company to pack up your stuff and unload it. Linn will be with you to supervise. Problem solved."

I remind him of something. "There aren't a lot of good memories here. I'll help you."

"Help me?"

"I'll stay and help you move. I'm sure Linn could use a hand."

He puts his hand through his hair. "Moving every time there's a problem is not a solution."

"But it's the only one that makes sense for this particular situation, and you're wealthy enough to make it happen," I remind him. "Use that to your advantage."

Melissa shakes her head. "Doesn't matter where I go. The kids at the new school only have to Google my name and it starts all over again."

That hadn't occurred to me. I'm not familiar with the insidious world of the Internet.

Her mother is a little more savvy. "You get off Facebook, get off Instagram and Tumblr and Twitter, delete all your accounts and your pictures along with them. Even if your name is on those terrible pictures, no one will be able to connect them to you. And if they do find you, you have no idea what they're saying, so their power is gone."

"It won't be too hard to have Kurt's accounts suspended, or those pictures taken down. You're still a child, after all. I'll get my lawyers on it. But I hope this a wake-up call, Melissa," her father says. "You do have some responsibility in this. Poor judgement, in fact."

"I know that, Dad! Geez."

She huffs off, like kids do when they know their parents are right but they don't want to hear about it.

"You're doing the right thing," I tell them. "Melissa sees that you two are together in this and that's a huge relief. She's had a rough time since the divorce. It's tough for kids to watch their parents break up."

"There she goes again, doling out advice about parenting." Jonathan leaves the room.

I look at Deanne. "I can't win."

Deanne sits down in the stool vacated by Linn. "Jonathan's always going to blame you for everything. He's like a broken record."

"He needs help, and I'm hoping to use this opportunity to mend a few fences. I understand his grandfather is still controlling his life?"

"You have no idea. To tell you the truth, if that old man was out of the picture, I think Jonathan and I would've had a chance together, but he's like an evil poison and I couldn't take it anymore."

"I know all about it."

THE NEXT DAY JONATHAN HUGS MELISSA, SAYS HE'LL SEE HER SOON, AND goes to work. An hour later Deanne and her new husband come by to help lug Melissa's stuff to their place.

"Grace, this is my husband, Andre."

I shake his well-groomed hand. He has this European vibe going on. I wonder if his name is really Andrew. "Nice to meet you."

"Enchanted. I've heard a lot about you. I'm so happy Melissa is going to be with us for the foreseeable future."

Complete hogwash, but he's doing his best. Melissa makes a face behind his back.

Andre turns out to be a great help, since he's the one carting her belongings to the car. It's like excavating a tomb. There are layers to get through. We're not moving her furniture, just her clothes, jewellery, toiletries, and a box full of hair dryers, curling irons, flat irons, hot rollers, and hair pieces. Hair pieces! I'd love to say something about this ridiculous stockpile, but I keep my big mouth shut—just looking at Deanne, I can tell her bedroom is exactly the same. I'll have the makeup table shipped to Deanne's address.

Melissa hugs Linn and me goodbye.

"Will you come over?" she asks me.

"Of course. I'd like to see your new digs."

"The door is always open, Grace. Thank you for everything." Deanne gives me a very sincere hug. I know she appreciates my support. And the fact that I didn't give her an earful about her benign neglect of Melissa while she was swooning over Andre. Deanne's had a scare and she's a smart girl. She won't let it happen again.

Even Andre hugs me. "You are welcome anytime."

I like this kid.

JONATHAN AVOIDS ME FOR THE FIRST COUPLE OF NIGHTS, AND I STAY OUT OF his way. Perhaps it's better if this conversation starts spontaneously. I'm nervous about it. I'll have to wait and see. He's at work all day of course, and Linn and I rattle around. We've become fast friends. She even asks me if I'd like to meet her sister's family. So off we go one afternoon to New Jersey. We have a great time, and the food! Bowls and bowls of the most delicious concoctions with vats of steamed rice, all of it on a circular Lazy Susan in the middle of the table. I'm in heaven. I even take pictures of the feast. It's times like this that I wish I'd travelled more. The world and its diverse cultures have so much to offer.

Christmas is only two weeks away, and New York City is quite a spectacle of lights and holiday cheer. Linn and I take a walk the next afternoon just to see the sights. There is something mesmerizing about the energy in this city, and while I can appreciate it, I find it very tiring now. Once upon a time it had me in its thrall, but that was a long time ago.

Linn points ahead to a corner shop. "I buy lotto tickets. Maybe get rich."

"Good idea there, Linn. I'll get some too."

We're in this tiny store that is stuffed to the rafters. You can get anything in here. While we wait our turn at the cash register, Linn tugs on my arm. "Over there is Kurt. I recognize him. He came to house a few time."

I look over and oh yes, central casting couldn't have done a better job. He's got perfectly highlighted and messed-up hair under his ball cap, which is turned to the side, with his jeans belted halfway down his ass and a quilted jacket over his hoodie. He's on his cell, showing his friends something, and they're busting a gut. Doesn't he think he's God's gift to the world? Even Devon didn't stink this bad.

I pull Linn out of the lineup and give her my phone. "Do you know how to take a video with this?"

"Uhh..."

Quickly, I show her the button. "Just keep the camera on me. I'm going to do something and I want it recorded for posterity."

She smiles. "Yes. Yes."

I go over to the slushy machine and fill an extra-extra-large plastic cup of blue slightly frozen water. Now I go into my feeble routine. I'm perfectly placed when I just happen to trip over my own big feet, sending a gallon of slush into the air and completely drenching my horrified victim and ruining his oh so lovely face, hair, phone, clothes, and gigantic running shoes.

"Oh my God! I'm so sorry! I don't know how that happened! Are you all right?" I reach over and wipe his chest with vigorous strokes, hopefully smooshing the coloured slush into his jacket permanently.

"Get the fuck off me, lady!" He brushes me away but I'm hard to get rid of. I keep mauling him.

"I feel so bad! Is there anything I can do?" I yell over to the cashier. "Do you have any paper towels I can use?"

Now everyone in the store turns around and stares at our blue boy. He's mortified.

"He needs help!"

"Stay away from me, you crazy-ass bitch!" Out of the store he storms with his entourage glaring at me.

Linn is rolling. She gives me a thumbs up.

When Jonathan gets home it's the first thing we show him. He smiles and shakes his head. "Only you could pull this off. And using my poor housekeeper as your accomplice."

"So fun!" Linn says.

The next day is Sunday and Linn departs to visit her sister. That means Jonathan and I are alone in this place, which makes my stomach upset.

I show up at his study door. "Could I talk to you?"

He picks up a handful of paper off his desk. "I'm trying to find a new apartment. Isn't that what you wanted?"

This study is too cold and unwelcoming. I need a better place. "Could you come into my room with me? I've made us some coffee."

"Your room?"

"I want to sit on the bed and you can sit in that very nice armchair that I'm sure has never been sat on before."

"You drive me crazy with remarks like that."

"You're right. I've got a big mouth. But please humour me."

When he sighs and reluctantly gets out of his chair, he is identical to Melissa. He's just this big kid wearing a grown-up suit. A big lost kid.

We settle ourselves and he sips the coffee to humour me. I gulp mine.

"Jonathan, I owe you the truth."

"What truth? Your truth? Why did you never tell me what happened at the compound? You told me your mother and sister left you, but nothing else. I had to hear it from Melissa."

"It was painful. You'd been through enough. But right now there's a lot more you need to know. I owe you the truth about your dad."

"Okay. Do I want to know the truth about my dad?"

"How can anyone move forward without putting the past to rest? And I think you, and me, and your father need some peace."

CHAPTER TEN

THEN

The first time I meet Fletcher officially is the summer after my Aunt Mae's death. I've been accepted at Dalhousie University for September and I know Aunt Pearl would have been pleased. My neighbour Bruce Samuels says he'll keep an eye on the house, but I'm worried about my aunts' car. I don't want to be responsible for it in Halifax, seeing as how I'm living in residence and the bus is readily available. And yet they loved it so much, I don't want to sell it. I happen to mention it to someone at the post office and he said I should speak to Fletcher Parsons.

"Oh yes, I've heard of him. He's up on the hill with all the cars in the yard. They say he's very good."

"He's the Muhammad Ali of mechanics."

I'm still chuckling when I drive my Pontiac into Fletcher Parsons's yard and get out to see if he's around. A dog and a couple of cats are hanging about but they don't bother with me. Just lift their heads to see if it's anyone important, then go back to their siestas.

"Hello? Anybody here?"

There's the sound of a drill coming from the garage so I go over and peek in. There's this big husky guy with grease smudges on his face and hands doing something noisy. I wait until he stops and then shout, "Hello!"

I scare the life out of him.

"Jumpin' Mary! I didn't see ya there." He takes a rag out of his back pocket and approaches me, wiping his hands as he comes. "What can I do for you?"

"Fletcher?"

"That's me."

"I hear you know cars."

"Don't know much else, but I do know cars."

"What should I do with this one?" I point behind me.

He takes one look at it and gives me a great smile. "Now that's a car. Bumper needs work, though."

"I'm leaving for Halifax and can't take it with me, but I don't want to sell it either. Do you know if I could store it somewhere? A man at the post office said I should ask you."

"Well now, there's a few places, but they charge too much if you ask me. You don't know anyone who could store it in their garage for a time?"

"No. My aunt died and I have no one else, so I'm kind of desperate."

"I'm truly sorry to hear that."

"Thank you."

He looks around. "Well, I'm not saying it's the cleanest place in the world, but you see that old barn in the back up there? I use it to store an assortment of car parts and whatnot, but if I move a few things around, you could put it there and I'd keep an eye on it for you. I'd cover it up of course."

"I didn't mean for you—"

"I know you didn't, but the space is there and you're more than welcome to use it. How long will you be gone?"

"I don't know."

"Never mind. Makes no difference."

"Are you always this nice?"

He throws back his head and laughs. "Don't know about that. Critters seem to like me."

I offer to help him move the stuff in his barn, but he says he'll be fine. I give him the keys and we look at each other.

"Well, see ya, then. Thanks so much."

"You're welcome."

I turn around to walk back to the car and stop. "What am I doing? Now I don't have a car."

"I was wondering when you were going to figure that out," he grins. "Why don't you keep the car until you leave and I can drop you off at the bus station when the time comes." He hands me back the keys.

"You see? You're so nice."

"Just one thing."

"What's that?"

"Your name?"

"Amazing Grace Fairchild."

"That's a name I'll remember."

MY DAYS AT UNIVERSITY ARE A JUMBLED MIX OF SHOCK, BOREDOM, AND FASCI-
nation. I'm in a residence with girls my age, but I am light years away
from them in life experience. My first roommate is insane. All she does
is blubber if things don't go her way. That's when Daddy sends her
money, or talks to her prof so she won't fail her course, and Mommy
comes in every few days with her favourite meals since the cafeteria
food is "disgusting."

I love the food here.

When I simply can't stand it any longer I see the Dean of Women at
the residence and ask for another room. She's a middle-aged woman
in a trim blouse and skirt. She hasn't taken her eyes off me since I've
come into the room, but I don't think she's listening to me.

"What's your last name?"

"Fairchild."

She hits the desk with her fist. "I knew it! You're related to Pearl
Fairchild, aren't you?"

It gives me a momentary jolt to hear Aunt Pearl's name. "Yes, she
was my great-aunt."

"She's died, then?"

"Yes."

"That's too bad. She was the smartest woman I ever knew. Pearl
was the one who encouraged me to go to university. I'm so pleased
you're here. You have her mannerisms. Even the way you sit in your
chair. Well, well. Pearl Fairchild. What a woman."

My request is granted. I'm given a room in Old Eddy, in the basement. There's not many rooms down here. It's rather shabby and forgotten. Most of the girls here are black. I wonder if that's a coincidence.

We become pals and I spend my evenings in their rooms, watching
them put oil in their hair before bed. What a production. They tease

me about being white and having an easier time of it. I assure them straight hair is just as problematic.

The day I'll never forget that year, is when one of my black friends gives me the rest of her can of Coke. I take it back to my room and ask my roommate if she wants a sip. She asks me where I got it, since Coke is a luxury, and I tell her Judith gave it to me. She refuses to drink from the can and tells me to throw it out.

I never speak to my roommate again.

Fortunately, the one thing I love is the learning. I read everything, and devour facts and ideas like they're Aunt Mae's ginger cookies. My professors love me and the feeling is mutual.

One professor in particular. Mr. Roman teaches my psychology class. The man is undeniably handsome, but it's his confidence that envelopes me and makes me feel like I'll be special, too, one day.

Our assignment is to re-enact the Second World War. Our class of one hundred is divided into countries and there are two or three trailers out behind the psych building that house the seats of our collective governments. Armed with knowledge about events after the First World War, we are given the task of trying to avoid another world war. All of us are certain that we'll stop the war entirely, since we're young, war is horrific, and we know better. We'll show them.

Our World War Two starts five years earlier. None of us can agree on anything and there are bullies on each team who refuse to budge from their almighty principles. Not to mention the guys shouting over the girls, because they're so damn important and what do we know anyway.

I'm close to hitting the emperor of Japan before I realize I need to retreat behind one of the trailers to cool down. As I reach for my matches to light a cigarette, Mr. Roman approaches and lights one for each of us.

"So what do you think, Miss Fairchild?" He blows smoke above my head. "What did you learn today?"

"That men are idiots."

He laughs. "You are a delightful creature, so different from the others."

"What do you mean?"

"When I look at you I see truth. You don't hide behind bullshit."

"Then I have a recommendation for your experiment. Divide it by sex and see what happens. My bet is the women will win every time."

He looks impressed and nods his head. "I think we should discuss this over lunch."

Lunch leads to more lunch and then dinners, and inevitably breakfasts.

I have a secret now, and I hold it to my chest like a gemstone. The great Professor Philip Roman is in love with me. He picked me out of all the girls on campus. An educated man who listens to every word I say. He tells me I'm smart and impossibly beautiful.

Now I understand love-making. It's supposed to make you feel good, not bad. We meet in his small apartment when he can get away.

"Maybe we could go to dinner sometime. Or a movie." I'm naked on the bed, in the crook of his arm, smoking a cigarette.

He takes a drag on his and pulls his fingers through my hair. "I want you all to myself. I can't bear to share you with anyone."

That's all he ever says. I sit up, annoyed. "At some point, we have to go outside."

Mr. Roman gives me a big sigh. "Do I really have to say this, Grace? I'm your prof. It would be bad form if people knew I was dating a student."

"If you knew that, why are you here with me? What kind of relationship is this? Are you ashamed of me?"

"Darling girl." He stubs out his cigarette and then grabs mine and flattens that as well. "Come here."

This always happens. He makes love to me and I'm helpless against him. Despite my annoyance, he's like a drug. All my life I've run away from men and now I'm rushing towards one. Philip makes me feel wanted, like I have someone I can count on. These are the best days of my life. I have friends at the dorm, my boyfriend, and great classes. Everything is working out very nicely, for once in my pitiful life.

And it gets better. I'm in social studies class, in the back of the room with my head beside the open window.

The guy next to me says, "Got a headache?"

I turn to him. "Yeah. How did you know?"

"My whole life is a headache. I can spot one a mile off." He grins and takes out a small aspirin tin from his pocket and offers it to me. "Take two."

I swallow the pills with a gulp of Pepsi. "Thanks...what's your name?"

"Aaron. Aaron Willingdon."

"Thanks, Aaron. I'm Grace."

"No, you're not. You're Amazing."

Now I'm suspicious. "Okay, how do you know that?"

His brown eyes crinkle at the corners and dimples bracket his mouth. "I'm a spy. No, a friend told me. One of your cohorts from Old Eddy. Judith Reddick."

"I love Judith."

We're still chatting when a TA we've never seen before walks into the room. She doesn't look much older than us, with her checkered bell-bottoms and bandana on her head. She proceeds to sit in the swivel chair behind the desk in the front of the room.

"I'm your substitute for the day. Open your books."

We dutifully open our textbooks and wait for further instructions, but that's it. She spends the entire time spinning in the chair.

Aaron leans over. "Lucy is in the sky with diamonds, I fear."

At first we smirk, then laugh and look at each other, wondering what we should do, but after a while it gets ridiculous. Aaron stands up, and he's very tall. I'm not sure how he fit under the desk. He says loudly, "Well, comrades, I say we make a break for it."

He grabs my hand. "Let's get some coffee."

The entire class follows our lead. For all I know she's still spinning.

Aaron and I head to a small coffee shop off campus. It never occurs to me to be worried about going anywhere with him. He has this big brother kind of feel. We settle in with our coffee and danishes.

"So tell me about yourself," he says. "You have a wicked look about you."

"Oh, I have the devil in me. Someone told me that once."

"I look at your big hazel eyes and auburn hair and see only angels flying here and there...through the air...a girl so fair...without a care..."

"I love corny people," I smile.

"Then you'll be enthralled with me."

Aaron and I become fast friends. He just gets me. I find myself telling him about the compound, something I never thought I'd do, but Aaron makes me feel safe. Even when I tell him terrible stuff, he never flinches. He will keep my secrets.

But after a while I notice that he doesn't say much about himself, or he'll change the subject when I ask him a question. It's annoying, but I can't stay mad at him. He'll make a goofy face or buy me a popsicle, or make me ride on the handlebars of his bike, both of us shouting at people to warn them, as we zigzag down the sidewalk.

After a crazy session in bed one afternoon with Philip, I ask my psychology expert how to get someone to talk.

"If they don't want to talk, it's damn near impossible. You could torture them I suppose, but somehow that doesn't strike me as your style." He kisses my hair. "Who is this person you want to know so much about?"

"Just a friend."

"A girlfriend."

"No."

He looks down at me from above. "Are you seeing someone behind my back, you wanton woman?"

"He's a friend."

"You tell your friend to keep his hands off. You're my property."

"I'm nobody's property." I push him away and get off the bed, grabbing my clothes off the floor.

"Grace! I'm kidding!"

"I have to go."

The next day a bouquet of red roses arrives at the dorm for me, with a small card. "I'm sorry. I love you. P."

I've never had a man give me flowers before. I show them to Judith.

"You got it goin' on, girl. You better find me a man like that."

With all the distractions in my private life, my grades suffer for the first time since before my aunts found me. Aunt Pearl would have had a fit, and I feel like I'm letting her down. I can't jump every time Philip wants me to meet him. Even Aaron takes up a lot of my time with his wonderful goofiness. I'm not sure when he goes to class. He makes me laugh like no one else, but I'm still no closer to figuring him out.

We are weeks away from dispersing for the summer, my first year over. What to do with myself weighs heavy. Getting a temporary job and leasing an apartment for a couple of months is imperative, but what do I want to be when I finish university? The thought of going to classes forever seems preferable to making a decision. So far nothing has reached out and grabbed me by the throat. Some of the girls know already that they want to be pharmacists or doctors or lawyers, although the vast majority are hoping to snag a guy before it's too late.

Someone suggests social work and I actually shiver. My experience with social workers makes my stomach knot, but I do see from this vantage point that they were trying to help me. Trouble is, they never looked at it from my point of view. They were bossy strangers who never let me speak, or even if they did, they'd tell me not to worry and that everything would be fine. But I wasn't clueless. I knew I should be worried and that things might not be fine and there's no reassurance strong enough to push those thoughts away. It's difficult to deal with a pissed-off mouthy kid all day, but my being rude and unco-operative was fear manifesting, and not giving me back my cat was unforgivable. I dream about Buddy still. It's not knowing what happened to him that makes me sad. He must have thought I didn't love him anymore. Nothing could be further from the truth.

I'm working in the library on a paper for the end of term when Aaron happens by and sits opposite me.

"Go away, Aaron. I need to finish this."

His lip goes down in an exaggerated pout. "Gee, thanks. I guess I'll give you the good news later." He starts to leave.

"Sit down, you jerk. Just hurry up because I have to finish this."

"I've solved your problem."

"I have many. Which one are you referring to?"

"Your lease."

"I need a really cheap apartment. You know that."

"This is very cheap. It's at my place. I have a spare bedroom. You can spend the summer there."

I look up from my paper. "Thanks, but it will ruin our friendship. I'll figure it out."

He says nothing, so I put down my pen. "You're a very sweet guy and I appreciate your offer, but I don't want to put you out. I need to stand on my own two feet."

Aaron leans back in his chair. His cheekbones stand out, like he's lost weight.

"Are you eating?"

"Perhaps you could live with me and feed me like a baby bird."

"Or you could become a fashion model. With cheeks like that you'd make a fortune."

"Well, don't say I didn't offer."

"I love you, Aaron. Thank you for even suggesting it."

He pats my head before he leaves. It's dark by the time I finish my assignment. Even though I won't take up Aaron's offer, it's like a warm piece of coal in my pocket. If things get desperate, he's around. Sometimes that's all a person needs.

A few days after that I'm not feeling very well and one of the girls suggests I go to the clinic to get checked out. It can't hurt, I suppose, but I make sure it's a woman doctor first. Dr. Lang listens to my complaints, my nausea and feelings of fatigue. She listens to my heart and takes my blood pressure and then asks me to lie down on the table. The minute she starts pressing on my stomach, I know. Even before she says she wants a urine sample.

"Is there any chance you could be pregnant? You're practising safe sex, I hope?"

"I'm a fool."

"Your periods stopped?"

"I guess so. I wasn't paying attention."

She looks down at me kindly. "Are you not in the habit of taking care of yourself?"

I avert her gaze. "Apparently not."

"The father is still in the picture?"

"Yes. He'll help me."

"It's scary, but your body knows what it's doing, as long as you take care of it. No drinking, smoking, or drug use. That's imperative. See me regularly so I can monitor your progress. I'll prescribe some prenatal vitamins." She takes out her notepad.

I want to die. "This isn't my first baby."

The sympathy in her eyes goes away. "You have another child?"

"No, I miscarried when I was fifteen."

"How far along?"

"Three months."

"Do you have a mom? Or any female relative."

"No.

Dr. Lang sighs and puts her hand on my shoulder. "I'll help you through this."

It's worse when people are kind to me.

It takes me a while to find the courage to tell Philip. I'm not so naive that I don't know that this is a potential problem, but I figure he's a lot older than I am and is probably ready to settle down and start a family. This isn't what Aunt Pearl had in mind for me, but I know she'd never throw me on the streets if she knew. Or maybe she would. She'd certainly call me a hippy-dippy; it's like I never look far enough ahead to imagine the consequences of my actions. I've let myself down for sure, and this little baby who terrifies me. It might decide I'm a screwup, too, and leave me like the last one did.

Philip and I are on our usual Tuesday night date. After pizza, we fall into bed and stay there. When he decides he's had enough, he pulls himself up, leans against the headboard, and lights a cigarette. "Want one?" He holds out the cigarette pack.

"No thanks."

He looks surprised. "Okay then. On a healthy kick are we?"

"Sort of."

It occurs to me that Philip often smokes so he doesn't have to talk. I'm guilty of that myself, but only with people I don't know. Philip knows me better than anyone.

"I need to talk to you."

He closes his eyes and inhales. "Sounds serious. Let me enjoy my ciggy."

I lay back down on the bed for a couple of minutes but he's not in any hurry, which annoys me, and I get out of bed and get dressed.

"I always know when you're pissed off at me," he chuckles. "You put your clothes back on. So why am I the bad guy now?"

I'm fully dressed before I answer. "I'm pregnant."

He takes the cigarette out of his mouth and glares at me. "Are you fucking kidding me?"

His anger frightens me a little. "Is this a big surprise? That's what we do. That's all we do. Did it never occur to you that this might happen?"

Philip pounds his cigarette into the ashtray and gets out of bed. "It never occurred to me that you wouldn't take care of it."

"So because you won't use condoms, I'm supposed to come up with another plan? I thought that meant you didn't care if I got pregnant, that you might even be glad if it happened. You say you love me. This is what people in love do."

He struggles into his jeans. "You stupid little girl. Why did you have to be so stupid?"

"What?"

That's when he takes a step towards me and holds his arms out like he's explaining something to a imbecile. "I'm married with three kids already! Why would I want one with you?"

"Married?"

"Of course I'm married. Don't pretend you didn't know that. Everyone knows that."

"I assumed you weren't married because you never told me you were. You chased me, remember? So that information was your obligation, not mine."

"This isn't happening. Do you hear me, Grace? If this gets out it will ruin my career. Surely you wouldn't be that selfish." He throws on his clothes on and jumps into his runners.

"What about me?"

He stops then and tries to collect himself. "You're right. There's you. You gave me such a fright I panicked for a minute." He reaches over and takes me in his arms, stroking my hair like it might give him some special power. "I'm sorry. You're right."

He steps away and picks up his wallet on the bedside table. "Here. Here's three hundred bucks. No, here's four hundred, just to be safe." He puts it in my hand. "Get an abortion, but please go to someone who isn't going to butcher you. I can't have that on my conscience. I've got to go. Put the key under the mat when you leave."

And he disappears out of my life forever.

CHAPTER ELEVEN

NOW

I knew it would be BAD. *To learn that your father isn't your father. My* mistake was made long ago, when I didn't tell Jonathan as soon as he could understand. My poor boy has gone white, his coffee forgotten long ago. He's dazed, like I hit him on the head. That's just what I did. Pounded him into the ground and uncovered a new reality that can't possibly be real.

"I'm sorry, Jonathan. I never should have gone along with keeping it a secret. Your father thought it would be best if you didn't know."

"Go ahead, pin the blame on him. According to you, my real father gave you money to get rid of me. My pretend father lied to me my whole life. You ran away. What did I ever do to deserve such a nurturing group of people? Excuse me."

He's a little unsteady as he rises from the armchair, and won't look at me as he leaves the room.

I get in the tub and brood until the water gets cold. Then I crawl into bed and stay there. Here's hoping Jonathan can get a little rest.

It becomes a waiting game. He disappears for about three days. I follow Linn around just for something to do, but I'm in her way. I spend hours at the movie theatre eating popcorn but have no clue what the films are about. On day three I find myself in front of Deanne's apartment building. It at least is only two storeys up.

"You're lucky you caught me in." She ushers me inside. "I stayed home today to catch up on some paperwork. Would you like a drink?"

"Whiskey."

"That kind of a day. Coming right up."

I wander around her living room. It's chic, but not over the top. It looks like a magazine cover, but one that people live in. There are newspapers on the floor and I see evidence of Melissa everywhere, which means she's not holed up in her room twenty-four-seven.

Deanne walks back in with two tumblers of whiskey. "I took a chance. On the rocks."

"Thank you, my dear."

We sit on either end of her sofa. She makes herself comfortable, tucks up her legs and holds out her glass. "Cheers."

I do the same. "Cheers." The whiskey tastes good on my tongue.

"I was going to call you and ask if you wanted to have dinner with us tonight—this is great timing."

"Oh goody. What are we having?"

She laughs. "Oh, Grace. Have you forgotten? I don't cook. It depends on what restaurant you'd like to go to."

"No wonder Jonathan divorced you."

"Oh, he had plenty of other reasons to get rid of me. Let's just say I lead when I dance."

"I think he misses you."

She reaches up and tucks her stylish hair behind her ear. "I doubt it. Jonathan and I were always better friends than anything else. He needs a woman who will let him call the shots. For a man who's worth a fortune, he has very little confidence."

"That is totally my fault."

"Why?"

I reach over and pat her leg. "He'll tell you when he's ready. Now, how's our girl?"

I end up offering to make dinner. Andre and Melissa are overjoyed to be eating at their own dining-room table.

"Mom, you really have to take cooking lessons. This quiche is so good. Gee cooks all the time in Cape Breton. Every meal is homemade. Did you make dessert, Gee?"

"Naturally. Coconut balls."

The minute I taste one with my tea, my longing for home overwhelms me. Wonder what Fletch and the critters are up to? No doubt Dora is skipping merrily up to our place with her baked offerings.

"Your mother has far more important things to do, like run a hospital. She can't do everything."

"Thank you, Grace. I'm glad someone is sticking up for me."

Andre reaches over for another coconut ball. "I have an idea,

Melissa. I'd be happy to pay for cooking lessons for you. Perhaps after school? Would that be something you'd like?"

This guy is trying very hard, and I see Deanne give him a grateful look. For someone who's still so young, he has a maturity about him.

Melissa likes the idea but she doesn't want to admit it. "Maybe. We'll see."

"What do you say to someone who makes such a nice offer?"

She makes a face at me but turns to Andre. "Thank you, Andre. That's very generous."

"Not at all," he smiles.

Later, as I help Deanne load the dishwasher, she turns to me. "Jonathan and I have made a lot of mistakes with Melissa. We let her get away with too much."

"Always a temptation with an only child. Deanne, you've done a lot right too, and you're here. That's everything."

Andre drives me back to Jonathan's. I'm almost out the door when I turn to him. "You're a good kid, Andre. Just keep doing what you're doing with Melissa and everything will sort itself out."

"Thank you, Grace. It's been tough."

"I can only imagine. Thanks for the lift."

As his tail lights disappear up the street, I stand outside Jonathan's apartment and smoke a cigarette. Some uptown ladies go by with their crocodile purses, fox collars, and mink coats. They make me sick.

"You should be ashamed of yourselves."

They give me a collective disgusted look, like I'm something to be scraped off their designer boots. The world is going to hell. I'm glad I'll be outta here sooner rather than later. Death doesn't scare me. Life does.

When I get back to Jonathan's apartment, I know right away he's home. There's a dark energy in here. I go to my bedroom and shut the door; he knows where I am if he wants to talk. To soothe my nerves I call Fletch. He sounds sleepy.

"How's she goin'?" he says.

"I miss you."

"We miss you too, don't we, fellas?"

"I suppose Dora's been up with countless cookies."

He laughs. "A few."

"What is it with that woman? She's got a perfectly good husband of her own."

"I'll tell you a secret. Might make you feel better."

"What?"

"She asked me to marry her once."

"When?"

"When we were in high school. Damnedest thing. Never heard tell of a woman asking a man."

"Obviously you said no."

"I told her I was too busy."

"And what did she say?"

"She said she'd change my mind. The woman is driven, if nothing else."

A thought occurs to me. "I bet she married Harvey just to live next door to you. Why are you still nice to her? She's been stalking you for fifty years."

He chuckles. "She's not harming anybody, least of all me."

"Well, she bugs me."

"The dogs are scratching on the door to get out. Take care of yourself."

"See ya, Fletch."

THERE'S A KNOCK. "COME IN."

Jonathan opens the door. He's haggard, but even in his casual clothes, he looks smart. Philip always looked sharp. Funny how things like that are passed along.

"Can we talk?"

"Of course."

He settles himself back in the armchair and I lean up against the headboard.

"Before you say anything, Jonathan, I want you to know how terribly sorry I am about all this. You were an innocent victim and never deserved to be lied to. I'm ashamed of what I did to you."

"I've been thinking about this non-stop for the last few days. I realize that you were only a few years older than Melissa when this happened to you. But you were a grown woman when you left me. How does that happen? Tell me why that was your only choice."

"You're not going to like it."

"I don't like any of this."

"Fair enough."

CHAPTER TWELVE

THEN

My shock lasts for hours. I don't have the strength to leave the apartment. There are no tears, just this frozen lump of disbelief that I have been so utterly duped. After a while I turn the anger I feel for him on myself. What is it about me that screamed victim to him? How did I make it rational in my own head that a university professor would be interested in me for anything other than sex?

Before I leave that apartment, I rip up his money into tiny pieces and leave the pile on the middle of the bed. Then I take a knife from the kitchen and stab the mattress with it, over and over again, leaving it there for him to find. I smash the mirrors, crush his packs of cigarettes under my heel, and pour molasses all over his clothes. Then I plug up the sinks and bathtub and leave the water running. The door to his apartment is wide open when I go, the key dumped in the nearest trashcan on my way back to residence.

Once I get back to my room, my energy disappears. It's an awful night, just me, my rage, and my baby. I don't know what to do. If I go back to Marble Mountain, I'll be the talk of the town with my pregnant belly on display. I can't do that to Aunt Pearl. If I stay here, I'll go mad. University means nothing anymore. What I need is a job so I can take care of myself and this child, who I feel sorry for already. What a shit mother I'm going to be. I can't give this baby a father, a home, or stability. Maybe I should abort it.

But it's the only thing that's mine.

Aaron eventually seeks me out. Exams have started, and when I don't show up, he comes and finds me. I'm sitting in the bleachers by the sports field watching a soccer practice when he runs up to me, his long hair curling around his neck.

"There you are! What's going on? Did you forget we had an exam this morning?"

"I didn't forget. I dropped out."

"Dropped out? Of what? Class or life?"

"Both."

"Are you crazy? You're at the top in all your subjects."

"Doesn't matter."

His face is full of concern as he takes my hand. "What's wrong? How can I help?"

"You can't save me from myself, Aaron. No one can."

"Maybe not, but I'm not leaving you here alone. You're my best friend." He puts his arm around my shoulder and leans in to hug me closer.

"I don't know what to do."

"We'll figure it out. You're coming back to my place."

He keeps his arm round me as we walk across campus and down the side streets of Halifax. So far I've managed not to cry. I'm too miserable to cry. We sit in his apartment on either end of the hide-a-bed, drinking soup out of a mug. It's embarrassing to tell him about my ridiculous behaviour, that I fell for the lies and the bullshit. A real country hick.

"This is not your fault," Aaron says. "Stop thinking it is. None of this is your fault."

"I know you're trying to be nice, Aaron, but it is my fault. I didn't use birth control, and I didn't question his never wanting to leave the apartment or be seen with me. Not true, I mentioned it once and he distracted me, but it was blatant and I chose to ignore it."

"He's in a position of authority and knows very well that he's in the wrong. Didn't stop him though, did it? And then he tells you to get rid of his kid. His kid! What kind of worm does that?"

"I trashed his place before I left."

"Good girl."

"It was childish."

"Felt good though, right?"

"Yep."

We watch a bit of television, each of us with our own thoughts. It feels nice to sit and not think. My eyes get heavy and I doze off. At one point, I rouse to find I'm covered with a blanket and there's a pillow under my head. I drift back to sleep and don't wake until morning.

Over breakfast, Aaron says. "I want you to come and live with me for the time being, while you look for a job. Obviously you can't stay in residence if you've quit school. I'll help you bring your stuff over."

"I'm imposing on your good nature."

"You're doing me a favour. Two is always better than one."

The first thing to do is tell the Dean of Women at Sheriff Hall that I'm leaving. She looks surprised. "Not for good, surely?"

"Afraid so."

"Are you going to another university?"

"No. I'm having a baby."

"Oh, Grace!" There is such disappointment on her face. Exactly how I imagine Aunt Pearl would look in the light of such news. "You've got your whole life ahead of you. You have such potential."

"I'm not dying."

"You might as well be." She gets up and starts pacing in her office. "I'm sorry. I shouldn't have said that, but it's so frustrating to see a bright girl like you waste her future like this. Anyone can be a mother! Not everyone can make the highest aggregate in all her classes. I had such hopes for you."

She sits back down behind her desk, thoroughly dejected. It's sort of touching.

"If your mother didn't have you, you wouldn't be here giving me flak. Have you thought of that?"

She tries not to smile. "I could wring your neck."

"Sorry."

"Is there anything I can do for you?"

"Yes. One of your psychology professors is a predator. He needs to stay away from young, foolish girls like me."

She looks grim. "Oh god. We've let you down."

I reach over and hold out my hand. "Thank you for your concern. I know you'll do the right thing."

She stands up and shakes my hand. "Rest assured. Good luck, Grace Fairchild. My admiration has not diminished, my dear."

Here I am again, leaving hope behind.

After I move in with Aaron, he comes tearing up the stairs of his flat. He hands me a piece of paper. "Roman's address. Don't let him off the hook, Grace."

Unsure if I want to do this or not, I take a bus over to his neighbourhood, and wander around until I find the street and then his house. It's no great shakes. Not what I imagined at all. There are a few toys around the yard and it has a sort of neglected look. Before I lose my nerve, I walk up onto the porch and ring the doorbell. A dog barks. Poor thing. I feel sorry for it, having Philip as his human.

The door opens and an ordinary looking woman answers the door. She's not gorgeous, she's not slim, and she hasn't dyed her hair in a while. There's a commotion behind her. Sounds like kids and plates crashing.

"Yes?"

"Does Professor Roman live here?"

"Yes."

"Are you Mrs. Roman?"

"What do you want?"

What do I want? I want a lot of things, but not this.

"Sorry I bothered you." I turn away and walk down the steps.

I'm almost at the sidewalk when she shouts, "You're not the first, you know!' before she shuts the door.

My job hunt doesn't take long, but then again, I'm not looking for a career. They need someone at the corner shop down the street, especially the night shift. When I tell Aaron, he shakes his head.

"No way. You're not working in a store by yourself at night. Find something else."

I stop stirring the macaroni in the pot on the stove. "I need to buy some groceries. I can't live off you forever."

"Stop talking."

We both find jobs that summer. He works at a flower shop, doing their accounting and general paperwork, and I'm a waitress and chambermaid at a bed and breakfast on Barrington Street. A job like this confirms my suspicions that human beings are disgusting. Who doesn't flush a toilet? My back aches by the end of the day after making umpteen old-fashioned beds, and whenever Aaron gets home first, he has a hot-water bottle waiting for me.

All day, every day, I think about the future. How am I going to bring up a baby alone? I still have a lot of Aunt Pearl's money in the bank, but it won't last forever unless I am very careful. The thought of coming to the end of my inheritance frightens me. If it comes down to it, I might have to sell Aunt Pearl and Aunt Mae's car. Maybe even the house. Then I change my mind and think I should just go back to Marble Mountain with the baby. So what if a few uptight hens squawk at me behind my back? At least I'd be safe.

But what happens if there's a snowstorm and I have no power? I'd be in the middle of nowhere. Is that a good idea with a baby? What if someone breaks in? I can't think anymore.

Then I have the brilliant idea of placing an ad in the Toronto and Ottawa newspapers, asking anyone who knows of a Trixie or Ave Maria Fairchild to please call my number. It cost me a bit, but if I can find my family, I won't be raising this baby alone.

In the end it comes to nothing. I have one caller who says he'd tell me what I want to know if I pay him a thousand bucks. Another tells me she once knew a Tricia Fairchild, but that she died long ago.

At the end of summer I find Aaron with papers all over the kitchen table. I go to the fridge and open the orange juice. "What are you doing? Don't you have your courses picked out already?"

"I need to talk to you. Sit down."

After I pour the juice, I take a big gulp and sit at the table. "What?"

"Hear me out."

"Uh-oh."

"Grace. Be quiet. Please."

"Sorry."

He picks up the papers in front of him. They look like applications of some kind. If I didn't know better I'd say he was in a sweat. "You don't know about me."

"Are you a killer?"

"Grace!" He starts again. "I'm leaving Halifax. I only came here to get away from my life. I needed a break and it did the trick, but I have to go back. Fortunately I met you and now I can't imagine life without you. I want you to marry me and let me raise the baby as my own."

I drink the rest of my juice to stop from laughing.

"Well?"

"How can you ask me to marry you? You've never kissed me. You're not in love with me. I adore you as a friend, but as your wife? I told you before, Aaron. I'm never getting married."

"Just listen!"

He seems so serious.

"I do love you, Grace. I haven't approached you because I knew you were seeing someone else. I just didn't know who. And then this horror happened to you and it wasn't the time to say anything. Just because I haven't drooled all over you doesn't mean I don't want to. I'm aware of the hurt you've been through. You might not think you're in love with me, but what is this, if it isn't love? We've formed this little family. I don't know where I'd be without you and I hope you feel the same way. My life is difficult, but it would be heaven if I had you and the baby."

"Why is your life difficult?"

"My father."

"What about him?"

"He is a very wealthy man who owns half of New York City. He thinks he owns all the people around him too. Like me, like my mother, before she ended up in a sanatorium. I'm a disappointment to him. But if I went home with you as my wife, and a grandchild on the way, an heir to his fortune, he would welcome us with open arms. I'm sure of it. And you would have the kind of life you've never dreamed of. And this child will have endless opportunities to explore the world and have the finest education money can buy. You need a father for your baby. You need to be protected from the world. I can't let you struggle here alone. We need each other, Grace."

All this is bouncing around in my head. He doesn't know what he's talking about. I grab his hand from across the table. "Aaron! You have every opportunity to fall in love with another woman and have your own child. Why would I take that away from you? You're not thinking clearly."

His head drops and he's still for a long time. Then he looks at me. "So you don't think you love me at all?"

"I don't trust men, Aaron. And you're a man."

"I'm a good man, in case you hadn't noticed."

"I—"

"Don't say anything. Just think about it. It's a happy ending for both of us. I do love you very much. I wish I was like you. You're brave and smart. You're a survivor. Quite frankly, I could use your strength around me."

"What are all these papers?"

"A marriage license. A passport application for you. If we marry in New York and the baby is born there, it will be an American citizen."

"I want my baby to be Canadian."

"It will have dual citizenship, which is always a bonus."

"I have a headache."

He gets up from the table. "We need more juice. I'll go get some."

I stand by the living-room window and watch him exit the building and walk down the street. He's such a funny character. A bit odd, yet sweet. Trying so hard to please his father. Thinking of me and the baby. I'd be set for life. I wouldn't have to worry about having a home, or bringing the baby up alone. I'd be able to keep the car and the farmhouse. We could go to Marble Mountain in the summer and I could teach the baby how to swim in the lake. I'd be a respectable married woman, not someone whispered about. There is really no reason I shouldn't do this.

Except it's wrong to marry someone when you don't want to be married.

I say yes anyway.

THE NEXT FEW WEEKS FLY BY. AARON INSISTS ON TAKING ME SHOPPING FOR NEW clothes. Anything I want I can have. He pays for everything. He sends me to an expensive hair salon, and I'm sitting under the dryer when it hits me. He's trying to make me look good for his father. Like I'm not good enough already.

He's in the shower when I arrive home. I walk into the bathroom and flush the toilet.

"Aaah! That's cold water! What did you do that for?"

"You're a jerk."

He peeks out from behind the curtain with soap bubbles in his eyes. "What did I do?"

"All this makeover stuff. You're trying to butter up your old man by making me look like a Barbie doll. That's revolting."

Now I storm to the bedroom. He eventually comes out with a towel wrapped around him.

"I'm not doing it to try and impress him. I'm trying to make it easier for you. You're going to be meeting lots of people and I want you to feel confident among them."

"Poor little orphan Annie, meeting all the big mucky-mucks. If I do this, Aaron, I'm not going to be anyone but myself. I don't give a shit how I'm dressed."

"That's another thing. Don't curse."

"Fuck!"

WE'RE MARRIED IN A REGISTRY OFFICE. THE FIRST TIME WE KISS IS IN FRONT OF the judge. It's nicer than I expected. Then we go out for hamburgers. In between bites I admire my ring. That was a complete surprise. A gold band with little diamonds circling my finger.

"I love it."

"I'm getting you a bigger one when we get to New York. We'll go to Tiffany's."

"That's not necessary."

"I'm your husband, Grace. I will buy you jewels for the rest of your life."

"I'd only lose them."

"Stop trying to be this macho chick. You're beautiful, Grace. I want to see you in diamond earrings and bracelets. You'll put all the other women to shame. My father thinks I'm a loser. With you on my arm, I'm no loser, and he'll know that the minute he sees you."

Oh, brother.

Before we go, I book an appointment with Dr. Lang, to make sure everything is okay with the baby. I'm six months pregnant and the baby is moving, but I don't have a big belly. Listening to the heartbeat makes it seem real. While I lie on the table I wish with all my heart for this baby to be a girl. I'm ashamed to say I don't want a boy. I'm afraid he'll come out and look just like Philip. How am I going to take care of a child that reminds me of a terrible moment in my life? So every night I pray to a god I don't believe in, just to cover all bases.

It's early October when we board the plane bound for New York. My instinct is to turn around and run, but when I glance at Aaron, he looks so happy. I do love this man. I'd be nowhere without him. He deserves my loyalty. If anything ever happened to me, Aaron would take care of my child. That's worth everything. I have to make this work.

I AM AN AMAZED GRACE AS I TAKE IN THE SIGHTS OF NEW YORK CITY. It's overwhelming and I'm not sure where to look first. Aaron asks the taxi driver to take us to Times Square, and then to wait for us with the luggage. We get out and I literally stand in the middle of the street with my mouth open.

"Aaron, pass me my camera!"

Now I'm a true blue tourist, snapping pictures left, right, and centre. I'm delighted with everything.

"Look at all the yellow taxis!"

"I know!" he laughs.

He gets a great kick out of me. Everything you could ever want is behind a pane of glass. "Can we go in a store?"

"Of course." We pile into the taxi once more and Aaron gets the driver to take us to Macy's. "Wait here until we get back."

"Sure thing."

Aaron grabs my hand and we run into the store. It's like a jewellery box. Everything sparkles and catches my eye. We ride up and down the escalator, and he grabs things I might like, buying them even though I protest. A pair of kid gloves, a scarf, a bottle of perfume with an atomizer. That, I'm thrilled with, because Aunt Pearl always had one on her dresser. I wrapped it in tissue paper and put it in the bureau drawer for safe keeping. Now I have a piece of her here in New York. How I wish they were with me to see this. Aunt Pearl would stick her nose in the air and pretend it was foolish, but she'd love it, and Aunt Mae would be beside herself, twirling in the aisles.

We go up to the baby section and gape at the cribs, the dressing tables and rockers. There is every kind of stroller you could imagine.

We buy plush toys and a huge stuffed giraffe. People stare at us as we try to shove it in the back of the taxi, but we don't care. There's only the two of us and baby makes three. We giggle in the back seat like school kids as we drive through traffic.

"I'm so happy," I say to Aaron.

He takes my hand and kisses it. "As long as you're happy, that's all that matters."

I lean over and give him a proper kiss. It surprises him, I can tell. "Just give me time, Aaron. I know you're suffering for the mistakes other men have made, but in time I'll get better. You wait and see."

"I love you today, Mrs. Willingdon."

"And I do love you, Mr. Willingdon. One day I'll show you how much."

It's almost dusk when we arrive at a large townhouse on a quiet, tree-lined street. Even I, who know nothing, can tell that this place reeks of old money.

"Are you ready?" Aaron smiles.

"Let's go."

The taxi driver helps us with our luggage, bags, and gigantic giraffe, depositing them on the front step. Aaron gives him a large tip, then takes out a key and unlocks the door. A large entrance hall is revealed, with marble floors and a chandelier.

"You have a chandelier in your porch?"

"It's not a porch. It's a vestibule."

"Excuse me."

The house is palatial. I hate it. It would be a catastrophe to break anything in here.

"Please say we're not living here."

"No. This is Dad's house. We'll have our own. We'll pick it out together. This is just in the interim."

A man in a suit comes from nowhere. "Master Aaron. Good to see you, sir. Let me take those for you."

"Thanks, Parker. Parker, this is my wife, Grace."

Parker tries not to look astonished. "Welcome, Mrs. Willingdon. I'm at your service."

"Thanks, that's not necessary. I can service myself."

Parker gives Aaron a quick glance and heads up the stairs with our luggage.

"Let him do his job," Aaron whispers as he hugs me. "It's the one pleasure he has in life."

"That's a lot of crap. I'm sure he'd love to put his feet up and stop running around after you lot."

Aaron laughs and laughs.

We have our own suite. A lovely bedroom with a large bathroom and walk-in closets. There are armchairs flanking a fireplace with an ottoman in front, great for warming your toes. A secretary desk is placed between the floor-to-ceiling windows. If I'm lucky, I'll never have to go downstairs. All the excitement has tuckered me out. I lie on the very comfortable bed with my arms wrapped around the giraffe.

"I'll let you rest." Aaron shakes out a throw and tucks it around me. "I'll be back up when it's time for dinner. Perhaps you'd like a bath. There are robes hanging on hooks in the bathroom."

"Thank you," I yawn.

I rest for a couple of hours, not quite sleeping. This place is still un-familiar to me, and it's hard to relax. But I do take Aaron's suggestion and have a hot bubble bath. I've never been in a tub like this. You can fit four people in here. It's odd to have so much room, and I find the water gets colder faster. I daydream about our old tub back on Marble Mountain. A tub with claw feet and a sloping back, just perfect for resting your neck and feeling cozy. I'm going to insist on one for our new house.

After waiting a while for Aaron to come back, I get impatient and decide to strike out on my own. I'll get lost, I'm sure, but it's a good excuse to snoop around. What's so noticeable is that all these rooms are empty. Why do you need all this if no one is here to enjoy it? Of course, if Aaron's mother wasn't locked away in a home, maybe it would be cheerier.

When I'm at the top of the main staircase, I hear raised voices com-ing from downstairs. It sounds like Aaron's angry. What kind of a father would upset his son on a day he brings home his bride? Aaron needs my support. I haven't even met his father and I hate him already. I'm grateful that I have on my new clothes, with my posh haircut and jewellery. Forget everything except that I'm Aaron Willingdon's wife, heir to a huge fortune.

My hands tremble.

When I appear at the doorway of the study, both men turn to face me, their animosity still thick in the air.

"There you are. Grace, come and meet my father."

I walk towards the man who looks like an older version of Aaron. It's uncanny. He's standing like an army officer, with neat dark hair and piercing blue eyes. The fact that he's good-looking bugs me. Somehow I imagined him hunched over in a wheelchair, a bitter, twisted old man.

"Dad, this is my wife, Grace. Grace, this is my father, Oliver Willingdon."

He puts out his hand, so I have to shake it. "Grace."

"Hello, Mr. Willingdon."

The three of us stand awkwardly for a few moments before Aaron's father says, "Would you like a drink?"

"I'll have a Coke."

"A Coke?" Oliver glances at Aaron. "I do hope your new bride is old enough to drink."

"I'm twenty-one."

"Only twenty-one? I never imagined you to be one to rob the cradle, Aaron."

"I'm twenty-six. Hardly an old man."

Oliver walks to his desk and presses a button. Parker appears. "We'll have a Coke, a Manhattan, and whatever the boy wants."

"The boy wants a Coke as well."

"Very good." Parker disappears.

"Aaron, why don't you come sit by me?"

"Sure thing." He sits on the couch next to me and puts his arm around my shoulders. I put my hand on his leg to stop him from shaking it.

"What part of Canada are you from?"

"Nova Scotia."

"I went there to golf once. Rustic."

"It's the best place on earth."

"Is it, now?"

Once our drinks arrive, Oliver sits down behind his desk. It feels like Aaron and I are students in a principal's office.

Oliver holds up his drink before taking a mouthful. "Tell me, Aaron. Why did you get married in Canada? Why not come here and have a grand affair? You're my only son. I would've wanted to celebrate that with my friends and colleagues from around the city. Weddings are always great for public relations."

"That's exactly why. It was our wedding, not yours."

"I see. Now tell me, Grace, what is the nature of your family's business?"

"We didn't have a family business."

"Your father?"

"Don't have one."

"Your mother?"

"Don't have one of those either."

"A girl with no family. How fortunate that you just happened to run into Aaron."

"Here we go." Aaron stands up and walks to the fireplace. "Grace knew nothing about my background. Money doesn't impress her."

"Is that right, Grace? Money doesn't impress you?"

I sip my Coke. "Not really."

"What does?"

"The truth. Loyalty."

My father-in-law watches me closely. He can't figure me out yet, and I think that makes him nervous.

"What do you do, Grace?"

"I was in university, but not anymore."

Oliver smirks. "Well, why would you be? You've found a more lucrative situation."

"Dad! Is it your mission in life to insult everyone you meet?"

"I'm just trying to figure out why this happened so suddenly."

I stand up and put my glass on his desk, nowhere near the coaster. "I'm pregnant, that's why. It's a pretty common situation. We're not the first, and we won't be the last."

Now Oliver looks at Aaron with surprise. "I wasn't expecting this."

"Neither were we," I say.

"I thought you might be happy for us, Dad. Haven't you always wanted a grandchild?"

"Yes, of course. This is very unexpected." He gets out of his chair and walks over to shake Aaron's hand. "Congratulations. You've become a man."

Then he comes over to me and takes my hand. "I owe you an apology, Grace. Please forgive me."

He looks straight at me but he doesn't mean it in the least. He knows I'm a big nobody, and as much as he might want a grandchild, it's killing him that someone like me is the mother. I only hope Aaron doesn't figure it out, because there's no way I'm telling him.

CHAPTER THIRTEEN

NOW

My back is sore. I've been sitting too long.

"Wow," says Jonathan. "Passing me off as blood kin to the Willingdon family. That didn't bother you?"

"No, not really. It didn't make one bit of difference. Mr. Willingdon wanted a grandchild and you needed a father. Besides, I thought maybe one day your dad and I might have more kids."

"Doesn't sound like it. You practically told Dad you didn't want him to touch you."

"I was young and overwhelmed. At some point I knew your father and I would be together. I was very lucky to have someone who was willing to wait for me to catch up."

Jonathan picks at a piece of thread on his sweater. "And you wanted a girl."

"That wasn't anything personal, Jonathan. When you were born we were very happy, but I was a wreck. I knew nothing about babies and you had colic. I'd cry while you were crying. Your dad would spell me and take you outside for a walk or a ride in the car. He was more patient than I was. I was always afraid I'd hurt you somehow, but your dad would throw you around like a little football and you loved it. To tell you the truth, it was very obvious you loved your dad more than me. He'd be the one who got the hugs and kisses. I'd get the throw-up and the tantrums. Although they say now that babies pick up on your energy. Perhaps that's why you liked to be held by your dad. I was more nervous."

"He was a good dad."

"What's your favourite memory?"

"When he'd let me ride him like a pony all over the living room. He'd yell, "Hi-Yo, Silver!""

"I remember that. He was always goofing around." I glance at the clock. It's midnight. "I don't know about you, but I'm beat. Can we talk some more tomorrow? Any chance we could take a drive or go for lunch? I think we need to get out of this bedroom."

Jonathan stands. "Yeah, all right. I can only handle so much in one stretch. This is hard."

He looks like a little boy. I don't care if he bats me away, I go over to him and put my arms around him. He lets me, but he doesn't hug me back. It's enough that he's still. I hear his heart through his sweater, just like at the doctor's office so long ago. I should be ashamed of myself for what I did to this kid. I should've known better. How do you live with your worst mistakes?

My sleep is restless. I dream about trying to find Jonathan in the woods but he won't come to me. Then he turns into Buddy and I have to chase him. Buddy ends up on the big rock by the bog, washing his paws.

"I'm sorry, Buddy." I put my hand out to pat him, but he hisses and scratches me before disappearing back into the woods. I don't blame him. I'm the one who lost him.

JONATHAN AND I END UP AT THE RESTAURANT IN THE ROCKEFELLER CENTER, the one that overlooks the skating rink and Christmas tree. We settle ourselves at a table next to the window and spend most of our time watching families skating while we wait for our lunch.

"I could never skate," I tell him. "I wanted you to play hockey like a good Canadian boy, but your father didn't skate either."

"Too bad. I would've liked hockey."

"You can still learn. You're not over the hill yet."

"Maybe, but I never seem to find the time."

"And you never will, unless you make it a priority."

He turns his face towards the window. "I miss Melissa. It feels strange to be in the apartment without her."

"She'll be with you soon. Once you find a new place to move into."

"I'm half thinking of buying back Dad's brownstone."

I put out my hand and pat his. "I think that's a wonderful idea! I loved that house. But will the people you sold it to move out?"

"People will do anything if you pay them enough."

I pick a roll out of the basket in front of us. "What's it like to get whatever you want?"

"I don't get everything I want."

"Oh no? Darn close."

"I didn't get you."

The roll is forgotten. My hands cover my face because I don't want to make a scene. It's a matter of getting myself under control.

"Mom?"

When I think I'm okay, I take my hands away and look at him. "This is the hard part, Jonathan. This is the part that will take your breath away and I want you to be prepared for what you're about to hear. Your father and I and your grandfather are all villains in this piece, and you might not want to talk to me ever again, but I have to take that chance. You need the truth so you can figure out how you're going to live your life from here on out."

"You're scaring me."

"I know."

CHAPTER FOURTEEN

THEN

The first years in New York are actually fun, except when I have to spend time with Oliver. He's delighted with Jonathan, and even treats Aaron with more respect, but when Aaron is out of the room, I can feel his hostility like a thick coat of glue. I understand him being ticked off that I'm not a high society girl like the friends Aaron grew up with, but I haven't put a step wrong and still he judges me. If Aaron knows, he's pretending not to. Aaron never did like to rock boats. And for some reason his father's opinion means a lot to him. Never having had a father, I can't relate, but I imagine trying to please an impressive man is difficult.

One thing that does puzzle me is Aaron's devotion to work. I never pictured him to be a businessman, and yet he spends long days and evenings toiling away for the Willingdon fortune. Jonathan and I have his full attention on weekends, and we have great adventures roaming through Central Park and visiting museums and the like. There's always something to do, and Jonathan loves whatever his father suggests. He also loves it when his grandfather takes him for the afternoon. I can't hold that against Oliver. He does love our son, but then Jonathan is too young to talk back to him. Just wait until we hit the teen years. It might not be so pleasant then.

I lead a solitary life. None of the wives I've met at parties have ever invited me to accompany them to lunch or the theatre, so when Jonathan is at school, I spend a lot of time browsing and buying in bookstores. My formal education might have stopped abruptly, but that doesn't mean I can't educate myself.

One of my other pastimes is making the house as nice as possible. Just knowing I can walk into a store and buy anything gives me a thrill. But while being married to money has its perks, it doesn't solve everything, and now that we've been married for six years I'm getting restless.

Aaron and I do sleep together now, but not often. Deep down I'm afraid my background bothers him and he's too nice to say anything. Or maybe I'm just not that great, because I'm always so on edge. Aaron is kind and I shouldn't worry so much, but now that the years are passing, I'd like another baby. I don't want Jonathan to be alone like I was. But so far nothing has happened.

We put Jonathan to bed one night and Aaron says he has go out and meet a client. "Only for a couple of hours."

"I'm alone here all day, Aaron. Why can't we be together to-night?"

He reaches over and strokes me cheek. "I'm sorry. I promise we'll do something tomorrow night. If it wasn't important I wouldn't go."

"How are we supposed to have another child if you're never here?"

He looks annoyed. "I am here, Grace. I'm here all the time. I can't help it if I have to work. Trying to please my old man is hard enough. I don't need to be told I'm not pleasing you either. I'll see you later."

So I sit in this large, gorgeous home and try to convince myself I'm not lonely.

FOR THE LAST FEW YEARS I'VE BEEN VISITING THE SANATORIUM WHERE AARON'S mom, Lydia, lives. Some days she doesn't talk much, but now that she knows me, she lets me sit and hold skeins of wool while she rolls the yarn into balls for her knitting projects.

Lydia is a beautiful woman but her face is vacant, like her life force left a long time ago and only her shadow was left behind. But she seems content enough.

"Jonathan got a hundred on his grade four math test the other day," I say proudly. "He takes after Aaron. All the Willingdon men seem to have a knack for numbers."

"Oh yes." She nods.

I look out the window at the spectacular grounds. God only knows how much it costs to stay here.

"Do you ever wish you could go home, Lydia? We miss seeing you every day."

"I am home."

"I mean with Oliver."

She throws the ball of yarn in my face. One of the nurses hurries over. "I believe Mrs. Willingdon needs her nap now. She'll say good-bye."

"Goodbye, Lydia. I'll tell Aaron you said hi."

As she's being led away, she looks at her nurse. "Who's Aaron?"

It's a hot July day in 1984 and Jonathan is ten. He and I are in a sweat packing everything he needs for summer camp in Vermont. Aaron says he'll try and make it to the community centre before Jonathan leaves, but that he might get stuck at work. He gives his son fourteen extra squeezes to last him for the two weeks he'll be away.

"I love you, buddy."

"Love you too, Dad."

I follow Aaron to the front door. "Are you kidding? All the parents will be there to wave them goodbye. You better show up."

"Will you get off my back? He's not bothered by it. He'll be too excited to even notice if I'm there."

"Wonderful. Thank you."

"I'll do my best, Grace. Are you going out to see my mother today?"

"I hadn't planned on it."

He puts his hand on my arm. "Why don't you? The house will be mighty quiet this afternoon, and I know how you get."

"All right."

He kisses my cheek. "Love you." And he runs down the stairs and jumps in a taxi.

I shut the door. Lately I'm always disappointed, but I shake it off when I hear my son hollering from the top of the stairs.

"They said we were going to have bonfires every night! Did you pack me some marshmallows?"

"Yes, they're in your kit."

"And I'll be learning how to sail. Grandfather is very happy about that. He says I can sail his yacht someday."

"Did he, now?"

Between the two of us, we bring down all his gear to the front door and go over the list again. Jonathan and I have breakfast together quickly and then we put all his stuff in the car and I drive us over to the centre where the bus is waiting. They said it will leave at eleven on the dot.

We join a mass of excited kids and happy but anxious parents. Jonathan has never gone two weeks without us in his life, but the fun of having his friends around twenty-four-seven is such a novelty for him. Only children often long for a sibling, and Jon thinks camp will be like having a big family vacation. I'm thrilled for him, despite knowing it will be too silent without him.

It's time to get on the bus. Jonathan has his arms around me.

"See ya! Don't get lonesome, Mom."

"I promise."

He looks around. "I don't think Dad is going to make it."

"Well, you know he loves you very much and he's super happy for you."

"I know. Bye, Mom." He wiggles out of my arms and runs to the bus steps.

"I love you!" I shout after him, but he doesn't turn around.

The parents huddle together trying to pick out where their kids are sitting. Jonathan is in the middle, in the aisle seat. He waves over the kid in the window. I wave back and blow him kisses as the bus lumbers out of the parking lot and disappears up the street.

Couples talk together as they walk back to their cars. There are a few of us who are here solo; I'm not completely alone. It just feels like it.

There's no sense going back to the house. On my way to Connecticut to visit Lydia I pick up fresh fruit and pastry. We can have a picnic outside if she feels up to it. It's a glorious day and she should be out in the fresh air.

When I get to her room with my parcels, she's not there. I go in search of one of the staff. They know me here. "Where's Lydia?"

"She has a visitor. They're outside in the garden, if you'd like to join them."

I MAKE MY WAY TO THE GARDEN AND REALIZE TOO LATE THAT OLIVER IS SITTING with Lydia. He spies me before I can sneak away, so I hold my chin up and continue across the lawn. I kiss Lydia hello.

"It's nice to see you, dear," she says.

"And you. Hello, Oliver."

"Grace."

I sit under the shade of the umbrella and pass Lydia a chocolate biscuit. "How are you feeling? You look well."

"Do I?"

"You're always lovely."

She smiles and looks away to watch a squirrel on the lawn.

"How often do you come here?" Oliver asks me.

"A couple of times a week."

"That's not necessary. She doesn't remember."

"Why wouldn't you want your wife to have company from time to time?

"She has me."

Maybe it's because I'm missing Jon already, but I'm not in the mood for bullshit. I take a pastry and throw small pieces on the ground for the squirrel. "Why do you hate me so much?"

"My dear, I don't think about you at all."

"I am your grandson's mother. I'm important in his life. Why do you want me as an enemy? It doesn't make sense."

Oliver reaches for one of the plums I brought with me. "You don't matter, Miss Fairchild. Your influence is secondary. I see the way Jon is with Aaron. They are a team. Mothers are overrated."

His ability to make me feel like less than nothing is astonishing. I'm speechless.

But Lydia isn't.

She turns to him. "I love Grace. I love Aaron. I love Jonathan. I hate you."

Oliver gets up and walks away.

Lydia doesn't say anything else after that. We sit together all afternoon. At times she pats my knee. A nurse comes over and says it's time she went inside. We kiss goodbye and I walk to the car, my hands trembling.

I stop at the nearest restaurant and order a chicken sandwich and coffee. It's the only way I'll be able to drive home. By the time I leave it's dusk and a beautiful summer night, but I drive with the heat cranked to keep from shivering. It's as I'm pulling onto our street that I remember it was only this morning that I said goodbye to Jonathan. Is that possible?

When I come in, Aaron rushes out of the kitchen. "Where the hell were you? I thought you were in a ditch."

"You told me to go see your mother, so I did."

"You stayed all day?"

"I'm a good daughter-in-law."

He smiles and comes over to hug me. "I know why you didn't want to come home. Jonathan's not here. You miss him, don't you? I have to say the place is pretty quiet."

I don't say anything. He holds me closer. "We're alone. How about we try and make this baby of yours? There's wine in the fridge. I'll run you a hot bath."

"Okay." My heart isn't in it. The truth is, this family makes me crazy. Maybe I shouldn't be in such an almighty hurry to find my own family. There seems to be nothing but heartache with relatives.

Aaron says, "Are you all right? You look pale."

"It's been a long day."

"Come my love. I'll try and make you feel better."

IT'S NOW SEPTEMBER AND JONATHAN IS GOING INTO GRADE FIVE. IT'S HARD TO believe that I was about this age when my mother and sister left me at that compound. Whenever Jon makes a fuss about something silly, I want to shake him and say, "You have no idea what it's like for some kids." But it's not his fault. He's a good boy, even though I continue to see him grow closer to his father and grandfather than to me.

Maybe I'm not a great mother. I'm doing what I think I should do, but sometimes I feel inadequate and that makes me ill-tempered. It's not just Jonathan who gets the brunt of it.

Ever since my meeting with Oliver about two months ago, I've had a hard time dealing with Aaron. I'm taking my anger at his father's behaviour out on him. Whenever he talks about something that went right for a change at the office, and how his father was so pleased, I want to gag.

Aaron also gets annoyed when I back out of dinner engagements at his father's house.

"He's going to notice that there's something wrong. What is your problem?"

"I don't feel like it."

He throws his hands in the air. "What has gotten into you? It's like you're all pissed off at everyone and everything. If this has something to do with your not being pregnant, that's not my fault. You hardly come near me. I'm not going to beg you to be with me, Grace. I have grave doubts about bringing another child into the world, when you are so obviously depressed or something. Did you call that therapist I told you about."

"No."

"Then I give up. Do what you want."

He stays out late just to punish me.

It's October when Jonathan is invited to spend the weekend with his chum Tommy from school. He's anxious to go and since we know the family, he gets the green light. Once again, as soon as Jonathan leaves my life loses meaning, but I don't want to sulk around Aaron this weekend. I book myself into an overnight spa experience I read about in a magazine. When I tell Aaron, he looks up from the paper as he eats breakfast at the kitchen table. "That's a good idea. Enjoy yourself. It might make you more relaxed."

"Which would be a relief for everyone, I'm sure."

"Now that you mention it." He grins.

I go over and kiss the top of his head. "I just need to do something different. Maybe I'll audit some classes at the university."

"Why don't you go to university? What's stopping you? I know how much you love to learn. Why didn't we think of this earlier?"

"You're right. I may just do that. What's on your agenda?"

"Paperwork, what else. I think Dad wanted me to drop by to see the plans for a new addition he's thinking of building at the back of his property."

"Why does he need more room? He rattles around there by himself as it is."

"Don't ask me. He doesn't explain himself and it's easier not to ask."

"Have fun."

"You too."

The spa experience is lost on me. Having people rub their hands over me is not my idea of a good time. Why didn't I think of that before? The massage and facial are torture. I'm surprised I get through it. The manicure and pedicure aren't as bad. Now they tell me to get in a sauna. This is the worst of all. The moist, heavy heat burns my lungs and as the sweat pours off me, it's like my inner anger seeps out with it. It dawns on me that the moisture on my face is not just sweat but tears. The lady said that might happen. "A cleansing of the body and soul."

I hate her. I hate everything.

When I limp out of the sauna, they want me in a cold shower. "It's bracing."

"This is bullshit. Let me out of here."

So I find myself in my car late on Saturday afternoon. There is nowhere to go. I've been in every museum and art gallery in this city more than two dozen times. Broadway shows are starting to bore me. I don't go to movies; I never have anyone to talk to about them after.

Maybe Aaron will be up for going out to dinner. Surely he's not busy on a Saturday night.

I let myself into the house and hear music upstairs. Good, he's home. I take my overnight bag that didn't see any action and open our closed bedroom door. There's Aaron, having the time of his life on our bed with a naked man. They don't see me at first. I wait until they do.

Aaron yelps and backs off the bed, covering his penis. The other man does the same. Two little boys caught with their hands down their pants.

"Grace! What are you doing here?"

They grapple with their clothes as I continue to stand, unmoving. If he expects a reaction, I'm not giving him one.

Aaron shoos his stunned friend away and he scurries past me like he's afraid I'll reach out and grab his hair. Aaron holds out his hands and walks slowly over to me.

"I'm sorry, Grace. I'm so sorry. It's meaningless. Something I do from time to time, like some people watch a porno movie. We haven't had much physical contact lately and I know that's no excuse—"

"Why didn't you tell me in Halifax that you were a homosexual?"

"I'm not!"

"I wouldn't have cared. It wouldn't have mattered in the least."

"Grace! I'm not. Don't judge me like this. It's a mistake, one I won't make again."

"You lied to me. Yet another man who used me to get what he wanted. A charade of a marriage to keep his father quiet. A dumb wife to produce the kid to keep his father happy, and the freedom to do what he wants because what she doesn't know won't hurt her. It must have made you feel great to know that you were saving me, despite the sacrifices you were making."

"I'm so sorry. I love you. I love our son! This makes no difference! It means nothing. It's an itch I scratch, that's all. You and Jonathan are my family. Not that guy. Not any guy!"

"Jonathan is my son, not yours."

He holds his hands to his head. "No, Grace. Don't do that. Don't say that. I know you're angry, but never say that."

"I'm taking him and I'm leaving this city. You and your father will have to console each other. Make sure you tell him why I left."

My bag and my purse are still in my hand, and I run down the stairs and out of that house, Aaron shouting behind me, "Don't go! Don't do this, Grace! I'll make it up to you."

Poor old Aaron. It's not entirely his fault, but there's the saying, *the straw that broke the camel's back.* He just happens to be that straw.

I run to my car and he chases me, but I see he has his car keys in his hand. He's going to try to get to Jonathan before I do. That is not going to happen. I pull out of our driveway and put my foot to the floor. I'm halfway up the street when I see his sports car tear into the road, almost hitting a car in the process.

Now it's a race. There are no thoughts in my head, only that I'm taking my son away from these two men. Sometimes that's all you can do, just run away from the master. It's the only way out.

I'm almost at Tommy's house when I glance in the rear-view mirror and see Aaron run a red light. A truck T-bones him in the intersection.

At the exact moment of Aaron's death, his car flies apart, pieces falling to the ground almost gracefully.

I'm out of my car and running. A crowd of people have gathered. I push them out of the way and stumble over to the smoking car.

"Aaron! Oh my god, Aaron. No."

Someone grabs me and takes me away before I can see him. I catch a glimpse of his blue shirt covered in blood. There are sirens and people shouting.

"I'm his wife! I'm his wife! Let me go!"

A medic insists I sit in an ambulance so I don't have to watch them scrape my husband off the road. I hold my head in my hands.

"It's all my fault. It's all my fault."

"It was an accident," he says.

"No, you don't understand. I have the devil in me."

We're taken to the hospital where Aaron is pronounced dead on arrival. I'm ranting; someone gives me a needle to take the edge off, but it doesn't. They finally let me in the room to say goodbye. Aaron is covered with a sheet.

A nurse looks at me sympathetically. "You might not want to see his face. Perhaps you should remember him as he was."

"I did this. I need to see the mess I made." Before she can stop me, I pull back the sheet and expose my poor, broken Aaron, who only hours ago was having fun in his bedroom. If I'd stayed at that spa, I never would've have known about this and we'd go together to pick up Jonathan and take him home for Sunday dinner.

I've killed Jonathan's father.

There's a commotion outside the room. It's Oliver, shouting and demanding to see his son. When he opens the door, he doesn't even see me. His face crumbles at the sight of the sheet and I back away as he approaches Aaron's body, whereupon he drapes himself over him and weeps.

I leave before he can talk to me and take a taxi home. I don't know what else to do. All I can think of is Jonathan. I need to be the one to tell him, before his grandfather does. I call Tommy's parents and ask them to drive Jonathan home. I don't tell them why, just say it's a family emergency and please don't let on to Jonathan.

It's almost half an hour before I hear my son at the door. He's not happy.

"Why am I here? I'm missing out on everything. You said I could stay for the weekend and we were having fun. Why are you so mean?"

Taking his hand I lead him to the stairs and pull him down beside me on a step so I can put my arm over his shoulders.

"Something happened to Daddy."

His face instantly pales. "What?"

"He had a car accident."

"Is he okay?"

"No. I'm so sorry Jonathan, but he died."

The sobs come fast and furious. All I can do is hold him and weep. We are two lost souls. Every time I glance at Jonathan's swollen face, I feel such overwhelming guilt. Why did I tell Aaron he wasn't Jonathan's father? He was the very best father he could be. No wonder Aaron panicked when I left. He knew me well enough to know that if I did get to Jonathan first, I was capable of disappearing with the boy forever.

The agony is relentless. I'm afraid to move as my son clings to me. How are we going to survive this?

Our front door bangs open and there's Oliver looking like Satan himself, completely dishevelled and raging. He points to me.

"You did this you nasty bitch! You killed him. I should've done away with you a long time ago."

"Stop it! You're scaring Jonathan."

Oliver towers over us. "He should be scared. His mother killed his father."

Jonathan looks at me with his big eyes. "What's he saying?"

"He's distraught, as we all are." I stand up and hide Jonathan behind me. "I want you to stop this now, Oliver. He's just lost his father. He doesn't understand anything and you're not helping."

"I don't give a shit if you think I'm helping or not. I've lost my only child and you're worried about what I might say? Witnesses told police there was a chase and a car matching your description was ahead of Aaron by only moments. That means it's your fault. You took my boy away from me and now I have no one, but that's about to change."

He reaches behind me and grabs Jonathan by the shirt. "You're coming with me. I don't trust your mother not to kill you too."

"Mom wouldn't kill me! Mom, tell him you won't kill me!"

I grab Oliver by the arm. "Stop it! Stop it! Give me back my son. He and I need to be together. This is monstrous! I'll call the police."

"Go ahead. Call the police. You'll find they're on my side. You're a nobody. You'll always be a nobody. You are to stay out of this child's life forever. Do you hear me? I never want you near him again, and if I find that you disobey me, you will suffer the consequences and so will he."

He picks up the shocked Jonathan and marches out the door with him.

"Stop it! This is kidnapping! Leave him alone!"

"Mom! I'm scared."

"It's okay, baby. Mommy's here and I'll get you back."

Oliver almost throws Jonathan in the back of the town car, then turns to me and sticks his finger in my face. "You come near either of us again and you're dead. And don't think I don't mean it. You're dead. I'll put a bullet in your head myself."

The last thing I hear before he shuts the door is Jonathan calling for me.

The car speeds away and leaves me standing there.

CHAPTER FIFTEEN

NOW

Our food is cold and untouched. The entire restaurant is buzzing while Jonathan and I are in this bubble of long-ago memories. Neither of us speaks; we just look at each other with pain on our faces. The energy it took to tell him and the stamina he required to hear it are overwhelming. I have nothing left and by the slump of his shoulders, I know it's the same for him.

"I don't remember the day Dad died. I don't remember any of it."

"Consider that a gift."

"Did you try and see me?"

"Of course I did. Once I made it into your grandfather's house, but he had me arrested for trespassing."

"Did you tell them you were my mother?"

"I told everyone who would listen to me, but your grandfather's reach was vast. It's very easy to brand a woman as a hysterical menace, someone to be put away and forgotten. When you have no one to vouch for you, people can paint you in any light they choose. After a while I had no mental or physical energy left. There was also you to consider. I didn't think you needed any more trauma in your life."

"I needed my mother."

"I know that now, Jonathan. I should've known better; I lived with that horror myself. But I think at the time I was so depleted in mind, body, and spirit, that I wouldn't have been any help to you. You would have been frightened by me."

"You should have tried."

"Yes, you're right. I should have tried until it killed me. I live with that regret every day of my life. If I'd said no to Aaron's plan and parted ways with him then, I could have gone back to Marble Mountain and raised you there myself. It was a scary thought at the time, but in the end I could have relied on neighbours and the few friends I had, and our lives would've been very different, and maybe even happier. That haunts me."

"But if that was the case, I wouldn't have Melissa."

"You see. Something good did come of it in the end."

"I thought you left me because I was bad. That you didn't love me anymore."

"Is that what your grandfather told you?"

"Pretty much. After a while I believed him."

I take a sip of water and so does he, our food congealed on the plates in front of us. The waiter asks if we need anything and Jonathan asks him to take the food away and give us two coffees instead. Once the warm liquid goes down my now-hoarse throat, I feel a little better.

"Did you ever get my letter, with my Marble Mountain address and phone number?"

"The one you sent to Tommy's parents? Yes, they gave it to me. I hid it from Grandfather, but I think now he might have found out about it, or even searched my room, because it was after that when he sent me away to boarding school. Probably so you couldn't find me."

"I thought maybe you'd get in touch with me when you were eighteen."

"No, I wanted to hurt you."

"I understand."

"It was Deanne who suggested I get in touch with you, remember? She said that you needed to know we were having a child."

"It was the happiest day in my life when you called."

"On the occasions we did meet after that, Grandfather would fake some kind of emergency to get my attention, but there was nothing he could do to stop me. I was a married man." He wipes his hand through his hair. "I can't believe this. He's insane."

"You need to be careful, Jonathan. It might not be in your best interest to say anything to him about the past. You now know what he's capable of."

"That will be my decision."

"I'm so proud of you. You are a credit to your father. Your real father. Aaron adored you."

For the first time I see Jonathan's eyes well up with tears. "I still miss him."

"As do I. He was a good, good man. I now know there are wonderful men out there. I'm sitting in front of one of them."

He grins at me. "You're my mom. You have to say that."

"Yes, I do."

We finish our coffee and put on our coats to leave. Jonathan holds mine out so I can slide into it. I take the opportunity to give him a quick squeeze and he hugs me back. Progress.

We go back to the apartment and say good night to each other. There is no energy to say anything else. I take a hot bath to ease my sore muscles and call Fletcher before I get too sleepy.

"How are things going?" he says.

"I passed a milestone today. Jonathan knows the truth and tonight I feel as light as air."

"Well, now. I'm very glad. Are you coming home soon?"

"Do you and the critters miss me?"

He laughs. "No, not really. I've had Dora up here almost every night bringing goodies. Her Christmas baking."

"Listen you, stop aggravating me."

"I must say, her coconut balls are pretty spectacular."

"You are going to be in big trouble when I get there."

"Say good night, Beulah." Beulah barks on command.

"Where is she? In your beard?"

"That's right. She's my beard warmer."

"I miss home. I'll be there soon."

"Good."

MY SLEEP IS SOUND FOR THE FIRST TIME IN A LONG TIME. IT'S LIKE I'M DRUGGED. It's almost ten o'clock when I emerge to see Jonathan on the living room sectional, staring out the window. The sky is the colour of steel. The moisture outside drips on the windows and there's an accumulation of snow down below on the street.

I'm still in my robe as I sit in the armchair opposite him. "Did you get any sleep?"

"A little."

Linn hears me and comes in with a cup of coffee. "Good morning, Grace."

"Linn, you're a life saver. Any toast going?"

"Right away." She hurries out to the kitchen.

"It will be Christmas soon," he says.

"The church ladies will be in a tizzy if I don't get back in a hurry. I'm in charge of the food drive and the craft table at the Christmas tea and sale."

"So you enjoy your life in Cape Breton."

"It's the place where I found peace."

"When you left after Dad died, is that where you went?"

"The only thing I could think of was to crawl back to Aunt Pearl and Aunt Mae's house. I literally had nowhere else to go. I had some clothes in a suitcase and my aunt's money in the bank when I got there."

"You didn't take your belongings? Or Dad's money? An insurance policy?"

"I didn't feel I deserved anything that your father and I shared, since I killed the man. I wanted nothing to do with your grandfather's money. Only your baby blanket. I put it in my purse before I left. The only other thing I took was the car, because I knew it would make leaving easier."

"So in 1984 when Dad died, until I got in touch with you in '97 about Melissa's impending birth, what did you do? That's thirteen years unaccounted for."

"Oh lordy. Do you really want me to open up that can of worms?"

"Might as well get everything on the table."

CHAPTER SIXTEEN

THEN

Oliver makes sure that I can't attend Aaron's funeral. There are security guards standing at the entrance of the cemetery. That's for my benefit. I'm hoping for a glimpse of Jonathan as I stand outside the gates, but I don't see him. Imagine not letting a child say goodbye to his dad. It's only about Oliver's loss. Jonathan and I are not even considered.

When I try to see Lydia, they won't let me in, saying if I show up on the property again they will call the police. Oliver obviously got to them first. The idea of never seeing Lydia fills me with longing. Pretending she was my mom on my visits made me feel needed. Will she miss me, or even remember me?

The only information I get is from the papers. Aaron's death is plastered all over the front pages. *Oliver Willingdon Suffers Tragic Loss.*

The time comes when I know I have to go. The thought of killing myself in the house is a temptation, but I don't want Jonathan to have to endure another loss—that is, if his grandfather would even tell him.

I drive straight through from New York City to Marble Mountain, stopping only at the border and for gas. It takes me roughly twenty hours. When I pull into the yard and see my poor neglected farm-house, something inside me breaks. There is literally a wrenching of my heart and my first instinct is to run out of the yard, down through the field, and out onto the shore. It's October; the leaves are turning and the lake is quiet in its welcome. I throw myself into the water and don't even feel the frigid cold. To lie with my head under and drift feels like the only relief I've had since I looked in that rear-view mirror.

Eventually I have to take a breath and my body protests the cold, but for that moment I was elsewhere.

It's a long slow climb back through the field, with my sodden clothes hanging off me. When I turn the key and take my belongings into the dusty, forlorn rooms, I strip off my clothes and wrap myself up in the quilts that I left in the cedar chest. My old bed beckons and I sleep for hours. When I wake I have no idea where I am, or even who I am. For one brief second I think that Aunt Pearl is downstairs and my heart leaps, but reality rushes in and I'm in the dark once more.

Eventually I have to attend to practical matters, and I hang my soggy clothes out on the line. Then it's the cleaning of the fireplace and stove and rinsing a few dishes. Once the water heater fills up I take a bath in my beloved tub, remembering that Aunt Mae would yell up the stairs to say supper was on the table about ten minutes after I had dipped my toes into a bubble bath. It annoyed me then, but I would give anything to hear it now. The junk food I grabbed at gas stations feeds me that first night, and I make my bed with sheets so I can sink back into oblivion and not have to remember. But for now the fire is ablaze in the hearth and the flames mesmerize me, to the point where I don't hear the pounding on the door at first. When I do, I'm startled and grab the fire poker before creeping into the front hall.

"Who's there?"

"It's Bruce Samuels, from up the road."

Not that I want him to see me, but at least he's not a murderer. I let him in.

"Well now, how's she goin'? I didn't know you were coming home for a visit. Nice time of year to come though. The colours are vivid on the trees this year. The house is just fine. When I smelled the smoke from your chimney, I said to Patricia, I better make sure that no one's broken in. You're not paying me to look after the house and me not do my duty. No sirree. I've kept a good eye on the place."

"Thank you, Bruce."

For the first time he really looks at me and I see concern in his eyes. "Are you all right, Grace? Anything I can do to help?"

My face crumbles. "My husband was killed and my father-in-law won't let me have my son."

Now this he wasn't expecting. I bawl. He's about as comfortable as a cat in a room full of rocking chairs, as Aunt Mae used to say. He has no choice but to pat my back because I'm clinging to his flannel jacket, but he's over his head and we both know it.

"Let me go get the wife. I'll be right back."

And when he and the wife do get back, I'm right where he left me, still sobbing. Patricia Samuels is a bit standoffish in general, but faced with my breakdown she becomes Mother Teresa. "Bruce, go up and get Erna and bring her back here. This is a two-woman job."

So off poor Bruce goes and comes back fifteen minutes later with Erna, who has sweets in one hand and a hot water bottle in the other.

Now that there are two women taking care of the situation, Bruce says he'll walk home and leave Patricia the car. She shoos him out the door.

They're on a mission. They put thick socks on my feet and make tea and feed me the squares Erna brought. The hot water bottle is against my chest, and I somehow have on my pyjamas and robe, though I don't remember changing. They prop me up in front of the fire again and sit on either side of me, and gently ask me what happened.

I must be spilling my guts, given the gasps and declarations of mercy coming from the two of them. I have to turn my head to look at them one at a time. It's like a tennis match.

"You can't tell anyone about this. If my father-in-law finds out you know, he'll have you killed."

"Oh my land!" Erna makes a sign of the cross. "You can't be serious!"

"I'd like to see him try!" Patricia yells. "Blasted foreigners. They have no business up in this neck of the woods. If you see him coming, you call me and Bruce will be down here with his rifle. Let your father-in-law put that in his pipe and smoke it!"

Eventually I drift off and they bundle me up so I can snore by the fire. They leave a note saying they'll be down for breakfast. When I find it in the morning, I'm horrified. I refuse to be the village's charity case, and I know these two. They'll have told every female from here to Whycocomagh by now, so I call Erna and tell her to tell Patricia that I'm very grateful for their help, but I need to be alone today and I hope they understand.

"Oh, certainly, child. Just call if you need anything."

I find two casseroles in my front porch, but no one bothers me.

I spend my time alone. People know I'm here and Bruce comes down and plows the snow from the driveway when we have a storm. I talk to people in town, just chit-chat while I buy groceries or go to the drug store. By now my story is old news and people are back to being preoccupied with their own lives.

Patricia and Erna suggest I join their rug hooking guild but I decline. My days are monotonous and I fill them writing letters to Jonathan so that one day he might read them and know that I think about him every day. I still write to agencies in my search for my sister, but nothing ever comes of my inquiries. It's lonely work.

When spring arrives it's clear I need to get a job if I want to continue to eat. The bulk of Aunt Pearl's money is still safe, but I don't want to use it, because if I do, then she's really gone. I'm qualified for nothing with my high school education, but I manage to get a job as a waitress at Wong's, the only Chinese food restaurant in Baddeck. They are kind and the locals have a habit of giving me hefty tips. They feel badly for me, and I accept their generosity because I need the money. The owners also let me take leftover food home for my meals, but after a year I'm heartily sick of chowmein and chicken balls.

The only downside to working there is seeing the families with kids come in and enjoy their dinner. Normal moms and dads who get to be with their children. Do they know how lucky they are? A young man comes in one night with his family and he reminds me so much of Jonathan, it's all I can do not to stare at him. I go home that night and cry until dawn. No mother should suffer the loss of her child. Sometimes I dream of killing Oliver Willingdon.

That fall on my way to work, my car makes a strange noise and sputters to a stop by the side of the highway. This is the first time it's acted up; I've been lucky so far with this car. If I have to buy a new one, I'll be in financial straits.

It's not too long before someone comes by and sees me standing by the side of the road. A guy with a ball cap on swerves over and shouts out his window. "Need help?"

"My car won't start."

"Do you want a lift?"

"Sure." I scramble into the cab of the truck. "I'm going to be late for work."

As we drive to the restaurant, he says, "You should ask Fletcher

Parsons what's up with your engine. If anyone knows, it'll be him."

That's right. I wonder if he still has my car. I give him a call.

"Not sure if you remember me. I'm the one who parked my Pontiac in your barn and forgot to come and get it."

"Amazing Grace Fairchild. Your car is fine, so no worries."

"My new car is a Toyota Camry and it's on the side of the road near the Red Barn. It died on me. Do you know if there's a towing company around that can take it to your place? Maybe you'll be able to figure it out."

"No problem. I'll see to it."

A co-worker drops me off at Fletcher's place after work. He's under the hood when I arrive.

"Hello again."

He straightens up when he sees me. "Hi, Grace. The bearing went in the idler pulley on the serpentine belt."

"Good grief, that sounds serious. I can't afford a new car."

"It's not serious. I'll have it ready for you tomorrow."

"What a relief. Thank you. How much do I owe you for the tow?"

"Nothing. I got it myself."

"Then what do I owe you?"

"It's on the house."

"How do you make a living if you keep offering things for free?"

"Don't you worry about that."

He drives me home and says he'll bring me the car when it's ready. He looks around at the house. "I remember my grandmother coming here. She was friends with Pearl."

"I miss Aunt Pearl."

"I thought she was sort of scary."

"Only if you didn't know her. Would you like some tea?"

"Don't mind if I do."

We sit at the kitchen table and drink our tea.

"I only have store-bought cookies." I pass him over a plate of digestives.

He takes a couple. "Thanks. My grandmother told me the Fairchild sisters were known for their beauty, back in the day. Strange that only one of them got married."

"Do only beautiful people get married?"

"Must be. I'm single." He has a great belly-laugh.

"Is your grandmother still alive?"

"Yes, she lives in Baddeck. Still spry and bossy. Everyone calls her Nan."

"You mean the small lady with blue hair who walks with a cane? That Nan?"

"Yeah, you know her?"

"She used to visit my aunts. She seemed like quite the character. You're very lucky."

"I am. She raised me. Where were you brought up?"

"Guelph, Ontario. I pretty much raised myself until my aunts found me."

"Your parents?"

"Don't know where they are. Listen, do you think your grand-mother would talk to me about Aunt Pearl?"

"She loves company and she'll talk your ear off. I'll ask her."

Fletcher arrives the next day with the car as promised and I drive him back to work. Once again I try to give him money, but he de-clines. "I make lots of money. Don't need yours. My Nan says to come by today at two. She'll have the kettle on. Her trailer is on the right, halfway up Buchanan St.

"Trailers seem to run in your family."

"I bought it for her when her place became too rundown. She loves it. It's surprisingly cozy."

Once again this gentle giant has come to my rescue.

"I don't know what I'd do without you. Thank you."

"No worries."

I knock on her door at two. This tiny woman, who Fletcher could pick up with one hand, comes shuffling to the door. "Oh dearie, come in, come in. You must be Grace, all grown up."

"Yes, and you're Nan."

"My word, you Fairchilds all have the same nose."

She motions me to an old plaid couch, but takes the tabloids off it first and shoves the television tray with her half-done puzzle to the side. The radio is blaring from the kitchen.

"I'll go turn that off. Milk in your tea?"

"Yes, please."

While she's gone I look around. This place *is* surprisingly cozy. Mind you, I'd never have three cuckoo clocks in a row or a hundred thimbles on a shelf, but I can see it suits Nan just fine.

She's back with our mugs and sits on the rocking chair by the couch. "Fletcher tells me that you want to know about your Aunt Pearl."

"Yes, I wondered—"

"She and I were good friends, and she didn't have many of those. Pearl never could tolerate nonsense and she wasn't shy about telling you. Oh my, the boys loved her, always trying to get her attention, but when her mother died she sacrificed herself and became the woman of the house. I was so mad at her. She deserved her own family, but she never complained. Her father wasn't the same after his wife died. Started drinking, although Pearl always denied it."

Nan leans forward. "I saw him drinking when I was over there once, but I never said anything to Pearl. She had enough to contend with, what with her two batty sisters."

"Her sisters were a handful?"

Nan rocks a little harder. "Handful? Does a bear shit in the woods? I mean, they were lovely girls, but not a brain between them. Rose was swept away by a handsome stranger. A year later she was dumped back on her own doorstep with a baby in her arms. Now I ask you!"

"Trixie was my mother."

She nods. "Yes, a sweet little thing when she was small. Rose always dressed her like a china doll, but oh my, was she stubborn. I remember the day Rose and Pearl were in the grocery store and Trixie wanted a treat. She had a tantrum right in the aisle, crying and kicking her feet. Poor Rose tried everything she could think of to get her to stop. Pearl heard the ruckus in the next aisle and came marching over. She took one look at Trixie, reached down and hauled her to her feet. 'You behave yourself. You're acting like a spoiled brat!' And Trixie spit on her! Pearl put her over her knee and gave her two good swats on the bum, which is what her mama should have done in the first place but some people are weak. And Trixie played on that when she got older."

"Oh?"

Nan touches my knee. "Rose and Mae were the dithering type, so Trixie would run to them and cry about how mean Aunt Pearl was, and Rose resented Pearl for trying to discipline Trixie. It was a mess. I hate to say it, my dear, but your mother broke your grandmother's heart."

"She broke mine too."

"Oh dear. That's not good. Whatever became of her?"

"I wish I knew."

Nan tsks and shakes her head. "Imagine. Not knowing what happened to your own mother. That's a sin, child. A real sin."

I take a slug of my tea.

"I heard rumours when you came back home, but I'm one to mind my own business. I'll just say I'm sorry for your troubles."

"Thank you."

"And I'll tell you this, young lady. Your Aunt Pearl thought the world of you."

I look up from my mug. "She did?"

"Never stopped telling me what a smart little thing you were. And she loved your spunk. She'd say, "That girl will make something of herself, you just watch. She's like the daughter I never had.""

At first I can't speak, and then I clear my throat. "Thank you. I'm so glad I found you."

"You come by here anytime. I like company. More tea?"

The days go by and I visit Aunt Pearl and Aunt Mae in the cemetery, bringing them flowers to leave at their graves. It helps a great deal to know that Aunt Pearl believed in me. What would she want me to do now? Can she feel my spirit draining away?

When I get back from the cemetery, I check the mail, only to find another lead in the search for my sister has come to nothing. This Maria Fairchild lives in Texas and has no siblings.

I have no family here, not my darling Jonathan, not my crazy aunts. There's only one thing to do at this point. I have to go back to Guelph. My best chance at finding my family is to physically be there, in case leads do come up. I'm wasting time here. I need to look people in the eye. Surely someone knows where they are. I close up the house once more and give the keys to Bruce. After that I drive up to the garage to say goodbye to Fletch.

"Are you sure you should be driving by yourself all the way to Ontario?"

"I'm not a weak little woman, as you know."

"The world's changed. It's not as safe as it used to be. Don't pick up hitchhikers."

"I promise I won't."

"Do you know when you'll be back?"

"I can't say, Fletch. But I will miss you." I reach over and give him a hug. He pats my back.

"Take care, Grace. I'll keep an eye on the house."

"Bruce is looking after—"

"And I'll make sure he's doing his job."

"Thank you for everything, Fletcher. You're the best friend a girl could have."

I hurry to my car and wave goodbye before I start sobbing. There he is in the rear-view mirror, waving back. My gentle giant.

THE COMPOUND WAS ON THE OUTSKIRTS OF THE CITY, FARM COUNTRY, BUT I forget exactly where. Just driving here makes my upper lip sweat. My mission is to find my relatives; I didn't think I'd go back to the camp. And yet here I am, driving up and down these country roads, trying to see something that looks familiar. Why would it? I never went off the property until my drive in the police car, which I only remember in bits and pieces.

For three days straight I search, each night going back to the motel defeated. It's not like I have any idea what I'm going to do if I find it, but I have this pull I can't explain. There's a diner near the motel where I go to eat. One of the older waitresses is friendly, or more likely nosy, but I'm so lonesome I talk to her anyway.

"I've worked here forever." She wipes the counter as I sit on a stool eating my ham and cheese sandwich and glass of milk.

"Did you work here in the mid-sixties?"

"Yep. Told ya…forever."

"Do you remember a fire in 1965 that burnt down the buildings in a commune around here?"

"Sounds familiar." She looks at an old fella at the end of the counter. "George, do you remember a fire here around 1965? Some sort of commune?"

"Yeah, the old Wainwright property. Weirdo religious hippie freaks burned the place to the ground. They almost burned the neighbouring farms too. People around here were glad to see them leave. Strange goings-on up there."

"Where did they go?"

"Who knows? Who cares?" George goes back to his coffee.

The waitress frowns. "He's a bit of a crank."

"Can you tell me where this Wainwright place is?"

The directions take me further afield than I realized, almost fifteen miles to the north. The closer I get, the more I tremble, but I need to see it. It's the last place I saw Mom and Maria, so it's almost like a homecoming, but in a terrifying way. I have a tiny, tiny hope that I may find something that leads me to them.

As I approach the property, I have a flash of recognition about the landscape. Something seems familiar and yet strange, but then I never lingered outside the gate, only looked at it from the inside.

I pull the car into an overgrown dirt driveway, but stay near enough to the highway that I can see it. When I get out of the car, I lock it and put my purse strap across my shoulder. My camera is in my hand. I'm still not sure if I'm going to use it.

The walk down the driveway seems long, but that's because I take baby steps, as if creeping up to surprise someone. Before I'm totally prepared, the compound comes into view. All the buildings are gone, but you can tell something used to be here, and the barn's foundation is peeking through the tall grass.

It's so much smaller than I remember. What I thought was a field is only a large backyard next to the woods. I walk around in a daze, trying to remember exactly where our bedroom was, the dining hall, the classroom. All the people are gone now, but did they take their memories with them? Do they live with them still? This place is quiet but the air is thick with the cruel things that happened in this space.

How could our mother bring us here? Why did she run towards something so dark? I'm so angry with her. I'm now the age she was then. Would I take Jonathan to a place like this? Would I let my son suffer like my sister and I did?

The barn is like an open wound. I don't go near it, but I feel it follow me everywhere. I remember the tree house and walk towards the woods, but it looks like it was burnt to the ground as well. My eye catches a glint of something in the dirt. I brush it away with my hands and find a spoon covered with muck. Helen and I used to take things so we could pretend the tree house was our home. I wipe it with my bottom of my jacket and put it in my purse.

Then I head for the bog, thinking some of the stuff I buried might still be there. But the hike into the woods is fraught with emotion. With the memories of my mother, sister, and me running, and then crouching behind the rock, all of us touching, our breath intermingled.

When I get to the big rock, I foolishly hope that Buddy will be sitting on it. Once again I wonder what happened to him. The guilt I feel about leaving him behind—is it the same guilt that my mother and sister felt, leaving me?

Rooting around in the dirt by the rock, I come up with one of the shoes I stole from a girl so long ago. I put it back; it was never mine. I sit on the rock and listen to the silence, and eventually I take out my camera and snap pictures of the bog, the surrounding trees, the rock itself, and the spot where we hid.

When I notice the shadows getting longer, I get up and leave the bog behind. Passing through the yard, I know there is no need to take pictures of phantom buildings and a destroyed barn. I'm glad they're gone. I have no wish to bring them home with me.

When I'm back in the car I take a deep, slow breath. Then I drive back to the motel and spend a long night looking at the ceiling.

It's too expensive to stay in motels forever, and soon I rent a room in a boarding house and start a job as a cashier at the local grocery store. I miss Marble Mountain, but I'm alone here or there, so I might as well focus on my mission.

My job at the grocery store lasts a year. On my days off I frequent social service departments in Guelph, Brampton, Waterloo, and Kitchener, the agencies that would have had my records. The foster homes that took me in were in this area—surely someone must remember something. Any information, no matter how small, I keep. That and look through the missing persons records at the police station, trying to find a paper trail, but it all leads to nothing. It's like they walked out the bedroom door and evaporated.

There's a woman who works with Children's Services in Guelph, a Mrs. Nearing, who's found some of my records from when I first left the compound. There isn't much in the file, just that I was being passed off to Kitchener Children's Services. But there is one reference that perks up my ears.

"It says here that you left the facility with only the clothes on your back and a cat."

I jump out of the chair. "Buddy! Is he still here? Where did they take him?"

"I'm sorry. It doesn't say. And I don't imagine the cat is still alive."

"There's no need to remind me of that!" I collapse back in the office chair. "I'm sorry. You're only trying to help."

She does listen carefully to what I tell her about the compound and she's found records of some of the other children who were relocated after the fire, but there's nothing on Maria. I check in with her too often. One day I knock on her door and can tell by the look on her face, she's exasperated.

"Sit down, Grace."

"Have you found anything?" I sit in the chair by her desk.

"No. If I do, I will call you immediately, but if I don't call it's because I have nothing. I hate to see you look so disappointed. You may have unreal expectations about this situation. It's been more than twenty years since the fire and anything could have happened to them. You have to accept that you may never know the truth and get on with your life. Do you have a life, other than working at the grocery store? Do you date, do you have friends, do you go out to dinner or a movie once in a while?"

"No."

"Grace, I hate to say this, but they may be dead. You could search your whole life and in the end find nothing. Then your life has been wasted as well. You need to make your own family, and stop obsessing about this."

"After losing my cat and spending four years in four different foster homes, I found my family. My elderly aunts took me in, but they died one after the other. I married and had a child, but my husband was killed in an accident I caused and then my son was taken from me by his grandfather. I've tried the happy family route and it isn't as wonderful as you people make out. I lose everything. That's why I keep looking. If there is any chance that I can find my mother and my sister, do you think I'd stop?"

She looks at me with such sadness. "I'm so sorry, Grace. You don't deserve this."

"I'm sure there are people worse off than me." I stand up. "Thank you, Mrs. Nearing. If you hear anything you have my number."

At work later that night, around suppertime, I look up after giving a lady her change and there in the last checkout aisle is Helen. I'm almost positive. It couldn't possibly be anyone else.

"Helen!" I startle the man taking the groceries out of his cart. "Helen!"

Her head comes up and she looks around.

"Helen! It's me, Grace. Amazing Grace!"

Helen finally puts her eyes on me and her reaction is instant. "Grace! Is that you?"

We run to each other ignoring everyone else in the store. We stay in each others arms and hold tight.

"I'm so happy to see you," I whisper.

"Oh, me too. Me too."

We let go so we can look at each other again, both of us incredulous. I can hear my manager yapping at me to get back to work.

"I have to work until nine. Can we meet for coffee somewhere?"

"Sure. How about the Tim's on the corner at nine? I'll go home and then come back. Or why not come to my place?"

"Let's just meet at Tim's for now. I'm still too shaky to go anywhere."

She laughs. "Okay. I'll be there."

She runs back and gets her groceries and I skedaddle back to my post. The man I was serving gives me a smile. "An old friend?"

"Oh yes. A childhood friend. They're the best kind."

Three hours never seemed so long. My stomach is chewed up. I'm terrified I'll wake up and this is a dream.

When nine comes I'm out of the store in a flash. I take the car and boot it down to Tim Hortons. I can see her sitting at a table by the window. When I get out of the car she spies me and waves. I quickly order a large coffee and hurry to her table. We embrace again before settling into our chairs.

"I would've known you anywhere, Helen. You look exactly the same!"

"Hardly, but thanks for saying so. I wouldn't have recognized you. You're only thirty-five and your hair is silver!"

"It turned that way a while back. I can't be bothered colouring it."

She reaches over and takes my hand. "After all these years, to finally see you. I was so sad after the fire. I never saw you again and no one told me where you went. Mom didn't know and everything was messed up after that."

"I went into foster care. A complete nightmare."

"We ended up in foster care too."

"But you had your mother."

"My mother had some sort of breakdown and couldn't take care of us, so we kids were split up. I see some of them from time to time, but you sort of lose track of each other. Did you ever find your mom and sister?"

"No. I've been looking for them. So far no luck. But now you're here and I feel so much better. Do you live right in Guelph?"

She nods. "I'm with a friend at the moment because my boyfriend and I split up a couple of months ago. I have a little girl now. Do you have any kids?"

"A son."

"Funny we haven't bumped into each other."

"I've been out east mostly."

Eventually we decide we both need a smoke, and then we need a drink, so we hop down to a local bar and sit in a corner. One beer leads to two, which leads to three, and now I have the courage to ask her questions.

"When we were at the camp, did the man ever sexually abuse you?"

Helen's eyes turn dark. "Yes. Did he do it to you, too?"

"To me and my sister."

"I was terrified of him. He'd just look at me and I'd cry, but he'd do it anyway."

"I'm sorry, Helen."

"When I listen to other kids talk about their childhood it makes me sad." Helen takes a gulp of her beer. "I don't ever remember having fun, except when we were together in the treehouse. It was so stressful all the time, waiting for someone to slap you or yell at you for displeasing God. I haven't darkened the door of a church since."

"Why did our mothers go with the man? Is he our father? Oh god, I hope not. That thought is worse than anything else." I shudder with a cold chill that sneaks up my spine.

"He wasn't my dad. Mom told me my father walked out on her before she went to the compound. I doubt he was yours. You look nothing like him."

"I don't think so either. But what was wrong with our mothers? They had to be crazy, or doped to the eyeballs. When they describe cults on television, I know that's exactly what we were in. Those women were brainwashed."

The two of us nod sadly at each other.

"Do you ever see your mom now?" I ask Helen.

"Not very often. She's always looking for a handout. She's got arthritis and claims she can't get around, but she's off to the liquor store often enough when it suits her. I'm much better off without her. I have enough problems of my own."

"Is there any chance that you know where the man is?" I didn't even know I was going to ask this question. I blurted it out without thinking.

Helen looks surprised. "Why would you want to see him again?"

"I want to ask him if he knows where my mother is. And my sister."

"The stupid bastard probably wouldn't tell you anyway."

"I want him to know that he didn't break me."

"I can ask around, but don't get your hopes up."

We promise to see each other again. When I get back to my room, I fall across the bed and sleep straight through until the next afternoon. Just knowing that Helen is happy to see me makes me feel a thousand percent better about everything. I have a friend and I don't intend to lose her again.

We meet regularly. I'm introduced to her daughter. She's a sickly little thing, her nose always running, with a hacking cough. I worry about her but Helen says she's fine, that's she allergic to lots of things. I'm not fond of the roommate. She looks like a hard character, but she's out most of the time. Fortunately Helen never asks me probing questions about my life; she's an easy friend. Not someone who's out for anything. But in the end she does give me something I was looking for.

She calls me. "I probably shouldn't tell you this, but I found Ed Wheeler. He lives in a ramshackle place on the eastern side of town, near the Esso station. People mostly leave him alone. They say he's nuts. There's no way you should go near this guy, Grace. Please don't."

"Don't worry, Helen. I probably won't. Thanks."

I go looking for him. I find his place quite easily and park on the other side of the road, and watch for a few hours. There's never anyone around. It becomes a bit of a ritual. If I'm driving by that way, I'll stop and check to see if there's any movement. In the end I think that maybe Helen's information is old. It doesn't look like anyone lives here anymore.

Fed up with getting no results, I step out of the car one day and walk right up on his property. It's overgrown and desolate, garbage strewn from one end of the lawn to the other, a rank smell permeating everything.

This is the perfect depiction of his soul.

I turn to leave and a movement behind the curtain in the window catches my eye. He's definitely in there. He's afraid of who I am, or what I represent. I go right up to his door and pound on it.

"Ed Wheeler! I know you're in there. Come out right now."

Nothing.

"Ed! I want to speak to you. It's about the camp on the Wainwright property. I have some information for you regarding some money you may be owed. By an insurance company."

"I don't believe you," he shouts from inside.

"Suit yourself." I call his bluff and walk back across the lawn towards my car.

"Hey, you!" He stands on his porch in his bare feet. The clothes he's wearing haven't been washed in weeks. Everything about him is yellow, like he's rotting from the inside out. "What money?"

I walk back towards him. There are no thoughts, only feelings churned up from the dark. I go right up to him and hit him as hard as I can right across the face. He howls with surprise and pain and tries to get back into the house, but I grab his shirt and give him an almighty kick, right where it hurts. He drops like a stone and writhes on the ground.

"I am Amazing Grace. Where is my mother, Trixie? Where is Ave Maria? You tell me, old man, or so help me…"

He's crying and can hardly speak. "Who? Who are you?"

"A little girl you raped over and over again because it made you feel powerful and mighty. But look what happened. You're on the floor cowering, just like I used to. Don't you remember, or did you have so many little girls, we just get muddled up in your filthy brain?"

"I don't know who you are! Leave me alone."

I give him another kick and grab his shirt. "Where is Trixie? The woman you beat every night. Where is she?"

"I don't know…she ran away. I never saw her again."

"And my sister?"

"I'm telling you I don't know."

"I'll kick you again, old man."

He leans upward and looks me in the eye. "I don't know! You have to believe me. I never saw them after the fire."

"They disappeared years before the fire."

"They did?"

This man has no brain left. It's been destroyed by perversion and drugs. He'll never be able to tell me anything.

I point my finger in his face. "You are going straight to hell, Ed Wheeler. You have the devil inside you and we all know what happens to evil people. They burn forever. The very thought of it makes me giddy. You tried to destroy me, but you didn't. You tried to possess me but you couldn't. I am the powerful one now. The tables have turned, you creep. You have no one. You are a big nobody. You will never cross my mind again, because I win, you bastard. I win."

I'm almost across the lawn when he shouts, "They left because they didn't love you. Nobody loves you!"

Don't look back.

AS SATISFYING AS IT IS IN THE MOMENT TO CONFRONT ED WHEELER, HIS last words manage to hurt me again. Why did I go and see him? There was nothing to be gained by giving him the opportunity to poke me with a stick. My little escapade backfires on me and I get very low.

Helen and her roommate offer me a joint one night and soon I'm getting high most days. I need to forget that my grand plans for finding my family are clearly not progressing. When I'm not at work, I go over to Helen's and sit on her couch just for something to do. While I'm wasted, I love Helen, but when I sober up it bothers me that Helen thinks it's okay to smoke up in front of her little girl. And yet I'm doing it too.

When her daughter stays with her dad, Helen has men over. It becomes a party very quickly. All the guys who show up are loser types. They think I'm a stuck-up bitch. At one point I smoke so much weed that I nod off. When I come to, there's a guy lying on top of me with his hand down my pants and his tongue in my mouth. Instantly, I give him such a shove he lands on the floor, cracking his head on the coffee table as he falls. I stand over him.

"You're a pig. Keep your hands off me."

I go to leave but he grabs my ankle, causing me to fall to the floor beside him. Then he proceeds to kneel over me and punch me in the face until I can't see because of the blood. Helen is screaming in the background and some guys pull him off me, but the damage is done.

Helen drives to the hospital high, but we get there in one piece. I'm such a bloody mess that they take me right in. My nose is broken and I've fractured my cheekbone. The doctor tells me I could have lost an eye.

When I'm eventually released the next day, my face a swollen wreck, Helen is there. I didn't ask her to pick me up. She must have been hanging around. She tries to hug me.

"I'm sorry, Grace! You'll never see that bastard again. I'll make sure of it."

"It's not your fault. I'm taking a cab home. I'll call you when I'm better."

"I can drive you home. You need someone to take care of you!"

Not you, my dear.

"I'll call."

My manager at work is annoyed that I'm taking a few days off, but he's always annoyed. The phone rings every night; I assume it's Helen. I don't pick up.

While I'm recuperating on my single bed I hear Aunt Pearl's voice. She's disappointed with me. I need to make it right. I'm furious with myself because I'm going downhill and I see that now. There is nothing for me here, but I stay in the boarding house until the worst of the bruising and swelling have gone down. Sitting in silence helps me. It's a little late to plan what I want to be when I grow up, but the times I've had someone to look after have been the most satisfying. To be needed by someone made me feel good inside.

Helen, fed up with not hearing from me, shows up at my door one morning. I invite her in.

"You look much better," she says. "I was worried. Why didn't you answer the phone?"

"I didn't have the energy to talk."

"Poor you. Well, once you're better we'll have some good times."

"I'm leaving, Helen."

Her face falls. "You are? I'll miss you terribly."

"And I'll miss you, but I need to get home. We'll stay in touch."

But we never do. I drive away and never see her again. I love my childhood friend Helen, but not the woman she grew up to be.

CHAPTER SEVENTEEN

NOW

"Do you mind if I stop to get more coffee?" I get up and start towards the kitchen. Jon is looking at me strangely. "What's wrong?"

"I can't believe you faced the man. Ed Wheeler. How did you get so brave?"

I look out the window before I answer. "It wasn't brave. It was stupid. Anything could've happened. And in the end, he managed to stick the knife in one more time. That eats at me sometimes. Excuse me."

Linn pours me another cup of coffee while I skedaddle to the bathroom. When I come back to collect my cup, she says, "Is very good thing, Mr. Willingdon listening to you."

"It is good, isn't it? But it's not over yet, god help me."

"Then I make lunch for two of you. Need strength."

"You're a fine woman, Linn."

She waves her dishtowel at me.

CHAPTER EIGHTEEN

THEN

Despite telling Helen I'm going home, I have no intention of going back. Not yet. I need to prove that Aunt Pearl's faith in me was not misplaced. I drive to Toronto and with the help of Aunt Pearl's money, enrol in the BScN program at the Lawrence S. Bloomberg Faculty of Nursing at the University of Toronto.

I'm the oldest student in my classes and at first I keep to myself, but over time my peers affectionately begin to call me "Ma'am," and we get along great. I have too many horror stories to tell these young girls. Nothing about my private life of course, but I've seen enough in my time, and these youngsters are just starting out. I embellish a lot, but they believe everything I say. It's kind of fun.

The other students try to get me to come out with them socially from time to time, but I stay away. I have no interest in foolishness anymore. Everyone must know it, because while I'm counting sheets in the linen closet on the ward one day, two girls pass by and I over-hear one of them say, "Ma'am has no life. How does she stand it? She's still so young and pretty."

That night I go back to my room in the residence and look at my-self. I've never thought of myself as pretty. My hazel eyes are notice-able, and my silver hair, but that's it. I look rather humdrum, if you ask me. But obviously I can't help but be flattered. I'm not forty yet. Maybe there is a little life left in me, despite my never-ending sadness over Jonathan.

It's in my second year that one of the residents takes a liking to me. His name is Albert and he's nothing special in the looks department, but he's clever and funny and he manages to bring his cafeteria tray to my table one supper hour, so I can't just jump up and leave. By the time I go back on the floor, we've made plans to go to a Silent Film Festival that weekend.

I haven't laughed like that in years. We have a marvellous time, to the point where we start a popcorn war in one of the theatres and the management escorts us out.

We end up having a bite to eat and when we get in his car at the end of the evening, I look at my watch. "It's getting late. I have an early morning."

Albert puts his arm across the seat behind my neck. "Please don't go, yet. We're having such a lovely time."

I smile at him. "Yes, we are. Thank you. It's been ages since I've enjoyed myself this much."

He reaches over and kisses me and I feel nothing at all. Bloody hell. But I pretend otherwise because I don't want to hurt him.

We date for most of my second year, but in the end, he knows there's something not quite right, and he's the one who ends it. He cries when he does and I feel wretched because he's clearly in love with me. In another world, we might have had a chance. I hope he finds a lovely girl someday because he deserves one.

No family member comes to my graduation, but I have plenty of classmates hooting and hollering when I cross the stage. I even see Albert at the back of the room. When our eyes lock, he blows me a kiss and goes out the door. It's the last time I see him.

NOW TO PUT MY KNOWLEDGE TO WORK. I KNOW I WANT TO GO TO A PLACE THAT needs the most help and I find myself at a medical clinic that deals with drug addicts and runaways, street kids and prostitutes.

The suffering I see here makes my life look like a picnic. I am no longer a victim, but a strong and independent woman, the kind Aunt Pearl would have been proud to know. The fact that it was her life savings that made it happen for me is a comfort when I'm by myself. She's always here. Aunt Pearl was my mother. I didn't have her long, but long enough to make a difference.

I try to make a difference for these kids, however briefly. Often it's not the cleaning up of their wounds that helps them, but the coffee, doughnuts, and having someone listen to them. I remember one young Inuit girl from up North. She was such a pretty little thing, when she wasn't being beaten by her john.

The last bandage goes over her ear and I tape it down. "This will hurt coming off. Some of your hair is under here."

"I don't feel pain anymore."

I hold her face in my hands. "Why are you here? You should go home if you can. Unless you're running away from them also."

"I don't have the money to get back."

I give her the money. She promises me that she'll go home. I'll never know if she did; I just know at that moment I couldn't sit back and do nothing.

Which is exactly how I feel when I decide to reach out to Oliver. Maybe with the passing years his hatred of me has subsided a little. Perhaps I can reason with him.

I manage to get through. "Hello, Oliver?"

"Who is this?"

"Grace. Don't hang up on me. I want to tell you that I've gone to university and I'm a nurse now. A respectable woman who shouldn't be punished her whole life. I need to see my son. It's time we put our issues aside and do what is right for him."

"He hates you. He never speaks of you. He's enjoying a privileged life in a boarding school in Europe. Why would he want to talk to someone who walked out on him and never came back?"

"Is that what you told him? That I walked away? That I didn't love him?"

"You will never be a part of his life. Forget he exists. He has the best of everything. He's forgotten you, Grace. Leave well enough alone."

When he hangs up, I smash the receiver into the wall over and over again. Men and their power make me want to vomit.

AFTER THREE YEARS OF DEALING WITH AN ENDLESS PARADE OF SAD, SAD STORIES, I find I'm tired and a bit burnt out. My yearning for Marble Mountain returns. I can find a job anywhere now and take care of myself.

I sold my car when I first arrived in Toronto to help defray some living expenses, so I have to fly home. Memories of meeting Aunt Pearl and Aunt Mae at the airport all those years ago make me smile. I rent a car for a week, until I can buy another one, and I know exactly where I'm going to go for advice on that front.

I pick up the keys at Bruce's house and both he and Patricia are happy to see me.

"You look wonderful!" Patricia says. "Wait until I tell Erna!"

My little house is in need of some attention, but it's still watertight, not too far gone. I have the entire summer to fix the place up. I want to plant a garden and get the field cut. A new lick of paint will help the exterior and a pretty new colour on the door will help. Shutters might look nice too, but it all requires a car. I drive the rental up to Fletcher's place.

For once he's not in the garage, but there are cars about, so I go over and knock on his screen door.

"Come on in!"

I go into his cozy kitchen. His face lights up when he sees me.

"Grace! You look amazing. Welcome home."

"It's good to be back, Fletcher."

He gets up and shakes my hand. It's nice to see him, but I'm more interested in the woman sitting at the table with him. She gives me a sour smile.

"Grace, this is my neighbour, Dora Trimm. She keeps me well supplied with sweets."

She practically simpers. There's something I don't like about her. "Hello, Dora."

She nods.

"She and her husband, Harvey, live next door. What can I do for you? Finally coming to pick up your Pontiac?"

"As much as I'd like to, I think a newer model would be best and I'd love your advice on what kind of car I should buy."

"I'd be happy to help you."

"Could you come visit some car dealerships with me? Maybe on the weekend? I know you're busy."

"I'd love to. How about tomorrow? I'll pick you up at nine."

"But tomorrow is Friday," Dora frowns. "You always work on a Friday."

"I'm taking the day off."

I get the feeling Dora hates me.

After that successful meeting, I go straight to Nan's house. She doesn't look a day older.

"Grace Fairchild! Oh my word, you're a sight for sore eyes."

We chat for two hours over our tea and I tell her about my nursing career. Nan is well pleased.

"Your Aunt Pearl's buttons would be poppin'!"

The next day Fletcher arrives on the dot of nine and we have a great day together. He tells me not to buy a new car because they lose value the instant you drive them off the lot, and then he takes me to a bunch of small local dealers where he does the talking. As soon as he introduces himself, I can see the salesmen deflate a little. Fletcher's reputation precedes him.

By the end of the day, I have another Toyota Camry, a 1995 Vienta station wagon. I'll be able to carry around a lot of stuff, like bags of sheep manure and flats of flowers. We go out to supper before heading back home, Fletcher driving behind me while I get used to my new car. The next Monday, he takes work off again and drives the rental back for me while I drive behind him. On the trip home we stop for ice cream.

Throughout the summer we see each other sporadically. I'm happy Fletch is my friend and we meet for coffee or share a pizza, but I am busier than a buzzing bee. My job at the local nursing home lets me spend time with fifty Aunt Pearls and Aunt Maes. I love them and they love me back. The stories that they tell me! Someone should write them down. A lot of them remember the Fairchild girls.

Birdy Cameron doesn't weigh much more than a bird, but her mind is a steel trap, at the ripe old age of ninety-five. She tells me that she has a "garbage" brain and that it retains all kinds of useless information. I pump her for every drop of memory she possesses.

"My grandmother Rose was the Fairchild sister who left Baddeck and got married and had my mom, Trixie. Do you remember anything about my grandfather? What his name was even?"

"Now let me think," she says, as she puts her almost transparent, fragile hand up to her head. "I know his name was Gavin Simms."

I quickly write this down on the back of my chart. "Was he from around here?"

"No, child. If he was, he'd have known better than to marry Rose Fairchild! She was as ditsy a woman as I've ever met. Only wanted to be happy. That's a foolish ambition, and it was bound to end in tears."

"Where was Gavin from? What happened to him?"

"Don't know that child, but the last anyone saw of him, he was being chased up the road by Pearl, who had a shotgun on her shoulder."

"Hot *damn*, I love that woman!"

Despite many conversations with the residents as I gave them their pills, I never do find out anything new about Rose and Gavin. Their brief romance is forgotten. Just as well. It didn't end happily.

That fall, Jonathan calls me.

"Mom?"

I'm sure this is a wrong number. "Who are you looking for?"

"Grace Willingdon."

My heart stops. "Jonathan?"

"Yes, it's me."

"Oh my god...*oh my god!* I'm so happy to hear from you! Please don't hate me. I couldn't bear that. I had to go because your grandf—"

"Mom, I don't really want to talk about details. It's hard enough to hear your voice. This isn't even my idea. My wife—"

"You're married? You're too young to be married."

"I'm twenty-three. I got married last year."

"Is she a nice girl? What's her name?"

"She's very nice. Her name is Deanne. Anyway, she thought you should know that we're expecting a baby."

I jump up from my chair. "A baby! You're going to be a father?"

"That will make you a grandmother. I hope you'll do a better job with this child than you did with me."

"Oh, Jonathan. I'm so sorry. Does this mean I can see you every now and then? Can I hold the baby?"

"I don't know, Mom. We'll see how it goes."

"Is Deanne there? May I speak to her?"

He passes over the phone. "Hello? Mrs. Willingdon?"

"Oh, Deanne, you have no idea what you've done. You've saved my life. Thank you, thank you for making him call me. We've been estranged for years and I want it to end. I love him so much."

"I thought you might. After only six months of pregnancy, I love this baby more than my life. I'll keep working on him. It will be nice to meet you some day."

"And you, sweet heavenly girl. May I talk to him again?"

He gets back on the phone. "Mom, I have to go."

"Please give me your telephone number. I'd like to call you every now and again. And I'll come to you. You just say when and I'll be down there."

"Mom. Let's just take it slow. You're a stranger. I'm overwhelmed enough with the thought of having my own child. I'll call you when the baby's born. Goodbye."

I whirl around in my living room with an excitement I had not thought possible. You're back. Your grandfather didn't win. We'll make it now. I wish I had someone to tell.

Fletcher.

The speed with which I drive to his place is unseemly and I hardly get the car stopped before I'm out the door. "Fletcher! Fletcher?"

He comes running out of the garage and when he does, he trips over a piece of equipment and sprawls to the ground in slow motion. It's like seeing a gigantic tree fall in the woods.

As soon as he lands I hear something break. He cries out in pain and I run to him. "Oh my god, don't move. I'll be right back." I throw my coat over him and run to the house and call an ambulance. Then back I go to hold his head until it arrives.

"You're going to be all right." I feel his neck for a pulse. He must be in shock; he looks at me but can't speak. "I've got you. You're going to be fine."

Of course he isn't fine. He has a broken hip that requires surgery. Every night after supper I go up to the hospital to see him. I run into Nan every time, as well as the dratted Dora.

A plan formulates in my head. I'm responsible for this injury and I have to make it right. Thankfully I find him alone one night at the hospital and he smiles at me. I take his hand.

"How are you feeling?"

"The doctor says I can go home in the next day or two."

"How can you go home by yourself? Be realistic."

"The doctor is organizing home care, because although Nan wants to, she's too feeble to help. This is just what I need. Strange women in my house."

I smile at him. "How about this woman?"

"What?"

"Hear me out. Winter's coming and I get lonely at my place. I caused this ridiculous accident and I feel I owe it to you to come and help. If you let me stay at your place, I can be of assistance. I can cook and clean and make sure you're all right and doing your physio. You're a dear friend, Fletcher, and I care about you."

"And I you, in spite of the fact you almost killed me. I'll take you up on your suggestion. We can live together for the winter and see how things go. I appreciate this more than you know."

I bend down and kiss his forehead. "We need each other. And after all you've done for me over the years, it's a privilege."

CHAPTER NINETEEN

NOW

"That was around fifteen years ago, and we're very happy with our arrangement. I stopped working after my diagnosis—I'm officially retired. Now you know everything."

To speak of the past is draining, but the fact that Jonathan wanted to hear my story makes up for it. He watches me as I bite into the hard toast that Linn left me a few hours ago. I chase it down with cold coffee.

"How come you never told me all this?"

"I didn't want to upset you. It's in the past and it's forgotten now. We all have trauma. You grew up thinking that your mother didn't want you and didn't love you anymore."

"And so did you."

"I'm a lucky woman, just sitting here with you."

He gets off the couch, walks over to me, and stretches out his hand. When I take it, he pulls me up and into his arms. "I'm sorry, Mom. I'm sorry I blamed you for everything. I do love you. I always have."

We hold onto one another for a long time. It's the greatest moment of my life.

Jonathan and I go over to Deanne's place for supper so I can say goodbye to Melissa before I go home tomorrow afternoon. We bring pizza with us and we eat way too much of it. Andre makes himself scarce after dinner so Jonathan and Deanne challenge Melissa and me to a game of Monopoly.

As I sit and laugh with these three precious people, I give thanks for ordinary moments. This is what life is all about. Just this. How I wish Fletcher was here. Maybe he'll come with me next year, or we can invite them to a Cape Breton Christmas. The future is wide open.

My granddaughter holds me close before I go. "Thanks, Gee. I love you."

Deanne also holds me tight and whispers, "Thank you for all you've done with Melissa."

Jonathan and I head home, listening to Christmas carols on the radio. We have an early night. I call Fletcher to tell him my flight gets in at suppertime. He says he and the critters will be there to meet me. I'm asleep by ten.

The next morning, I have my last blissful bath in this marvellous tub and pack my things. There's not much. I can carry it on the plane.

Jonathan is already at the dining-room table and smiles at me when I show up. Linn is there with the coffee pot.

"Good morning, all. Oh, thanks, Linn. Would you like to come home with me?"

She giggles as she pours.

"Linn, bring out our special breakfast, please," Jonathan says.

"Right away."

The orange juice is freshly squeezed. I must do that when I get home. Linn brings a whole platter of buttermilk pancakes to the table.

"Linn! How marvellous!"

"Not me. Mr. Willingdon made these."

"Just for you," he grins.

They're the best damn pancakes I ever tasted.

I'm reading a magazine later in the morning when Jonathan comes into the living room.

"Would you mind if we went somewhere first, before going to the airport?"

"Not at all. I'm ready now."

"Great. Let's go."

Linn and I exchange fond farewells. I will miss her delicate presence and graceful manner. Too bad I couldn't learn a few lessons from her. I'm as delicate as a moose.

We're in the car driving before I ask him where we're going.

"To see Grandfather."

My stomach turns. "Oh no. Don't do that to me. I'm having such a nice time. He'll ruin everything."

"He can't ruin anything anymore, Mom. We won't let him. I need you with me. Please?"

He says he needs me. "Of course."

It's heartbreaking to see Oliver's house again, thinking of the day Aaron and I walked in so many years ago. Nothing looks like it's changed. A great soulless place, devoid of love and happiness.

Jonathan knocks on the closed study door and Oliver tells him to come in.

When he sees me behind Jonathan, his face goes white.

"What is she doing here?"

Oliver is like Dorian Gray. He's still a handsome man, even in his eighties. His hair is white and his face is full of wrinkles, but time has treated him kindly. The only concession to old age is his walnut cane with brass handle. He slams it down on the floor a few times.

"I said, what is she doing here? She's not welcome in my house."

"If she's not welcome, then I'm not welcome."

Oliver's eyes narrow. "What are you saying?"

"I'm saying the days are over when you can ignore my mother. She is and always will be my blood, and I'm giving you fair warning. If you do not treat her with the respect she deserves, then I will have nothing to do with you."

He gets out of his chair. "Have you gone mad? How dare you speak to me this way? I've given you everything."

Jonathan marches up to him. "You've given me a lifetime of misery. I was a lonely, sad little boy who just lost his dad and only wanted his mother and you denied me that. You took her away from me and filled my head with lies."

"She's telling you nonsense. Don't listen to her. If you want her in your life then you're a fool. See her as much as you want, but I will never welcome her in my home. And if you don't watch it, you'll be turfed out as well. I still own this company, in case you've forgotten. I don't have to stand for this insubordination. I don't care how long you've worked for me. I can take everything away in the blink of an eye."

Jonathan straightens his shoulders. "As can I."

For the first time Oliver looks hesitant. "What are you talking about? You wouldn't dare leave this company."

"I'm resigning as of today. I already have a new job lined up. Believe it or not, there are other business leaders in the city who are clamouring for the chance to work with me and can't believe the lengths you've gone to in trying to implicate me in your money schemes. They know the truth and now I can write my own ticket. So you're on your own, Grandfather. Just the way you like it."

The shock on Oliver's face is almost frightening to look at. "But this is madness! How can you walk away from your own flesh and blood?"

Jonathan turns to me. "I believe I'll let you answer this question, Mom."

I step closer to this miserable old man and glare at him. "He can walk away because he isn't your flesh and blood. Jonathan isn't Aaron's son. And Aaron knew that and loved him anyway."

"You're a liar! Get out of my house, you miserable bitch!"

"Gladly." I spin around and walk to the door, Jonathan behind me .

"Jonathan, wait! She's crazy! Don't listen to her."

Jon stops at the threshold of the door. "I've been your puppet long enough. My mother came here and helped save my daughter, and while she was at it, she saved me. She's done more for me in a month than you've done in a lifetime. I hope you and your money are very happy together. Believe me, we won't give you another thought from this day forward."

He slams the study door and we hurry to the car, both of us shaking. Jonathan drives out onto the street but he parks in the first space he sees. He covers his face with his hands.

"Are you all right, Jon? Are you sure you know what you're doing? How did you get those other business people to—"

"I lied." He uncovers his face and catches his breath. "I don't have a job. I don't know what I'm going to do."

"Oh, shit."

He turns and laughs at me. "Oh shit, is right. But that felt so good. You have no idea how glorious it is to be released from prison."

"I have an inkling."

THE GRACE WHO LEFT IS NOT THE GRACE WHO COMES HOME. I RUN AS SOON AS I get off the plane. The minute I see Fletcher I give him a squeeze. "I am so happy to be home."

"We sure missed you."

My crazy hound dogs go out of their minds when they see me walking towards the car. It makes me laugh to see their nose prints on the car windows. After a joyful hello we settle in for the ride home. Then I pause. "Where's Beulah?"

"My grandmother has kidnapped her. They get along like a house on fire."

"Beulah seems to get along with everyone she meets."

We catch up on each other's news as we drive home. I can tell that Fletcher is well pleased that Jonathan and I have patched things up. He always knew how much it weighed on me.

"The ladies at the church have called about five times in a complete tizzy over some tea and sale. You'd think the Apocalypse was coming. Without you, they're panicking."

"It's nice to be wanted."

We go to pick Beulah up but she's on Nan's lap sound asleep and Nan waves us off, so we go home without her.

"You're right. We may never get her back."

Fletch has a pot of homemade beans ready for us. He even bought corn bread. We eat in comfortable silence as the dogs gobble up their supper and the cats purr on the counter. Then Fletch heads for his recliner while I do the dishes. I pour a cup of tea and start the crossword puzzle, but something doesn't feel right. That's when I remember my cigarettes. I pull them out of my purse and look at them. With all the drama going on, I haven't had one in two days. If I can go without for two whole days, I can go for three. And it upsets my son and granddaughter to see me smoke. Out with the trash go the cigarettes.

I join Fletch and we watch a bit of television. Then I get ready for bed and pick up my book that's still on the nightstand. At eleven, I hear Fletch bank the fire, let the dogs out, let them in. His bedsprings groan, my signal to turn out my light.

"Night, Fletch," I shout.

"Night, you old bat!"

It's so good to be home.

THE CHRISTMAS TEA AND SALE IS IN TWO DAYS. I RUN DOWN TO THE CHURCH hall where I know the ladies are setting up and charge through the door. "I'm here."

"Fat lot of good that will do," Delima sniffs. "We don't have enough crafts for the craft table, thanks to you."

The ladies buzz around the tables getting things ready. Everything does look very nice, but the craft table is paltry. "I'm sorry. I had a family emergency and was called away."

"You better think of something quick," Delima says.

Gladys Nicolson tsks. "We'll just jiggle some of the stuff around and add to Grace's table. Not worth arguing over."

Delima puts her shoulders back. "I am not arguing. I'm merely pointing out that she needs more items on her table."

"Don't worry, I'll think of something. As a matter of fact, I have it. Gotta go."

"Go? Where?" Delima sounds annoyed. I'm already out the door.

At the Christmas tea and sale, my craft table is an enormous hit. I have Beulah in her sweater, showing off all the other colourful fleece dog sweaters in all sizes I've sewn up in the last forty-eight hours. Everyone is mad for them. Beulah is obviously the drawing point, and my table is busy from the minute we open until we close. The Golden Collar Dog Grooming owner bought five! There are a few ladies who shall remain nameless that are mightily miffed that I've done so well, almost six hundred dollars. The rest of them are grateful that the coffers will be full.

On Christmas Day we go down to Nan's for dinner. We bought her a new television and she's tickled pink. Fletcher even got her a remote that has very large numbers on it so she can see what she's doing. Now if she'll just remember how to use it. We write the instructions down and leave it on the coffee table. She picked up Avon soap for me and a pair of slippers for Fletch as well as bags of treats for the dogs and cats. Exactly what we needed. Fletch and I don't exchange gifts. We write cheques to our favourite charities, which naturally include the local animal shelter.

That night at home we stay up a little later, finishing off a bottle of bubbly while we enjoy our small tree lit up in the dark.

"I'm half in the bag, Fletch."

"I'm all the way in! Who knew champagne had such a kick?"

"How did we get so lucky?" I slur. "I mean, we live like a married couple, but we have none of the crap that goes along with it."

He downs his glass. "You mean the romance? I think there's something wrong with us. I mean, I love you very much but I've never even hit on you. For that matter, I haven't hit on anyone in my whole life."

I jump out of my chair and sway in front of him. "Get out! Never?"

"A few times in high school, in between trying to stay away from Dora, but I never felt the need to be with anyone. They probably have a word for that now. Thank god, I don't know it. I was just born a bachelor and I'm perfectly content with that."

"So if I make the huge mistake of kissing you right now, you'd be disgusted?"

Fletch chuckles. "No doubt about it."

"You shit head!" I jump in his lap and give him a great big smack. "How was that?"

He looks perplexed. "Not bad, actually, but I am drunk."

"Well, I guess I'll be staying a dried up old prune, which is fine by me." I get off his lap, stretch my arms over my head and yawn. "Shall we hit the hay?"

"Might as well. It's been a great Christmas."

We shuffle around, putting the house to bed, and I wait for Fletch's bed springs to creak. That's when I hear him shout, "The old farts were nestled all snug in their beds!"

I answer, "While visions of coconut balls danced in our heads! And Mama in her long johns…"

"…and I in my cap, had just settled our brains for a long winter's nap!"

"Good night, you old fool."

"Night, Gracie."

I'M NOT SURE WHY I WAKE IN THE MIDDLE OF THE NIGHT, BUT I KNOW INSTANTLY something is not right. The dogs are whining. Maybe someone's in the trailer. You hear of break-ins at Christmas time.

"Fletch! Fletch! Wake up!"

When he doesn't answer me I jump out of bed and hurry to wake him up, but he's already awake, and he's in a sweat.

"What's wrong?"

"Don't panic. You should call an ambulance."

I immediately call 911 and unlock the side door and turn on the outdoor light. Then quickly to the bathroom to get a baby aspirin, which I put under Fletcher's tongue. "It's okay. They'll be here soon. Just stay calm, I'm here with you."

"Shouldn't have had a second helping of plum pudding," he whispers.

"You're going to be fine. I won't let you die.

"Good."

FLETCH IS WHEELED INTO SURGERY AND, THANKS TO THE STARS IN THE SKY AND the wind on my hill, he makes it. He's in the hospital for a couple of weeks after his quadruple bypass surgery and he's given a stern lecture to lose a lot of weight. I assure the doctors that I will take care of it.

"You're going to be the healthiest man in Cape Breton," I tell him.

"Not sure I like the sounds of that," he frowns.

"You'll do as you're told."

He smiles. "Bossy."

The day Fletch comes home, who comes roaring up the driveway but Dora Trimm. It's like she has some weird telepathy that tells her Fletcher is within range. She's carrying two armfuls of baked goods. I throw on my jacket and go out the door into the cold, my arm held out in front of me.

"No, Dora. Fletcher is on a diet and he won't be needing any of your baking from now on."

Her face falls. "A little isn't going to hurt him. The poor man needs a treat now and again."

"Fletcher needs to lose weight. We almost lost him, no thanks to me or you."

"You're blaming me? I cook for Harvey, and he hasn't had a heart attack."

"Consider yourself lucky."

"Then I'll make low-calorie desserts. Do you have a problem with that?"

I reach over, grab her tins, and fling them into the snow. They burst open and shower the dogs with cookies, much to their amazement.

Now I have my finger in her face. "You need psychological help with your obsession over Fletcher. He doesn't love you, Dora. He's your friend, nothing more. And guess what? You're married! Go home and love your husband and leave this poor man alone."

She bursts into tears.

Honest to god.

So I bring her into the house and make her a cup of tea. Thankfully Fletcher is in his bedroom. The only snack I have is Melba toast and peanut butter, but she gobbles them up as she sips her tea.

"Fletcher was always nice to me in school and not many kids were."

"Why's that?"

"My nickname was Dumb Dora. I have dyslexia, you see. Back then people just called you stupid, but Fletcher never did. And he listens to me. Fletcher always seems interested in what I have to say. The only thing Harvey ever does is talk about fishing. Who can have a decent conversation when it's always about mackerel?"

"Look, Dora, I apologize for throwing your baking in the snow. I know you have a generous heart, but Fletch gave me a fright, and I have to do everything I can to protect him. Do you understand?"

She nods sadly.

"Perhaps you can find some low-calorie recipes I might try after all. That would be helpful."

Dora looks a little brighter. "Okay. I'll bring some over."

"Would you mind calling first? Fletcher needs his rest. When he's ready for company I'll let you know."

I help pick up the now empty tins and she's on her way. My dogs come inside, sit in front of the fire, and fart all afternoon. Must have been those oatmeal raisin cookies.

A FEW WEEKS AFTER FLETCHER COMES HOME, WINTER ARRIVES WITH A VEN-geance. We listen to the howling of a nor'easter battering the trailer. Sometimes the wind literally screams as it rushes down the hill.

When I take a peek out the kitchen door, all I can see is blowing snow so thick it looks like we're being splashed by an ocean's surf. I worry about all the feral cats around the neighbourhood and in town. I've started a program whereby the church ladies and I are raising funds to build cat shelters. Only Delima refuses to participate.

"We used to drown kittens when I was a kid," she says matter-of-factly at a church meeting.

"And that is why I will hate you forever, Delima."

She gives me a filthy look. "You have a screw loose!"

Fletcher frets about me bringing wood in for the fire, and doesn't want me to run the truck with the snowplow attachment to clear the yard. He gets a friend to come up and do it, which annoys me.

"I'm perfectly capable of driving a truck back and forth."

"I don't want you out on that slippery snow more than you have to be. If you break a hip, we're done for."

I pour him tea with lemon.

"I hate tea with lemon."

"Tough."

The next day, I get an email from a social services office in Toronto. I had written to them asking if they had any records for a Trixie and Ave Maria Fairchild. I'm trying to reach every city and town in Ontario and cross them off the list. It's a lot of work, but there's nothing else to do on these dark winter nights.

Dear Mrs. Willingdon,
I'm afraid there is no record at all for a Trixie Fairchild in our jurisdiction, but I did come across an A. Maria Fairchild who used our bereavement services a few years ago. I've enclosed an address and phone number. I do hope this is helpful to you.

Sincerely,

Bernice Brown

I literally run to the phone with the number and call long distance. "Hello?"

"Yes, is this A. Maria Fairchild?"

"Yes."

"Oh my god."

"Who is this?"

"I'm sorry. My name is Amazing Grace Fairchild! Does that name ring a bell?"

"No."

"Are you sure?"

"Yes, I'm sure."

"Is your name Ave Maria Fairchild?"

"No. It's Anna Maria, but people call me Maria."

"Oh. I'm sorry I bothered you."

"What's this about?"

"Nothing. It doesn't matter. Thank you anyway."

I hang up and run to my room. I don't even answer when Fletch asks me what's wrong.

Lying on the bed snivelling is not something I do often, but for some reason, hearing that woman's voice made this more personal. If only she were my sister and not some stranger on the other end of the phone. What would that be like? I'm not sure I have the stamina to keep this up forever. I'm so weary of always being disappointed.

There's a quiet knock on my door. "You okay?"

"Come in."

Fletcher comes in and sits on my bed. So do all the other critters in this place, except for Beulah, who's keeping Nan company tonight.

"It's not Jon or Melissa, is it?"

"No, they're fine." I fill him in.

Fletch stays quiet for a long time. It's very comforting to sit like this and not have to go over it in detail.

He eventually takes my hand. "Grace, ever since my heart attack, I've been doing a lot of thinking."

"That's a first." I smile.

"Now, I want you to hear me out. We are getting to an age where anything can happen to either of us. We need to make plans."

"Plans?"

"Don't laugh! Promise?"

"Fine! What?"

"I want to marry you."

"Hell's bells! Are you crazy?"

Fletch gets off the bed and starts to pace. The room is only big enough for him to take three steps before he has to turn around. "If something happens to me, I want you protected. I want you to have this trailer, and my business, which you can sell to the highest bidder once I'm in my grave. We need to make things legal in case one of us falls into a coma and only family members have the authority to pull the plug. That kind of thing."

"But—"

"We love each other, Grace. We're a family and we're best friends. How we conduct ourselves in our own home is our business. We belong together, but we need to make it legal so neither one of us has an issue about anything in the future. What do you think?"

I look at him. "I think you are the best man I've ever met, and I love you very, very much. I would love to be your wife. You're right. We need to protect each other."

I jump off the bed and into a big bear hug. We hold each other for a long time.

"Oh god! I just thought of something!" I shout.

"What?"

"How are we going to tell Dora?"

FLETCH AND I GET MARRIED IN THE LOCAL COURTHOUSE ON VALENTINE'S DAY, as a private joke. Nan and Beulah are our witnesses. Then we go home and have salmon and spinach salad for supper, with low-fat pudding and a tablespoon of lite Cool Whip for dessert.

Once Fletcher drives Nan home and takes our Beulah with her (I miss that dog!), I'm as jumpy as a flea on a hot coal.

This is my wedding night! To a man I won't be sleeping with! What is the protocol for a situation like this? I did buy a new flannel nightgown instead of my usual flannel pyjamas, but it's not like he's going to see it unless I go to the fridge for a glass of milk.

"Your hubby is home!" Fletcher sings as he comes through the door. "What do we do now?"

"I'll do my crossword in the living room with you instead of the kitchen."

"Perfect."

We spend a pleasant couple of hours. Then it's time for bed. We go through our ritual.

"Should we try sleeping together?" I ask him.

"You mean…"

"I mean me sleeping in your bed or you sleeping in mine. Nothing else."

"I suppose we could."

When I head to Fletcher's room, the animals actually seem miffed.

We go to bed. "Good night, wife."

"Good night, husband."

We even kiss good night and settle in.

"Can I close the window a tad?" I ask. "It's cold in here."

"Really? Okay."

So I get out of bed and close the window. Then back into bed.

"Stop taking all the blankets," he says.

"I'm not taking all the blankets."

"How many pillows do you have against my back?

"Only two."

"But I have no room."

"Your feet are like blocks of ice!"

We both sit up and I get out of his bed. "I'll see you in the morning, husband."

"Okay, wife. Would you open the window on your way out?"

CHAPTER TWENTY

It's summer, and Fletcher has lost seventy pounds. I've lost ten, which means I look like a scarecrow, but Fletch looks mighty fine. We walk every morning and again in the evening after supper. He's only allowed to sit in his recliner if he walks.

The phone rings one hot July afternoon.

"Hi, Gee!"

"Melissa! How are you, dear?"

"Really good. Can I come for a visit and bring my friend Juniper?"

"Jupiter?"

"Juniper! Like the tree. We call her Juni."

"Some parents should be shot."

Melissa giggles. "You sound like Aunt Pearl again."

I do, too. "When are you coming?"

"Now? Can we stay for the summer?"

"You can stay forever but you'll have to help me get the house ready."

"No problem! Yay!"

"Is your dad around?"

"Yeah...DAD!"

What is it with kids? They scream right in your ear.

"Mom?"

"Hi, Jon. Is this okay with you and Deanne?"

"Sure, if it's not too much trouble. I don't want them to be a burden if Fletcher is still on the mend."

"No, he's never been better. I'd love to have them."

"Juni's a great kid, a complete nerd. You'll like her."

"How are things with you?"

"Getting better. The new job is great and so is the house."

He hadn't been able to afford to buy Aaron's house back, so he'd moved to a small townhouse. Just as well. There were a lot of memories in the old place, though Jonathan says they are mostly good.

"I'm glad. Has your grandfather eased up on you?"

"He's stymied because I don't react. He held sway over business leaders long ago, but this is a new world and his reputation for being difficult is catching up with him. As a matter of fact, he might be in trouble over fraud issues. It could get nasty."

"Nothing more than he deserves."

"He doesn't concern me anymore, but I do have some news. I have a girlfriend."

"Wonderful. I'm happy for you."

"Her name is Whitney and she's a pharmacist. Deanne introduced us, if you can believe it. They work at the same hospital."

"I'm as happy as a pig in shit."

He laughs.

THE GIRLS ARE MAD ABOUT THE FARMHOUSE. JUNI JUMPS OUT OF THE CAR AND twirls around in delight. I'm afraid she'll fall and hurt herself, she's so tall and slight. She reminds me of a daddy-longlegs. Her hair is shaved on one side and down to her shoulder on the other, and I have to say it suits her.

Now she's clasping her hands. "It's just like Anne of Green Gables! I didn't know houses like this even existed anymore! You were right, Missy! It's glorious!"

"Wait till I show you the beach."

The two of them take off and I'm the sucker taking in their luggage. But they do more than enough work when they get back, helping me clean and organize the place. Now the windows can be open, and Melissa takes great delight in shaking mats out of them. I show Juni how to hang clothes on the clothesline and you'd think I'd given her a gift. "Thank you! I've always wanted to do this."

That night we have a small bonfire on the beach. We huddle under blankets and look at the stars through the sparks.

"Didn't I tell you, Juni? Can you believe it?"

"It's…heavenly."

"Girls, whenever life seems overwhelming, remember to look up at the stars at night and know that your worries amount to nothing in the face of such wonder."

"Wait until I tell my dad!" Juni says. "He'll freak!"

We toast marshmallows until our hands are sticky, and then burn our fingertips taking hot dogs out of the embers and off our branches. Juni hasn't stopped smiling. "Mrs. Willingdon, do you think I could come back here again, sometime in my life?"

"You better."

We put the fire out, gather up our things, and head for home. We take turns sharing the bathroom while we get ready for bed and then say good night. Just as I crawl into Aunt Pearl's bed, there's a small knock at the door and Melissa opens it slightly.

"Come in."

She tiptoes over and sits on the edge of the bed. "Thank you for letting Juni come here. She really needs it. Her parents are going through a divorce and she's been very sad. I knew this place would cheer her up."

I reach out and take a curl of her hair. "What a lovely friend you are. Are things better now?"

"Oh, yes. Dad's new place is really nice and homey."

"Did Linn go with him?"

"Yes. She likes it better there too, because she's closer to the ground."

"I know what she means. And your new school?"

"It's school, but the kids are nicer. Juni is my best friend. We just get each other."

"And boyfriends?"

"I'm not interested. They're all jerks."

"They are jerks, until you find the one that isn't."

"Fletcher looks great, by the way."

"Doesn't he? I'm so proud of him. I'll let you in on a little secret. We got married."

She jumps up with a yelp. "What? Without me?"

"Sorry, I didn't know you'd want to be there."

"Of course I would!"

"Jeepers. Calm down."

"Let's have another ceremony right here! Right now, while Juni and I are visiting. We can be your bridesmaids! Please! Please say yes!"

I laugh at her. "Don't be crazy."

"You can get married in the field! And we'll make you breakfast. Come on, Gee! You're always saying we're such a little family. We need to be with each other for things like this. It's once in a lifetime!"

"Gotta ask Fletcher."

"He'll say yes. He loves you."

I can't believe that Fletcher does say yes. So now we've been hi-jacked by two teenage girls. They've already decided that Beulah will be the ring bearer and I need a dress.

"I don't wear dresses."

"Gee! If you don't wear a dress you're depriving Fletcher of his dream come true."

If only she knew he couldn't care less.

"Think about it! Besides, Fletcher already told me he's buying a suit."

"A suit! What a waste of money. When will he ever wear that again?"

Melissa folds her arms. "At my wedding."

"And mine," Juni says.

So off we go to Sydney to look for a dress. They give me an anxiety attack showing me all the choices there are. "How am I supposed to pick? This is a nightmare."

"We'll choose." They stuff me in a dressing room and shortly af-terward start flinging garments over the door. Is there anything worse than being in front of a mirror trying on clothes?

"I look ridiculous!"

"Show us."

I open the door and make a face. The front of the dress is baggy where my breasts should be.

"Hmm. Can you wear fake boobs?"

"Nah, I'd be fiddling with them all day."

In the end they choose a very simple sleeveless silver dress, to go with my silver hair. I have to admit, I like it. They pick the shoes and a delicate shawl that I can wrap around my shoulders if it gets cool.

But we don't spend all our time on wedding plans. Most mornings the three of us take the canoe out on the lake just after sunrise. The water is like a pool, with a thick, almost velvet look. I tell them to stay quiet and listen to the cries of the loons, which they do up to a point, but they are girls and their gums start flapping before too long.

Then we go in for a swim and afterwards the two of them bask in the sun on the shore while I read under my floppy hat.

Every day I am grateful that this is my life. My granddaughter and her friend make me feel like a mom, but I'm not going to waste these golden moments thinking about what I missed with Jonathan. I'm looking forward now, not backward.

We go up to visit Fletcher, hard at work in his garage.

"Well, hello ladies. Having fun at Camp Gee?"

"It's the best place in the world," Juni says. "Is the whole island like this?"

"Why don't we find out?" he says.

The next day the four of us go on a road trip. Nan babysits Beulah and Harvey and Dora look after our other critters, despite Dora's upset over our nuptials.

We take the girls over the Cabot Trail. One afternoon we go on a whale tour, watching humpback, minke, and pilot whales cavort in the water. Another boat tour takes us to Bird Island, which has a large population of puffins, with eagles watching as we pass. I can't count how many pictures Juni has taken, but her phone is likely to blow up before much longer.

I've never enjoyed Cape Breton more than I do now, seeing it through her eyes.

We're having a picnic in Cheticamp when I go to the car to get my sweater. As I walk back to the picnic table, I see the three of them in a huddle, obviously making plans, no doubt about the wedding. The last thing I want is a production. But then I think, what the hell? I've had an entire lifetime of not being celebrated. Get out of the way, Amazing, and let this happen.

THE GIRLS WILL TELL ME NOTHING ABOUT THE CEREMONY. NEITHER WILL Fletcher.

"Just show up," he says.

"I live there. I have no choice but to show up."

"About that," he says. "I'm spending the night before at the farm and we want you to stay in the trailer. It's the girls' idea of romance. Just be at the farmhouse at ten in the morning. Everything is taken care of."

"Are you sure—"

"Zip it. For once you're going to do as you're told."

"The girls—"

"SHHH."

The day of our second wedding, I get up before dawn and take the dogs out for a walk on my hill. There are large grey billowy clouds gathering in the east. Uh-oh. They do say rain is good luck, but what do they say about standing in a field under a big tree? We'll be very well-dressed lightning rods.

My morning routine is the same as usual, until someone knocks at the kitchen door.

"Come on in."

It's Joan, our local travelling hairdresser.

"What are you doing here?"

"I have instructions to make you look divine."

"But I don't need—"

"I also have instructions to tell you to keep quiet."

"But how—"

"Just sit."

She proceeds to take out her hair salon on wheels. Joan makes a good living catering to women who might not be able to get to a hairdresser's on their own. Nan is a great customer. Joan also caters to the ladies at the old folks' home. Her skills may be middling, but her manner has cheered up more old souls than I can count, and that is priceless.

Joan washes my hair in the kitchen sink.

"I just washed it in the shower."

"Don't care. It's a process."

She wrings out my scraggly mop and nearly takes the forehead off me. "Ow!"

"Stop being a baby."

Now she sits me down, takes a towel, and goes at my scalp with the same intensity I use when drying the dogs after we're caught in the rain.

She leaves the towel over my head and walks away.

"Is this part of the beauty regimen?

"Can't find my hair dryer." I hear her rattle through her bags.

"I have one."

"No, no. I'll only be a second."

Eventually she whips off the towel, then takes her thumb and holds it to my scalp while she yanks a comb thorough my tangled hair.

"Ow! Do you do this to all your old ladies?"

"They love it. Most of them haven't been touched for weeks."

Despite her technique, my hair does look very nice once she pulls a straightener through it.

Finally I get rid of Joan and put on my dress. I do a couple of twirls in the mirror. I even dab on a little blush, mascara, and lipstick that Melissa left for me.

Donald and Daffy and Tom and Jerry tell me I'm beautiful. "We'll be back soon!" I tell them.

I'm about to get in my car when who comes up the driveway but Bruce Samuels. It looks like he's washed his truck. He gets out and waves me over, still spry in his eighties.

"You look mighty fine, Grace. I'm your chauffeur. We gotta get a move on."

Away I go in Bruce's truck, bouncing over the potholes to Marble Mountain. When we get to the laneway I ask him to stop and let me out.

"Ya sure?"

"Yes, please. I want to walk under the trees."

"Okey-doke. I'll tell them you're coming."

The truck disappears down the lane and I close my eyes. Take a deep breath, Grace, and enjoy this moment.

As I walk along under the curved branches of the silver birch, poplar, and maple trees, I think of my great-aunts. My fingers touch Aunt Pearl's pearl necklace. What would've happened to me without those two fine ladies? How I wish they could be here.

The farmhouse comes into view. There must be twenty cars parked all over the lawn.

"Jumpin'... Who have they invited?"

There are pots of geraniums on the porch and silver balloons in bunches tied to the rails. Melissa and Juni run out the front door and over to me, giving me great hugs. They look lovely, both of them in summery dresses.

"When did you get these?"

"Fletcher bought them for us. I told him not to, but he insisted. Now come with us. You have to do what we say."

They pull me by the hands into the living room and yell, "Ta-da!"

Jonathan smiles at me. "Hi, Mom."

I cover my face and tears fall. He comes and hugs me. "Now stop it. I'm here to celebrate with you, not watch you blubber."

"Yeah, Gee! Your mascara will run."

Jonathan passes me a handkerchief and I dab my eyes. "Thank you for coming. I can't believe it. Does Fletcher know?"

"Of course he knows. We had quite a party here last night."

"And I missed it! Thanks a lot."

He laughs. "We did feel kind of guilty about it."

Melissa starts jumping around. "We have to hurry. They're ready."

"Okay, okay, but first..." He reaches into his pocket, takes out a velvet jewellery box, and opens it, revealing an exquisite diamond brooch. "This is from Grandmother. She wants you to have it and sends her love."

My hand goes to my throat. "Lydia remembers me?"

"She does. Let me put it on."

I look at myself in the mirror. "I'll cherish this forever."

I'm in a daze and I haven't even seen my groom yet. Juni hands me a bouquet of wildflowers, Melissa picks up Beulah, who has our gold bands tied with a bow to her collar, and Jonathan takes my arm.

"May I walk you down the aisle?"

All I can do is nod.

As we walk out the back door, I can see our guests gathered under the oak tree, flanking the same county judge who performed our ceremony a few months ago. Everyone is standing. Nan is here, and Bruce and Patricia Samuels, Erna and her husband and the ladies of the church, Janet Pickup and Gladys Nicolson, among others. Dora has had the good sense to stay away. There's a very attractive woman standing off to the side looking shell-shocked, but I only give her a quick glance before my eyes land on Fletcher.

It's incredible. It's Fletcher, but it's not Fletcher. He looks fantastic in a suit. Why did I ever think he wouldn't? But there's something else. He's shaved his beard. He looks about twenty years younger.

"Is that you?" I holler over the fiddle someone's playing in the background.

"It's me! Get over here, beautiful!"

I'm almost giddy. When our little posse finally gets close enough, Fletcher reaches out and gives me a big hug.

"Hello, wife," he whispers in my ear.

The minute the judge starts the ceremony there's a huge rumble of thunder and the wind picks up. We all look anxiously at the sky and then try to ignore the increasingly darkening skies.

The judge leans over and asks Fletcher, "Do you want me to stop? We can continue in the house."

"No, sir. Keep talking!"

So as the wind howls and the ladies hang on to their dress hems, the judge hurries through our vows in a rather unseemly fashion. At the next rumble, Beulah decides she's had enough and wiggles out of Melissa's arms. She has to chase the dog around the tree to get the rings.

Just as he pronounces us man and wife, the skies open and huge drops of rain pelt down. Everyone screams and takes off back to the house. There is utter chaos for the first ten minutes, finding towels to dry everyone off, but by the time that's done, the church ladies have effortlessly put out the brunch and we all tuck into a marvellous meal of eggs, bacon, pancakes, waffles, fresh fruit, and muffins, washed down with gallons of tea. The girls even made an angel-food wedding cake for us because it's low in calories. It's demolished in minutes, along with fresh strawberries.

Jonathan waits until my mouth is full to introduce me to Whitney, the pharmacist girlfriend. She still looks overwhelmed. No doubt the poor girl has never attended a wedding like this.

"It's nice to meet you, Mrs..."

"Technically I suppose it's Mrs. Fairchild Willingdon Parsons, but please call me Grace. Have you ever been to the Maritimes before?"

"No. It's very...quaint."

"It's that, all right."

I can tell that Jonathan is nervous. He must like this woman a lot. When I get a chance I sidle over to Melissa. "Do we like her?" I toss my head at Whitney.

"She's okay. A bit needy."

"Good. That's perfect for your father. He needs to be someone's knight in shining armour."

"Ugh."

I'm so happy the girls thought of this, and I'm even happier that Fletcher agreed. Melissa was right. These are the moments when families need to be together.

Fletcher comes over and takes my hand. "If you don't mind, folks, I'm taking my bride away for the night. Thank you, everyone, for a very special day. We'll never forget it."

"Juni and I will clean up, Gee. Don't worry about a thing."

I kiss my family and wave goodbye to my friends. Fletcher opens the front door for me and I gasp.

The Pontiac is in the yard, shiny, polished, and looking brand new, now that the bumper is fixed.

"Oh, Fletcher!" I jump up and down. "Thank you."

He puts his arm around me. "Couldn't have a wedding without the whole family here."

The minute I sit in the front seat a rush of memories come at me. I swear I can still smell my aunts' perfume. My head leans against the leather seat, and I let their essence surround me.

"This is the best wedding gift ever," I smile at my husband.

We drive to the Keltic Lodge, the windshield wipers going constantly. The gorgeous views of Ingonish are shrouded in fog and misty rain, but we don't even notice. We enjoy a scrumptious meal of scallops and lobster and toast our wedding day with a bottle of bubbly.

Then we hold hands as we go back to our room with its two double beds and shut the door on the world.

We stay for another night, but then we're bored and missing everyone, so we hop in the car and go home, this time with me driving.

"I was Melissa's age when I learned to drive this car. I can't believe Aunt Pearl and Aunt Mae let me behind this steering wheel. It's the size of a hula hoop."

"Are you going to let Melissa drive it?"

"Are you nuts?"

We get back home and have a great reunion with our furry buddies, unpack our overnight bags, and get dressed in our normal ratty clothes. Fletcher heads out to his beloved garage.

"I'll be back whenever!" I shout out the Pontiac window.

"Have fun."

When I get to the farmhouse, I can hear voices down by the water. I cross the field, stopping to hug our wedding tree, and continue down to the shore. The girls are drifting on circular tubes that Jonathan must have bought them. He's sitting on the sand and Whitney is folded up on a towel, trying not to get a speck of sand on her. Her expression is pained, as far as I can tell under her floppy hat and sunglasses.

"Hi, Gee!" Melissa waves both arms at me.

"Hi, Gee Gee!" Juni has decided that's what she wants to call me.

I wave to them before I plunk my arse down by my son. "Hello, you two. Did you have fun while we were gone?"

"It's been an experience." Jonathan turns his head away from Whitney and winks at me. "Wouldn't you say so, Whitney?"

"Oh yes. It's lovely here," she says. "Really nice."

"Come back any time. We'd love to have you."

She lets out a scream. "Jonathan! What is that horrid bug? Get it off me!" Whitney flaps her arms around trying to get rid of the horsefly buzzing around her head. When that doesn't work, she leaps up and runs down the beach, still flapping her hands about.

"She's a city girl."

"I gathered. When are you guys heading back?"

"Tomorrow."

"So soon?"

"Sorry, Mom, I can't take any more time off. And I believe it's time I took the two amigos home. Wait until Deanne sees Melissa. The two of them are as brown as berries. I've never seen her look so good. Thank you for that."

"This has been the best summer of my life—I thank you right back."

Jonathan insists on taking us out for supper that night and Fletcher and I both have baked salmon and asparagus, with fresh fruit for dessert. Fletch tells us he's lost another five pounds, so high fives all around.

Saying goodbye isn't easy. The girls cry and hug us and we thank them for our wonderful wedding. I hug Whitney goodbye and try to ignore the look of intense relief on her face that this ordeal is nearly over. She did her best, and that's something.

Fletcher and I stand with our arms around each other as Jonathan's rental car drives out of the yard, both girls hanging out the window waving and blowing kisses. Jon toots the horn and they're on their way.

We close up the farmhouse and head home. It's only after we get back to the trailer that we realize how tired we are. It's been a long summer and I can't wait to get back to our normal routine.

A week later, after our evening walk, Fletcher and Beulah head for the recliner to doze. I wash up the dishes and drink my tea at the kitchen table, with the crossword puzzle in front of me.

The phone rings.

"Hello?"

"Hi, Mom."

"Jonathan! Nice to hear from you. What's up?"

He hesitates.

"Jon? Is everything all right?"

"Mom, I found your sister. I found Maria."

CHAPTER TWENTY-ONE

All my life I imagined how it would feel if I ever had the chance to contact my sister, and my reaction is the complete opposite to the one I had anticipated.

"I have to go."

"Mom?"

I put down the phone with a trembling hand and run outside to the yard, where I get sick to my stomach. Fletcher finds me bent over, retching. He holds my shoulders.

"Grace, are you all right?"

"I can't…"

"You can't what?"

"I can't do this." When I lift my head, the world around me tilts. Fletcher steadies me.

"Whatever it is, we'll get through it. I'm here for you, Grace."

"Everything was perfect and now this…oh my god." I cling to him, trying to understand why I feel like my world is falling apart. I'm crying now and Fletcher very gently leads me back to the house, sits me in a kitchen chair, and passes me some tissues. Both the dogs are at my feet, looking very concerned.

The phone rings again.

"I'm not ready…not yet."

Fletcher answers the phone. "Hi, Jonathan…She's a bit overwhelmed. What's going on?…I see. Look, she'll call you back when she's collected herself…Don't worry, I'll take care of her…I know you didn't mean to frighten her…Yes…Okay, we'll call you later."

He puts the phone down and gives me a sympathetic smile. "You're in shock, that's all. Give yourself a chance to digest this. It's a good thing."

"No! It's not! I'm so angry! How could she leave me and just get on with her life, never trying to find me or be with me? I don't want her to come here. I don't want her!"

I run into my bedroom and slam the door. This terrible darkness comes over me and it's like I'm nine again, hiding in the blankets on the bed. All the anguish I felt during those three days waiting for my mother and sister to rescue me comes back with a vengeance. How does that happen with only a few words spoken? My life is finally my own, and now this horrible sadness and loneliness punch me in the gut. Was it really there so close to the surface all these years? Have I made no progress? I'll be collecting a pension cheque soon. Do I still not know who I am at the age of sixty? It's pathetic.

And now I have a fear of the unknown. My life is out of control once more and that is a terrible thought.

I emerge from my bed cave and walk from window to window as Fletch and Beulah sit on the recliner.

"I'm so angry! I thought I wanted this, but I don't. I'm fucked up, Fletch! I want to disappear or hide or something. I don't want her to know how much she hurt me."

"Listen, Grace, you don't owe her anything. If you don't want your sister in your life, then there's nothing to be done. Jonathan did say he hasn't spoken to her—she knows nothing about this. You're not under some time crunch. It's your decision and you shouldn't be hasty."

"Blah, blah, blah. How do you know how this feels? Everyone thinks they know what I need and what I want. No one else I know had their whole family disappear."

"My parents died when I was a kid."

"But you had your grandmother."

"And eventually you had your aunts. Stop blowing this up into something bigger."

"Thanks a lot."

"Stop being angry at me! I didn't do anything. And stop being angry at the world. You're not helping yourself."

"Why is this happening?"

"Everyone is afraid of ghosts." He gets up and puts Beulah in my hands. "There is something you should consider, however this turns out. Your son has spent six months trying to find something that he thought would make you happy."

Fletcher leaves the room.

It's two nights later before I call Jon.

"I'm sorry, Mom…"

"Jon, please. There's nothing to be sorry about. I appreciate your gift more than you can know. I'm just sorry I wasn't prepared to hear it at that moment. Please know I love you dearly for doing this for me. I will never forget it."

"I should've stayed out of it. It's your life and I had no business interfering."

"Are you kidding?" I laugh. "I've waited my whole life to have my family interfere in my business!"

"Still…"

"I'm not interested in doing anything about this right now, but how did you find her? For years I hit only brick walls."

"It's a different world, Mom. The Internet makes things happen and I hired a detective agency—"

"You *what*?"

"Why not go to the experts?"

"You did that for me?"

"We both know what it's like to be without family. Since you came back to me, I wanted your family to come back to you."

"You're quite a kid."

"I'll have the information here for you when you're ready…or not."

"Where is she?"

"In Toronto."

"I could have passed her on the street."

"I have her name, address, and phone number."

"Well, I might as well write it all down, I suppose."

He gives it to me and we say goodbye. I put the scrap of paper on the fridge door with a magnet and look at it. Maria Evans. So, she married. I wonder if she has children. Not that I care.

The next day we're out of fresh veggies and I tell Fletcher I'm off to the store. He sticks his head out of the garage. "Could you drop in and see Nan? She sounded stuffy on the phone yesterday."

"Sure. I'll pick up some things for her, too."

As I walk to my car I happen to look over at the trailer and there are the three dogs in the window watching me go. Beulah is perched on top of the bookcase, while the other two are at floor level. Fletcher made a staircase for her once we discovered she loves looking out the window. Beulah climbs up and surveys her kingdom most days, ready to sound the alarm when any strange car pulls in the yard, which is all the time. Then I notice the two cats, Tom and Jerry, in the kitchen window. You'd think I was leaving them stranded on a desert island. "I'll be back in an hour. Geez."

The first stop is Nan's. Last night's snowfall is on the porch, so I take the small shovel she has leaning by the door and proceed to push it aside, then I knock and go in. "Nan! You here?"

"Yep, hold your horses!" she hollers from the john. The toilet flushes and she soon emerges drying her hands with a towel.

"Wasn't expecting you today."

"Fletcher asked me to call in. He thought you might have a cold."

"A cold? What gave him that idea."

"He said you were stuffy."

"I was peeling onions. Want some tea?"

"A quick cup while you make a grocery list. I'm off to the Co-op—whatever you need, write it down."

She gives me my tea and starts to hunt through her cupboards. "I'm out of canned tomatoes and I need some more macaroni." Then she starts on the fridge. "Margarine, eggs, and whipping cream." She bends over to look in the vegetable crisper. "Fletcher mentioned Jonathan found your sister. Have you been in touch yet?"

"He had no right to tell you that."

Nan straightens up and shuts the fridge door. "Is it a secret?"

"I suppose not, but..."

She sits in the chair beside me. "He's worried about you."

"He's angry at me, more like."

"There's lots of things Fletcher doesn't tell you."

"Excuse me?"

She nods. "Sometimes he's afraid of you."

"Fletcher! Afraid of me?"

"A lot of people are afraid of you. Didn't you know that?"

"Why, for god's sake?"

"He's worried you'll leave, and I've heard from a few sources around town that you throw things, like cookie tins. You have a temper. Pearl knew it; she bore the brunt of it."

"I'll leave? He says that? We just got married. Twice!"

"He knows you're quite capable of disappearing, like you've done many times before. He's insecure about it. I doubt he even knows. It's a grandmother's intuition."

"A grandmother's intuition is usually right."

When I get back out to the car, I have to sit for a minute. Has my anger been on display...an obvious thing, even to strangers? Fletch shouldn't be stressing about anything. Not with his heart.

As I go up and down the aisles of the grocery store I'm in a flap and not paying attention. I crash into someone's grocery cart so hard I wrench my neck. People stare at me.

My hand goes back to cradle my neck. "Who was the idiot who left this cart in the middle of the aisle?"

As it happens, my doctor turns around with a jar of dill pickles in his hand. "That would be me. Are you all right, Grace?"

"Obviously not."

"Come to my office in the morning."

"Never mind. I'll take a couple of painkillers."

"I'm not talking about your neck."

After I deliver Nan's groceries and get home to put away my own, I immediately go to the garage, where Fletch is gabbing with his cronies.

"May I speak to you for a moment?"

"In a minute."

"Now."

All the men turn to look at me at once.

"I'd like to speak to my husband without half the village listening in!"

"Excuse us," Fletch says. He comes towards me with a look of thunder, takes my arm, and walks me back into the house. Once we're safely out of earshot he turns to face me.

"Don't you ever speak to me like that again in front of my friends. Despite what you may think, I can only be pushed so far. I know you're upset about your sister, but taking it out on me is not going to help you. In fact, you should think seriously about getting help for your anger. It's hurtful and I'm not going to spend my golden years tip-toeing around it. I've managed to live most of my life without you. I can do it again."

"You'd leave?"

"Of course not. I'd kick *you* out. Now stop taking me for granted, Grace! I'm not one of the dogs! I don't know why, but I feel I can say these things now that we're married."

"Don't leave me!" I'm hysterical. The thought of Fletcher not wanting to live with me anymore never occurred to me, and now it's a giant sword stabbing me in the heart. "Don't go! I'm sorry! I never meant to give you a heart attack. Please don't go!"

I grab his shirt and press my face into his chest. He puts his arms around me.

"I'm not going to leave you, Grace."

"I will never take you for granted again, Fletcher. You are the only thing in my life that's good."

"That's not quite true."

"But it was true for so many years," I gulp. "I have no idea why you put up with me."

"Because when you aren't being a shrew, you're quite nice to have around. Now, what was so urgent?"

"I can't remember."

"Then I'll be outside. What's for dinner?"

I wipe the sweat off my face with my sleeve. "Umm…cabbage rolls. Tell the guys I'm sorry."

"Don't worry, they have wives too."

Once he leaves, I sit at the kitchen table and tremble. I'll be waiting outside the doctor's office in the morning.

THE UPSHOT IS, I'M ON SOME MILD ANTI-ANXIETY MEDICATION AND I HAVE TO have "talk therapy." Something I would've pooh-poohed only weeks ago. But I will do anything to make it right with Fletcher, and if it means me telling some stranger about my problems, then so be it.

Turns out, it's surprisingly easy to spill your guts. It's also surprising to hear that I'm not crazy and my reaction to even the thought of meeting my sister was totally appropriate…for me. I'm not a bad person for not wanting to see her. The psychiatrist says I have to prepare myself for something like that, and it's obvious I'm not ready. No biggie.

The relief is overwhelming. What prisons our minds can be. He said with my history of abandonment and having my son taken from me, he's surprised I'm as normal as I am.

Who knew?

All fall, Fletcher and I are content. We continue to walk the dogs twice a day to get our exercise. Now Fletch even joins me walking up the hill, which he couldn't do before. We celebrate his hundredth pound gone with sparklers. It took him eleven months, which is amazing. His doctor is thrilled and says he's fit as a fiddle. This makes my heart sing. Whenever someone mentions how good Fletcher looks, he always says, "Couldn't have done it without Grace. She's the reason I'm here."

The lead-up to Christmas is in full swing. I'm railroaded into doing the advent calendars for the church fundraiser because Delima said she shouldn't have to do them two years in a row.

"God forbid," I whisper to Gladys at our meeting. She grunts.

"Something else I'd like to bring up for the minutes," Delima announces in a clipped tone. "I've decided I need to retire from napkin duty. From now on someone else will have the responsibility."

Napkins? "I'll do it for all the suppers and events. We can have themes and seasonal colours. Maybe I can sew up a few samples to show you what I have in mind."

This sets my elderly ladies abuzz. It feels good to make them happy.

"I don't think so." Delima throws me a look over the glasses hanging on the end of her nose. "We've always used paper napkins. You can't keep washing cloth napkins. They'll stain."

"Maybe so, but you're retiring. You don't have a say anymore."

"Just so you know, Grace, the napkins are always white. White paper napkins. It's been ever thus."

"Time for a change."

"I withdraw my motion."

"You are a lunatic."

"I'll be a lunatic with white paper napkins."

Fletcher just about wets himself when I tell him of this exchange. "What's killing me is that this is actually a job!"

The advent calendars become the bane of my existence. I start to understand Delima's reluctance. All I do is cut out bits of felt and squeeze globs of hot glue everywhere. It's bad enough making the trees to attach to the banners, but the small ornaments that go into the daily pockets have me up at night. Delima tells me she wants one row of sequins outlining every tree, so I impatiently press one lousy sequin at a time into the glue and burn my fingertips. Nan helps me one day when she comes to see her beloved Beulah. We're at the kitchen table cursing up a storm.

"You listen to that crackpot," Nan tsks. "Who appointed her the queen of advent calendars? You should stay away from that lot. They're crazier than a bag of hammers."

"You never joined a church league?"

"Who needs the aggravation? I've never met a more judgemental bunch in my life."

"I can't believe I'm defending the church, but they have their good points. All the money they raise is funnelled into projects for the less fortunate."

"I was a less fortunate, and no one darkened my door when I was trying to raise Fletcher on my own. Don't get me started."

When the phone rings I gingerly pick it up with my fingertips, trying not to glue myself to it. "Hello?"

"Hi, Gee! It's me!"

"Hello, you. What's new?"

"We're going to Florida for Christmas. Wanna come?"

"No thanks, honey, but have fun."

"Oh, we will. Juni is coming with us."

"Don't her parents want her home for Christmas?"

"Remember that divorce thing? The battle is still raging—she's coming with me as a not-so-subtle way of letting them know neither of them are winning."

"Good for her. And your mother? Won't she miss you?"

"Oh, she will, but she's too sick to notice."

"Sick?"

"She's having a baby. Isn't that gross?"

"A baby! So you'll have a half-brother or sister! How marvellous."

"That part is cool."

Jonathan gets on the phone and wishes us all the best for Christmas. He sounds very happy and relaxed. Whitney is living with them now, which I think is a bit hasty, but no one asked my opinion so I'll keep it to myself. When I finally get off the phone, I give a big sigh.

"I love it when they call to tell me happy news. It makes me feel like I'm surrounded by family."

"What am I, chopped liver? I don't see any of them sitting here sacrificing their fingers for your sake."

I lean over and kiss Nan on the forehead. "You're the best."

"Remember that."

Every year I buy two Christmas arrangements to put on Aunt Pearl's and Aunt Mae's graves. This year we have snow, and the graveyard looks peaceful in its white finery. Lots of snow has stayed on the fir trees, making them even more beautiful. The day is cold and crisp, with a robin's-egg-blue sky peeking from behind the clouds rushing by. I love the silence of this place. My aunts rest easy here. As I admire the pine and holly berries against their headstones, I think while this is a lovely place to be buried, I'd prefer to have my ashes scattered over my hill. Unless Fletcher already has a plot somewhere, but I doubt it. We should discuss these things, I guess. It's hard for me to believe I've weathered sixty years. Inside I'm still twenty. Aunt Mae used to say, "When I look in the mirror my mother looks back at me."

What does my mother look like, if she's even alive? I'll never know unless Maria can tell me something. I push the thought aside quickly. I bend my knees to touch the ground in front of Aunt Pearl's marker with my gloved hand. "My loyalty will always be to you. I should have told you I loved you long before I knew you were dying. I hope you knew I did, despite my nonsense."

Can't forget little Aunt Mae; I touch the snow where she lies too. It gives me comfort to know that these two sisters are together forever, throughout the seasons, while days turn into nights for all time. I doubt it will happen for me.

A BRAND-NEW YEAR IS UPON US, AND AFTER THE EXCITEMENT OF CHRISTMAS it's always a bit of a let-down. No more "Merry Christmas" to shout across the street. The village is in for its long winter's hibernation. Fletcher and I and our furry family spend our evenings in front of the fire. Fletch still dozes through his television programs, but he doesn't snore anymore. My new project is knitting sweaters for penguins. After an oil spill, even when penguins are cleaned off, they can still poison themselves by preening, so knitters across the world are making colourful little sweaters to try and save them from man's stupidity. I've got half of the church women doing it and we send off a parcel quite frequently. The only one who says it's hogwash is Delima.

"A sweater for a penguin? What's next? Pyjamas for polar bears?"

I'm cutting up grapefruit for breakfast one morning in February when I get a call from Jonathan.

"Mom, Grandmother died."

"Lydia died? Oh no, I'm so sorry. I didn't know she was ill."

"She died in her sleep. Natural causes, they said. I was wondering if you'd like to go to the funeral."

"Yes indeed. Lydia was so kind to me. I suppose your grandfather doesn't want me there."

"I didn't ask him one way or the other. I want you there. The service is on Friday."

Fletcher stays to keep the home fires burning, and once more I find myself in New York, only this time I'm going without the heartache and uncertainty. Both Jonathan and Whitney pick me up, and Whitney is a completely different girl on her own turf. Bright, bubbly, and so welcoming. As long as she never comes back to a Cape Breton beach, she'll be fine.

The townhouse is adorable and the two of them are like excited kids showing me around. There's nothing like a woman's touch to bring a home alive. Linn and I have a great reunion and Juni comes tearing down the stairs with Melissa to jump into my arms. All of us sit around the dining-room table and gossip for hours while we obliterate Linn's pad Thai. She remembered I loved it.

"We should be penpals," I tell her as I help put the dishes in the dishwasher.

"So fun! Yes!"

Lydia's funeral is held at St. Patrick's Cathedral, a magnificent church in the heart of New York City. There are hundreds of people here; the Willingdon name is well known in this part of the world. Oliver's cronies, his business associates, politicians, and even celebrities, the kind of people Lydia had such a hard time with. But I'm grateful that Jonathan and Whitney's friends are here to support him and even some of Melissa's chums show up. Deanne and Andre are also with us, and the dear woman looks quite peaky. I give her tummy a pat and tell her how pleased I am.

Oliver doesn't acknowledge anyone as he sits in the front pew; it's easy to avoid him. I don't want to upset the man. Lydia was his wife, for better or worse, and I know this must be a terrible day for him.

The ceremony is long, with communion. I don't go up to the altar but spend my time thinking about the wonderful woman I knew as my mother-in-law. Her brooch is pinned to my coat, which Jonathan noticed right away before we left the house.

The burial is private—only immediate family proceed to Green-Wood Cemetery in Brooklyn.

Oliver doesn't speak to any of us, not even Lydia's family from California. He stands alone, not wanting anyone near him. The rest of us are on the other side of the grave. It's while I watch him there, staring at the graves of his wife and son, that I feel something let go inside. My intense hatred for him seeps away. He's an old man who's lost his entire family.

Once the last prayer is read and people begin to depart, walking slowly arm in arm, I turn to Jonathan. "Go ahead, I'll only be a moment."

He gives me an uncertain look. "All right. We'll be in the limo."

As I approach Oliver, he keeps his head down. Only when I stop beside Aaron's grave does he speak.

"Leave me alone."

"I loved Lydia. She was a wonderful woman. I needed to pay my respects."

"You have. Now leave."

"Oliver, I want to tell you that I forgive you for taking Jonathan away from me. I need to let it go so I can move on. The night Aaron died was horrific and I realize the despair of losing your only child made you crazy."

"No, you did that. A girl from some backwater, with no education or breeding. It was laughable."

I look away for a moment and compose myself. "I also want to tell you that I'm sorry Aaron and I lied to you about Jonathan. It wasn't fair to any of us, least of all Jonathan himself. It was a big mistake and I regret it."

He takes two sudden steps and gets right in my face. "You took my grandson away from me. You made him hate me. Everything I worked for, he's throwing away. My life's work is up in flames because of you."

"You can blame me if you want to; it makes no difference to me. But let me give you some advice. Family is all there is, and you have one last crack at it. Jonathan and Whitney could have ten babies in the future. Melissa could have as many herself. You have a whole new group of people coming along that can belong to you, if you let them. Or you can live in your house alone until you die, surrounded by your stockpile of money. You should choose wisely."

When I turn and walk away from the man who caused me such misery, my heart feels much lighter. By forgiving him, my relationship with Oliver is finally over. He can't hurt me anymore. I scramble into the limo and sit back in the seat with a sigh.

"You okay?" Jonathan asks.

"Yes." I give his hand a squeeze.

When I get home, I'm going to call Maria.

CHAPTER TWENTY-TWO

It takes me three days to work up the nerve to call her. Fletcher promises to
stay in the garage and not disturb me. Why I need to be alone, I haven't
figured out yet. The poor dogs and cats are corralled in two separate
rooms, all of them confused and annoyed. I place a glass of water on
the table and a box of tissues. The last thing I put near the phone is
the spoon I found at the compound. Not that Maria had anything to
do with the tree house, but it was there when Maria and I were sisters.

My hands are shaking when I pick up the phone. What is her voice
going to sound like? What if she hangs up?

"Stop it!" I yell at myself. I dial the number and it starts ringing.
The wait is torture, but no one picks up. There doesn't seem to be
an answering machine, either, not that I would've left a message. In
my mind I see her ignoring the ringing phone because somehow she
knows its me. I slam the phone down. "I don't want to talk to you
either."

Everyone is allowed out of their allotted rooms. I grab my winter
jacket and march to the garage. Fletcher looks up from the hood of a car.

"She didn't answer," I tell him.

"She's not home."

"No, she just didn't answer. I don't need this."

"Stop spiralling and take a deep breath."

"I'm going for a walk."

"Good."

The big dogs come with me as I climb the hill to try and heal my
bruised ego, which is totally ridiculous. Fletcher's right. The poor
woman is probably out shopping with a friend, or she's gone to Cuba
for a holiday. Just because she didn't answer the first time I tried to
reach her doesn't mean she's rejected me again. Stop being a baby.

But I try several times to call over the ensuing weeks and no one
answers. Jonathan checks back with the detectives and they assure him

it's the right number and that a Maria Evans, formally Maria Fairchild, is living there.

Now I wish I hadn't bothered, because my mood is definitely darker.

Fletch comes in for his midday meal, a tuna salad stuffed into pita bread. Tom and Jerry rub up against his legs hoping for a flake of tuna to drop. "You should go to Toronto. Go knock on her door."

"Why would I waste the money?"

"Because you're sad, Grace. You're sad. Do us both a favour and rip this bandage off once and for all."

So on April 1 (so appropriate), I'm standing in front of a small non-descript brick building in Scarborough, east of Toronto. It's rundown, almost like it's given up. Inside is not much better. The place hasn't been painted in years. What a depressing place to come home to.

Her apartment is on the second floor and as I make my way up, various smells of cooking and rotten garbage greet me. I proceed down the corridor and look for her apartment number. I hear music blaring from behind one wall and arguing behind another. There's also the faint wail of a baby crying.

"Oh, Maria. How did you end up here?"

I'm now face to face with her closed apartment door. Do I want it to open? My stomach feels sick, but I take a deep breath and knock.

Silence. I knock again and put my ear to the door. There's no sound from inside. My disappointment is deep. To keep preparing for an encounter, only to have it turn into nothing, is killing me. This is going to have to stop. I did my best. Fletcher is home waiting for me. My family is complete.

There's a noise behind me. A middle-aged man in his undershirt peeks around the edge of his door. "Are you knocking for me?"

"Sorry, no. You couldn't tell me when the lady who lives here gets home?"

"Someone said she's in the hospital."

Unbelievably, that has never occurred to me. "Oh no. Do you know why?"

"I mind my own business. All I can tell you is that she's a drunk." With that he slams his door shut.

"And you're an asshole!"

The rest of the day I spend on the phone, calling every hospital in the city. No one's heard of her. Tears fall off the tip of my nose as I dial. A drunk, he said. My beautiful Ave Maria, with her golden hair and lovely, creamy complexion. What godawful things happened to her? My heart might break right here in this lousy motel room.

I'm down to my last two phone numbers. Once more I explain that I'm looking for my sister, whom I understand has been admitted to hospital. I give them her name, address, and phone number and ask them to check. The girl puts me on hold. It gives me a chance to blow my nose.

She comes back on. "Yes, we have a Maria Evans from the same address listed here. She's on the fourth floor, room 410."

"Thank you so much!"

Maria is close. It's so much to take in that I call Fletcher and tell him the news.

"I'm sorry to hear she's ill. It's a good thing you went."

"The man from the apartment across the hall says she's a drunk."

"Oh dear. Be careful, Grace."

"You were the one who told me to come here!"

"Just don't jump in with both feet. Perhaps you could talk to her doctors before you introduce yourself. She may not be up to such news. Don't be hasty."

"You're right, but I just want this over with. I'll call you tomorrow. Everything okay there?"

He chuckles.

"What?"

"Dora came over today with cold chicken and a salad, dressing on the side."

"That was nice."

"You've sure changed your tune."

"Harvey is a mackerel expert. The woman is starved for normal conversation."

My sleep is fitful, and I spend most of my time staring at the alarm clock. After all these years, I'm getting my wish, so how come it feels like I'm going to my execution?

THE HOSPITAL ELEVATOR OPENS ONTO THE FOURTH FLOOR. MY LAST CHANCE TO stop this. The doors start to close again, but I reach out and push them back. Once I get my bearings, I see the nurses' station on the right, halfway down the hall. That's where I head.

"Excuse me, could you tell me what room Maria Evans is in?"

The young man looks at the computer. "Room 410. She's in the far bed."

"Thank you."

I walk exactly how I did when I went to the compound, taking small, reluctant steps. Completely around the fourth floor. If I'd started in the opposite direction, hers would have been the first room. Doesn't matter, I needed that time to prepare.

The room is made up of curtained walls, most of which are pulled back to some degree. One of the beds is empty, but the other two have elderly women in them who are in desperate need of a hairdresser. I give them a quick nod and head to the last bed on the left. The curtain is completely around the bed, and I'm unsure if I should intrude.

"It's okay, dear," one of the patients says. "She's in there, but she likes quiet."

"Thank you."

My heart pounds as I peek around the curtains and instantly I get the shock of my life. She looks like Aunt Mae. A very sick and thin Aunt Mae, but still. There's immediate relief that I know this woman after all. She looks like family.

Her eyes open as I walk towards her. "Maria?"

She doesn't respond.

"Ave Maria, it's me. It's Grace, your sister, Amazing Grace."

I reach out to touch her hand but she pulls it away.

At this point I'm overwhelmed. "Don't you remember? I'm your sister. We haven't seen each other in a very long time."

She tries to focus, but the effort seems too much. Her head sinks back into the pillow and she shuts her eyes.

"You're tired, I'll come back later."

Whether she hears me or not I don't know, but I immediately leave the room and go in search of a washroom so I can lock myself in and stop hyperventilating. When I look in the mirror I'm as white as a sheet. I splash some water on my face so I don't faint, and then I sit on the john and rock back and forth.

She's so ill. I've come too late. If only I had looked for her when Jonathan told me that night on the phone. All these months wasted, and it's no one's fault but my own. How could I have been so selfish?

I'm not sure how long I'm in the washroom, but eventually someone wants to get in, so I gather myself and walk to the nurses' station. The same young male nurse is at the desk.

"Excuse me, where can I find Maria Evans's doctor? I'm her sister from out of town and I'd like to speak to him."

"He'll be here at one. I can mention that you'd like to see him."

"Great. Do you know where I can get a coffee?"

"We have a cafeteria on the lower level."

In four hours I've had three extra-large cups of coffee and an overpowering urge to smoke, but instead I stuff my face with two brownies encased in cling-wrap that just happen to be by the cash register to entice the inevitable impulse buyer like me. They are delicious, more so because I haven't had a sweet in months. All I do is sit at a cafeteria table and shake my foot, trying to keep myself together.

At a quarter to one I'm at the nurses' desk once more.

"I'm here. I'll just wait outside the doors on a chair in the corridor. Please don't forget to tell him."

"Sure thing."

An hour and a half goes by before a clean-shaven man with a stethoscope around his neck takes a peek out those same doors. I hold my hand up and he comes over and shakes my hand before sitting himself.

"Hello, I'm Dr. Orrell. You wanted to speak to me?"

"Yes, I'm Maria Evans's sister, Grace, but we lost contact when we were girls and I've just now found her. You're not her family doctor, are you?"

"No, she doesn't have one as far as I can tell."

"Is she dying?"

He gives me a sympathetic look. "I'm afraid so. She has stage four breast cancer."

"Damn. It runs in our family."

"Unfortunately, Maria was already compromised when she arrived here. It's very clear she's been an alcoholic most of her life. On top of that she also has early onset dementia."

"Oh god, dementia's in the family as well. I'm too late, aren't I? She won't remember me, or be able to tell me anything of her life."

"Often their long-term memory is much better than their short-term, so it might be possible for her to remember you, but as she's so ill, it's hard for her to communicate. She's here because there's no-where else for her to go."

"So she doesn't have a family?"

"No one has come to visit."

"What a terrible waste. I wish there was something I could do."

"There is. Our nurses are very busy; having a family member be able to sit with her would be a real blessing."

"How long does she have?"

"A few weeks, perhaps. We never know."

"Thank you, Doctor. I appreciate you filling me in."

He shakes my hand again. "If you could let them know that you're her next of kin. There are papers to be filled out."

"Certainly."

I'm so drained at this point that I leave the hospital without going back to see her. I need to gather my wits about me. When I get back to my motel room, I fall on the bed and lay there until the outside street lights turn on. Then I call Fletcher and tell him that I'll stay here until she dies and bring her back with me to be buried beside Aunt Pearl and Aunt Mae.

"Do you want me to come?" says Fletcher. "I can come and stay with you, if you want."

"No. No, I need to be with my sister, just the two of us. I want to take care of her until the end."

"Well, don't you worry about anything. I've got it covered."

There's nothing more wonderful than a man who takes care of everything.

Except two men who take care of everything. Jonathan calls me half an hour later.

"Mom, I'm sorry to hear about your sister."

"It's a bitter pill. I should have reached out sooner, but I'll do my best for her now. At least she'll be with family in Cape Breton."

"Look, I want to make things easy for you. I've booked you into a nice hotel closer to the hospital and you can collect your car rental tomorrow at the front desk."

"But Fletcher—"

"I've spoken to Fletcher and told him I want to do this for you, and he's okay with it. Also, when it's time for you to come home, just give me the name of the funeral parlour and I'll take care of it, as well as your plane ticket."

"You don't know what this means to me," I manage to squeak out.

"I do know, Mom. I love you."

My son loves me.

I'M IN TORONTO FOR THE ENTIRE MONTH OF APRIL. EVERY DAY I SPEND AT THE hospital in a chair by Maria's bed. She doesn't know who I am, but I notice after a while that she visibly relaxes when I walk in. I feed her like a baby bird and cut up fresh fruit in tiny bites to slip onto her tongue. She likes bananas the best.

The nurses know me by name and one of them will always stop and chat for a moment while attending to Maria. I've also become friends with the ladies in the other beds, but mostly I pull the curtain around my sister's bed so I can have her all to myself. She lets me hold her hand now.

I rattle on about how much she hated when I mimicked her behind her back. She'd chase me but I'd run like the wind and she'd give up. Or the time we tried to make breakfast in bed for our mom, but we spilled a glass of orange juice all over everything on the tray.

"Do you remember my friend Helen? She and I would play in the tree house."

She tries to say something, but it's garbled.

"Yes! We were always together. I think you remember her, don't you?"

That reminds me of the pictures I brought with me, to show her my life back home, thinking maybe she'd enjoy them. So one day when she's a little clearer, but oh so weak, I prop her up with pillows all around and lean over to show her the photographs one by one.

"This is my husband, Fletcher, with our dogs. Do you see the tiny one? Her name is Beulah, and she's as saucy as anything."

She's looking at the photo, which is great. It almost feels like she's with me. Please let her stay like this for a few more minutes.

"And this is my son, Jonathan. Isn't he handsome? He lives in New York with his daughter, Melissa. Do you see her blonde hair? That's what your hair looked like when you were a little girl. That was the last time you saw me and I saw you. You were twelve and I was nine. I missed you very much when you left. I missed Mama, too."

She starts to fidget so I go through the photos like a deck of cards to find one she might like. That's when I come upon the pictures of the woods at the camp and the bog. I didn't know they were in this pile, but this is perfect.

"Look, Maria. Do you remember the woods where you and me and Mama used to walk? And here's the rock we would sit on. And here's the bog. Look. Do you remember the bog?"

She grabs my hand and squeezes it with a strength that's surprising. She shakes my hand to and fro.

"Yes, Mama! That's right! I don't know where she is. Did she ever find you? Were you together at all? Did you miss me, even a little?"

A tear runs down her cheek, but she laughs. A guttural laugh.

When the nurse comes over, I ask her about it. "With Alzheimer's patients, their reactions are not always the correct one. If she shed a tear, she might be happy, or if she laughs, she might want to cry. It's an emotion and a release. It can bubble up any time. You can never really know what it means."

That's enough for today. Gathering my belongings, I take one more moment to stroke her brow. She stares at me. I kiss her forehead and tuck the blanket around her before I leave.

I have a quick fast food meal on the way back to the hotel. I take a bath and watch television for an hour. Then it's lights out. I'll try a few more pictures with her tomorrow.

The hotel phone rings at five in the morning. Maria died sometime in the night. Why didn't I stay with her? She was alone in the end.

There is so much to do and yet a weariness takes hold and shakes me to my core. Even holding the cellphone up to my ear seems too much, so I lie on my side and let the phone just rest against my cheek. Fletcher picks up on the first ring.

"Hey, Gracie, I had a weird dream about you last night. You were trying to make me eat coconut balls."

"That's nice."

"Not really."

"Maria died."

"Oh no. I'm very sorry, Grace."

"It's a good thing. She's found peace at last. Call Jonathan and tell him. The hospital knows I'm coming in later to deal with the formalities, and then I'll contact the funeral home. After that I'm going to get the landlord of her apartment building to let me in so I can gather her belongings, such as they are. I'd like something to remember her by. Look, I have to go. I know I just woke up, but I'm tired."

"You've been looking for her your whole life. You're allowed to be tired."

"Talk later."

I hang up the phone and weep into the pillow. My only contact is gone, and she was unable to tell me anything. The disappointment is vast.

Much to my surprise, Jon and Fletch fly in to be with me that night. They didn't have to do it, but it's such a relief to see them at the door.

Fletch opens his arms and I jump right into them, while trying to kiss Jonathan at the same time.

"You have no idea how good it is to see you!"

"We could hardly let you deal with all this by yourself."

I fill them in on the past month, and how difficult it was to not be able to communicate with her.

"I'm sure you did, Mom. Maybe not with words, but you were there to hold her hand. She felt you with her."

"You're right. At least that's something."

The dismantling of someone's life is a bureaucratic ordeal. Papers to fill out and agencies to inform, each province with its own way of dealing with the matter. We spend a good deal of time on the phone and at the hospital. Then we go to the funeral home to discuss our options.

We decide on cremation; it will be easier to bring her home this way. The funeral director asks us if we want to see the remains.

"It's up to you if you want to go in," I tell them.

They both say they will. I'm glad to be able to share this with someone. I want Maria to count.

Her casket is top of the line. When I depart this earth, I want a pine box, or even a cloth shroud. Just plant me and go your merry way. But since Maria went without her whole life, we want her to feel special. It sounds silly, but it makes sense to us.

She looks better in death than she did in life, her face calm and serene.

"She does look like Aunt Mae," Fletcher says. "It's uncanny."

"For some reason that makes me happy," I confess.

"She looks like you, too," Jonathan says. "She must have been pretty."

"She was pretty. That's how I want to remember her."

It's time to leave. I kiss her one final time and whisper in her ear, "I'm bringing you home with me. You'll be safe now."

We get in touch with the landlord and make an appointment to see Maria's apartment in the morning.

It's been a very long day, but we take the time to eat dinner at a nice restaurant, to lift our sagging spirits. Fletcher orders grilled haddock, God love him. He hasn't put any of his weight back and clearly all the exercise does allow him to indulge a little, which is why he orders a piece of cheesecake.

"You better order two pieces," he tells me. "You've lost weight since you've been here, and you look a little peaky."

"Then I'll have the deep fried cheesecake."

"Deep fried! Lord have mercy."

I'm desperate for normal conversation. "How's Melissa?"

"You mean, how are the girls. Juni lives with us now."

"You're kidding?"

"Her parents are insane and actually like the idea, which shows you what kind of nutjobs they are. The girls are into theatre and fencing, of all things. Half the time we never see them."

"And Whitney? Things are still good with you two?"

Just the way he lowers his head and smiles tells me the answer.

"You love her, don't you?"

"She's a pretty wonderful gal."

I reach over and pat his hand. "That makes me happy."

"On a different note, Grandfather has prostate cancer."

"Well, I wouldn't wish that on anyone. He keeps in touch, then?"

"Surprisingly, yes. At first I thought it was an anomaly, but he often calls me. I've gone with him a few times for his chemo. Melissa and Juni went with him, too. I think he gets a kick out of Juni.

"Who doesn't?" Fletcher laughs.

Our desserts come and they are out of this world. Strange how something sweet in your mouth can take the pain away, if only for that moment.

"How's Nan?" I say with my mouth full.

"She needs a knee replacement."

"Poor dear. Maybe it will give her a better quality of life. She shouldn't be in pain."

Then it's up to our rooms, where tonight Fletch and I crawl into the same bed together. He takes me in his arms and I'm safe.

"Thank you for coming."

"I wouldn't be anywhere else."

"Who's looking after the critters?"

"Beulah is at Nan's and Harvey and Dora will take the dogs out and feed the cats."

"I dream of home. Just a little bit longer." I fall into a deep sleep.

THE SUPER FOR MARIA'S APARTMENT LOOKS LIKE HE JUST GOT OUT OF BED. HE passes us the keys.

"You're responsible for any damages," he warns us.

"How would you be able to tell? This whole place is a disaster."

"Ain't mine, lady. Talk to the owner, if you can find him."

"We'll bring the key back when we're finished."

"You better have that stuff shifted by tomorrow at the latest." He shuts the door in our faces.

"Charming."

I'm afraid to open this door. We are invading Maria's personal space, leaving her open to scrutiny and judgement. No one would want people rooting around their cupboards or bathroom cabinets. She can't defend herself from our prying eyes.

"Maybe we should just leave it alone."

"Mom, do you really want strangers to do it?"

Jon gives me the push I need, but when I open the door, I gasp before I'm even over the threshold. There are so few things in here, absolutely the bare minimum. Her bed is a mattress on the floor and she has only one broken sofa, with not even a television to keep her company. There's an overpowering smell of nicotine and beer, with piles of empty cans in the corner. The kitchen counter is full of empty chip bags and fast food wrappers.

"Oh my god, I can't bear it."

Fletcher brought a few cardboard boxes for us to put her treasures in, only there aren't any.

"Why didn't I call her? Why? How could she live like this? How did she let this happen?"

"Mom—"

"That doesn't require an answer! I'm just pissed off, dammit! Even her sheets are filthy. She had enough money for beer! Why couldn't she wash her sheets?"

I'm aware I'm rambling, but it's like my feelings are throwing up all over me. If she was here right now I'd shake her. Why didn't she get help?

The smell of this apartment is closing in on me. "I have to get out of here." I throw open the door and run down the hall and the stairs to stagger outside. Let them deal with it. I can't cope with anything else. Since Jonathan has the car keys, I slide down the passenger door and sit on the driveway with my back against the car, keeping my eyes shut to try and block out the look of that apartment. I truly wish I'd left it alone; I don't think I can stand much more of this.

Eventually Fletcher and Jonathan come outside and walk over to me. Fletcher has a small box with him.

"What could possibly be in that?" I shout, like it's all his fault.

"The only things we could find were a couple of books and a few trinkets. I threw in her sweater and there's a small bottle of cheap perfume. Also a hand mirror."

"We told the super that a removal company will be here in the morning to take away what little remains," Jonathan says. "After that I've made arrangements for a cleaning company to come in and deal with the mess."

"Thank you both. I'm sorry I shouted."

"Mom, I can't even imagine what you're going through. Here, take my hands."

He pulls me up and the three of us set off, leaving the sad space behind.

AT THE TORONTO AIRPORT WE SAY GOODBYE TO JON. HE'S FLYING TO NEW York and we're on a plane to Halifax and then Sydney. I'm carrying my sister's ashes in my tote bag. There's a sense of satisfaction that I'm able to bring her home, but a lingering melancholy that Maria's life was so terrible. I keep thinking that if I'd only found her even a few years ago, she might have been able to tell me something of her life, and whether she knew whatever happened to our mom.

Still, I am grateful for small mercies, and the idea that I can bring Maria back to Cape Breton to lie with our family members in the graveyard in Baddeck instead of some anonymous grave brings me great relief.

But in the end I don't put her in the graveyard. I keep her with me. Her urn is on my windowsill. I can't bear to part with her just yet.

CHAPTER TWENTY-THREE

In the morning, I leave to get some groceries and pick up Beulah, but first I drive into Harvey and Dora's yard. We bought a few carton of beers for Harvey and bottles of wine for Dora to thank them for looking after things while we were away. Nothing's changed in this household.

"Why, thank you." Harvey seems mighty pleased. "I'll crack open a few the next time I go fishing."

Dora gives me a pained look. "How's Fletcher?"

"Fletcher is great. Although I think he was missing your low-fat offerings. Better rustle something up and get over there quick."

She beams at me. "Perfect! I have a cauliflower-cheese recipe just begging to be made."

It doesn't take much to make some people happy.

When I walk in Nan's door on my way home from the grocery store, Beulah is on her lap. Poor Nan has her upper dentures in a glass on the side table and she's snoring to beat the band. The house looks pretty messy.

"Nan…it's only me."

Beulah raises the alarm when she charges over to try and climb my legs, so I pick her up and give her several kisses, while her little tongue goes a mile a minute.

"Who's there? Oh, it's you." She reaches over and puts her teeth back in her head. "Good to see you. You've been away a long time."

Before I sit on the rocking chair I bend down and kiss her cheek. "I missed you, Nan. And this little critter." Beulah is still jumping in my lap.

"You're not taking her home, are you? It's lonely here without her."

Nan does seem rather down.

"How did you make out while I was gone?"

"Not good. Not good at all. My knee is acting up. Can barely move some mornings. But don't worry about me. I don't want to be anyone's burden."

I fix up some macaroni and cheese for her supper and deliver it on a tray with a cup of tea and a scone so she can watch television. Naturally, I leave Beulah with Nan; they both seem content with the arrangement. During supper I tell Fletch about our conversation.

"Hopefully things will be better once she gets her knee fixed," Fletch says, "or do you think it's more than that? She's never minded being alone before. Do you think we should explore a senior's home?"

"Who said anything about that? She'll come here and be with us."

He smiles. "Are you sure? I know it's asking a lot. I work all day and you'll be stuck with her. You know how she can get."

"One temperamental old broad won't break me. Not after what I've been through."

Fletcher leans over and kisses my cheek. "I love you, Mrs. Parsons."

Nan's temperamental, all right. She refuses to leave her trailer. "I don't want to live with anyone else, including you."

Fletcher sighs. "You have difficulty even cooking. You can't stay here alone. Your knee—"

"To hell with my knee. I'll crawl if I have to. You're not going to shove me in your back room so I can rot away doing nothing all day."

"Be reasonable…"

"Why don't we move her trailer onto our property? That's what trailers are for."

Both Nan and Fletcher seem dazed by the suggestion.

"That's a great idea," Fletch says. "How about it?"

"Just as long as you don't come barging in on me. You have to knock first—you have no idea what I might be doing."

We don't want to think about what that means.

It takes a good part of the summer to get our property organized and ready for the new trailer. Fletcher kitty-corners it to ours, and builds a large deck that joins the two. We set up a nice outdoor seating area, with a table and umbrella, lots of chairs, and even a rocking chair so Nan can knit in the shade but still warm her bones. The animals are already thrilled with it.

We spend days packing Nan's fragile things into boxes for the trip over. I discover that Nan is a real packrat, which is kind of great—I find a few pictures of her and Aunt Pearl when they were young girls, sitting around a campfire with other friends. They look happy and carefree. It's nice to see Aunt Pearl like this. You forget that elderly people are just young people who've been hanging around for a while. Nothing changes inside. Perhaps that's why our childhoods still have such sway over us.

The arrangement works beautifully. Nan is already spending more time outdoors than she has in years, and no matter who comes calling, they have to stay and chat with our resident busybody. Dora comes almost every day with some treat or other for her and the two of them talk themselves blue in the face most afternoons.

Beulah provides the comic relief. She runs around in circles in the yard, and Daffy and Donald chase her until they're worn out. They are fast friends now, and most of the time they sleep together in a furry pile. Sometimes you can't even see Beulah until she opens her eyes and yips.

It's while we drink sweet lemonade out on our deck that I end up telling Dora and Nan the story of my childhood, and the search for my kin. Dora bawls her eyes out. She really is a lovely, generous woman and is quickly becoming a good pal. It's freeing to be able to tell people the story of my life. I'm not ashamed or guilt-ridden or broken down by it anymore. It happened. It's over. Life goes on.

The phone rings one morning, and it's Melissa to tell us she has a new baby brother.

"You should see him, Gee! He's perfect. I didn't know babies were so little."

"That's wonderful news! Send pictures."

"Just go on Facebook. Mom's put up about a hundred already."

"That's a good idea. So what's the baby's name?"

"Ryder."

"What?"

"Ryder...like a horseback rider, only with a y."

"Oh dear."

"Stop going all Aunt Pearl on me," she laughs.

"Fine! So what are your plans for fall?"

"Juni and I were both accepted at Barnard College. Isn't that fantastic? I want to go into women's studies or comparative literature and

Juni is in dance! Dad says we have to live at home for the first year, but second year we can get an apartment together."

"Wow. I can't tell you how proud I am. You've got the world by the tail, honey. Enjoy every moment."

When I hang up, I sit for a while in utter contentment. My granddaughter will be a Barnard College graduate. Wouldn't Aunt Pearl be thrilled? The relief that Melissa has found her feet again is powerful. So often there are crossroads in your life, when things can go right or horribly wrong. We never know when something we say or do will turn a person's life around. I think the night of Jonathan's phone call helped Melissa more than he could have anticipated—not that I take all the credit. We've all grown a lot since the day I landed in New York.

Nan insists on knitting a sweater, hat, and booties for the baby. I'm pretty certain this child will be dressed to the nines, with Deanne as his mother, but an old-fashioned gift is always appropriate. A baby quilt seems a lot easier to me, and I'm halfway done when I read a magazine article that says modern mothers don't put anything over their children in the crib, for fear of suffocation or SIDS. Well, maybe she can put it on the floor for the baby to lie on. It's hard to keep up with the times.

I spend my mornings on the computer looking at Ryder's pictures and selfies of Melissa and Juni. Now that I'm not looking up missing persons sites, I like to go through my Pinterest boards while I drink tea. Naturally they are full of pictures of animals, but it's the art that captivates me. It's like being back in New York at a museum.

Dora's grandson Felix sets Skype up for me. It's ridiculously easy and I don't know why I thought I couldn't do it myself. Now I can have a real live chat with Melissa, holding baby Ryder in her arms.

"This is beyond amazing," I tell Fletcher. "It's like they're in the room with you."

There's less socializing on the new deck now that summer's over, but there's still plenty of it at Nan's. She, Dora, Gladys Nicolson, and I play tarbish or crib a couple of times a week. It keeps us entertained and I can see a real difference in Nan's mood. She's cheerful and chatty and ready for anything. Why didn't we think of this years ago?

In September, Nan goes in for her knee replacement. She says it was a piece of cake. Hard to believe she's in her eighties. I hope I'm that spry at her age.

Since I'm on call with Nan while she recovers, I spend a lot of time at her place, but when she naps I tend to my own chores, thanks to the new baby monitor that Fletch bought me. We put one speaker in Nan's room and one in our kitchen. Nan knows to holler into it if she needs me.

Today it's time to muck out this bedroom, but the first thing I see is the urn with my sister's ashes on the windowsill. At first it was a comfort, but now I'm starting to feel a little selfish. Would I want to linger in someone's bedroom, gathering dust, after I'm gone? I'm going to have to stop waffling soon.

The urn reminds me of the small box that Fletcher gathered from Maria's apartment. It's been in the top of the closet since we got home, and I've had no desire to see the contents. Fletch told me what was in there and it's not much, so why am I staring at it now? Just open it and have it done with. Perhaps I can bury her things with her. Reaching my arms over my head, I take down the box and sit on the bed with it. It's so sad. This is all there is to say she lived. Her sweater is dirty and pilled, with food stains and a cigarette hole in the cuff. I'll wash it and fix the hole. There's a small thistle pin, the kind you wear on a coat. The back pin is broken and it's quite tarnished, but I can have it repaired. The hand mirror is cracked. I'll fix that too.

There are two books at the bottom. One is a paperback, some romance thing with a chesty woman and a swashbuckler on the cover. That I'll donate to the book mobile. The other is a small and worn, hardcover book. When I turn it over I discover it's a copy of *Alice's Adventures in Wonderland*.

I'm back at the camp. Maria decided to put on a play. Helen and I both wanted to be Alice, but Maria said that was her role. She made me the Queen of Hearts and Helen the White Rabbit. The other parts were chosen by Maria too, with all the kids clamouring to be part of it. We worked on it for a couple of weeks and the younger kids loved it. They made us do it over and over again. Even some of the mothers were in the audience. I'd forgotten all about it; the bad memories wiped out the good ones. Working on that play with my sister is definitely a great memory.

It must have been for Maria as well.

My sister never forgot me. Some part of her wanted me with her. When she had nothing to her name, she kept that book. Oh, how I wish we could have shared our stories with one another. I hold the book to my heart, a gift I will cherish forever.

As I put it down I notice a bookmark of some kind, so I open the pages and retrieve it. It's a small document that has been folded up for a long time. It's probably nothing, but I unfold it anyway.

It's a birth certificate. Maria had a child with her husband, Terry Evans. A little girl named Trixie Grace Evans, born in Toronto on June 13, 1970.

I stare at the paper, afraid to believe it. If this is true, I have a niece. A niece named after our mother and me. Further proof that my sister loved me. That she loved our mom. We are a family, despite having been torn apart by horrific circumstances. This connection is real and can't be taken away.

Fletcher finds me sitting on the bed with the birth certificate still in my hand. "Why is it so gloomy in here?" He turns on the light which makes me squint. "Any supper going? If not, there's a vegetarian pizza in the freezer."

I hold the paper out to him. "I have a niece named Trixie Grace. Do you know what this means?"

He smiles at me. "Everything."

CHAPTER TWENTY-FOUR

I'm not making the same mistake again. My search for Trixie begins immediately. My computer is smoking, but despite my hours of searching, I can only get so far. There are a few Trixie Graces on Google, but none with the last name Evans. That's not to say that she isn't out there. Lots of people aren't on the Internet. But Canada 411 doesn't come up with anything, and neither do Facebook or Linkedin. So I call Jonathan.

"Can you give me the number of your detective?"

"Who are you hunting for now?" he laughs.

"Your cousin."

"Cousin?"

"Can you believe it? Maria gave birth to a daughter named Trixie Grace in 1970, which means she's four years older than you are. She was born in Toronto and I have to find her. She can fill in the gaps."

"But I thought you said Maria didn't have any family. No one was at the hospital with her. Surely a daughter would want to be with her dying mother."

"As we both know, life isn't simple. Maybe they lost touch as well."

"Wow. I'm really happy for you, Mom, but you've gone through so much already. Are you sure you want to do this? I'd hate to see you disappointed. What if she wants nothing to do with you or us?"

"It's a chance I'll have to take. I remember Aunt Pearl's words when I received her letter. She wrote, '*Kin is kin. We can't abandon you to the mercy of strangers now that we know you exist.*' I'm not suggesting she needs my help, but now that I know she's out there, I can't ignore her. Do you understand?"

"Of course. I'll get Mr. Smith to call you."

"His name is Smith?"

"Probably not," he laughs.

"While I've got you on the phone, how are things?"

He hesitates. "Grandfather is going downhill. It's only a matter of time now. I didn't want to bother you with it."

"Are you okay?"

"I'm in a good place. He actually apologized to me."

"When you come to the end of your life, you want to leave this world unburdened. I'm glad he apologized. I never thought that would happen."

"Me neither."

MR. SMITH IS ON THE CASE. EVERY TIME THE PHONE RINGS I JUMP. NAN SAYS I'M a flea on a hot stove. She's doing well; we get her up and exercising every day and her quality of life has vastly improved. It does our hearts good to see her so happy. While she recuperates, I ask her if she would mind talking into a small recorder, to share her memories of growing up in Baddeck. It's important to keep these stories in the family.

Often Dora and I sit in Nan's living room while she chatters away, and we listen to what life was like for her as a girl. It's got Dora thinking she should do the same for her grandchildren, and I think some of the other women in the community might feel the same, so I mention the idea to the church ladies as we serve tea and sandwiches to Earl "Diddy" Durdle's family after his funeral.

We're in the hall kitchen getting ready. Delima adds more milk to a pot of tea. "Who wants to go digging up that nonsense again? It was bad enough to live it once."

Gladys unwraps another platter of ham and relish sandwiches. "Do you ever say anything positive, Delima?"

"Sure. I'm positive it's a stupid idea."

I giggle in the corner while I put a variety of squares on a platter. Janet Pickup sticks up for me. "Well, I think it's a marvellous idea and we should keep it in mind, perhaps do something for our families for Christmas."

Delima starts pouring the tea into Styrofoam cups. "And what exactly would you talk about, Janet? The time you got caught in the barn with Little Dan Angus McIntyre?"

Janet turns bright pink. "Delima! I was never in a barn with Little Dan. Now, Diddy was another matter."

All the ladies hoot with laughter, but once the family starts pouring in, we sober up and tend to our task. I notice at one point Janet goes over to Diddy's wife and gives her a hug.

What happens in a Baddeck barn, stays in Baddeck barn.

THE CALL COMES THROUGH ONLY A FEW WEEKS LATER. MR. SMITH HAS located a Trixie Grace Bailey, nee Evans. She lives in Fredericton, New Brunswick. So close! He gives me her address and phone number, which I stare at for a while.

No, I'm not going to call her. That would be too much of a shock. I'll write to her first. Then if she doesn't want anything to do with me, it will be easier to walk away.

Not really.

I wait until all is quiet, with Fletcher and critters flaked out in front of the television.

Dear Trixie,

You don't know me and I don't know you, but we are family. I'm your mother's younger sister, Grace. We were parted through no fault of our own and spent our lives alone. I always wondered what happened to Maria and it's only recently that I found out.

I'm sorry to tell you this, but your mom had breast cancer and dementia and was in a very bad way when I finally got to meet her. I stayed with her until she died and she was peaceful and at rest in the end. I brought her ashes back here to Cape Breton with me because I didn't realize Maria had a daughter. I found your birth certificate in a book after her death.

You may not want to hear from me. I'm assuming since you weren't around that you and your mother were estranged and I'm sorry if that's the case. But I do hope you want to talk to me. I would love to hear about her life and I feel I've been given a second chance with you.

Despite the fact that your mother may have been a disappointment to you, (I know she was an alcoholic), I have some wonderful memories of her as a young girl and I'd like to be able to tell you about them. I'd also love for you to meet my son, your cousin Jonathan. He has a daughter who's off to university in the fall. Do you have any children?

There is a family homestead here that you might like to visit, and I can tell you about my great-aunts who saved me when I was a young girl.

I could ramble on, but I'll close for now. I'll put my address and phone number on the card and please feel free to reverse the charges if need be.

Kin is kin. I hope you feel the same way.

All my love, your Aunt Grace. xo

Patience is not my strong suit—the wait for Trixie to get back to me makes me crazy. Once again I'm in a vortex of frustration of my own making. Why do I never listen to people? Both Fletcher and Jonathan were worried about my attempt to contact my niece and I pooh-poohed their concerns. Now, four weeks later and with no response, I wish I'd listened to them.

Oliver Willingdon dies in October. Jonathan thinks it best if I don't go to the funeral and I agree. He leaves his entire fortune to Jonathan. While Jon is pleased that they made up, the money represents a massive responsibility and he's unsure of his ability to cope. I tell him I have every faith in him and obviously his grandfather did too. Melissa and Juni are already badgering him about their philanthropic causes. They'll keep him on his toes.

In the meantime, I'm restless. Why can't I just put this aside and get on with my life? It's like I can never relax, knowing I have a niece out there. Maybe I will always be unsatisfied. Perhaps I should call her, but if the letter didn't move her, why would the sound of my voice change her mind? Do I really want Trixie to tell me to go away?

This time I don't ask for advice, seeing as how I never listen to it anyway.

I just pick up the phone and call her. "Hello, Trixie?"

"Maybe, but if you're a bill collector, I've never heard of her."

"It's Grace, your aunt. Did you get my letter?"

"Oh! Good News Grace, telling me my mom is dead. Thanks a bunch."

"I'm sorry—"

"Not like it was a big shock. I assumed she died years ago of liver failure."

"So you were estranged? I thought you might be."

"Estranged is the wrong word, Grace. We were pissed at each other. She didn't like me and I sure as hell didn't like her. We did the cordial thing and just never crossed paths."

"That makes me sad. There are so many things I want to ask you about her."

"Don't bother. She was a sad, grumpy bitch most of the time. I'd say you got off lucky avoiding her all these years. Look, I hate to burst your bubble but my drug dealer is here and it's important that I talk to him, so I gotta go."

"You're pulling my chain, aren't you, Trixie? You're trying to be a smartass so I'll go away, but I want you to know that your mother was a great sister to me while I had her—"

"Bully for you, but I'm not interested in regressing. It irritates my shrink to no end. Ciao." And she hangs up.

What an odd choice of words. She can't regress. So she's trying to survive her upbringing too, despite her tough-as-nails veneer.

I've gone about this the wrong way, asking her about her mother. What I need to do is ask her about herself. Her life and her dreams. Maria's life is over, but Trixie and I are alive; it's our relationship I need to nurture. I don't want to be tarred with her mother's brush. She needs to see that a relative can be supportive and kind, not someone to be overcome. Because despite her saucy mouth, I like her. She reminds me of me.

Now to plan a strategy, which means a long walk on my hill. The dogs and I head out.

It's almost Halloween and the ground is cold but I sit on the grass anyway. The dogs gather round. I see Tom and Jerry making their way up the hill, but they mosey and pretend they aren't interested, the way cats do. They might not make it up here before I have to leave.

It's windy, a kite-flying day. This hill was made for a kite and I can't believe I haven't flown one here. Maybe I'll have to drive to Fredericton to buy one.

Fletcher doesn't approve of my plan when I wander down to the yard to tell him. He's just coming in for supper.

"She told you she doesn't want to take it any further. You should respect that."

"She doesn't know me."

"This is how stalkers are born."

In response, I shake the dish towel I'm taking off the line at him. He keeps going. I yell, "You're not the boss of me!"

"Thank Christ for that."

Surprisingly, Dora thinks I should go. "The minute she sees you she'll be overwhelmed by the family connection. It happens all the time on that show, *The Locator.*"

Nan is on the fence. "Maybe send her some pictures instead, but don't get your hopes up."

"Wait a minute, that's a great idea. I'll take pictures of all of us! That way she can see what she's missing."

"She'll take one look at me and run for the hills," Nan shouts. "Leave me out of it."

But I don't. I arrange for a photographer to come over. Both Nan and Fletcher are being big babies about it, so I apologize ahead of time to the poor woman. "Just ignore them."

"Kind of hard to do if I have to take their picture."

It doesn't go well at first.

A formal pose of the three of us around the recliner is hijacked when all the dogs try to get in the picture at the same time. After a lot of barking and shouting we come to an agreement. Beulah is front and centre on Nan's lap. Daffy stands with Fletcher to one side, and Donald is at my feet as I sit on the arm of the chair. We discover later that Tom and Jerry have photo-bombed every shot, and that's after they refused to be in the picture with us.

Cats!

The photographer takes candid shots as well, and these are my favourites. She takes pictures of Fletcher working in his garage and Nan playing solitaire. She follows me up onto the hill and takes a really nice one of me poking my head out from behind a tree. I ask her to take shots of our view and also the trailers. I'm not ashamed of them. This is where we live and love.

It's one of the best things I've ever done for myself. All of us are thrilled with the results and we frame a couple of the more formal poses, but the others I have tacked up on my bulletin boards so I can look at them every day.

I get in touch with Melissa and she sends me an avalanche of pictures from the New York crowd, all of them on the computer of course, but she tells me how I can transfer them to an external drive and take them to get printed. Isn't technology marvellous?

Melissa and Juni are now nineteen, though Melissa looks younger than she did at sixteen, when I travelled to New York to sort her out. She's a striking girl, all cheekbones and bright red hair, at least for this month. She dropped out of Barnard College when she realized that fashion is endlessly more enjoyable than literature or anything else and now attends fashion school. She sounds giddy on the phone whenever we speak.

There's one picture I adore of her and her little brother, Ryder, who is now fifteen months old. He's a chubby little Buddha and Melissa has him up in the air as he smiles down at her. Their noses are exactly the same. It makes me want to weep with joy.

I'm putting the pictures in an envelope to send to Trixie when I get a call from Juni. She calls every month or so just to chat.

"Gee Gee, I need some advice."

"Fire away."

"My parents are getting back together."

"Holy shit! You're kidding."

"That's what I said! I've watched them fight for years and now suddenly everything is bliss. They even want to have a vow renewal. Can you believe that? It's so...desperate! I told them I want nothing to do with it."

"Don't be so foolish. You are their only child; of course they want you with them on their special day."

"But—"

"Juni, my love, the world can be a terrible and hostile place. Don't ever turn down the chance to celebrate love."

"But—"

"You're frightened that it won't last. Understandable, but guess what, buttercup? You need to suck it up and go anyway. Now, is there anything else?"

"I'm dating a really nice guy. He's from Japan and he's dreamy.

Eugene Yokohama."

"Sounds perfect. Bring him up this summer and we'll have a lobster overdose."

"I love you, Gee Gee."

"Love you right back, little one."

After that I turn the phone off. I need to compose another letter to my niece.

Dear Trixie,

Just indulge me for a few moments and take a look at your family.

Because this is your family.

I've put everyone's name and relationship on the back of the pictures so you don't get us all mixed up. Some of us are gorgeous and the others not so much. Some of us have money and others have zilch. There are a few lovely dwellings and others that look like the ass end of a cow, but all are equally comfortable.

Some of us have courtside seats to the New York Knicks in Madison Square Garden and box seats to watch the Islanders at the Coliseum, and even at Yankee Stadium, but I promise you the rest of us have diddly-squat. We're all equally comfortable.

We have a lot of crazy dogs and cats because who can get through life without them?

We have a summer farmhouse that sits on the shore of the Bras d'Or Lakes. In the summer we swim and have bonfires there. It's a nice place to hide from the world for a time.

Your mother and I said our farewells, so I will not bring her up again. But wouldn't I love to know you! What's your favourite ice cream? What do you do for fun? Do you like to dance or yodel??

If you'd like to get in touch, we are here for you. If you'd rather not, then we completely understand. Have a wonderful life and know that your Aunt Grace loves you very much.

Grace

P.S. Did you know my first name is Amazing? Isn't that amazing?

Fletcher asks me what I said in the letter, and I tell him.

"You mentioned Madison Square Gardens, the Coliseum, and Yankee Stadium? Like that has any relevance to the situation? Did you ask Jon if he even has seats?"

"No."

"That's so you."

A WEEK LATER I GET A PHONE CALL.

"Aunt Grace?"

"Trixie! It's so good to hear your voice!"

"Don't get all sappy. The only reason I'm calling is that my boys are basketball fanatics and they said they'd pound the shit out of me if I didn't get in touch with you."

"I love them already."

"You can have them. They're eating me out of house and home."

"Does this mean you'd like to get together sometime?"

"Maybe, if only to touch your hair. It's the exact colour of mine and it's freaking me out. You look more like my mother than my mother did."

"How neat is that? This is so exciting! What are your boys' names?"

"Jeremy and Nate. Big hulks who live at home because of the goddamn economy. I've also got one of their girlfriends and my granddaughter, Sunni, for the time being, so you could say I'm a bit stressed."

"When can I visit?"

"Jesus…you wanna come here already? I don't have any room."

"I won't stay with you. I'd just like to meet everyone."

"We're not that special, but seeing as how you're so anxious to know us, how about taking us to New York for a basketball game?"

"Oh…I…"

"You see! I knew it! Don't go running your mouth off about how privileged you are if you have no intention of sharing it with us, Auntie Grace."

"Wait a minute! Don't take that tone with me. You know nothing about what I intend to do, but I know one way of not getting a trip to New York and that's to demand it. And just so you know, I can be just as badass as you. I have no intention of being steamrolled, no matter how much I want you in my life. Do I make myself clear?"

"Geez…calm down. I only wanted to see if you were serious."

"All right. So do you want to meet me or not, Trixie?"

"After that? Not really."

"You're a rig, do you know that?"

"And you're a tool. We're even."

I burst out laughing. I like her.

CHAPTER TWENTY-FIVE

It's like I'm in a dream.

I'm standing in front of Trixie's apartment door. My niece is only a few feet away. I can hardly breathe!

Knock, knock.

A black kid answers the door and I immediately deflate. "Bloody hell. I thought this was the right address. Sorry." I look at my piece of paper again. "But it says 120 and this is apartment 120, isn't it?"

"Yeah. You've got the right place. You must be Aunt Grace."

"Yes! And you are…?"

"Nate."

I reach out and pump his hand. "Nate, how the heck are ya? "

"Great."

The rest of the family pours in. Trixie looks exactly like me, only bigger-boned. It's freaking me out a little. The older boy, who must be Jeremy, is a handsome dude, with a tiny Chinese girlfriend and the sweetest little baby I've ever seen, resting on her hip.

"How is it possible that you have the world's nicest-looking family?" I shout.

"It's a terrible burden. Hello, Aunt Grace."

We hug each other and then with her arm around my shoulder she introduces her family. "This is Jeremy, and his girlfriend, Jiao, and their baby, Sunni; the one with the dimples is Nate. Say hello, everybody."

They all come forward at the same time with cries of disbelief.

"No way! You're like an old mom!" says Nate.

"You're charming," I say.

"Great to meet you." Jeremy shakes my hand and doesn't take his eyes off me. "I can't believe we have a relative we never knew about."

"A relative with centre court seats!" Nate adds.

I hold out my hand. "About that. Apparently I was mistaken.

Jonathan doesn't have season's tickets, but he said if you visit he'd set something up."

It's impossible not to be happy, looking at their excitement.

"Is there any chance I could hold that baby? She's precious! How old is she?"

"Thirteen months." Jiao hands her to me. "She's usually good with strangers."

I reach over and take her in my arms. She's so tiny and light. "What a sweetheart you are!"

She stares at me with her finger in her mouth, not quite sure about things. I see her look at her grandmother and then me again. "Even she can see the resemblance! How about that?"

Trixie puts her hands up. "Okay, knock it off, everyone. Let the poor woman take her coat off."

Jiao takes her baby back and I try and gather my wits. "I couldn't get some water?"

"Frig water. Do you want a beer?"

"Great."

We settle ourselves in the kitchen of this modest apartment. There's not a lot of space, but this seems to be where they hang out. There's sports equipment around and a lot of baby toys. It's lived in, as it should be.

Gradually I find out that Jeremy works as a bus driver, and Nate is currently "finding himself" at Community College. It's hard to believe that Jiao has her master's in nursing, when she looks about fourteen. They want to know all about us, so I fill them in. Nate tells me he loves cars, and gets excited when he hears about my 1955 Pontiac. I promise him someday he'll see it.

Eventually they leave Trixie and me alone with our beer. We make short work of the bowl of chips, and soon she opens another bag and dumps it in.

"This is the extent of my canapes," Trixie laughs. "Never did get the hang of cooking. Not much time for extracurricular activities."

"How lucky you are, with two amazing sons and that beautiful grandchild."

"Sunni is pretty cute, like her mother. They have the same temper, too. You should see the way Jiao bosses Jeremy about. She's this tiny little thing but she rules the roost. I can't wait until they can get a place of their own."

"Do you have a husband?"

"Not anymore. He decided to break up a fight at a corner store and got himself stabbed in the process. Nate was two at the time. I've never forgiven him for dying like that."

"Oh, Trixie, that's awful."

"What's awful is that I was left on my own. His family never liked me, so they weren't much help. I have this awful habit of surrounding myself with people who let me down."

"It must have been so difficult raising sons on your own. How did you keep them out of trouble? It certainly seems like you've done a great job."

"They were always in trouble, but I used to embarrass them in front of their friends by dragging them out of parties or trailing them in my car. I told them point blank that I would kill them if they ever got themselves killed like their daddy. It's running after them that turned my hair white."

"I admire you."

"Don't. I'm not a great mom. I yell and scream too much. It's a habit left over from trying to scare the shit out of them so that they'd listen me. Me and my wooden spoon."

"Sorry...the admiration is still there."

"Suit yourself."

"How do you make your living?"

"I'm a seamstress."

"That is insane! I like to sew too! But I'd never be able to make a career out of it. Do you have your own shop?"

"Hardly. That would require money. I work from here. I have a steady stream of regulars, thank god."

"I make dog sweaters. That's the extent of my talent."

"Mom used to sew some."

"Did she? Oh gosh, that makes me so happy. We all have a connection somehow."

"She used to save buttons. I loved that jar. I took it with me when I left. She probably missed that more than me."

"I doubt that very much. Would I be able to see it?"

"They're only buttons."

"Please."

She gets up and leaves me at the table. My heart is so full already and I've only been here a couple of hours. She brings it back and hands it to me. It's an ornate jar and every button in it is different and special, not your ordinary variety. Some of them look like costume jewellery.

My eyes well up with tears.

"Ah, hell," Trixie says. "Don't go bawling."

"I'm sorry," I sniff. "It's just that they belonged to her. I missed her so much when I was growing up. I thought she left me behind and forgot about me, but she didn't."

Trixie makes a face. "She didn't think of you that much, if she didn't tell me about you. She never talked about anything from before I was born."

I put down the jar with a bang. "Then you know nothing about what we went through as children. We were trapped in a cult and we were sexually abused. You name it, it happened to us, so don't you dare say mean things about her. Your relationship is your own business, but when I think of my sister, I think of the little girl with long blonde hair that used to wipe away my blood with her hands, who always made sure I got extra dessert, and kept me company at night when our mom was getting beaten up and raped by the same twisted man who was raping us."

She doesn't answer back this time. So ends day one of our family reunion.

Over the rest of the weekend, I end up telling Trixie everything I can remember about her mom, and she tells me of a father who disappeared when she was a baby and a mother who was emotionally unavailable, as if she was afraid to love her daughter in case something happened. The drinking got worse as Trixie got older and sometimes she was taken away from Maria by social services. It was a bad situation all around. If only Maria had reached out for help. I'm sure her guilt about leaving me behind was one of the reasons for her inability to cope. I tell Trixie that. It was a pain so deep, she couldn't tell her daughter about me, because then Trixie would ask, "Why didn't you go back and get her?"

By Sunday, we are emotionally drained. The boys have been in and out the whole time, with Jiao taking Sunni out for most of the days to give us some space.

I'll say goodbye to them tonight, seeing as they have to work tomorrow morning. There's a part of me that would love to call Fletcher up and tell him to come and get me, for I am weary beyond belief. But the drive home alone will afford me the time I need to rehash everything that my niece and I shared with each other.

What I do know is that I love Trixie with all my heart. She's a good, good person who's had some unlucky breaks that she didn't let defeat her. I know she still has a lot of anger towards her mother, but I believe I've given her an opportunity to look at her mom in a more sympathetic light.

I INSIST ON TAKING THEM OUT FOR DINNER. "MY TREAT! WHATEVER YOUR HEART desires!"

"Even appetizers and desserts?" Nate wants to know.

"All of it...the more the merrier!'

We have a jolly old time with Sunni in a high chair banging her sippy cup with delight. I take a million pictures with my phone.

While we sip our coffee and eat our cake and ice cream, I tell them my plans for the summer. "Just let me know what weeks are good for you guys, and I'll have the farmhouse ready for you. My granddaughter, Melissa, and her friend Juni will be down at some point too, so we'll have to coordinate who's staying where and when, but I can't wait to see Sunni at the shore. I'll buy her beach toys and we'll keep them at the farmhouse for whenever she visits."

"That sounds really nice," Trixie sighs. "I can't remember the last time we had a vacation."

"That's because we've never had one," Nate says.

"You're right. We've never had one."

"You have a standing invitation for the rest of your lives."

It's ridiculous how hard it is to say goodbye to them. We part in the parking lot; I'll go back to the motel and they'll head home.

I hug them all and save my biggest for Trixie. "Goodbye, honey.

Take care of yourself and call me whenever you want to. If you ever need anything, I'm always here, okay?"

"Okay, Mom."

When my lip quivers, she hits me. "Don't get all sappy! Jesus, you're a pain."

"Fine! Take off, will ya?"

I march to my car and they toot the horn as they drive by.

WHEN I PULL INTO THE YARD AROUND SUPPERTIME THE NEXT DAY, FLETCHER and Nan are at our kitchen table with a big bowl of spaghetti and meatballs waiting for me. God, I love being home.

Naturally I tell them about my trip and I whip out my phone to show them the pictures. I can't wait to hear what Nan says.

She stares down at the picture. "What am I looking at?"

"We're at the restaurant. Look, they're all waving."

"You got the wrong family. These people are black."

"I know! Isn't that fabulous? And look at Jiao and baby Sunni, they should be in commercials!"

"How did they end up black?"

"How do you think, Nan? Trixie married a black man. These are his sons. What I wouldn't give to be such a gorgeous mocha colour. You know some day, the whole world will be like this."

"Where's the mother?"

I take the phone back and wipe my finger across the screen. "Here."

"Merciful heavens! She could be you!"

"Let's see." Fletcher reaches for the phone. "Wow! That is incredible."

"I know! It's beyond my wildest dream to know that I'm related to this fabulous family. I can't wait for everyone to meet each other."

Fletcher and Nan say they'll do the dishes because I look beat. I take a bath, crawl into bed, and am joined by my best buddy, Beulah, who tries to get as close to my face as possible. I'm drowning in fluffy fur when sleep overtakes me.

NATE AND I BECOME INTERNET BUDDIES; HE HAS TIME OFF BETWEEN CLASSES, unlike his brother. Then he becomes friends with Melissa and Juni, and suddenly Jonathan knows what's going on in Fredericton before I do. Every Sunday becomes Skype day and we get to see Sunni bouncing on one screen and Ryder on another.

I hold up the pets so everyone can see them and when I show them Beulah, Trixie falls over laughing. When I tell her how much she cost, the hilarity ends.

"Jesus Christ Almighty! Do you know what I could do with eight thousand dollars?"

Jonathan butts in. "Gee, Mom, I can't imagine why you think you and Trixie are related."

"What's that supposed to mean?" Trixie wants to know.

"He means you swear like me."

"When I hear something that's batshit crazy, yes, I do."

It absolutely blows my mind that with these computers, you can connect with your family on a daily basis, if need be. People who haven't even met are joking around like they've known each other all their lives. It might be my imagination, but I think there's a little harmless flirting going on between Nate and Juni. I'll keep my mouth shut. I wonder if poor Eugene Yokohama knows.

Three weeks before Christmas, Jonathan and Whitney tell us they're getting married and that she's expecting a baby in the new year. We hoot and holler our good wishes.

"It's just a small affair," Jonathan says, "but we'd like you all to come."

"Thank you," Trixie says, "but I can't afford—"

"It's on me, cousin."

"It's too much—"

"Shut your gob," I yell at her. "Just enjoy the party!"

And so commences the best time we've ever had. A private jet flies into the Port Hawkesbury Airport to pick Fletcher and Nan and I up, then it wings over to Fredericton and picks up Trixie's crowd, who are so beside themselves they can't stop laughing. It's the first time I've seen a genuine smile on Trixie's face.

She settles into a seat beside me. "I can't believe this is happening."

I pat her knee. "Obviously Fletcher and I don't take advantage of

Jonathan's wealth all the time, but it sure comes in handy for a special treat now and then. And you and the boys deserve it."

"This is the nicest thing anyone's ever done for me, and I haven't even met Jonathan, not properly."

"You'll love him, but he can be a bit of a prig about swearing."

"I'll be on my best behaviour."

"Fuck that! Forget everything and relax."

A couple of town cars are at the airport to pick us up and drop us off at our luxury hotel, the Strand on West 37th Street. We have three suites that join together and I get such a kick out of the reactions of not only the Bailey crowd, but Fletcher and Nan too. Nobody can believe that this is how some people live.

My New York family meets my Maritime family in the lobby. Even Deanne, Andre, and baby Ryder are here, along with Jonathan, Whitney, Melissa, Juni, and my old pal Linn. There are sixteen of us in all. The entire chaotic scene gives me chills. After so many years of feeling alone in the world, this eclectic mix of people seems like a dream. They all belong to me in one way or another.

Jonathan takes us to a swanky restaurant, the type that has dribbles of food on the plate instead of a homemade meal. It costs him a fortune, so I don't tell him that we're all going back to the hotel to order pizza afterward.

Whitney looks wonderful. A little weight suits her, and it's obvious she and Jonathan are madly in love. I can't believe the difference in Jonathan. He's become his own man and laughs easily and often. And now that they've both moved on, there is no discomfort between him and Deanne. She is excited about Whitney's baby and can't wait for play dates with Ryder.

Jonathan takes me aside at one point after dinner and looks around to make sure no one is listening.

"Whitney wants to keep it a secret for now, but I want you to know that we're having a little boy and we plan on naming him Aaron James, after both our dads."

Aaron's face swims in front of mine, the laughing boy who made my life bearable in Halifax so long ago. His funny, silly demeanour and protective presence. The tender love he gave my son.

I hug my boy close. "Thank you. Thank you."

He kisses the top of my head.

And true to his word, Jonathan gets Trixie, Jiao, and the boys court-side seats to a Knicks game and even takes them back to the locker room to meet the players. He also insists on buying them Knicks jerseys. By the time they get back to the hotel, where Fletch, Nan, and I are babysitting Sunni, Jeremy and Nate are completely blissed out. They talk over each other describing their night.

Trixie's eyes sparkle as she hugs me good night. "Your son and my now favourite cousin, Jonathan, have made my boys happier than I've ever seen them. We will never forget this. Never."

"It's just as much a thrill for us as it is for you. Jonathan never had a sibling and I know he missed that. To suddenly have a first cousin is amazing for him. He told me so."

We spend the next day touring the city, but poor old Nan is completely at a loss with the noise and confusion of the traffic and begs off after only a few hours. Melissa and Juni become the tour guides as I go back to the hotel with Nan. Once she goes down for a nap, I take a minute to put my feet up and am just drifting off when I hear a light knock on my door.

It's Trixie.

"I came back as well. I can't keep up with those youngsters."

"Is Fletcher still going strong?"

"He's leading the pack."

"That makes me happy."

"May I talk to you for a moment?"

"Sure. I'll order some tea."

We settle ourselves once the tea arrives with an assortment of sandwiches. Trixie is on her second cup before she begins.

"I've had a hard time sleeping lately."

"All the excitement, I guess."

"No. It's because of my mother. Ever since you told me about what happened to her, I've been feeling very guilty that I didn't make her life a little easier. I was a mouthy brat who spent most of my life hating her for her weakness and her drinking. Now I'm ashamed of that. It was easier to blame her and pretend that everything was her fault."

"Are you sorry I told you? Maybe I shouldn't have said anything."

"No. The truth is always better. It's just more uncomfortable for me."

"Listen, Trixie, you were a little girl who needed protection and your mother wasn't able to provide that. Of course you resented her; she wouldn't want you to beat yourself up about it now. When I was in her apartment I was so angry with her. I couldn't believe she let herself down like that, and it bothered me that I was furious with her, but the emotions were real and needed to be felt. That's all. Acknowledge it and let it go."

"It's not easy."

"I know."

She looks out the window at the spectacular view. "I also want to tell you that I loved my husband. I know I said I couldn't forgive him for dying, but I didn't mean it. I just hated the world for taking him from me. Jesse was a good man, I never wanted anyone else."

"I wish I'd known him."

Her head goes down and her voice quivers. "It's all my fault that he died. I'm to blame."

"I'm sure that's not true."

"We were arguing about nothing, like you do when you're tired and the kids are underfoot. I told him to leave me alone, to go get some milk or something. That's why he was in that corner store. He saw a man start to beat his girlfriend and he intervened. If I'd just shut my mouth, he'd still be here."

She struggles not to cry. I get out of my chair and sit beside her, taking her hands in my own. "I know exactly how you feel. I blamed myself for my husband's car accident as well. I know how it destroys you for a long time. It's a terrible burden and ultimately does nothing but cause pain. You didn't kill your husband any more than I did. Forgive yourself. Jesse would want you to. And think how proud he must be with the way you've raised his sons. You honour his memory every day being a strong mother. You are a wonderful person, Trixie. Even if your mother never said it, she knew it. Believe me."

Now the strong and sassy Trixie does cry. I'm sure it's been many years, if ever, that she's let herself be vulnerable in front of anyone. I rub her back and stay beside her, just to let her know I'm here.

Eventually her tears dry up and she wipes her eyes with the linen napkin that accompanied our lunch.

"Thanks," she says.

"Any time. Why don't you have a hot bath? It's my cure all for everything."

"Good idea."

She hugs me before she leaves and I have to pinch myself once more that she is my sister's child. It feels like I'm hugging Maria too.

That night Jonathan, Whitney, Melissa, and Juni stay at the hotel, along with Whitney's relatives. The wedding is in the morning, beside the rooftop garden at the top of the Strand Hotel. There'll be brunch after.

We're all up early. Melissa has arranged for a stylist to come to the hotel and do our hair and makeup. I think Trixie is more excited about this than anything else. It's not often she gets to spend time doing girlie things. Jiao is also thrilled and it makes me happy to see them laugh together.

"So how is Eugene Yokohama?" I ask Juni.

She blushes. "We're just friends."

"Tell her why," Melissa smirks.

"No reason!"

"She likes Nate. Did you know that, Trixie? Juni likes your son!"

"Hush up, Melissa!"

"All the girls like Nate, so join the club."

"Speaking about boys, any new ones on the horizon?" I ask Melissa.

"My career is too important. I don't want a creepy boy tying me down."

"I'll remember you said that," I laugh.

I help Nan get dressed in a pink suit I bought her in Baddeck. I also bought something new so Jonathan would be proud. The dress and jacket cost too much if you ask me, but I do look nice. Fletcher gives me a wolf-whistle.

"You are going to be prettier than the bride."

"You are earning big brownie points for that, mister."

"Good. I love seeing you look so happy."

"Oh, I am. More than I deserve."

"You deserve everything, Grace."

"I don't deserve you."

"Well, that's true."

I whack his arm as we leave our room.

Whitney is breathtaking in her fitted lace gown, and Jonathan stands proudly as he takes her hand. It's a simple ceremony, over in ten minutes, and we all burst into applause as they kiss one another. Brunch for the forty or so guests is served swiftly and with great fanfare. Everything is delicious and Fletcher says he's off his diet today as he heads for the waffle bar.

About two hours later, it's all over, but later that night we get together to go to a Broadway show and then dinner at an Italian restaurant downtown. Linn is at the hotel babysitting Sunni, so it's a real date for Jeremy and Jiao, who spend the whole night holding hands.

And seemingly in the blink of an eye, it's over. We hug goodbye with promises of summer visits at the farmhouse and endless thanks for a fabulous time, all of us knowing that the next morning, we'll be back in our usual routine, but with memories to last forever.

When we fly into Fredericton, the boys give me bear hugs, and it's torture to say goodbye to our little Sunni. I'm mad about this kid.

Trixie holds onto me for a long time. We don't need words.

Back to Cape Breton, back to our humble abode, where a lot of pissed-off pets are ready to let us know that it was a pretty crummy trick leaving them behind. But they don't sulk for long. That's what's so awesome about animals. Too bad humans don't catch on.

Poor old Nan is tuckered out. "I can't imagine living in that city for more than a few days. It's like losing your breath in the rush. Thank God I live in the country. I'm never leaving again."

Once more I head down to Harvey and Dora's with gifts for their kind babysitting duties. "I hope one day we'll be able to return the favour. You two should go on a cruise or something."

"I'd love to go on a fishing trip to Scotland," Harvey says.

"You would," Dora grumps. "Why not Paris?"

"I can't speak French."

"You're hopeless! One day I'm just going to leave and you won't know where I am!"

"Promise?"

WE HAVE A HARD WINTER, LOTS OF BLOWING SNOW AND BLIZZARD CONDITIONS. We're not used to it anymore. Our winters have been mild for a few years, the snow usually turning to rain. I've noticed the bad weather is getting Nan down. No one is travelling much on the roads, and she has no interest in venturing outside, so she's not seeing anyone. I mention it to Fletcher one night at supper.

"She's really down in the dumps. I wonder if I should take her to the doctor."

"Everyone gets a little low in the winter. Do you think it's serious?"

"I'm not sure. I'm going to keep an eye on her."

My afternoons consist of sitting with Nan doing my best to cheer her up, offering to play Scrabble or a game of Crazy Eights. She shakes her head listlessly. Not even Beulah makes her happy, and finally I make an appointment with her GP. She tells him she sometimes has chest pain.

Fletcher is upset. "Why didn't you say anything?"

"No sense in worrying you."

The doctor sends her to a specialist, who diagnoses her as having congestive heart failure, brought on by coronary artery disease.

When we bring her home with her medication, she tosses it aside. "All these fancy terms. I'm ninety-three! I'm going to die of something. What difference does it make? If it's not this, it'll be something else."

"Don't say that," Fletcher says.

Nan looks at the both of us. "I'm tired. I love you both dearly, but I'm tired. All of my close friends are gone. All that's left is sitting in front of the television day after day. I hope and pray I die in my sleep. Promise me you won't moan and groan when I'm gone. I've lived longer than I had any right to. I've spent decades without my husband and daughter and son-in-law. I'd like to be with them now."

Nan dies in her sleep two weeks later. Can someone wish themselves dead? Her heart was failing, but it was also breaking. I'm glad she's at peace.

We have a private funeral. I tell the family to stay where they are. Only Fletcher and I need to be there.

It's horrible coming home knowing the trailer next to us is empty. Beulah is also in a bad way. She knows something has happened and she spends her days looking out the window at the trailer. Sometimes I take her over to sit on Nan's couch for a few hours. It's good remembering how happy Nan was about moving up here on the hill. We shared some good times.

It's a strange feeling when your elder dies. It dawns on you that you are now the older generation. There are no more buffers between you and death. They say you get wiser as you get older, but I don't feel any wiser. More grateful, perhaps. It took more than six decades for me to grow into my own. A slow learner, but I did get there.

Nan's funeral makes me finally come to terms with burying my sister. I call Trixie and ask if she'd like to come on a weekend and be with me when I do. After she agrees I realize I've been holding my breath.

We wait until Easter. Nan's little trailer makes a perfect guest-house, which we hadn't considered until now. Maybe everyone can come for the summer at the same time.

Only Trixie and Fletcher and I are at the burial. The minister says his prayers over the grave and it's done. Trixie doesn't cry, but I see her shoulders ease when the ceremony is over. I have the same reaction. A great weight has been lifted. One wish I've had since childhood is fulfilled. I know where my sister is and I can come and visit her whenever I want.

I take Trixie down to the farmhouse so she can see where her grandmother grew up.

"This is beautiful." We walk down through the field towards the water. "Why would she want to leave here?"

"She was young. All youngsters want to explore the world."

"I wonder what would have happened if she stayed? A nice normal life, instead of dragging you and my mother around, putting you both in harm's way."

"Who's to say what would've happened? My Aunt Pearl called Trixie a hippy-dippy."

"An irresponsible hippy-dippy."

"She had her good qualities."

Trixie looks at me. "Sorry. I shouldn't talk about your mother like that."

"All of us think our mothers have to be perfect, better than anyone else. It's too bad we don't see them as people until we grow up ourselves."

"The ones who get off the hook are the fathers."

"Do you know who your father is, Trixie? Have you ever thought about trying to find him?"

"No, thank you. I have all the men I want in my life."

Fletcher has supper waiting for us when we get back. We spend a nice evening in front of the fire, and in the morning Trixie starts her long journey home. Before she gets in the car, she turns to me.

"You're the best. Thank you for seeking me out and not taking no for an answer."

"Sometimes being stubborn comes in handy."

Later that night she calls us to tell us she made it home safely. Fletch and I retreat to our chairs and watch a little television, Beulah on Fletcher's lap and Tom and Jerry on mine. The wind is blowing a gale outside, but it's warm and cozy in here.

It doesn't take much to make a person happy.

AARON JAMES WILLINGDON IS BORN ON THE FIRST OF MAY AND IS A HEALTHY eight pounds.

Personally I think all babies are pretty hideous at first, but it's amazing how you ignore the misshapen head, stork bites, and rashes when it's your own flesh and blood. All we see is blond fuzz, a button nose, and the most beautifully shaped lips.

I resist the temptation to immediately fly to New York. The new parents need this time to themselves, and I can look at all the Instagram photos his father is posting. Melissa calls me in tears.

"You should see how perfect he is! I honestly see a resemblance between Ryder and Aaron. Oh gosh, they are going to be such good pals. It almost makes me want to have a baby of my own."

"Really?"

"Of course not! But he's so cute!"

After six weeks I can't stand it and quickly pop down to New York. Aaron is beyond adorable at this point. His mom seems to be a natural, and Jonathan is an old pro. Holding Aaron in my arms is like Christmas morning, pure delight. He always falls asleep when I have him, so I'm allowed to hold him quite a bit. He and I rock together and I sing songs from *The Sound of Music*.

I only stay for four days, which probably feels like four weeks to Whitney, but she's a good sport. I make sure I run over to Deanne's and make a fuss of Ryder too. Deanne tells me she's pregnant again.

"How old are you?"

"Too old for a two-year-old and a newborn, that's for sure."

"Doesn't matter. It's marvellous news. Make sure you look after yourself."

"I hope it's another boy. I can't imagine trying to raise another teenage daughter in my late fifties."

"Good luck, my dear. You're going to need it."

BEFORE WE KNOW IT, IT'S SUMMER ONCE MORE AND THE NEW BRUNSWICK gang comes for two weeks to stay at the farmhouse. Melissa and Juni show up for a week and they stay in the trailer, though we spend most days down on the shore. I make big picnics and on really hot days Fletcher joins us in the water.

Nate and Juni are still smitten with each other, but I pretend I don't notice. Nothing ruins a romance faster than an adult catching wind of it. But Trixie sidles up to me one afternoon to whisper in my ear. "I hope she doesn't break his heart."

"She might. It's called life."

Nate is enamoured with Fletcher's garage and can't believe his good fortune when we let him drive the Pontiac a couple of times. He follows Fletcher around when he's not teasing Juni.

Sunni loves to splash in the water. Is there anything sweeter than a little one at the beach? Of course, we're not the ones running after her. Her poor parents don't get much rest.

It's such a pleasure to see Trixie relax. She actually looks years younger than when I first met her.

As for me, I've never been more content. It's like my whole life has been leading up to this moment.

Which is why I'm pissed off that my cancer's back.

CHAPTER TWENTY-SIX

I *think.*

I'm telling no one until I have some tests, and maybe not even then.

My first clue is how tired I am coming back from meeting my grandson, Aaron. I did nothing the entire time I was there, but when I get on the plane to come home, a great exhaustion falls over me. I put it down to travelling, but when I don't feel up to volunteering for the Red Cross, I get an uneasy feeling.

Fletcher shrugs. "So what if you want a year off? You run around for them every year. Time for new blood to take over."

I still try to help out in the church hall, but I have an accident while making dinner for the community play. I pick up a large pot of cooked potatoes and can't quite get it to the sink. Lucky for me the water splashes in the other direction and no one else is in the immediate vicinity.

Delima's beside herself. "What do we do now? Supper's almost ready!"

Gladys to the rescue. "There's a huge box of Minute Rice here. We'll have that." She starts pouring the rice into another large pot.

"We can't have rice! We've never had rice!"

"There's always a first time."

Everyone says the rice is a nice change.

It's a beautiful September and Fletcher suggests we take a trip around the trail. "Maybe we can spend another night at the Keltic Lodge."

It takes everything I have to agree that it's a great idea.

When you're in your own routine, you can get away with being quiet. Fletcher spends most of his day in the garage, so he's not with me, but here in the car is another matter.

"You're not saying much. Not having a good time?"

I pat his knee. "I always have a good time with you. I think I'm just missing everyone. It's been such an incredible year, but with Nan gone, it feels lonesome."

"I know what you mean. The other day I heard some gossip and I started over to the trailer because I knew she'd love it and had to stop halfway there."

"What was the gossip?"

"That Harvey and Dora might be getting a divorce."

My mouth drops open. "And you didn't tell me?"

"I forgot about it after that."

This news shocks me. "She put up with him for forty-five years and now she decides life would be better without him? Wow."

"You get older, you realize your time is limited."

Makes sense to me.

When we get home I invite Dora up for lunch. Might as well hear it from the horse's mouth.

"Is it true?"

Dora shoves a sandwich in her mouth. "Yes and no," she mumbles.

"Explain yourself."

"I told Delima and Janet Pickup that I was thinking of getting a divorce. Naturally, it made the rounds of the village and got back to Harvey."

"What did he say?"

"'Wanna go to Paris?'"

"You sly dog!" We high-five each other. "When are you going?"

"In a few weeks. Can you guys look after the critters?"

"Of course! It will be nice to pay you back for all the free baby-sitting."

I GO DOWN TO TAKE THEIR TWO ROTUND LABS OUT IN THE MORNING, BECAUSE I find I'm too weary to deal with them in the evening. Fletcher brings them up after supper and takes all the dogs out for a walk on the hill. The first time I don't join him, he gives me a funny look. I pretend I'm busy.

But after a while I can't ignore the pain in my hip and go to my doctor for tests. "Don't tell Fletcher."

"I can't tell him, but you should."

"Wait until we know."

The phone rings a couple of days later and the doctor wants to see me. Nothing good ever comes from this. I really want Fletcher with me, but I can't face it if he's with me, so I go alone. He thinks I'm shopping for a couple of new outfits. Men are so gullible.

I wait for my death sentence in his office. He comes in and sits down with a resigned air. I guess it's true that body language accounts for most of our communication.

"Well?"

"It's back."

"How long have I got?"

"I'm not answering that question. I've had people live for years when I thought they'd be dead in months. You don't want to put a thought in your head that will take root. You had great luck with chemo the last time. I think that's the course of action again."

"No. I'm not wasting the rest of my life feeling like shit." I stand up. "Gotta go."

"Grace..."

"Thank you, Doctor. Don't call the house."

The hospital hallway is endless. I'm walking but I never get to the front door. I'm in a deep well and just need to make it to the top so I can breathe.

It takes me forever to get to the Pontiac in the parking lot. It's like a mirage in the desert that keeps fading in and out. When I finally open the door and get in, I feel embraced by my wonderful aunts. They comfort me as I cry. I hoped the doctor would say I had arthritis and my red blood cells were low. Anything but this.

Right now, deep inside, I'm still nine-year-old Amazing Grace, but when I look in the rear-view mirror, an older woman looks back at me. When did that happen? All my days of fighting took a toll.

I have no business driving the car and should call Fletcher to come and get me, but I feel like I need to get home on my own.

As I drive home I decide I'm going to tell Fletcher right away, but I don't have to. When I pull into the driveway he's sitting on the patio in his grandmother's rocker. He stands up when I get out of the car and we look at each other.

He knows.

I put my face in my hands, and the next moment he has me in his arms. Then he picks me up as if he's carrying me over the threshold and takes me into the house. He sits in his recliner with me in his lap and strokes my hair gently.

"It's all right. I'm here."

"I'm sorry, Fletcher. I'm so sorry."

"Hush now. We can do this. You did it before and you'll do it again."

"I'm not going to go through that again. I want to be present while I'm here."

He doesn't say anything.

"Is that bad?'

"Hell yes, it's bad! Are your seriously going to tell me that you refuse to fight for yourself, when you have everything to live for? We have a family now! A great group of crazy people who want to be with us, who want us in their lives. And you're going to disappoint them by giving up? That's not the Grace I know, and it's not the Grace they know. So you're going to pick yourself up and face this with as much determination as you did the last time. You've got this! For god's sake, you're a grandmother to Aaron, and like a grandmother to Ryder, Sunni, and Finn!"

"Who's Finn?"

"Oh yeah, Andre called. Deanne had a little boy this morning."

"Wonderful."

"They need you hollering at them on the beach next summer. Now, I made some chicken soup. Would you like some?"

"Yes."

He takes me by the hand and we have supper together. The dogs and cats watch us as we eat.

You take all this for granted. You do it every day of your life, eating with your loved ones around you, but you hardly ever stop to think about what a gift it is. How fortunate we are to have this quiet time at the end of the day.

Life is in the ordinary moments. And I want a few billion more.

Fletch is right. I've got this. I start my chemo immediately, much to the doctor's relief, but I still don't tell my family.

About a month into treatment, Trixie calls to say she might come down for the weekend. Without thinking, I say, "Sorry, I'm busy with chemo this weekend."

"Fucking hell!" she yells. "Just fucking, fucking hell!"

She slams the phone down.

I love her.

I call her back and she lets it ring about six times before she picks up and gives me shit. "How dare you make me love you? How dare you not be here for me and my boys? You are a selfish bitch and I hate you right now!"

I can't stop laughing. She begins to chuckle too and soon we're gasping for air.

"Stop laughing, Grace! It's not funny. Why didn't you tell us?"

"Why should I? You'd only worry. Now I beg you, do not tell the others. I don't want anyone fretting, because I'm beating this bastard again."

"Oh, I have no doubt you'll beat it. All you have to do is give the big C one of your almighty pissed-off looks and it'll shrivel like a pecker in ice-cold water."

"I'm so glad I can talk to you. This makes things a thousand times easier."

There's silence on the end of the phone. I think I hear sniffling.

"Sorry, Trixie. I didn't mean to burden you with this."

"It's okay," she says quietly. "I'm just not ready to have the boogeyman put you in the bog."

"What?"

"It's something my mother always said when she'd threaten me with something. 'You don't want the boogeyman to put you in the bog.' What a stupid thing to say to a kid. It scared the crap out of me."

"Oh my god." I'm lightheaded. I can hear someone moaning, but I don't know it's me.

Trixie yells into the phone. "What's wrong, Grace? What's wrong?"

"The boogeyman killed my mother and put her in the bog."

CHAPTER TWENTY-SEVEN

"Who killed your mother?"

"That's why I was never able to find her! Maria must have seen him do it and run for her life. They didn't leave me behind, they didn't forget me! Ed Wheeler told everyone that Maria ran away and Mom went after her and they believed him. That's why your mother was so messed up. Who wouldn't drink if they saw their mother being murdered?"

"Who's Ed Wheeler?"

"The man, the man I told you about, the man who raped me and my mother and your mother. Someone who managed to destroy a whole family with his disgusting depravity. I'm going to kill him. Do you hear me? I'm going to kill him!"

"Grace, stop it! He's probably dead now anyway. You're using up precious energy. I'm going to hang up and I want you to tell Fletcher. He'll know what to do. I'll call you later tonight. I have to go."

She hangs up and I understand why. She has her own guilt and sorrow to deal with.

I don't seek out Fletcher because I can't get off the chair. My mind whirls as all the little signs drift into place like fresh snow. Mom went out to find money and food. Ed somehow suspected what she was doing and dragged her out to the bog to confront her. Maria went looking for Mom, and must have eventually run to the bog to check.

How did Ed kill Mom? Did he strangle her? She always had red marks on her neck. Or maybe he held her head down and drowned her, then slowly watched her disappear into the muddy water and sink to the bottom of the muck.

Maria had to run away. If she'd come back for me, he might have killed us both. She protected me by leaving. But how does a twelve-year-old with no money make her way in the world? The only scenario that comes to my mind is horrific. If she was in foster care, there would be records, and I was never able to find any. She obviously didn't go to the police—or did she? Maybe no one believed her. We'll never know what she endured.

When Fletch comes in for supper, I spill the whole story. His shock is as drastic as mine. All he keeps saying is "What? What?" Like he can't comprehend what I'm saying, and who could? Things like this don't happen to people you know. The big bad world always happens to other people. I should know better.

"What should we do?" he says.

"I am going to finish my chemo before I do anything, because I have a fight on my hands, and I need to be strong. You say I have a lot to live for? You bet your bottom dollar I do. I'm going to find my mother's body and bring her home. And then I'm going to find Ed Wheeler."

"Grace—"

"If this man is still alive, I want to see his face when I tell him I know what he did to my mother. He thinks he got away with this. Well, I'm about to burst his stinking bubble."

"Grace, please. I don't want you to burn out."

"I'm burning *up*. And that's a good thing. I'm too busy to have fucking cancer."

I COMPLETE MY ROUND OF CHEMO LIKE I SAID I WOULD. SO FAR IT SEEMS TO BE working, but that's almost the furthest thing from my mind these days. I've reprogrammed my brain not to wallow in self-pity. Lots of people get cancer and lots of people are cured. I'm going to be one of them.

The family still doesn't know about the cancer, but I tell them how I'm meditating now, and going to yoga class. I'm also swimming to build up my strength and Fletcher and I and the critters still walk every day. Yesterday I even made it to the top of my hill.

Dora bought me a juicer and spent a whole week showing me how to use it. I've never had so much green goop in my life. Fletch and I have bought a dehydrater, too, to dry fruits and vegetables.

I know I still have to wait for the test results, but I'm confident that the things I'm doing are helping me beat this. It's time to tell Jonathan my plans.

Jonathan meets Fletch and I in a hotel in Guelph, a far cry from the crappy motel I stayed in the last time I came looking for my family. The farm is only twenty minutes away. We sit with our morning coffee in the dining room of the hotel.

"Mom, you look like you've lost weight. Are you sure you're no overdoing this diet business?"

"My appetite hasn't been great since I found out about this. It's only temporary. I'll feel much better soon."

"Look, Mom, I understand that your suspicions may very well be true, but what if you're wrong?"

"I have to know one way or another. If the police find my mother's body in the bog, then I can finally put her to rest."

Fletcher takes a sip of coffee. "Do you think the police will investigate? Or even take you seriously?"

"There are case files on me floating around Guelph, Brampton, Kitchener, and Waterloo that say I was raped. They wanted me to testify. There's also a social worker's files on the children who went into foster care after the fire. On top of that I can always get in touch with Helen and she can verify that Ed Wheeler did indeed abuse us and that he was in charge there."

Jonathan nods. "We can always hire a Canadian detective to look into all this."

Fletch laughs. "I think you're looking at her."

No time like the present. We drive right to the police station, where we ask to speak to the police chief. He eventually shows up and introduces himself as Chief Doug Howard and asks us to come into his office. It takes me about half an hour to explain the situation. He doesn't do much talking, but he does seem to be listening.

"So this would've been when?"

"When I was nine years old, in 1962. That's when they disappeared. The fire wasn't until 1965. That was the year they asked me to testify against him, but I was too frightened. He was still living in

Guelph when I lived here in 1988. Is there any way you could track him down, or find out if he's alive?"

"First things first. We'll have to go back and look through the records and see if all this adds up; we need a probable cause to conduct an investigation."

"How many Bibles do I have to swear on to convince you that I know with absolute certainty my mother's body is in that bog? I know it's been fifty years and that's about as cold a case as you're going to get, but my mother deserves peace and I deserve to have her back."

Fletcher puts his hand on my arm. "Grace, calm down. He's here to help you."

Take a deep breath. "Sorry. It's been a tough time."

He passes me a pad of lined paper. "Why don't you write down the facts and we'll take it from here. Let me know where you're staying and I'll be in touch if I find out anything."

"But you can do it soon, I hope?"

"Mrs. Parsons, police work is not quite how they portray it on television. We don't solve things in sixty minutes."

"We realize that." Jonathan glances at me. "We very much appreciate your time and being kind enough to hear us out. This has been a terrible burden for my mother, not knowing what happened to her only parent all these years, so the idea of being this close to finding out is naturally making us anxious."

"I'll do the best I can."

It takes me another hour to write everything down and by then I'm done. Once more we head for a hotel, where Jonathan takes out his credit card.

"You can't be paying for everything," Fletcher says. "We can contribute."

"Please let me do this. I owe my mother."

"Well, I'm buying dinner."

We don't hear anything for two days. I beg Jonathan to go home because I feel guilty that he's missing his family, and tell him we can handle it.

"I see more of my family now than if I was home, thanks to email,

Skype, texting, tweeting, and the actual phone. Believe me, I'm not missing anything. And I can do my work on my laptop."

Fletch and I look at each other.

"Remember the old days, Grace, when you left and people didn't see you until you got back?"

"That was often a good thing."

The phone finally rings and it's Officer Howard asking us to come to the police station. We try not to get a speeding ticket on our way there. He ushers us into the office.

"Well, I can tell you that Edward Wheeler is alive."

"Naturally. Evil people live forever."

"He's in prison for sexual assaults against children."

"Gee, there's a surprise!" I shout before Fletcher again touches my arm.

"Sorry."

"We found your records from after the fire, when you went through the foster care system, and we also have confirmation that the fire was indeed in 1965 on the old Wainwright farm, which is now owned by someone else. Based on the validity of all the facts, I think we can go ahead and search the property."

I want to run out of the office there and then, but once again we have to wait for bureaucracy to shift itself. That takes another two days. Fletch and I play cards to pass the time while Jonathan works away in his room.

The morning we are to go out to the site, I'm up before the sun rises. Fletcher's still sleeping so I get dressed in the bathroom after my shower to avoid waking him. I have to wipe off the steam on the mirror, and when I look at my face, the truth is there for everyone to see. What's going to happen today? If there's nothing in the bog, what do I do? And if there's something…what do I do? My teeth are already chattering.

None of us can eat breakfast, so we head out right away to meet the police at the farm. The car is silent. It's all been said.

For some reason I expected the place to look the same as the last time I was here, but it's completely different when we turn down the driveway. Someone has built a large two-storey house and resurrected the barn, which is actually quite beautiful, painted red like in storybooks. It even has a wrought-iron weather vane in the shape of a rooster.

"I'm not sure where I am," I whisper to Fletcher.

We get out of the car and stand among the police vehicles, vans, and a tractor-trailer that brought in the backhoe. The people who live in the house are on their back deck, looking nervous.

Chief Howard comes over to us. "Good morning. I'm glad it's not raining. Makes our lives a lot easier. Now, if you would follow me, Mrs. Parsons, I want you to show our machine operators exactly where to dig."

"I need my husband and son with me. I can't do this alone."

"Of course, I understand."

As I walk towards where I think the entrance to the path used to be, I'm suddenly not so sure of my hypothesis. It's all changed. I don't recognize anything.

"I'm sorry…this is very different. It's been a long time."

Chief Howard doesn't seem worried. "It will come back to you. Take your time."

Stop freaking out and focus! I try to judge where the tree house used to be. When I look over my shoulder, I realize I can use the barn as a landmark. It was farther away from the bog than this, so I keep walking, everyone else trailing behind me. Going on instinct alone, I take a step into the woods.

The first time my sister and I go to the bog, our mom takes us there. She makes us run faster and faster, telling us to hurry up. I laugh with delight as we tear through the woods, stumbling on the wet ground as we wave branches out of the way.

"Over here!"

We hide behind an outcropping of rock and then sit, leaning against the warm hard surface.

My heart races. "Did I do good, Mama?"

She nods. "You're the fastest."

"I can run faster than the devil himself."

My sister turns on me. "Shut up, Grace. You can not."

"I'm Amazing, thank you very much! Amazing girls can do anything!"

Suddenly I'm at the rock, with no recollection of how I got here. "There's the bog." I point.

"We'll take it from here," Chief Howard says. "I want you to go back to the house and we'll keep you updated."

"Can't I stay here?"

Fletcher takes me by the shoulders. "Let them do their job. Come with me."

I follow Fletch and Jonathan back out of the woods as the workers and equipment roll in. The owner of the house comes over to us.

"Are you sure I'll be compensated for the damage to my property? They'll have to push trees over to get that thing in there."

Jonathan says, "Don't worry, sir. I'll take care of it."

Yet more money he's handing out like candy. What am I doing to everyone?

The lady of the house asks if we'd like to sit on the porch while we wait. She even gives us cups of coffee, but then she retreats inside and leaves us be.

We don't talk to each other, just listen to the machinery endlessly grind away deep in the woods. The tension is unbearable. I have to move. I go down into the yard and wander aimlessly, keeping my mind blank. There's a horse in the field by the barn, eating grass by the fence. He ignores me until I tear a handful of weeds and hold it out to him. He comes over with a lazy step and his soft lips nuzzle the palm of my hand.

"Hello, you."

He lets me pat his nose and forelock while I breath in his wonderful horsey smell. "I'm glad you're here."

Just being close to this creature makes me feel better. I'm not even sure how long I stand with him.

The machinery stops.

Fletcher and Jon stand up on the porch. I run over to them. All of us stare at the woods, willing someone to come and tell us what's happening. Eventually we sit down again; it's almost an hour before Chief Howard walks out from among the trees and heads our way. I descend the porch stairs and walk towards him.

When he gets close enough, he takes me by my shoulders. "We found her."

He steadies me when my knees buckle. My head falls onto his chest.

"Thank you," I whisper. "Thank you."

JONATHAN LEAVES FOR HOME THE NEXT DAY. FLETCHER AND I WILL WAIT HERE for the forensic reports and for my mother's remains to be released and cremated.

"I will never forget that you were with me when we found my mother, your grandmother. It made a terrible day a little less painful."

"I'm glad I could help." He gives me a big hug and then reaches out to hug Fletcher as well. "I'll call when I get back to New York. Keep me posted and let me know when you guys finally make it home."

"Will do."

He gives us one more wave before he jumps in the taxi that will take him to the airport.

Fletcher and I go back to our hotel room. The television's on but we're not watching, just lying on the beds, trying to absorb what's happened. I sleep a lot, which Fletch says is a good thing. "You're mentally exhausted. You need to rest."

Three days after we find my mother, Chief Howard calls us to meet him at the station, which we do. He says her remains have been sent to the funeral home, and the undertaker is waiting for our instructions.

"As near as we can tell from the autopsy, your mother was probably strangled before he put her body in the bog."

I nod sadly. "That's what I thought."

"Now, do you want to be involved in this investigation? It will be tough to prosecute, seeing as how it happened so long ago and the only witness is now dead."

"I'm not going to immerse myself in this for one more second. My mother is coming home with me. I've already brought my sister home. That's all the resolution I need. He's in jail where he belongs. Although there is one thing I'd like to do."

"What's that?"

"See him one last time."

Chief Howard looks at me. "Are you sure about this?"

"I want to look in his eyes when I tell him I know he murdered my mother."

"I'll see what I can do."

CHIEF HOWARD IS MY HERO. WHILE FLETCHER WAITS IN THE RENTAL CAR IN THE parking lot of the Central East Correctional Centre in Lindsay, Ontario, I'm in a waiting room with other visitors trying to keep my mind blank so I don't hyperventilate. We're escorted into a room with tables, the chairs on opposite sides. The prisoners are escorted in single file and join their relatives right away. Ed Wheeler shows up at the door and looks around.

Seeing him so old and pathetic helps me. He's a wreck, his disgusting deeds etched all over his face. The prison guard points in my direction. I'm in the chair when he shuffles over and takes a seat. He has no idea who I am, at least not for the first few moments—and then my silver hair must trigger a memory, because his eyes are suddenly wary. He's still a cagey bastard, playing this meek old man, but his eyes are the same as they always were, black wells of nastiness.

"You know who I am, don't you? Grace Fairchild, from the compound."

"Never heard of her."

"You know who I am. Amazing Grace, the little girl you tortured for your own pleasure. You know my sister Ave Maria, another child you forced yourself on. Maria is a successful, beautiful woman, and she told me that you killed our mother, Trixie Fairchild. Surely you remember Trixie? You used to pull her out of our room almost every night."

"You're crazy."

"You strangled my mother when you found out she was going to run away. You killed her and threw her in the bog. Maria saw you do it. She was hidden behind the rock."

His body tenses up and he glares at me. "That's a lie."

"Guess what? We found her body there just a few days ago. The police know you did it. And after Maria and I haul your ass into court and prove it, you are going to spend the rest of your life in jail."

"You have no proof that I did it. Why're you still so interested in me? You keep coming back. Must mean you liked it."

"I came here to tell you that you didn't win. You didn't get away with it. You didn't get one over on me. You and I and Maria all know what you did to my mother, and you will pay for that, whether it's in this lifetime or the next. Now, why don't you slither out of here and go back to the prison cell that makes up your world, you disgusting piece of shit."

I stand up, gather myself, and spit right in his face.

Then I walk out and never look back.

CHAPTER TWENTY-EIGHT

It's the day of my mother's burial.

Trixie's ashes will be interred in a plot beside her mother, Rose, her aunts Pearl and Mae, and her daughter, Maria. Five Fairchild women, together at last.

Besides these five, and Fletcher's Nan, (who makes six), seventeen other members of my family arrive to be with me today, including babies and the housekeeper.

I count them over and over again. Six plus seventeen is twenty-three. Twenty-three people who belong to me. Me. A woman who thought she was alone in the world.

It's cold and there's a stiff breeze in the cemetery. The pastor does his best to make himself heard. I told him to just stick to the basics. The entire village of Baddeck knows what happened to Trixie Fairchild, and we don't need to be reminded of it. We're not remembering how my mother died. We're celebrating the fact that she is home where she belongs.

WE HEAD BACK TO THE TRAILER WHERE DORA, JANET, GLADYS, AND EVEN Delima have a feast waiting for us.

The joint is full to bursting and all I see are happy faces, kids crying, people laughing, and even some flirting. Linn has the church gals enthralled with her recipes, and the dogs are stealing food from everyone's plates when they think people aren't watching.

Melissa asks if she can make a toast. Everyone gathers around.

"I want to say how proud I am of my grandmother, Gee. She never gave up on any of us, and because of that Trixie and her posse are now in our lives forever. Aunt Pearl, Aunt Mae, Aunt Rose, Trixie, and Maria are celebrating the fact that we're together today. So let's raise our glasses to the Fairchild women!"

"The Fairchild women!" everyone's voices ring out.

I hug Melissa.

Fletcher makes eye contact and tosses his head towards the door. I grab a sweater and go outside with him.

"Wanna walk up the hill?"

"Yes."

The two of us head out arm in arm. The cold breeze has died down, thankfully. The sun is trying to shine through the clouds but it's losing the battle. It's late summer now, time for people to get back to those ordinary lives full of ordinary moments.

Fletch and I sit in our Adirondack chairs and look down on our property. We can hear the shouts and merriment through the windows. Jeremy and Nate are outside throwing a football around while Juni cheers from the porch.

My cell phone rings, and I glance at the screen. It's the doctor. Pretend everything is normal. "Hello?"

"Hey, Grace. It's Frank."

"I know who it is. Tell me."

"It's gone."

"Fuck right off!" I hit Fletch in the chest with my arm. He wasn't expecting it.

"Enjoy your party. See you in six months."

"You old dog! Thanks, Frank!"

Fletcher gives me a look. "That was the doctor? And?"

"I'm fine. It's gone. See ya later, ya little bastards."

Fletch jumps up out of his chair and drags me with him.

"Let's go tell Trixie!" I say.

"Not yet! This is our celebration." He twirls me around and around, up on our hill. If anyone is watching, they'll think we're nuts.

But Fletch and I have always danced to our own damn tune.

OTHER BOOKS BY LESLEY CREWE

available wherever fine books are sold and online at nimbus.ca

Relative Happiness
978-1-77108-209-9

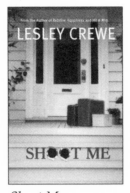

Shoot Me
978-1-55109-782-4

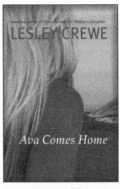

Ava Comes Home
978-1-55109-860-9

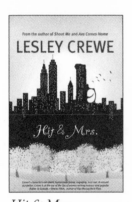

Hit & Mrs.
978-1-55109-725-1

Her Mother's
Daughter
978-1-55109-774-9

Kin
978-1-55109-922-4

Chloe Sparrow
978-1-77108-158-0